## WATCHER IN THE WOODS

He stared through the binoculars at the camp. Ever since he'd learned they were coming back, he'd been planning.

After a few moments, he stuffed the binoculars back in his pack and returned to the site of the pit. He was digging a grave. A big grave, enough for three. It wasn't quite finished yet, but it was close.

In his mind, he was already laying the fir boughs over its top. Maybe a thin wire mesh to hold the boughs in place. Something weak enough to drop them into the hole when he was ready for them.

Brooke.

Rona.

Wendy.

With a determined smile, he picked up the shovel and began digging in earnest . . .

## Books by Nancy Bush

**Published by Kensington Publishing Corp.**

# THE CAMP

# NANCY BUSH

ZEBRA BOOKS
Kensington Publishing Corp.
www.kensingtonbooks.com

# THE
# CAMP

# Prologue

She didn't believe them . . . didn't believe *him*. He'd told her a lot of things she didn't understand. She loved him. She truly loved him. But not in the way he maybe wanted. She couldn't tell, and though she'd tried to explain her feelings, she knew she hadn't been heard.

She hurried along the trail until she came to the ledge above the lake. The fog was below her. It had crept in like it always did, sliding over the deep green depths of the water, a downy gray blanket beneath a darkening sky that tonight felt as evil as some had described it.

She *wasn't* sick. She didn't need medical help. She didn't need her soul saved.

She'd made a mistake coming here. She just needed to get away.

The camp's outdoor lights were still on and visible from where she stood; tiny, yellow stars of illumination. But as she watched, the fog reached to the shore and flowed stealthily over the ground and then upward, long gray fingers obscuring the last glowing pinpoints until the camp went completely dark.

She squatted down on the ledge, feeling she should make herself smaller, just in case someone was looking for her.

She glanced north, in the opposite direction of the camp, and shivered. The fog was coming from that direction and working its way up the side of the cliff. Soon it would reach her if she didn't run.

An owl gave a lonely hoot, then cut itself off as if startled.

The girl jumped to her feet and whipped around, facing the forest. Was someone coming?

Then she heard him, moving quietly but approaching her direction, appearing at the edge of the woods, a dark shape heading toward her in the gathering gloom. He was in a ski mask and carrying white flowers, she realized. She recognized him by the way he moved, but her heart started an erratic tattoo in her chest. She loved him and feared him. What was he carrying in his right hand? Queen Anne's lace, maybe? Plucked from the trailside? And was that a metal goblet in his other hand?

*What?*

"These are for you," he said, thrusting the flowers under her nose. She automatically sucked in a deep breath, reaching up to grab the bouquet and push it back from her face a little as he bent down and placed the goblet on the ground. She thought she recognized the goblet from somewhere but just couldn't remember where. On a shelf, maybe. Or mantel?

She took a step forward, feeling too close to the edge of the trail. She couldn't let herself fall into the lake. It was a long, long way down and she doubted she would survive.

She could hear her heartbeat in her ears. Was he expecting her to drink something? Was that why he had the goblet? She didn't think that would be a good idea.

"What are you doing here?" she demanded.

"Looking for you, my love." His tone was light, almost singsong.

Immediately she was on alert. "I wanted to take a walk before it got too dark."

"You were avoiding me."

"Why are you wearing a mask?"

"I don't want anyone to see me."

His honesty was one of the things she'd told herself she loved about him. He never lied to her, even when he uttered truths she didn't really want to hear. "You don't want them to know you're looking for me?"

"I know you're trying to leave. I'm here to help you on your journey."

"What do you mean?"

"Sometimes love is so cruel."

She was feeling strangely light-headed all of a sudden. Something was wrong. Terribly wrong. She noted then that he was also wearing rubber gloves. Were her hands stinging? Her throat tightening?

Behind the mask his eyes were clear but the fog was surrounding him, blurring the edges. "I'm not sick," she tried to say, but her voice came from a long, long way away and she stumbled a step. And now she *felt* sick, but it wasn't her soul that was at risk.

"I—"

She never got to finish her thought because his hands suddenly encircled her neck, closing her windpipe. She dropped the flowers and tried to pry his fingers loose, but she couldn't. Her head was spinning. She envisioned a spiral of fog, wrapping her up like a spider cocooning its prey in spun silk. The spiral would whip her around and around, carrying her upward before dropping her into the depths of the water.

Her fingers scrabbled desperately against the pressure of his, digging hard, but she couldn't release his hold. When she lost consciousness and went limp, he held her carefully and then helped her body collapse to the ground.

When she stopped breathing he released the pressure on

her neck. She'd dropped the flowers. Carefully he plucked them up, then tossed them over the ledge and into the fog, knowing they would drift down to the water far below.

Then he laid her on her back and folded her arms over her chest. He picked up the goblet and held it high above her before gently tipping it. A trail of ashes ran from the lip and into the fog. He leaned over her closely, making certain most of the ashes had found their way to her.

*You should really burn her. Cleanse her.*

But the flames might be seen, even through the fog. The scent of the fire would carry to the camp.

When he finally stood he realized he could no longer see her. The fog had done its duty. Now he needed to melt back into the forest or risk falling into the lake himself. He would wait there for a while. Better to let time pass with this gray menace surrounding him.

He glanced back to where he knew the camp was, but the fog blanketed his vision. He could barely see more than a few inches into its thick depths. Still, he imagined them all sleeping in their bunks. The young campers and the sex-starved counselors. His lips twitched.

Arianna had been there.

Carefully, he squatted down and leaned over her, feeling his way. He let his hand travel over her face, mapping her features, and leaned in to kiss her.

Wait. Was that *a breath*?

He bent down and saw that her eyes were open. Black pools. Filled with terror.

She was still alive!

Wrapping his hands around her neck once more he squeezed with all his strength, smashing his lips to hers at the same time. He kissed her as long as he could without taking a breath, his lungs screaming. He then gulped air and then kissed her hard again. She didn't wriggle much. Her strength was already gone.

He stayed that way until there was no heartbeat. No chance of revival. The fog had kept moving and was now thinning, drifting away from him. He gazed at her slack features and waited, making sure she was really dead.

Finally, he rose and looked back at the camp. The lights had winked on again as the fog passed, though less could be seen as the hour had grown later. Stealthily, he headed down the trail.

He needed to not be missed.

# Chapter 1

# Camp Love Shack

**Then . . .**

Emma Whelan sat on the cold carpet of pine needles around the campfire, narrowing her eyes against the smoke. It was dark outside, no ambient light to push back the deep woods beyond the blood-orange glow off the spitting and grasping flames, rust and maize heat devils dancing toward the sky. Across the campfire, the boys' faces were up-lit, gallows-like. And beyond them the lake was a black void, a seemingly endless placid surface that stretched to the other end, though Fog Lake was barely half a mile long, both shores along its width in sight of each other.

"Sure you don't want some?" one of the boys asked, holding up a joint and pointing it in Emma's direction.

At seventeen Emma was no stranger to weed. She'd done her share of experimenting but she'd never cared for the high. She'd abused alcohol some, too. Got drunk just enough times to regret some of the things she'd said and done, and so her interest in marijuana and booze had fallen off a cliff.

Rona, seated a few spaces over from Emma, jumped up and circled the fire to take the joint, press it between her lips, and inhale deeply. She kept her eyes on the guy who'd offered it up, Donovan, even though he was still looking at Emma. He liked Emma, she knew, but she didn't care. She was used to male attention. But his interest in her had clearly pissed off Rona, which amused her.

Brooke, on Emma's right, said, "Joy's not leaving us overnight by ourselves. She'll be back."

"Nah, she's gone," another one of the guys answered. That was Lanny. Kind of a douchebag. Kinda funny. Emma wasn't sure what she thought of him. "The sad sack's not here. We've got the place to ourselves till tomorrow afternoon, so party on, dudes." Lanny got to his feet and did an impromptu bump and grind with his hips, part sexual, part plain stupid. He wore baggy shorts and a camp T-shirt and made goofy faces. His ears stuck out from beneath a shaggy haircut of brown hair. Everyone laughed and even Emma smiled.

Joy, who was kind of down and mopey, was the midthirty-ish director of the summer camp owned by Mr. and Mrs. Luft-Shawk. The Luft-Shawks had tried to entrench the name "Camp Fog Lake" but everyone still called it Camp Love Shack not only because it sounded like their names, but also because it had the reputation of being a hot, hook-up place. Emma could attest to that last part. She'd spent an exploratory half hour with Donovan behind the mirror, a space about the size of Mom's broom closet, but in truth her mind had been set on someone else. Donovan and his ilk were just a summer distraction and when he'd tried to jam himself into her standing up, Emma had pushed back as far as the space would allow and let him know that was the end of whatever was between them.

As if realizing her thoughts had touched on him, Donovan, who'd stretched out on the ground after passing the joint, roused himself again and sat up. His longish hair was dark in the shadows but she knew it was brown, streaked blond from weeks in the sun as a lifeguard at the lake. He had a great body, strong arms and chest that showed beneath the unbuttoned white shirt he'd tossed on over a pair of khaki shorts. All the girls wanted to be with him, which was, truthfully, why Emma had considered giving him a whirl behind the mirror. But like Lanny and Owen, Donovan was really just another horny guy looking to get laid. None of them knew the first thing about how to treat a woman. Hell, how to treat another human being. Bring up the word "relationship" and they would run away as if chased by a hive of hornets. Respect, consideration, and basic kindness were foreign concepts as well. All they were good for was quick sex with a hard body, if you were so inclined. She didn't even like kissing him or his ilk and had gotten a reputation around the camp for "no mouth stuff." They were all too eager, too slobbery, too much tongue. Took the thrill of a summer fling right out of it.

There was another guy who'd caught her eye. He wasn't hanging out with any of them around tonight's campfire and was a bit of a mystery, which was what intrigued her the most. He wasn't part of the camp as far as she could tell. She was still debating on him. A last hurrah before the rest of her life began. Just thinking about the future made her happy and anxious and determined all at the same time.

She glanced over at Rona and Brooke. They were both regarding Donovan reverently. They knew he'd been with Emma and they wanted a crack at him themselves.

*Good luck, girls.*

"You know why it's called Fog Lake, don't you?" Donovan said. He arched a brow for effect and threw a glance over at Brooke and Rona.

"Let me guess. Uhhhh . . . because of the fog?" Rona smirked at him. She was medium height with short, dark hair that flopped into her eyes in a cute, boyish way and yet she was all curves and knew how to use them. She slid a look Emma's way as if to say, *I've got his attention now, bitch.*

Emma could feel herself rise to the challenge and reminded herself that this summer was just a pause before the beginning of her real life. Let Rona have him.

"Not just a fog. It's this dense curtain of—I'm not making this up—water crystals and tiny cells that are part plant and animal in origin," Donovan said in all seriousness.

Emma squinted her eyes at him. Was he for real?

"Animal?" Brooke questioned, cocking her head. She swept back the curtain of light brown hair that fell across her face. She, too, was medium build; both she and Rona were a bit shorter than Emma. Brooke was seemingly more reticent than Rona, but Emma had caught her assessing her more than once with those green eyes and suspected Emma Whelan had been a very lively topic amongst the "three hottest chicks at camp, after Emma," according to the boys. Those chicks included Rona, Brooke, and their third friend, Wendy, who was seated one over from Brooke.

Now Wendy, who up till this point had been sitting like a statue, stirred. She was petite with curly brown hair she tried to constantly tame into a ponytail. Her elfin chin quivered slightly, and she complained, "You're just trying to scare us."

"No shit," was Lanny's jovial reply. He grinned and waggled his fingers at her, as if he were throwing a hex on her. Wendy shrank into herself and hid behind Brooke.

"So, the fog is alive?" Emma questioned dryly.

Donovan shrugged. "It's not regular fog. It's thicker. And it moves in slowly and creeps across the lake and hangs there. After it recedes, dead bodies have been found. Ask Joy, if you don't believe me."

Emma said, "The fog kills people. It's alive and it kills people. Let me write that down."

"People die when it comes around," Owen Paulsen jumped in quickly, shooting a glance toward Donovan. He was shorter and more compact, with longish, dark brown hair and was Donovan's lieutenant, always ready to defend his friend and maybe catch some of his hero's hand-offs where the ladies were concerned.

"So, the fog can think, too," said Emma. "Very evolutionary of it. If it was just made up of plant crystals, well then, the killing would be more reactionary, like plants, I suppose. But made up of animal crystals . . . that means it can *think*. If that's the case, the fog might actually know who it's killing."

"Shut up," said Donovan with admiration.

Lanny groaned. "You sound like a teacher."

Rona stately flatly, "The bottom line is: stay away from the fog. Fine with me."

"That's right. Don't go out in it," warned Owen, once again looking to Donovan for support. "When it rolls in, just stay in your cabin and don't come out."

Donovan said in a hushed voice, "The last time it crept over Camp Love Shack there was a body left on Suicide Ledge." He glanced back in the dark to his left, as if throwing a look in the direction of the infamous slab of rock that daredevils used as a means to launch themselves into the lake. That was how people died. By underestimating how far out you needed to leap in order to avoid the lurking boulders in the water just below the surface of the lake far below.

"I heard about that," said Wendy, poking her head out from behind Brooke like a frightened bird. "She was left on the ledge with her arms crossed over her chest and covered with ashes."

"A sacrifice," said Owen.

"That's a myth," Rona said with a snort.

"No, it's not." This from a boy named Ryan. Emma hadn't paid much attention to him to date. She thought about that other guy, the one who interested her, but it was probably best to forget him, too.

"The fog is nothing to fuck with." Donovan's tone was sharp, bringing the attention back to himself. "But it only comes early in June, so we've ducked it this year."

"Lucky us," said Emma.

Emma knew she was pushing him but didn't much care. Donovan was the kind of guy who didn't like being questioned, but Emma was the kind of girl who couldn't stand letting guys like Donovan get away with their bullshit, so she just met his gaze blandly.

Rona said, "Well, I'm glad we missed it."

"June gloom," said Brooke.

Emma rotated her shoulders as they were growing stiff. "Good story, Donovan, but I think I'm heading to bed." She stood up and swiped small twigs and branches from the back of her jeans.

"Not just a story. Truth," insisted Donovan. For all his looks to the contrary, he was no laid-back surfer boy–type.

"They've found a body in the lake once, maybe twice," granted Emma. "But those were probably swimming deaths."

"And the one on the ledge," reminded Wendy.

"Don't leave," Donovan said to Emma. "Sit down, sit down." He motioned with his hand patting the air for her to reseat herself on the ground.

"My butt is numb."

"That's part of the fun of Camp Love Shack," insisted Lanny.

They all chorused for her to stay, the girls a little less enthusiastically than the guys. Emma thought about it. Truthfully, if the camp director planned to be away for a while, it was nice to at least be unchaperoned. Sure, she would've rather had more sophisticated company, but what the hell.

"You sure you don't want some?" Donovan squeaked out, holding smoke in his lungs from a big hit, extending the roach toward Emma.

"No, thanks."

"A beer?" Lanny held one up from the cooler he'd sneaked into camp, waggling the bottle back and forth, trying to entice her.

Emma knew they all looked at her as if she were a pariah. She hadn't come to make friends, and she'd been standoffish from the start. She had other things coming up in her life. She'd just been putting in her time as a camp counselor this summer before her senior year in high school.

But . . .

"Okay," she said, slowly sinking back down, and she could almost hear the unspoken "Finally!" from the group.

"June's over and I, for one, am enjoying this 'fogless' night," stated Brooke firmly.

"The fog comes when the fog comes—June, July, August, whenever," said Lanny. His tone was surprisingly serious for him. "None of us are really safe, but that's what makes Camp Love Shack so cool."

"Let's not talk about it anymore," murmured Wendy.

"Why not? Bring it on," declared Rona. "Any fog in the forecast?"

Rona was one of those girls who talked big and kind of acted like she was one of the guys. You could never trust which way she would land on any issue. Sometimes she sided with her friends, sometimes she didn't. Emma had determined right away that she was untrustworthy and always looking for attention.

Emma took a long swallow of the beer. It was nicely cold and fizzed its way down her throat. She'd steered clear of beer since the time she'd drunk a warm one that a friend had pilfered from one of her parents' parties and hidden under her jacket. That same weekend Emma had gotten sick on orange juice and vodka, which pretty much put paid to her interest in alcohol altogether. That friend had since moved away and now Emma was kind of a lone ranger where girlfriends were concerned.

"The dead girl on the ledge wasn't a fable," Donovan assured them.

Rona moved over and wriggled herself between Donovan and Lanny. "Yeah, but the girl on the ledge took her own life. She took some drug and overdosed. Probably didn't even intend to kill herself. Was trying to make a statement to some guy at that cult place over there." She waved a hand in the direction of Suicide Ledge and the trail that led all the way from the camp to the commune about a mile further on.

"Haven Commune," said Ryan.

They all looked at him.

"It's not a cult," he tried to assure them.

"How do you all know so much?" Lanny queried. He'd sat back down cross-legged and was poking at the fire with a stick. A cascade of sparks flew upward, scarlet and orange fireflies moving frantically against the dark sky.

"I can read," said Rona. "Something I could teach you how to do, if I had the inclination to do so, which I don't."

The boys all protested loudly at the dig, but grinned like the dorks they were.

Emma pressed Rona, "She died of an overdose?"

"She was from that *cult*." She threw a look at Ryan, daring him to argue with her. "They all use drugs and have sex with everybody and chant and pray to the devil."

Emma laughed out loud. She couldn't help herself. Ryan immediately protested that he knew people from the commune, and they were totally normal. He sounded a little too anxious to convince them to Emma's ears. Donovan gave Rona a friendly shove and she shoved him back and pretty soon they were tickling and almost wrestling, and Emma decided Rona was going to get what she wanted from him after all. Well, fine. She finished her beer and screwed the bottle base into the dirt and pine needles to keep it from falling over, then lay back and looked up at the stars. The night was deep and clear.

As if reading her mind, Lanny intoned, "The fog rolls in,

covers everything in a cold, gray blanket, then recedes, leaving a trail of death in its wake."

"You asshole," said Rona on a laugh.

"Shut up," said Wendy at the same time, sounding like she meant it. Emma turned her head to look at her, but she was still obscured by Brooke.

"Look who's scared," sniggered Owen.

Brooke ordered, "Stop it, you guys."

Which made them double down on their teasing.

Suddenly Donovan was above Emma, his hair falling down on either side of his head, holding himself above her by stiff arms, staring down at her.

"Get off me," she said conversationally. She really wasn't in the mood. And where was Rona?

As if answering the question, Rona suddenly leapt to her feet into Emma's field of vision. She stood in the center of the group, almost in the campfire. "Okay, shut up, shut up. All of you. Time to play Truth or Dare, only it's just truth, so you morons don't do something stupid and kill yourselves and leave us to explain why you're all dead."

"No dares? Bullshit, I'm not playing," declared Donovan, but even so he jumped to his feet in one lithe move as well. Owen and Lanny and Ryan were still seated but they all heartily agreed with him.

"You're all playing," Rona ordered to their collective groan.

"Fine, then you have to answer with the truth, too," warned Lanny, pointing at each of the girls individually.

"Absolutely," Rona agreed with a lift of her shoulder.

"You first," Donovan told her.

"Fine. Go ahead. Ask me anything."

"Did you fuck Steve Burckman?" Donovan shot back immediately.

Wendy gasped and Brooke declared, "Donovan!"

"Well?" His gaze was fixed on Rona.

Unlike her friends, she was unperturbed. "Steve Burck-

man's an asshole. Let's get the rules straight here. Whatever
the question is, it should be asked of everyone. So, if you
want to know who someone slept with, you ask, 'Who's the
last person you slept with?' You can't be so specific—"

"Was Steve Burckman the last person you slept with?"
Donovan cut in.

"Shut up, asshole. I never slept with him," she snapped
back.

"We're not asking that question!" Brooke stated loudly.
"I'm not discussing my love life."

"Like you have one," sniggered Lanny.

"What's the point, then?" asked Owen.

"We need a different question. How about, 'What's the
worst thing you did that really pissed off your parents?'"
Brooke suggested.

"We'll take Brooke's question," agreed Rona.

"Too tame," groaned Lanny. "Ask something else."

"Nope. That's the question. Brooke asked it, and it stays.
I'll start." Rona began walking in a slow circle around the
campfire and Emma eased herself up into a cross-legged sitting position, curious.

"I was fourteen. It was the summer before high school
and I was with my cousin who'd just turned eighteen and
he and I were the only ones awake at this backyard bar-
beque party at my aunt's."

"Uh-oh," said Owen. "Sounds like a sex thing."

"We started kissing. No big deal. A little touching. Just a
little experimentation."

"Maybe a little statutory rape," drawled Donovan.

"It didn't go near that far." She glared at Owen as if he'd
said it. He raised his hands in all innocence. "But our parents
caught us and my cousin got a blistering with a hack paddle,
and I got grounded for all of freshman year." Rona reseated
herself by Donovan.

"Your *cousin*?" squeaked Wendy, which made all the

guys laugh and then pretend like they were barfing their guts out at the thought.

"Oh, stop it," said Brooke tiredly.

"What'd you do?" Owen asked her.

Emma had seen the way Owen looked at Brooke and wondered if Brooke had noticed.

"No. My turn," Lanny interrupted. "My mama caught me with enough ganja in my room to get the whole town high. She threw me out of the house, and I had to live with my dad and stepmother, the wicked bitch of Laurelton, for half a year before she let me back in."

"What about you?" Owen asked Brooke again. "You're the one who wanted this stupid question."

Emma slid her eyes to Brooke, who lifted a hand to brush back her hair, a move meant to buy time. Brooke then shrugged and said, "I took out my mom's car when I was fifteen before I had my license. When I drove back home my dad was standing in the picture window, waiting for me. They'd gotten home before I did and man, I was in serious trouble. Couldn't see my friends. Grounded, like Rona."

"This is a dumb question," said Owen, bored.

"What about you?" Donovan asked Emma.

Before she could answer, Ryan demanded the same thing of Wendy.

"Sorry. I don't have any story," she answered. "I haven't done anything to piss my parents off. I'm the good girl."

"Bullshit, Wendy," said Rona on a short laugh. "You just haven't got caught yet."

"You know something we don't?" Lanny asked Rona, who just shrugged.

Brooke seemed about to say something but held it back.

Emma looked at Rona, then Brooke, then Wendy. The three of them had all just graduated from Laurelton High together. Emma still had another year of school at River Glen, but felt light-years older.

"Emma?" Donovan turned back to her. All of their faces, ghoulishly lit by the fire, seemed to stare at her with black eyes. A bat swooped over them and then another before they headed north, in the direction of Suicide Ledge. Out of the corner of her eye Emma thought she saw movement in the trees just outside the camp clearing. She glanced quickly that way but there was nothing she could see.

"You're stalling," said Lanny.

They were all waiting with bated breath. Emma smiled to herself and thought . . . *A bunch of fourth graders . . .*

"Actually, the 'pissed off' stuff is still coming," she told them.

"What does that mean?" asked Ryan.

"Shut up." Donovan's eyes were on Emma.

"My mom doesn't know it yet, but I'm getting married soon."

That caused a moment of surprised silence, then Lanny cried, "Married?"

"Are you pregnant?" asked Owen.

"Yeah . . ." Rona was staring at her like she'd grown a second head.

Emma laughed aloud. "You should see your faces!"

"You're joking," accused Brooke.

"This is truth," Rona reminded.

Emma just shrugged. She wasn't about to explain herself.

Owen was next and told them he'd stolen some beer out of the neighbor's garage refrigerator. His parents had been embarrassed and the neighbor had suggested Owen mow their very large backyard for the entire summer, which pretty much sucked. Donovan was questioned about what he'd done and he said he'd taken up with his dad's girlfriend for a while after they broke up, which hadn't gone over well with dear, old Dad. Like Lanny, he was shipped off to the other parent for a while. Ryan never got around to saying what he'd gotten in trouble for, other than muttering his dad was a hard-ass and didn't like anything he did.

The campfire broke up soon afterward with everyone drifting back to their bunks. It was Ryan who slipped up beside Emma, matching his strides to hers as she headed to her cabin. "Are you really getting married?" he asked her somewhat earnestly.

"What'd you do to piss off your parents?" she countered. This was the first time he'd even spoken to her directly.

He glanced back toward the surrounding fir trees. The half moon had been obscured by clouds, but it broke free and shone brightly on the edge of the woods. For a second Emma thought she saw a white hand on the bole of a tree but she blinked and it was gone.

"Got involved with the wrong girl," he said with a kind of half chuckle.

"And your parents found out?"

"Them and everyone else. Hey, do you think we could hang out some? Summer's almost over and I don't want it to be."

Emma felt differently. She wanted this interminable summer to end. "Sure," she said, more to ease away to the solitude of her bunk than because she was dying to spend more time with him.

"Tomorrow. Maybe we can go swimming or take a walk, or something."

"Sure," said Emma at the door to her cabin.

Ryan smiled in the moonlight. He had nice teeth, she thought.

"Tomorrow," he repeated and gave her a jaunty salute.

Emma went to her bunk and lay on her back, arms crossed behind her head, staring up at the bunk above her. She had the sense that life was going to begin for her, a new door opening to her future. She thought of fooling around with Donovan behind the mirror and made a face. Probably a dumb move.

Outside her window, she heard, "Psst. Emma . . ."

"Go to bed, Donovan," she said, bored, and rolled over.

* * *

Sometime in the night she woke to a cry outside. She sat up and opened the slats above the screened window. Holy shit. Was that fog, creeping in like a thief, slowly moving inside? It was August. Maybe it hadn't heard that it wasn't allowed this late in the summer.

Shivering, she rose from her bed and stared through the window into the night, smothered now in a layer of dark gray. Well, it was here. Feeling a strange inner quailing, she stepped back from the window. Grabbing her flashlight, she headed outside, surprised that the door was already unlocked. The now cooler air feathered against her skin, causing a shiver. She wanted to look inside other cabins and assure herself that everyone was in bed, but if she flashed her light she might scare whoever was there.

Instead, she felt her way through the dark and fog around her cabin. She stopped when she was closest to the lake, hearing scraping, heavy breathing—and maybe crying? She hesitated, realizing she'd heard a piercing shriek, and that's what had wakened her. Should she turn on her flashlight? Would it even penetrate through this gray curtain? New noises sounded. Was that someone dragging one of the canoes over the scattered stones by the lake?

A few minutes later she heard footsteps and saw a quick burst of illumination from someone's flashlight. It was several people, trying to stealthily make their way toward the cabins. Emma shrank back, her fingers feeling the rough cedar shakes of her cabin's wall. She worked her way noiselessly back toward the doorway and sneaked inside ahead of them. She saw a few more quick stabs of light as the group came forward. One of them was crying. A girl.

Wendy.

She was being helped along by Brooke and Rona.

Emma quickly climbed into her bed and stayed stock-still as she heard the faint squeak of cabin doors opening and closing. She shut her eyes. Their collective breathing was stuttered and Rona shushed them. A beam of light swung her way and seemed to pause before passing over her. Had they seen her when she was outside? Or had the fog made her invisible?

When all was quiet Emma opened her eyes again, gazing into the dark. What had they been up to? She decided she would talk to them the next day about it, maybe cut one of them—Wendy, the weakest link—from the herd and find out.

But she never had the chance. The next morning the fog made it hard to see anything and Joy, who'd returned sometime in the night and was apparently affected by the tales of the "sentient" fog as well, kept everyone inside. It took several days for the weather to clear and when it did it also became clear that Ryan wasn't around. Emma caught up with Wendy, who admitted the three of them had been out, but the fog had swept in so suddenly it had scared them. They'd been down by the lake, sharing a joint, and had just run for cover. She swore they hadn't seen Ryan at all.

But then when Ryan didn't appear that day, the three friends had to admit to Joy that they'd been out at the lake, but they hadn't seen him. Joy reported him missing to the sheriff's department. The search extended to Haven Commune, but there was still no sign of him. He was just gone.

In the days following, Emma noticed something else. The three "hot chicks" were pretty cool to one another. Though they pretended to still be friends and were totally concerned about Ryan, the Laurelton High girls' friendship had hit a wall. They seemed to have stopped talking amongst themselves. Was it something to do with Ryan? Somehow Emma didn't think so. She thought back to what she knew of them and considered she might have an inkling of what caused the rift, but kept it to herself. Rona, sensing Emma's interest, demanded, "What do you know?" but Emma, as ever, simply ignored her. She just wanted to go home. All summer she'd distanced herself some from the camp shenanigans, and now she was completely over them.

The last days of camp Emma kept her eye on the three "friends." The consensus about Ryan was he'd just left. Joy apparently knew that this was within Ryan's MO from his overbearing parents and she was more pissed than worried that he'd used her camp as a jumping-off point. The guys seemed to consider Ryan some kind of hero now that he'd bailed. If they noticed Rona, Brooke, and Wendy's estrangement, they didn't care. Summer was over. They'd either scored with them or hadn't. From Emma's point of view, that's all the guys had cared about anyway. The last night they tried to get everyone around the campfire again, but no one was interested.

In the middle of that night Emma heard a loud noise. A shout. Her eyes flew open. Outside the window flashlights bobbed white in the darkness, an uncoordinated light show. Deep male voices reached her ears.

She climbed out of her sleeping bag and ran outside, but stopped short. Joy was standing by one of the lodge posts, a black jacket thrown over her sweats and T-shirt—Emma's sleeping garb as well. When Joy didn't see her, Emma stayed in the shadows and just listened.

Marlon, the camp handyman, broke from the group of flash-lighted seekers and told Joy in his gravelly voice that Ryan had been found. His body was floating on top of the lake.

But that wasn't all. A girl from Haven Commune was dead as well. She'd been found lying on the slab at Suicide Ledge, her arms crossed over her breast, ashes strewn over her body.

*So, there were ashes*, Emma thought, grasping onto a random thought as she inwardly reeled from Ryan's death.

"They were lovers," Marlon rasped. "He killed her and killed himself."

"Oh, my Lord . . . my Lord," whispered Joy.

Emma pulled her shoulders in.

Suicide Ledge had claimed another.

The next day, Joy closed the camp and it stayed that way for nearly twenty years.

# Chapter 2

Emma looked straight ahead at Miss Kacey, her therapist. She understood what Miss Kacey was saying, but she wanted to clap her hands over her ears because Miss Kacey said the same thing over and over again, and it was nothing Emma wanted to hear.

"We've talked about this, Emma," Miss Kacey was saying patiently. She was always patient. "Your injury has made it difficult for you to really consider all the possibilities, even hidden dangers, that being a surrogate for your sister might entail. Pregnancy comes with a lot of responsibility."

"I'm responsible," said Emma.

"Yes, you are. Very responsible. But you know you don't have the same problem-solving skills that you did before the accident."

"It wasn't an accident."

"No, it wasn't," the therapist agreed, momentarily at a loss to continue.

Emma couldn't quite remember the attack during her senior year of high school that had left a jack-o'-lantern-shaped scar on her back and had caused her head to hit the fireplace mantel, causing permanent damage. But she could remember being scared. She squinched her shoulders together at the memory even now, though it had happened a long, long time ago. Lots of years. Decades, she'd heard Jamie say. Decades were lots of years.

"I've talked to Jamie," Miss Kacey said. "It seems that your sister and her husband already settled on a surrogate. Isn't that right?"

Emma wanted to carry Jamie's baby. She'd told her she wanted to have a baby for her and Cooper, but Jamie had said it couldn't happen, and then Miss Kacey and that baby doctor Emma had gone to see, Dr. Simmons, had looked at Emma with sad eyes and said it couldn't happen. Her brain wasn't good enough.

"She's a friend of Theo's." Emma didn't want Theo's friend to be the surrogate.

"She's been a surrogate before."

"My body is good. It's just my head," Emma said seriously. She'd told Miss Kacey this again and again.

"You know that Jamie is responsible for you. It would be very irresponsible of her to have you be her surrogate. The courts won't allow it."

"The courts don't know me."

Miss Kacey nodded and said, "But, Emma, even if they did, they would not legally allow it."

"You said that last time," said Emma.

"Well, yes, because it's the truth. And until you accept that you can't be your sister's surrogate, I'll likely say it again." She smiled, but it was kind of sad. "This wish you have for them . . . it's lovely, Emma. You have such a big heart. We all know that. You want what's best for Jamie and your family. That's important."

"I want to give them a baby."

"They know."

Emma couldn't think of anything else to say. They weren't going to let her give Jamie and Cooper a baby. They were going to let Mary Jo be their surrogate. It made Emma's head hurt to think of that, so she pushed it aside.

Harley came and picked Emma up from her session. "How was Miss Kasey?" Harley asked as Emma buckled herself into the middle back seat, where it was safest. Harley Woodward was Emma's niece and, though she'd been driving for quite a while now, Emma still didn't like to be with her that much.

"She said I couldn't have a baby," said Emma.

"Yeah, well . . . yeah."

Harley nodded. Just like Miss Kacey nodded. They all nodded at her. "She says that every time."

"She speaketh the truth, Em. It's hard to accept. I get it. But you don't want to be pregnant now anyway. I just graduated. We're going to have fun."

Emma's chest tightened. "But you're going to Camp Love Shack."

"Camp Fog Lake," Harley corrected.

"You're going to be a CIT—a counselor-in-training—like me."

"Yes, I am."

"It's not safe there. You were supposed to go to London, England." Emma leaned forward and met her niece's eyes in the rearview mirror.

"True." Harley did want to go to London. She still did. That was what she'd asked for as a graduation gift and her mom and Cooper were trying to give it to her. But Cooper's daughter—well, stepdaughter, but really like a daughter to him—Marissa, Harley's best friend, was set to go to college in Colorado and there was only so much money, so Harley had taken the job at the camp to make some cash before her trip. Right now she was scheduled to head to London in the fall and start school winter term. Though her mom and Cooper wanted to send her to the college of her choice, Harley's plan was to live at home and attend Portland State and major in criminal justice. Or something police-ish, like her stepfather the detective. She wasn't sure, yet.

"I'm still going," Harley told Emma. "Just gotta earn some of the green stuff first." She put the car in gear.

"The green stuff?"

"Money."

"Oh."

"Why don't you want me to go to Camp Fog Lake?" Harley asked her. She'd asked Emma this same question a number of times with no real answer. Emma had been a counselor-in-training there the summer before the attack that had irretrievably altered the path of her life. Harley had done her research and knew a guy had supposedly killed his girlfriend and himself in some ritualized way that had maybe happened before and it had unfairly turned back on the camp, causing it to close. But the new owner had opened it up again, and she was the camp director, too.

"You have a job at Ridge Pointe," said Emma.

Harley still worked for Ridge Pointe Independent and Assisted Living, although she'd cut her hours down toward the end of senior year. She'd made a point of putting in long hours and getting good grades, keeping her options open.

But Harley's reasons for attending Camp Fog Lake were more than just about making money and/or exploring the camp's myths. Her ex-boyfriend, if you could call him that. Ex-guy she dated for a while when she was a sophomore was more accurate. Anyway, Greer Douglas had graduated and basically disappeared from Harley's life. Oh, sure, they'd texted and kept in contact, sort of, but that had pretty much been the end of it. Then she'd learned through social media that he'd taken a job at the camp, not as a counselor but as an on-site maintenance person. Over the last year he'd already been repairing a lot of the buildings and helping construct new ones. His new girlfriend knew the camp owners, apparently. So, he was going to be there all summer. As soon as she'd learned about Greer's plans, she'd moved her search to his girlfriend, Allie Strasser, checking her social media posts—Harley had stooped to being a lurker so she could learn what Greer was doing—and had discovered Allie had applied to be a counselor at Camp Fog Lake. Harley had then talked Marissa into becoming a CIT, too. Mom's friend, Theo, had helped them get placed there because she knew the camp owners as well.

The only problem was Greer and Allie seemed pretty serious, and Harley knew she could face some hard truths if she went. But she still wanted to go. Allie was very active online and Harley knew a heckuva lot about her. She'd attended Laurelton High, which was kind of a River Glen High rival. Harley certainly felt like Allie's rival, though she'd never met her. Talking Marissa into being a CIT at Camp Fog Lake had been no small feat as Marissa's boyfriend, Cam Dornbrenner, whom she just started dating a few months before graduation, seemed to be sticking around River Glen for the summer. Luckily Mom hadn't wanted Harley to go off to camp alone, so she'd joined in to convince Marissa to go. Even Marissa's real mom, Laura, who wasn't known for agreeing with anything Mom and Cooper suggested, had jumped on the bandwagon. Harley kind of thought, though they didn't say it, that the parental units didn't much care for Cam. Harley silently agreed, but Marissa was wild about him. Anyway, the parents wanted a little distance between Marissa and Cam, so in the end Marissa had been pressured into going to the camp and had finally, reluctantly, agreed.

"What was it like when you were at Camp Fog Lake?" Harley asked Emma. This was a question she'd asked many times before, but Emma always answered as if the conversation were new. "Can you remember?"

"Camp Love Shack," corrected Emma.

"Okay," Harley said equably.

From the back seat Emma stared through the windshield in that intense yet blank way she had. Long moments passed, but Harley waited. Her aunt's mental processes were mysterious and unpredictable. Huge gaps of Emma's memories were missing and her neurons seemed to fire in fits and starts. The attack that left her aunt in her current state had happened before Harley was born so she'd never known Emma any other way.

"I saw some boys while I was there," she finally said.

"Saw? Like looked at them? Or . . . dated them?" asked Harley.

"I never saw that Ryan again. He drowned and they were like Romeo and Juliet. You know who they are?" Emma's head swiveled Harley's way.

"Not personally," said Harley lightly.

"They were star-crossed lovers. That means they were unlucky."

"Really unlucky," agreed Harley. "But the guy, Ryan? I thought he killed that girl. The one found on the ledge. That's a little more than unlucky. That's premeditated murder." Harley hadn't come across anyone named Ryan in her research, although a boy named Christopher had drowned the year Emma was at Camp Love Shack, and a girl named Fern was the one who'd been found on the ledge, though the cause of death was listed as unknown. Privately, Harley thought the powers that be had swept that one under the rug.

"I never saw him again. They wouldn't let us go down to the lake. You can see the ledge from the camp, but you need binoculars."

Now it was Harley's turn to take her eyes off the road for a moment and gaze at her aunt, who was staring blankly through the windshield. Sometimes Emma said things that meant a lot more than the words. You had to read between the lines.

"Did you see the ledge through the binoculars?" she asked

casually, turning her attention back to the road. She didn't want to scare Emma into clamming up again, but she was really interested in learning all she could.

"I didn't have the binoculars that night. He did."

"That night? What night? Are you talking about Ryan? You mean, the night he *died*?"

Emma frowned. "He was going to see me tomorrow, but he died that night."

"The night he drowned he was looking through the binoculars toward the ledge?" Harley reiterated.

Emma cocked her head in her way that meant she was thinking hard. "He looked through the binoculars."

Harley pulled into a visitor spot in front of Ridge Pointe Independent and Assisted Living. Normally she dropped her aunt off beneath the portico at the main doors, but she wanted to keep the conversation going for as long as Emma allowed. Harley intended to go to the camp armed with as much background on the place as she could get.

"Why did you park?" asked Emma.

"I just wanted to keep talking a minute. You said this guy Ryan was looking through the binoculars at the ledge the same night he drowned?"

"I didn't see him again," she said.

"Could he have been looking at the ledge where the girl, Fern, died?"

"I don't think so. Do you want to stay for dinner?"

Harley had to pull herself back. Sometimes it seemed she was on some kind of breakthrough with what happened at the camp, that Emma was on the verge of telling her something new and vital. But it never quite worked out that way. "Why don't you come to dinner at the house? I gotta pick up something at the store for Mom for dinner, but you could join us." Harley knew her mother, Emma's sister, wouldn't care if there was one more at the table, especially as it was Emma. It was Emma who sometimes resisted.

Emma said, "Twink came into the dining room even though

she's not supposed to. She rubbed against Jewell's legs and Jewell 'howled like a banshee.' That's what Donna Dentworth said. Jewell thought she was going to die, but nobody's died in the month of June or May, so we're lucky. Not star-crossed."

Twink, short for Twinkletoes—a name Emma abhorred, which is why she'd shortened it—was the black-and-white cat that prognosticated death around Ridge Pointe. If the cat curled up into your bed with you it was a bad omen. Many times the people she crawled in with were found dead the next day or several days later. Although this information about the cat was definitely newsworthy, Harley wanted to get back to the camp. "Why don't we—"

"Jewell's sure she's going to die. Mr. Atkinson wants to get rid of the cat. I know you don't like Twink, but I do. She can't go anywhere near the dining room anymore. She needs a new home."

"Hey, I'd take Twink. She's totally creepy and cool. But back to the night you saw Ryan with the binoculars. I—"

"I think I could catch Twink and bring her to Jamie's."

"What about Duchess?" Harley asked, reminding Emma of her dog, who was at constant war with the cat.

"Duchess lives at Ridge Pointe," explained Emma, giving Harley a look that said, *You know that*.

"So, you want us to take Twink while you and Duchess stay at Ridge Pointe?"

"You just said you would."

"Okay, but this requires further discussion, Emma. Come have dinner with us. I'm leaving for Camp Fog Lake in less than a week and I can't take the cat. We should talk about it with Mom and Cooper."

"Don't go to Camp Love Shack. It isn't safe," Emma said again.

"Camp Fog Lake. I've got to go, Emma. I told you. I have a job there. And I want to go."

"But you might not come back."

"I'll come back. But Emma, I want you to think hard about the night you saw Ryan with the binoculars. The guy who drowned."

"Okay . . ." she said uncertainly.

"I don't want to confuse you, but I think his name is Christopher. That's the name of the guy who drowned while you were there."

"That's Ryan."

Harley stopped pressing for a moment as Emma had dug her heels in. "Okay. Maybe I'm wrong." She knew she wasn't, though.

Emma said slowly, "If you jump in the lake from the ledge, you die. It's too high and the water is concrete."

"Concrete?"

"That's what Joy said."

"Who's Joy?" asked Harley.

"The camp director. She said the water is concrete, but she's a liar. It's just water."

"She's not the camp director anymore, Emma. It's someone named Hope. And I think she meant that if you hit the water from that high up, sometimes it's like hitting concrete. You have to break the water tension, which sounds easy, but if you have enough velocity, it can be like running into a brick wall."

"Are you really smart, Harley?"

"Why, yes, I am, as a matter of fact." Harley grinned. "I'm a high school graduate, Emma."

"So am I. But I'm not smart."

"Oh, yes, you are!" Harley was adamant about that.

"I have a handicap."

"You know yourself, Emma," Harley said. "And that's worth a lot."

Emma's only response as she reached for the door handle was, "I need to walk Duchess before dinner."

"Okay, I'll come with you. But Emma, you *are* smart. I learn things from you all the time."

They both climbed out of the SUV and started toward the portico and the sliding glass front doors that opened into the facility's reception area. She couldn't handle it when Emma denigrated herself, even if she was just relating what she felt was the truth.

Emma was silent for a time, then said, "Maybe he saw those people on the ledge."

"People? Are we talking about Ryan now?"

"Ryan had the binoculars. It's kind of confusing." Emma had reached the portico and was peering inside. Directly ahead stood a stacked stone fireplace in the middle of the room with a grouping of chairs around it. Behind it lay the wall that separated the small bar and the dining room from reception.

"Did Ryan see Fern and someone else on the ledge through the binoculars?" Harley tried.

"I don't think so."

"Emma, this is important. Can you remember what happened with Ryan and the binoculars?"

"He didn't tell me. He told . . . Joy. She had the binoculars." Emma's attention was suddenly caught by something inside the building. "There's Twink!"

The mostly black cat streaked across reception straight at them and placed her white paws on the glass door, meowing piteously. Her weight wouldn't open the door. "And there's Mr. Atkinson!" Emma stomped on the pad that opened the door. Twink was out like a shot, leaping and running past them in a blur of black and white while the facility's director, red-faced and portly, stalked purposefully toward the door, looking none too happy as Harley and Emma entered through the still open door.

"I wish you hadn't done that, Emma," he said tightly. "That cat went into the dining room again."

"To Jewell?" asked Emma.

"What difference does it make? Ian taught her some bad tricks."

Ian had worked at Ridge Pointe before Harley but was no longer there. A shame, in Harley's opinion, as he'd been a good guy with a sense of humor. He'd liked Twink and slipped the cat whipped cream and table scraps whenever he could. Like Harley, Ian had shared a distinct dislike for Mr. Atkinson, who now greeted Harley with a stiff "Hello, Harley,"

"Hello, Mr. Atkinson," Harley responded politely. She might privately think he was a dick but she still liked working part-time at the facility and didn't figure he needed to know that.

At her room, Emma collected Duchess, whose shaggy brown coat looked like it could use a trim. The dog was medium-sized and glad to see Harley, who felt the same way. Harley realized she was going to have to table the discussion about Ryan, the girl on Suicide Ledge, and Camp Fog Lake in general or risk having Emma shut down completely.

Jamie clipped a Mister Lincoln from the rose bush, the bright red rose nodding its heavy head as she joined it with the others she held gingerly in her hand, careful of thorns. The lovely, dense aroma of the flowers filled her senses and she closed her eyes for a moment. Her mother's garden had been neglected somewhat. No one was as death on weeds as Irene Whelan had been, certainly not Jamie. The last few years had been a huge change for both Jamie and Harley, who'd moved from California back to Oregon upon Irene's death. Up to then Emma had been living at home under Irene's care, and Jamie had needed to take over after her mother's death. Since then, Emma had exhibited an independence that their mother possibly hadn't seen, and had requested to move to Ridge Pointe. Sometimes she waffled on coming back to live at the house, a decision Jamie was letting her make on her own.

Jamie inhaled and closed her eyes. Their move from California had been good for all of them and since returning Jamie had reconnected with Cooper Haynes, her major crush from high school, and this past April they'd gotten married. Cooper's stepdaughter, Marissa, now spent more than half her time with them and both Harley and Marissa had just graduated from River Glen High. Cooper had no children of his own and he and Jamie had both wanted to have a child together, but had learned they would need a surrogate as it was very unlikely Jamie would carry a child full-term. It still got Jamie whenever she recalled Emma sincerely declaring that she would be their surrogate, which was lovely but totally improbable. Emma didn't fully understand the nature of her own disability. She knew she was compromised in her thinking, but sometimes cause and effect were a slippery concept for her, and she really felt she could be the one to help them out. She still did.

Jamie walked back inside the house with the roses, their velvety petals tucked tightly together as if hiding secrets. She pulled down a clear glass vase and arranged the small grouping, setting them on a side table in the living room that sat in front of the window to the street. Looking through the panes, she saw Harley's Outback pull up across the street. She watched as Emma, Harley, and Duchess spilled out.

She suddenly wanted to burst into tears. If she hadn't just had her period—unpredictable as they were these days given her quasi-working uterus—she might have thought she was pregnant, but no, this was something else. With Harley's graduation and the joy of marriage to the man she loved, and now the beginnings of a new life as she'd just learned today that, through surrogacy, she was going to be a mother again, Jamie was a mass of wildly seesawing, unprocessed feelings.

One of the roses bent its heavy head toward her as if nodding in agreement. Somehow it reminded her of how her mother would admonish her when she felt Jamie was being too dramatic. She smiled faintly at the thought.

So, what was this knot in the pit of her stomach? The one that had been there ever since Mary Jo's phone call saying the in vitro had taken?

Joy? Apprehension? The thought that her and Cooper's baby was growing inside Mary Jo felt surreal. It was happening! It was *really* happening. She was thrilled, but . . . but . . . what did she know of Mary Jo Kirshner really anyway? Theo had vouched for her, but Theo hadn't grown up at Haven Commune, like Mary Jo had. She'd only visited the place. Haven Commune, coincidentally, was located near Camp Fog Lake. Jamie, for probably ridiculous reasons, didn't feel entirely comfortable about that. People had died at the camp. Harley was all over the history of the murder/suicide of two lovers who'd died the same year Emma had been there.

Jamie shook her head at herself. So what? This was a time for celebration, not fear. She forced herself to push her uneasiness about Mary Jo aside. Maybe it was all the lore surrounding the camp that was affecting her . . . and the fact that Emma had been at that camp scant months before the attack on her person had changed her forever. Though the two events were unrelated, it just felt . . . portentous, and not in a good way. Then today she'd gotten an email inviting parents and alumni to a weekend at the camp around the Fourth of July, followed by a call to their home phone, which was the number the camp had on record for Emma, who'd attended the camp's last season. The tragedy of deaths that summer had closed the camp for good . . . well, until now. Jamie remembered asking Emma about it at the time, but Emma had been closemouthed, completely disinterested in confiding anything to her younger sister when she'd returned, even though Jamie had been burning with questions at the time. If either of them had known what was to come, maybe they would've tried harder to communicate, but it hadn't happened.

As her family walked inside, Jamie checked on the chicken-and-rice dish and pan of roasted carrots, mushrooms, onions, parsnips, and broccoli currently bubbling in the oven.

Her thoughts seesawed back to Mary Jo. She and Cooper were having a baby. *A baby!* She should be jumping for joy.

"Hi," Jamie greeted them all as she closed the oven door. "You staying for dinner?" she asked Emma. Duchess ran right over to Jamie, tail wagging, eager to help and she smiled and patted the dog's head before turning back to wash her hands.

"Harley invited me," said Emma.

"It's perfectly fine," Jamie assured her over the rush of the water.

"Harley has questions for me." Emma spoke loudly, too, as Jamie shut off the tap.

"Lots of questions," agreed Harley.

"Joy's not there anymore," Emma told Jamie seriously.

"New camp director's name is Hope something," volunteered Harley, giving Jamie an inkling to what they were talking about.

"Well, how about this? I've been invited to parents' weekend, and Emma got a call about being an alumna. Maybe we'll see you there."

Emma blinked, her blue eyes blank. "Who called me?"

Jamie explained about the phone call from someone named Tina associated with the camp and a subsequent email message. Harley looked at Jamie in consternation and asked, "*You're* not going to go, are you?"

Jamie smiled, some of her tension dissipating. "What? You don't want me there?" She clutched her chest in mock horror.

"Mom . . ." Harley's lips curved.

"You need to stay away," stated Emma, firmly missing the banter entirely. "So does Harley."

"Too late for that. I'm going," said Harley.

Jamie glanced back at the clock. Cooper would be home soon and she really needed to talk to him. She'd been the one gung-ho for the surrogate. He'd gone along with her, but cautiously, and now it felt like their situations were reversed. It was big news and good news, and she wanted to share it with him alone before telling anyone else. She pushed away the flutter of anxiety that tried to take hold again.

"Mom, I don't really care whether you go or not," Harley said after a moment.

"Thank you, honey."

Emma said, "Bad things happened there. I saw him go in the lake."

"Who?" Harley and Jamie asked at the same time, and then Harley added, "That Ryan guy?"

Emma cocked her head, a sure sign she was thinking that over carefully.

"Haven Commune is right by the camp," Jamie remarked. "That's where Mary Jo grew up."

Harley and Emma looked at her and even Duchess, sensing something possibly momentous, stopped chewing on the dog toy she'd found behind one of the dining room chairs and looked up, ears pricked. Jamie hadn't meant to sound like she was making such a proclamation, but clearly something in her voice had reached them.

"Your potential surrogate? She's one of those *cult people*?" asked Harley.

"Ryan said they were nice," said Emma.

Now Jamie and Harley switched their attention to her. "The cult people?" Harley asked again, this time carefully.

Jamie understood how she was feeling. You had to be cautious when you were trying to talk to Emma, if you really wanted something from her. You could scare her into forgetting the point if you spoke with too much emotion, allowing the flotsam and jetsam that floated in her mind to get in the way.

Now Emma stated clearly, "He said they weren't a cult."

The rumble of Cooper's SUV could be heard as it turned into the drive and headed down the long approach to the back door. It was barely five thirty, but he'd said he'd be home early tonight and Jamie had made dinner with that expectation. She hoped to finish up and then maybe go out with him somewhere for an after-dinner drink or just quiet time together. She hadn't counted on Emma, though. It wasn't much of a problem as Harley could take her home, or maybe Emma would spend the night, though she struggled with too much of a break in routine. It just made it harder to carve out some time for her to speak freely with Cooper. As the thought crossed her mind, she watched Emma line up the salt and pepper shakers on the table and place them carefully in front of the napkin holder. A tell that she might be feeling stressed and needed to redefine order in her life.

"That Ryan guy said he wanted to see you the night before he died?" clarified Harley. "*That* night."

"I didn't kill him."

"I know that, Emma," she said patiently. "But do you think someone did?"

Jamie was about to intervene, certain Emma would start to hyperventilate because it's what often happened when she was confronted with feelings and fears from her past, whether the threat was real or imagined, but the words died in her throat when she realized this time Emma was in control of herself.

"Who?" pressed Harley.

Emma leaned forward and Harley leaned toward her.

She said something Jamie couldn't hear because Cooper pushed open the back door at that exact moment and sang out, "I'm home," and Duchess leapt up with a little bark of happiness, rushing toward him. As he came down the hall toward the kitchen, trying to tug the rope toy from Duchess's mouth, Cooper stopped short at the frozen tableau in front of him.

"What'd I miss?" he asked.

"Nothing," said Harley, who'd been on the edge of her seat but now had pulled back. "I thought it was a murder/suicide." She turned her eyes Jamie's way. Jamie flicked a look toward Emma, but Emma was watching Duchess wrangle playfully with Cooper. Cooper, brown hair falling forward, couldn't disengage from the dog and was grinning as Duchess decided it was time to play.

"I'm going to change," said Harley and took the steps two at a time, which caught Duchess's attention. The dog turned around, her flaglike tail swooping out behind her as she rushed up the stairs after Harley.

"Dinner's in, uh, ten," Jamie called after her. Cooper, freed up, washed his hands at the kitchen sink, then swept Jamie close and nuzzled her neck until she grinned and slapped at him. "You're tickling me!"

Emma said in her flat way, "I want Twink to live with us here."

Jamie and Cooper slowly pulled apart.

"The cat?" Jamie asked.

"Mr. Atkinson thinks Twink is bad for business," said Emma.

"Hmmm." Cooper was faintly amused and trying not to show it. Well, yeah, Twink was bad for business. Who needed a "death prognosticator" amongst their elderly clientele? "Maybe you should ask the cat if she wants to leave," he suggested as he reached into the refrigerator for a beer.

"Twink won't answer me."

Cooper pulled out a bottle opener from the junk drawer and snapped off the cap, eyeing his sister-in-law.

"Twink doesn't talk," Emma pointed out. "But she plays with Jewell's feet in the dining room, even though she knows she's not supposed to. Jewell will probably die."

Harley's steps clambered down the stairs. She appeared in sweats and socks." The cat plays with her feet?" she asked as she rejoined them.

Emma nodded gravely. "And then Mr. Atkinson will chase her out."

"I think we need to talk this over, Emma," said Cooper.

"We need a little time to think about it," agreed Jamie. "And who's to say Twink would stay with us anyway? You said she was missing for a while, but then showed up again at Ridge Pointe. She seems to think it's her home."

"Ridge Pointe *is* her home. But it can't be with Mr. Atkinson there." Emma was clear on that.

"Too bad he's not the one Twink's after," said Harley, coming into the kitchen.

"Harley," Jamie admonished her daughter. Harley shrugged and grabbed up a couple of cherry tomatoes from the bowl on the counter.

"I'm saving those for the salad," said Jamie. Then, "What did you two talk about over there?" She inclined her head to where Harley and Emma had quietly conferred earlier.

"I told Harley that I didn't want her to die," said Emma seriously.

"And I told her the girl committed suicide and that's not in my plans," Harley stated firmly.

"Well, that's good news," said Jamie.

"Yes, it is," said Emma.

Cooper suggested, "Let's table all this talk about the camp for now."

Emma lifted her chin. "Jamie, I know you don't want me to have your baby, but I would like Twink to be mine."

As Jamie struggled for some kind of response, Harley put in, "What about Duchess?" The dog perked up and wagged her tail. "Duchess hates the cat."

"Hate is a very strong word," said Emma sternly.

"Dislikes intensely, then. Mom, I'm gonna go over and see Marissa. I don't know why she's not here for dinner."

"After dinner. Please!" Jamie called as Harley turned toward the front door. "After dinner. I asked Marissa to dinner but she's with her mom tonight. You know that."

Harley lifted her hands as if in surrender and came back to seat herself at the table. Cooper joined her. "Can I have one of those?" Harley inclined her head to the beer.

"Twenty-one," Cooper said amiably.

Jamie sighed. This was their funny little exchange damn near nightly. She should be glad they liked each other so much. Harley could just as easily resent her stepfather. But Jamie felt so anxious and tense these days about just about everything that she failed to see the humor. After she talked to Cooper she needed to tell Harley and Emma that it looked like Mary Jo was pregnant, but she'd hoped to have a better time. But when would that be? Before Harley went to camp, or after? Probably before. But when? Now? In a day or two? And maybe Marissa should be privy to the information at the same time. The baby would be part of her extended family as well.

"I wish you weren't going to that camp," Jamie said with more emphasis than she'd planned.

"You, too? Why? Because it's haunted?" asked Harley.

"She also doesn't want you to die," said Emma.

"I told you. I'm not going to die. Bring in the death cat. I'll prove it."

The timer went off and Jamie yanked on her oven mitts and pulled out the casserole. "Dinner's ready," she stated firmly. "Harley, finish setting the table. Emma, you can help. You, too, Cooper."

Cooper, Emma, and Harley all looked at one another at Jamie's sharp tone. Duchess saw the exchange and gave a yip of worry. Without another word they all pitched in to help, then sat down to the meal.

# Chapter 3

It was getting on 6:00 p.m. when Brooke Daniels surreptitiously glanced at the clock as she listened to the droning voice of her boss, Franklin Lerner, who was complaining to his top foreman about the length of time it had been taking one of the landscape crews to mow a yard. It didn't matter that it had rained solidly the months of April and May, and the ground was so waterlogged that it was hard to cross the lawn without sinking into it. Brooke did the books for Greenscape, which consisted mostly of entering data into the landscaping company's computer and making sure everything balanced with the checking account and balance sheet. She'd been doing it for nearly a year and sometimes, like today, she wondered if this was the extent of her life, working at Greenscape, waiting to kick-start her stalled life.

By the time she was able to wrap up her day, it felt like an eternity had passed, but in truth it was only another half hour. She reached for her shoulder bag, which she kept stashed under her desk, and then took one more gander at her email.

The heading jumped out at her: CAMP "LOVE SHACK" REUNION!!!

Her heart froze for a beat.

She stared at it, feeling the freeze slowly extend to her core and down her limbs. She'd spent years forgetting about that camp. Forcefully blocking the memories. But now she could feel a door crack open inside her mind like a lifting of the lid of Pandora's Box, the ills clamoring to be set free. With an effort, she slammed it closed.

"No."

But her index finger was poised over the email. She stared at her lightly peach-covered nail. Saw how the digit trembled. She had to curl her hand into a fist to stop the urge to see what the message contained.

The email had clearly been sent and resent, addresses added in a long string. In the middle of the pack Rona's name flashed out at her like a neon warning.

Swallowing, Brooke shut down her computer. Grabbing her coat, she set her jaw and pushed out of the office and to the front door of the meandering one-story concrete building. She threw a glance at the still-threatening gray skies as she skipped around water-filled depressions in the parking lot tarmac, her mind churning. June rain. June gloom. And at the camp, maybe June . . . fog?

A reunion?

Fat chance.

She climbed into her dark blue Ford Explorer, a gift from her husband—more like a castoff, really—and drove away, blind to everything but the email header still imprinted in the forefront of her mind. Had Wendy's name been there, too? She hadn't seen it. But then she hadn't seen much of anything after absorbing that headline.

She'd spent nearly twenty years trying to forget that camp.

As she pulled into her spot in the apartment complex, she glanced at the time. Six forty-five. She dashed up the stairs to her second-floor unit. Since she and Brody had split, this one-bedroom Laurelton "Luxury Apartment Home" had been her abode. Did she love it? No. Did she want to move back with Brody into their spacious ranch with its mid-century modern vibe? Yes . . . maybe. Was it going to happen unless something changed between them? No.

But tonight she'd agreed to attend a cocktail party with him. A work affair, of some kind. The kind of affair she normally abhorred, but what else was she doing?

Brody had offered to move out of the house ten months earlier, when Brooke had said she was leaving, but she hadn't wanted him to be the magnanimous one. She wanted to be mad at him. She wanted it to be his fault that the marriage had foundered. A friend at work had asked Brooke what had happened, and Brooke had no ready answer. They'd met, fallen in love, gotten married and then . . . God knew. A niggling thought dug into her brain, one that was constantly aggravating her because there was a grain of truth in there that wouldn't go away no matter how hard she tried to ignore it.

*You never let him really get close. Purposefully never let him get close.*

She squeezed her fingers hard around the steering wheel. A mental picture of the email spread across her mind.

*It's all Camp Love Shack's fault, isn't it?*

"Camp Fog Lake," she corrected herself.

*Sure thing, Brooke. Camp Fog Lake. That's going to make it better.*

The truth was, it would always be Camp Love Shack to anyone who'd gone to the place before the twenty-year shutdown. Especially those, like herself, who were there that last season it was open.

But her failed marriage was Brody's fault, too, she reminded herself. He, too, was secretive, especially in his dealings at Daniels Century Prime, never fully letting her know what his business was about even though before their marriage she'd been in finance as well. Still . . .

Dropping her purse on the bed, she took a quick shower and then brushed out her shoulder-length brown hair. The blond highlights she'd so scrupulously kept in place until she'd left Brody were nearly buried beneath her true color: mousy brown.

She was in the process of threading the thin metal wire through her left pierced ear, the one that always gave her fits, when she heard her doorbell ring insistently.

*BZZZZ! BZZZZ! BZZZZ!*

Brody. Jesus, he was early. He was always early. She wished he'd let her drive herself, like she'd planned. Why in God's name had she agreed to go with him? They were well on the road to divorce.

Throwing a last glance at herself in the mirror, she smoothed the lines between her brows. If she didn't watch it she was going to have a permanent scowl. Her green eyes stared accusingly back at her, but her mind drifted past them to a scene from the past, from the camp, as tendrils of fog curled around the bodies grappling on the ground.

*BZZZZZZZZZZZ!*

"Coming. Shit. Hold your horses."

When she threw open the door he was leaning against the jamb. Was it a practiced pose? Maybe. Maybe not. He was always kind of like that. Relaxed. Capable of handling his emotions. Setting things aside instead of making his life utter chaos, which she could admit she tended to do.

He glanced down at her hand and saw the earring nestled in her palm. "Need some help?"

"No." She ripped out the other earring and turned back toward the bathroom. She had another memory of him trying to guide the earring through her left ear while she let her hands slide down his body and across his crotch. The silent grin that stole across his face as he still attempted to thread the earring through. The bubble of laughter that escaped her and then the two of them lost in lovemaking, up against the bathroom counter, stumbling to the bed, sliding down to the floor, clothes flung with abandon. That had been before a cocktail party, too. One they hadn't made.

"You're early," she complained. "I'm not ready."

"Well, hurry up."

She was completely aware of him in her living room. It had always been that way. He had lean good looks, a head of brown hair faintly touched by gold. His eyes appeared dark brown, but up close they were a lighter, tawny shade. She'd seen them sparkling with repressed amusement, and flinty and hard. Tonight they'd projected polite interest. They hadn't had much in-person contact since the split. A lot of terse telephone conversations and texts, but no physical presence. The last month or so tensions had seemed to dissipate some, maybe more on her end than his. She hadn't fully asked him why he wanted her to join him tonight, nor had she examined why she'd agreed.

*You wanted to see him.*

Well, yeah, but just for curiosity's sake. The marriage was over. It didn't mean they couldn't be civil, maybe even nice to each other. "Friends" was probably pushing it, but in time, maybe.

She'd met him when she'd worked at East Glen Bank. He'd been in investments in a larger financial institution than hers, and then had gone out on his own. At his encouragement, she'd drifted out of the financial world completely during their marriage. She'd dreamed of children, a family life, but it never seemed to be the right time.

*Whose fault was that?*

She smoothed an imaginary wrinkle on her royal blue dress. It had three-quarter-length sleeves and a boat neck. She had a pair of matching pumps, but opted instead for black sandals with a comfortable heel. Cocktail parties were notorious for not having enough chairs and she'd be damned if she would spend another night ruining her feet.

Picking up a small clutch, she took out her tiny wallet, phone, and a tube of lipstick from her everyday shoulder bag, placing the bag in a side nightstand drawer before tucking the black clutch under her arm and heading back to the living room. "Ready?" she asked briskly.

"You look nice," was the response.

She grabbed her coat, went to the door before him, and let herself out, locking the door behind them. They drove out of Laurelton and into neighboring River Glen in his Tesla. He pulled into the street level lot behind the River Glen Grill and found a space. The cocktail party was at the top of the building, a new event area atop the penthouse apartment, not far from downtown River Glen.

They took the elevator past the penthouses to the roof of the building. The doors opened onto a ballroom with floor-to-ceiling windows on three sides. It was large enough to cover at least half of the building's square footage. Brooke looked through the windows. She was at the center of River Glen's commercial district, but her gaze reached past it and toward the row of elms that she knew lined Clifford Street. She looked beyond them to where she knew the border to Laurelton lay. Her and Brody's rambling Craftsman-style home, which Brooke had remodeled down to a gnat's eyebrow, sat just across that border.

Brody got her a drink—a lemon drop martini—and that's the last she saw of him for a while as he was swept up by business associates. She gazed at the fake trees lining the back wall with their array of twinkling crystal lights, then turned to look out the windows once more. The sky was darkening with clouds. June gloom settling over the area. Brooke kept a lookout for Brody, generally aware of where he was, but stayed across the room. She caught sight of him as a dark-haired woman in a tight red dress touched his elbow. He turned around and smiled at her warmly.

She knocked back the rest of the lemon drop and went to the bar to order another. It might be over, but that didn't make it easy.

"Can I get you another one of those?" A young man who couldn't be much beyond his midtwenties nodded toward the empty glass she was placing on the bar.

"Why not?" Brooke smiled at him. "It's a lemon drop."

"You here with Brody Daniels?"

"How could you tell?"

"I saw you come in with him." He turned to the bartender and ordered her drink, then turned back. "I'm Tom Hennessey." He held out his hand and Brooke shook it.

"Brooke Daniels."

He pretended surprise. "The wife?"

She had a feeling he already knew it. Just something about his trying way too hard to seem casual. His eyes were dark and his chin was strong and dimpled. He had a three-day growth of dark stubble that wasn't unattractive and his hair was styled back with product. He'd had his nails done and there was something so GQ about him that she asked, "What do you do, Tom? Manage hedge funds and REITs?" Those were Real Estate Investment Trusts. "Run the investment-banking department of some venerable financial institution? Crash business cocktail parties?"

"I'm someone's date, too."

"Really?" She looked around. "Whose?"

"Hers."

He indicated the woman in the red dress who, along with Brody, had suddenly become aware that Brooke and Tom were talking together. The woman said a few words to Brody, apparently a goodbye, then hustled over to slip her arm through the crook of Tom's arm. Tom looked faintly amused and the woman gave Brooke a wide smile of greeting that didn't quite meet her eyes.

"Hi, I'm Jacqui Dortland," she said.

"Brooke."

"Brody says you're his . . . wife? So glad to meet you. I'm trying to talk him out of his merger and to come with us.

We're Tumwater Financial and we've been in business for years under different names. Your husband is just what we're looking for in our stable of professionals."

Brooke slid a glance across the room toward Brody, who met her eyes and gave a small shake of his head, meaning he had no interest in Jacqui in any form. Brooke couldn't decide whether she was annoyed or amused; she knew Brody so well. But underneath it all she could feel a deepening anxiety and she prodded it, seeking to see what was really bothering her. No surprise that it had nothing to do with any of this. It was the message from Camp Love Shack's director. Hope something or other.

*Camp Fog Lake*.

Momentarily she was thrown backward in time . . . remembered shivering uncontrollably as she and Rona grabbed the six-person canoe and dragged it through the fog to the water's edge . . .

"What?" She came back with a jolt, realizing Jacqui and Tom were looking at her expectantly.

"I said, do you want to join us for dinner afterward?" Jacqui asked. Her tone was a little tight, as if she wasn't used to being ignored.

"I can't. I'm sorry. It's gotta be an early night for me. I joined Brody tonight as a favor to him." Let them figure that one out, she thought, as she left them and meandered in Brody's direction. He saw her coming and waited for her.

"Ready to go?" he asked.

"I've been ready since I came here. Why did you want me here? I'm not in this world anymore and I don't want to be."

"I'll get our coats."

Outside, he touched her elbow and led her back to his Tesla. He drove in the opposite direction of her apartment and when Brooke protested, he said they needed to eat and he was taking her to a spot he'd found on Portland's west side.

It turned out to be an unremarkable door with AU REVOIR written on it. *Goodbye?*

Inside was a small dining room with tables set along floor-to-ceiling windows that looked out on a courtyard, each table circled by light, silk curtains that obscured them from the rest of the room while giving the patrons a view of the courtyard. The maître d' took them to a table for two and pulled back Brooke's chair, murmuring that their waiter would be back with them soon to take their drink order. He drew the curtain, and Brooke was left staring across at her husband. She turned her attention to the view outside the window. A central fountain with clipped box hedges surrounding it threw out splashes of diamond-bright water that flowed into a cache basin to be collected and pumped upward again.

She watched the fountain for long moments before asking without looking at him, "What are you doing?"

"I wanted to see you."

"You could have taken me to McDonald's for that."

"No, I couldn't."

Now she turned toward him. The truth was she already liked the restaurant's French ambiance and if the cuisine matched it, she would remember the place, although the money it might take to eat here would probably decide whether she returned or not.

"I don't want a divorce," he said.

"Oh, come on."

"I've changed my mind."

Her temper rose. "You don't get to just change your mind."

"Give me a good explanation about why you want a divorce. You've never said. You just drifted away. No. Correction. You were never there in the first place."

"You've been to a shrink. You're speaking shrink-talk."

"I've tried to get past your defenses but your walls are too high. I thought that you would come back to me if I gave into your decisions. That you wouldn't travel this path."

"I don't know what you're talking about." But her heart was thumping, and she could feel her face flush.

"Something happened to you. Something you can't let go of."

The panic she felt was out of proportion to his words. The waiter returned at that moment, and Brooke turned to him gratefully. "A lemon drop. No . . . um . . . make it a vodka martini. Skyy, Grey Goose . . . whatever."

"I'll have the same," said Brody and when they were alone again he turned his gaze on her with an intensity that made her quiver inside. "Alcohol isn't going to save you. Get as drunk as you like."

"I will," she said tightly. She picked up the menu but the words swirled before her eyes. He'd tried this before and she'd managed to brush him off. She was kind of thrilled by the attention but she knew better. She might have her secrets but he was a master at blue smoke and mirrors, something she'd always sensed but ignored far too long.

He lapsed into silence and so did she, only speaking up when they both ordered, *boeuf bourguignon* for him; Lyonnaise salad for her. It was delicious, but she could hardly eat more than a few bites because her head and body were fighting off emotions she didn't want to address.

He talked some more but she barely heard him. She declined dessert and coffee, refusing to admit that the drinks had given her a headache.

At her apartment she tried to say goodbye at his car and hurry to the outdoor stairs alone, but he was right on her heels. When she opened her door she felt him right behind her, literally breathing down her neck. She didn't even try to slam the door on him. She'd already calculated if that would work and determined it wouldn't. She would have to freeze him out with an icy demeanor, but when she marched into her living room and turned around he was right there, pulling her close, kissing her on the mouth and neck and cheeks. She had her balled fists on his chest but she didn't resist. She didn't want to resist. Did she love him still? Had she ever? She'd married him; that much was true. She'd wanted to be married. That was also true. But her reasons— and his, too—for actually walking down the aisle were complicated.

But right now his tongue was lightly touching her ear. He knew her weak spots, and he was making her insides turn to liquid. She wanted to drag him to her bed and make love. It had been too long.

The email headline flashed like neon inside her head again, and she thought of the camp.

"I can't, Brody," she murmured, pushing away.

He doubled his efforts and Brooke closed her eyes and swayed against him. He was still her husband. It didn't matter that she didn't trust him, maybe didn't even like him that much anymore. She still wanted him.

*Oh, hell . . .*

She stopped fighting and let her hands slide up his shirt. When she unbuttoned his top button, his hands slid to the zipper on the back of her dress. Moments later her dress was pooled by her feet and she was helping him with his belt.

They fell on the couch together with Brody still half-dressed. Both of them were chuckling, their mouths curved with laughter as they kissed, but then he stripped off his pants and boxers and with a muscular twist pulled her beneath him. Brooke grabbed his buttocks and soon they were thrusting against each other, both of them seeking control. When Brody tried to pull back, she muttered fiercely, "Don't stop."

"Relax. We've got all night," he answered.

Brooke forced herself to let him pick the tempo. She wanted to scream at him to hurry the hell up. But then her body responded of its own accord and she let go, riding the moment until they both reached a climax together.

When he collapsed against her she was already staring at the ceiling and seeking to control her breathing. At the camp she'd engaged in some fumbling-around sex with Owen Paulsen. She'd wanted Donovan. They all had. But she'd settled for Owen because he'd pursued her.

That could almost be said of Brody, too, she realized with a painful pang of self-awareness. She'd settled for Brody because he'd pursued her.

She struggled beneath him and he raised himself on his elbows. Brooke pushed away from him and quickly gathered up her clothes, carrying them into the bedroom. She tossed the heap on the floor of her closet and grabbed a terrycloth robe, wrapping the sash around her tightly before returning to the living room. Brody had managed to retrieve his boxers and was putting a leg through his pants when she returned.

"This doesn't mean anything," she said.

He zipped up his pants, grabbed his shirt, and shoved his arms through it. "I gotta be honest, Brooke. I know your secret."

That gave her a chill, but she just smiled tightly. "I don't know how many times I have to tell you, there is no secret."

He lifted a hand to dismiss her. "Have it your way, but there's something I have to tell you."

She crossed her arms and waited. He always changed tactics to get her to unburden herself. They would thrust and parry until one of them got angry and ended the argument.

"Brooke, a man came to me and told me he was a PI and that you were having an affair with Franklin Lerner's son."

Brooke's mouth dropped open. She almost laughed. This was new. "What?"

He regarded her soberly and she realized that he was deadly serious.

"You're kidding. This is a joke. Franklin's *son*? He's like fifteen or sixteen. *A kid!* Who told you that? Who is this guy?"

"I don't know. He came to my office a few days ago."

"It's bullshit. Bullshit!" When he didn't respond, she snapped, "You think I had sex with a *teenager*?"

"Calm down. I didn't say I believed it."

"Oh, thanks for that. Your show of support is mind-boggling."

"Brooke, what are you into? There's some reason he came to me."

"Goddammit, Brody . . . Who is he? Why did he come to you about me?"

"You're my wife. I think he—"

"We haven't lived together for months. How does he know me? Who's behind this?" She was trembling with outrage. This was so Brody. Blindsiding her when she sought any independence. But this?

"The guy gave me his card, which proved to be a fake."

"Oh . . . great . . . okay . . ." She waited, holding herself back from completely losing her shit.

"I followed up and found out he was an entire fake. I don't know what's going on. I decided to talk to you directly."

"Jesus, Brody."

"I'm trying to figure it out," he said with extreme patience. "Maybe you can tell me why this came up?"

He was fishing. A new and utterly repugnant tactic that infuriated her. "You couldn't have mentioned this *before* we had sex?"

"You're the one who wanted it."

"Get out. Just get away from me."

"I'm not making this up, Brooke. I'm going to get to the bottom of it. I promise." He buttoned his shirt and slipped into his shoes. She stalked to the door and threw it open.

As he walked outside, she said tightly, "No one's said that about Lukey and me. You made it up."

"Lukey?"

"What're you hoping for? That it's true?"

"You're unfair, Brooke."

"Well, pardon me."

"I know a private investigator. A real one. I'll ask him to look into this guy. Find out who he is and what his game is."

"Do that."

"I know it's not having sex with someone underage, Brooke."

"Really? Coulda fooled me."

"If you were just honest with me . . ."

He was waiting for her to . . . what? Explain herself? Was this his way of coming at her from another angle, hoping to expose her secret?

He lifted a hand, maybe realizing her temper was reaching the boiling point. "Maybe it has to do with me. Maybe someone's trying to screw up the merger and trying to get to me through you. It would help if you told me the truth."

"What merger?"

"Never mind."

"What merger, Brody?"

He just shook his head and stalked across the room and out of the apartment. She listened for his retreating footsteps and then hurried into the kitchen to look out the window to the parking lot, watching his ground-eating strides cross the tarmac to his Tesla. There was no roar of the engine coming to life. The electric car slid silently away.

Brooke slumped against the counter. She felt exhausted. Pulling herself together with an effort, she grabbed the clutch purse from where she'd tossed it and strode into her bedroom. Taking her phone from her purse, she scrolled through her emails till she found the headline she was looking for: CAMP "LOVE SHACK" REUNION!!!

Carefully, she tapped her screen, opening the email. She read through it, heart in her throat. The details of the "fun-filled weekend for alumni and parents!" barely registered. Still carrying her phone, she headed on unsteady legs into the bathroom. She gazed at herself in the mirror, leaning close, staring at herself accusingly.

Her secret?

Instead of her own green eyes reflecting back at her she saw other images. Herself. Clawing at a face. Her body rolling painfully along the pebbled shore, locked in an embrace she didn't want. Her legs, staggering after Rona. Her arms dragging the heavy canoe and then rowing, rowing, rowing. Other arms rowing, too. Fog over everything. The corpse's white face staring upward at them, rivulets of black blood coursing over his eyes.

She swallowed hard.

They were all in it together.

*Murder.*

# Chapter 4

Harley watched Emma and Duchess walk inside Ridge Pointe and she felt a moment of melancholy. Emma moved with a flat gait that went along with her flat tone of voice. Though Emma's disability normally didn't get to Harley, she knew how much Emma had wanted to be Mom's surrogate, and it felt unfair that she couldn't be. This Mary Jo person whom Theo had found seemed okay. She had a couple of kids of her own and had been a surrogate for someone else already, so maybe it would work out. Still, it made Harley feel sad for Emma, who probably would have done just fine as Mom's surrogate. It just couldn't be.

And what the hell was going on with Mom? She was tense and irritable all the time. Not her usual self. Maybe the whole surrogate thing was getting to her, too. Truthfully, Harley had been really gung-ho about the possibility of a baby a couple months back, but now she wasn't sure. Everything felt wrong and she really, really wanted to go away to camp.

Greer . . .

She felt a little sick to her stomach when she thought

about her ex-boyfriend. Could she really even call him an ex-boyfriend? They'd dated his senior year and then he'd gone off to college the following summer and that had kind of been it. There was no big declaration of love and there'd been no messy breakup. He'd just left, and communication had petered out and eventually stopped. If he came home for holidays she didn't know it, though she did drive by his dad's place now and again. And, of course, she checked on Insta and other social media, and so kind of kept up with him, although he'd never held a big presence anywhere on the internet. But that's how she'd learned about the camp. When Allie's name had popped up on his account, she'd moved to try and see what she was doing. Turned out Allie wasn't picky about who saw her posts and there was a picture of Greer, his arm around her, smiling down at her. Shouldn't have hurt, really. If someone told Harley the guy they'd dated a few years earlier had a new girlfriend, she would have told them, "Get over it."

She drove back to Clifford Street, lost in thought. She'd said she was going to see Marissa, but she'd changed her mind. Marissa was madly in love with Cam and Harley was a little tired of hearing about it. In the beginning Harley had been all for Marissa's first real romance, but now she felt Cam was just okay. Actually, no. Scratch that. Cam Dornbrenner was just another horny creep, in Harley's biased opinion. A pain in the ass. Up until this past spring Marissa had spent most of her time with Harley at Mom and Cooper's, but ever since Cam came into the picture Marissa had been hanging out at her mom's place because she lived in the same neighborhood as Cam's family.

But, at least Marissa was going to camp with her. Hallelujah! She just hoped Marissa could put Cam out of her mind long enough to have a good time.

"Mom?" Harley closed the front door behind her, but there was no sign of her mother. "Mom?" she tried again as she cruised through the kitchen. She and Marissa had made Rice

Krispies treats the day before and she dug into the cookie jar, snagging the last square, biting into the gooey, crunchy confection. Their earlier meal had been kind of strained.

"I'm upstairs," Harley heard the muffled answer.

She took the stairs two at a time. She wished Emma and Duchess were still here. How would it be with a cat?

*And a baby.*

"Where are you?" Harley mumbled around a mouthful of Rice Krispies.

"Cleaning your bathroom."

"Oh."

Mom struggled with Harley's haphazard housekeeping skills. Harley had to admit she was not the best with domestic chores, especially when it came to washing, sorting, and hanging up her clothes. She could hear the television in Mom and Cooper's bedroom and figured that's where Cooper was.

She walked into her own room and looked around. The tassel from her mortarboard lay in a silky tangle of blue and white on her dresser. Graduation had only been a few weeks earlier but already felt like it was in the distant past. She closed her eyes and fervently wished herself into Greer's arms, then smiled bitterly at the stupidness of that thought.

"Get over it. Get the hell over it. Get the fuck over it," she whispered, angry at herself.

*Don't go to the camp. Don't torture yourself.*

Oh, she was going. Was it likely a mistake? Yes. But too damn bad.

She sat down on her bed. It was dangerous to go, but not because people had died there. That was all just old stuff that she was interested in because she wanted to be armed with information and a good eerie tale. The reason she, Harley, shouldn't go was because somehow the camp director, Hope, was connected to Allie, and that's why Allie was going to be there, and that's why Greer would be there, too. According to what she'd gleaned on social media, Greer had been hired by Hope (urged on by Allie) as an all-around aide to the camp maintenance crew.

Was it a sick act of masochism to be around Greer and Allie? Undoubtedly, though she just wanted to see for herself that it was really over. Sure, it would be great if Greer suddenly tossed Allie aside and ran back to her. Harley certainly entertained herself with visions of just such a reunion, but the practical side to her nature also wanted closure. If Greer was truly with Allie, like forever and always, then Harley had to get over it, one way or another. Maybe then she could move on. Go to college. Take that trip to London. Experience the rest of England and Great Britain as a whole . . . the continent . . . eat at that restaurant in the Eiffel Tower . . . sun herself on the Greek isles . . . climb the seven hills of Rome, or something. Get the hell away from River Glen and Greer Douglas.

Brooke's phone buzzed at 10:30 p.m. It was plugged in silently on her nightstand but its light flashed and she read the phone number across the illuminated square before it blinked off. Not one she immediately recognized. She let it go. If they wanted her they could leave a voice mail. But then the phone lit up again as the caller rang back. This time she reached for it, feeling a low-level dread, the same dread that had been following her since being with Brody, hearing him say all those things that had made her want to cover her head with her pillow.

She unplugged the phone from its charger and answered carefully, "Hello?"

"You got the invitation from Camp Love Shack?"

A thrill of fear traced a line down Brooke's spine. She recognized the voice immediately. Rona. She hadn't spoken to her old friend in years. An email here and there. An invitation to her weddings, which Brooke had sent regrets to. A chance meeting outside an eatery in downtown Laurelton where both of them had stared at each other for an awkward moment too long.

"Did you get it?" Rona asked again. "Are you going?"

Brooke struggled to sit up in bed, turning on the bedside lamp. Warm yellow light spilled across her white matelassé coverlet with its diamond pattern, dispelling lingering ghosts. "No."

"I am."

Rona sounded as tough and militant as always. Nearly twenty years and it felt like yesterday. Gooseflesh rose on Brooke's arms in spite of herself. "Why would you do that? I'm not going back there. I can't believe you're going."

"It's only a weekend."

"I don't care if it's five minutes. I don't want to ever go back there!"

"My daughter, Kiley, is going."

Brooke sank back against her pillows, staring up at the ceiling. The annoyance in Rona's voice was edged with anger . . . or possibly fear. Rona's first marriage had lasted less than five years, but she'd gotten Kiley from it, and Brooke had watched the girl grow up in the series of Christmas cards that had arrived over the years. Rona's second marriage was still ongoing, as far as she knew.

"Come with me," Rona urged. "I want to see the place again."

Brooke heard the old persuasion in Rona's voice and was frustrated with herself for feeling even the tiniest bit swayed. Or, was her ambivalence now because she just wanted to run away and forget her current problems?

"I need to make sure Kiley's okay. She's headstrong . . . And I kind of want to know what really happened," added Rona.

"Rona, I'm not going. I'm not going to revisit bad times."

"Doesn't it eat at you? Not knowing?"

"No."

"They found Ryan's body in the lake. You and I know it wasn't Ryan who killed her."

"I don't want to think about it!"

"That girl on the ledge? Fern? She wasn't his lover."

"Yes, she was. And it was Ryan's body they fished out. They're not going to say it was Ryan, if it wasn't. It was in the paper and on the news and he wasn't at camp anymore. It *was* Ryan, and I don't know what happened and I don't care."

*And what about what we did?*

"Ryan died, but I don't think it had anything to do with what happened to Fern."

"Another tragedy. That damn place is evil and haunted."

"That's why I'm worried about Kiley, but she's not listening to me."

"Can't you stop her?"

Rona laughed shortly. "Oh, sure. That's how it works. If I try to force her into anything, she'll just run to her father and he'll take her side, and he and I will get into another big fight."

"Rona, I'm not going. I . . . hate that place. It's terrible."

Brooke heard the frail tone of her voice. She didn't want to think about Camp Love Shack, and she didn't want to think about Brody, and she didn't want to think about what she and her high school friends had done.

"Just think about it," urged Rona.

Brooke laughed aloud.


Rona waited on the other end of the line, wondering if Brooke was getting a bit hysterical. Maybe she'd counted way too much on this phone call with her old friend. At one time she'd been able to coerce and cajole Brooke, but those days appeared to be long over.

She stared through the white pane windows of her cottage at the edge of Silver Creek Park, the five acres of wooded property the locals had saved from the developers. She gazed past the Douglas firs and the one majestic coastal redwood that anchored this end of the park, but her eyes were blind to the lush greenery of the deciduous trees, the maples and aspens and shrubbery as she thought back to those last weeks at Camp Love Shack. She'd expected Brooke would be stubborn. That hadn't changed in all these years. Brooke always wanted to hide her head and cover her ears. Always had. Caution or cowardice, pick your descriptor. But she'd thought she could talk her—or maybe guilt her—into going anyway.

Brooke, after an uncomfortably long moment, said, "Something weird happened."

Rona was only half-listening, working on how to wear Brooke down.

"Someone told Brody I was having sex with the teenage son of my boss."

Rona came back to the moment with a bang, choking out a laugh. "You're kidding."

"I don't know. Brody says he thinks it's maybe something to do with him and his business. A smear campaign of some kind."

"And they came after you? Why? When did this happen?"

"Just recently, I guess." A pause. "It's not true."

"You don't have to tell me that. There's no way you've changed that much. Do you and Brody even still have sex?" she asked, amused.

"Jesus, Rona."

"Just asking."

Another pause and then, "Brody and I have split up."

"Oh." Whoops. That was a misstep. "Sorry. I didn't know."

"Doesn't matter. But I'm not going to Camp Fog Lake. What about Wendy? Why don't you ask her to go with you?"

A scene flashed in front of Rona's eyes. Wendy on her back with him above her. Her eyes turning to Rona. Her mouth opening on a scream. Shivering, she shook off the memory with an effort.

Rona had been friends with Wendy since third grade, even before Brooke moved into their school district, but they'd been estranged for years. None of them had felt comfortable with one another after the events at Camp Love Shack. But now Rona needed their support.

"I'm calling her next, but I wanted to touch base with you first. I want you to go with me. It's just a weekend. Two nights."

"Or take your husband," Brooke said pointedly.

Rona snorted. Husband? He was no husband. They hadn't been intimate for years. That's why she'd accused Brooke of the same thing. She tried a different tack. "I heard the new camp director has wanted to put the place back together for years and she's finally doing it. The camp's hers. But she's been working against its reputation."

"How do you know so much?"

"I read. I watch the news." Rona tried to keep from sounding like a smart-ass but wasn't sure she was successful. She knew a lot more about Brooke, too, than she probably realized. And Brody.

"What happened to Joy?"

"She closed the camp and quit it all, I guess. This new one, Hope Something, is about ten years younger than Joy, closer to our ages."

"Well . . ." Brooke drew a breath and Rona could tell she was about to end their conversation.

"I'm not giving up on you, Brooke. I'm going to do some digging before we go back."

"You can't talk me into things anymore. I've got to take care of stuff around here. I've got to find out who's spreading those vicious, unfounded rumors about me. Brody says

he's on it, but I need to deal with this. I mean . . . goddammit!"

"I get it, but—"

"I'm not going back, Rona," she cut her off.

"Bet the sheriff's department knows a lot about Ryan and
that girl and . . . other things."

"What other things?"

"When that parents/alumni weekend invitation email
showed up, it was like it was meant to be."

"You're not listening. I don't want to ever go there ever
again."

"I need help with Kiley and I know you're just the person
who can talk to her. You were always good at that. She doesn't
listen to me at all, but she will you. If I go alone, she'll just
blow me off."

"Oh, c'mon. She doesn't even know me."

"All the better. Just talk to her, listen to her. I get too
pissed off when I'm with her. I tell myself not to yell at her,
but I can't help myself."

"What am I supposed to say to her? Don't stay at the
camp? Your mom wants you to come home? It's dangerous
here? People die? We *made* people die?"

"We didn't make people die!"

"Yeah, right." There was a fatalism in her voice. Then,
"Does she know?"

"Of course not. But I don't want anything bad to happen
to her, like it did to us."

"Like it did to Wendy," Brooke corrected.

"Like it did to all of us," Rona retorted.

"We weren't the victims."

"Weren't we? Really, Brooke. Weren't we all victims?
This has followed us around for twenty years. We were good
friends, damn it. We should be again. And we will be. Starting now. Meet me for lunch."

"Goodbye, Rona."

"Saturday. Before Kiley leaves."

"Saturday's no good."

"Sunday then. At Lucille's."

"Jesus," Brooke muttered, and the line went dead.

Well . . . hell . . .

Discouraged, Rona stepped away from the window and turned around, her phone still at her ear. The shadow of a man stood in the doorway in a pool of moonlight and for a moment her breath caught in a gasp before she recognized her husband. She immediately felt a spurt of anger. He'd said he wouldn't be home till late, yet here he was. Sneaky fucker. Always trying to catch her out.

"Eavesdropping?" she demanded.

"Who were you talking to?"

"Do I ask you who you're talking to?"

"You're going to follow Kiley to the camp." He didn't actually accuse her, but it sort of sounded that way.

"I sure am. And Brooke's going with me."

"Really?"

Well, no . . . not yet anyway. But his lazy mocking tone made her half crazy. What in God's name had ever possessed her to marry him? she asked herself, but she knew the answer. She'd thought maybe she could have that suburban life that had been upended when Zach had suddenly said he was in love with someone else even though he'd assured her he still loved her, too. Hah, hah, hah. He just couldn't give up being the "good guy" even when he'd been screwing around behind her back, practically from the moment she'd said, "I do." Hurt and furious at his abandonment, she should have let her anger cool before heading down the aisle again. Her second marriage wasn't any better than her first. And in truth, she wasn't really the type of woman to raise children, either. She hadn't done the best job with Kiley. No PTA or mother-helping, or soccer, or bake sales, or whatever the hell. She had managed to work in real estate over the years, and had once owned several take-and-bake pizza outlets, which had done okay, but nothing spectacular, and later on she'd been glad to sell the whole kit and caboodle. She'd taken classes in finance and had toyed with the idea of working for someone like Brooke's husband, but she'd never quite got that whole plan off the ground. At one point she'd even half seriously thought of grabbing Kiley and running away. Just up and leaving and going . . . somewhere else. But that wouldn't have worked and truthfully wanderlust didn't run in her veins. She just wanted something other than the life she was living.

"What about Wendy?" he asked now.

Wendy. Wendy was a problem.

Rona had told Brooke she was going to contact Wendy next, but she had no intention of doing so. Wendy had gone religious. Like super religious in a way that made Rona question what was really going on there. Her husband, Caleb, had led the way into his church for her, but Rona wasn't convinced his congregation didn't practice some kind of strange and mystical rites of their own making. She remembered Caleb from high school and he'd been popular but sort of weird then, too. She doubted he'd improved with age.

"I'm going to watch TV," she said, brushing past her husband as he stood in the way. To her annoyance he followed her to the open doors to the den. Rona would have slid them closed, but he stood in the aperture. She blocked him from entering with her body.

"I'm going to the camp, too," he said.

"The hell you are." She laughed out loud.

"You weren't the only one invited."

She looked at him, really looked at him. He was tall, putting on weight, not terribly, but enough to remind her that neither of them was getting any younger. His T-shirt strained over his chest. He worked out, though, and his upper arms were strong. His blondish hair had grown a shade or two darker, but his blue eyes were just as sharp as they'd always been.

Donovan Keegan. He'd been there when Zach had

thrown her over and she'd gratefully fallen into his arms. She should've just had an affair with him and skipped the rest, like she'd done at the camp. If he knew what had really happened there, he'd never said, but her deep-seated fear was that he would suddenly remember. He knew something, but it was a subject they didn't discuss.

*Tell him you're leaving him.*

The words hovered on her tongue. She could taste them. Instead, she said coolly, "Not gonna happen, Donovan."

"You can't decide for me."

"What are you going to do? Screw around with the alumni, or maybe the newbies at camp like you did before?"

"I didn't screw around."

"Of course you did. I know you were with Emma Whelan. I *saw* you with her, but you weren't my husband then, so whatev."

"We didn't make love."

"'Make love.' That's what you call it?"

He ignored the jibe. "Do you think she'll be there?"

"Emma? No. Not since she became a . . ."

He was waiting for her to go on. When she didn't, he said, "What were you going to say? A *retard*?"

"I would never say something so awful and politically incorrect!" she flashed. "What do you take me for? You're such an asshole, Donovan! Emma's handicap is a terrible tragedy that shouldn't have happened. I don't know what she's like now. I've just heard she's not the same and she needs to be taken care of. God, Donovan. Just leave me alone!"

With that she grabbed both of the double doors and slammed them firmly in front of his face, nearly smashing his nose. Bastard. What the hell had she ever seen in him? He'd had sex with practically every vagina at Camp Love Shack. Even Emma Whelan, whom Rona had been incredibly jealous of. She'd wished all kinds of bad things on Emma and look what had happened. Yes, of course, it wasn't her fault, but she always felt a twinge of guilt for hating her so much and then learning she'd been forever changed by ugly circumstances beyond her control.

Rona flipped herself onto the couch. But Donovan . . . and Zach before him. All they ever did was screw around on her, no matter what Donovan said.

"You can really pick 'em, girl," she muttered, snapping on the remote. She'd had to have Donovan. Had to. And when the opportunity had arisen she'd snatched at it, realizing too late that Donovan had had his day in the sun in high school. Now he was just a middle-aged man with nothing to offer but a decent paying job.

And the fact that he might be keeping her—their—secret.

Friday morning, Jamie was up at dawn. She slipped on a robe over her thin pajamas, tucked her feet into a pair of sturdy mules, and walked onto the back porch and down the steps into the yard. She'd had a difficult night and wasn't sure what was truly bothering her.

*You should be grateful. Grateful! You're having a baby. Yours and Cooper's and it's what you want.*

"It is what I want," she whispered aloud, meaning it.

The roses were in shades of gray in the dim light, their petals weighted with dew in the damp chill of morning. She could still smell their sweetness, however, and she closed her eyes and breathed deeply.

*I don't like Mary Jo.*

There. She'd said it to herself. She didn't like the woman who was going to carry their baby. Mary Jo was too homey, too sweet, too . . . nourishing, maybe, if there was such a thing? Jamie didn't trust her, even though Mary Jo had already had two children of her own and had served as a surrogate for another family. Mary Jo really had all the bona fides you wanted in a surrogate, and Theo had recommended her and Jamie trusted Theo, who'd been such a good friend to both her mother and to Emma, but . . . but . . .

But Mary Jo worried Jamie. She should be ecstatic that the pregnancy had taken. Should be shouting it to the rooftops, or at least alerting Cooper . . . and Harley, too, who would be the baby's half sister. But she was reluctant to share the news and it wasn't because she was worried that Mary Jo would lose the baby, a very real possibility, but her fear was something deeper, more instinctive.

*Do you think she'll try to keep the baby? Do you think some of Mary Jo will rub off on him or her? Do you think she'll try to stay in your life from here to forever????*

That was getting closer to the crux of it. Her child's life had barely begun and she already wanted to snatch it away from Mary Jo. She didn't want Mary Jo to be the third side of a triangle that included her and Cooper.

"You need to get over it," she scolded herself aloud.

But now Harley was intent on going to that camp, which was near the commune that Mary Jo hailed from. Haven Commune grew produce that they sold in markets all across the region and was fairly self-sustaining. It was well recognized and a source of county pride.

*But those deaths . . .*

At different times two young women's bodies had been found on the ledge above Fog Lake. The deaths were a lot of years ago, but they were similar in nature, both laid out like sacrifices. Had the girls come from the commune? Jamie had very little information on the first one. She wasn't completely sure if she'd been covered in ashes or if that was just a myth. But the second girl's body was definitely sprinkled with ashes. Maybe on the rumors of the first girl's death? If the sheriff's department knew, they weren't saying anything.

One thing for certain, though, a boy Emma had gone to camp with had died in the lake at the same time the second girl was positioned on the ledge. That was a fact, and Harley was all over this information, trying to squeeze something more out of Emma about it, but Emma had gone to Camp Fog Lake when she was in her most secretive phase of high school, a few scant months before she was attacked. Jamie doubted she would remember much about it, and there'd never been any discussion about Haven Commune at all. Emma, at seventeen, just hadn't had much interest in anything outside of herself.

*Mary Jo doesn't live at the commune and hasn't since she was married. She was just a girl when that second girl was found on the ledge. She doesn't drink, do drugs, indulge in any kind of risky behavior. Heck, she barely drives. She lives on a farm. She's a homebody who loves being pregnant and helping others. You are* lucky *she chose to be your surrogate. If Theo hadn't spoken up for you, she would have chosen some other couple.*

She heard the upstairs shower running and returned to the bedroom and then into the bathroom. Cooper was in the shower, behind the curtain, getting ready for work. The rushing water drowned out Jamie's approach, so she yelled, "I think I'm going to that parents' weekend at the camp!"

Cooper looked around the curtain, his brown hair darkened by water. "When is that?"

"Fourth of July weekend. I'm not going to make you go. In fact, I don't want you to go. You need to stay home and take care of the . . . cat."

"*What?*"

She chuckled, throwing off some of her misgivings. "You said you had some work over the Fourth."

"I promised I'd work that weekend," he agreed. "But . . . *the cat?*"

"Okay, you work and I'll go to the camp."

"Get in here," he said, sweeping back the curtain and inviting her beneath the spray.

She flung off her robe and stripped off her pajamas. "Oh, and uh . . . Mary Jo called." She lifted her right hand in a thumbs-up gesture as she joined him behind the curtain. A slow smile crossed his lips, but he looked at her closely.

"You okay with this?"

Jamie forced her own features to relax as she slipped up against him. "Yes," she said, dragging him beneath the spray and kissing him with water cascading all around. Cooper grinned and Jamie did, too, and they both tried not to choke and sputter as water ran into their mouths, breaking them both into laughter.

There was no need to infect him with her irrational fears. And it was all going to be all right anyway.

"We're going to be parents!" he said in her ear.

Jamie's heart flipped painfully, but she nodded and forced her smile to stay pinned in place.

# Chapter 5

Late on Saturday the sun broke through the gray cloud cover that had persisted the first weeks of June. Jamie, Cooper, Harley, Emma, and Marissa pitched in to have a picnic in the backyard, a kind of wedding reception/graduation party mash-up as Jamie and Cooper had gotten married in April at a small ceremony and Harley and Marissa had just graduated from high school. Neither event had generated a big party; no one had wanted one. But now, as Harley and Marissa were about to head out to camp, they'd managed this impromptu gathering. Jamie laid a red-and-white-checkered tablecloth over the white, foldable table and they all brought a chair from the dining room. Amidst barbecued chicken, potato salad, watermelon wedges, and strawberry shortcake oozing with whipped cream, they congratulated one another, and Jamie finally folded her napkin on the table beside her plate and said, "We have an announcement."

Harley had pushed her strawberry shortcake aside with a groan, declaring she was going to pop, but looked up sharply at her mother. "Mary Jo's pregnant!"

Jamie smiled faintly and Cooper said, "Got it in one."

Feeling Emma's eyes on her, Jamie regarded her sister, who was seated directly across the table from her, and said gently, "I wish it could have been you."

"I could do it."

"I know, Emma. I know you could. But circumstances wouldn't let that happen."

"Wow," said Harley. "I mean . . . wow. Feels weird."

"It's wild," said Marissa. She was looking at her stepfather, her expression hard to read.

Cooper said gently, "Hey, you and I are always going to be good. Doesn't matter. As far as I'm concerned, you're a Haynes."

Marissa nodded and Harley saw her cheeks pinken as if she was holding in emotion with an effort.

Harley raised her glass of lemonade and elbowed Marissa to do the same when she didn't seem to be tracking. "C'mon."

Marissa lifted her own lemonade and everyone else followed suit. Jamie held up her glass of white wine, Cooper his beer, and Emma her water.

"To a wonderful summer ahead and the new addition to our family," said Harley.

Jamie examined her daughter closely, but she seemed okay with it. Actually, she seemed distracted. Something else going on there, she thought.

They clinked glasses and took sips and Emma said, "It won't be a wonderful summer if Harley and Marissa go to that camp. People die there."

"Those were suicides," Harley answered before anyone could say anything. "Really sad and messed-up people, and it was terrible, but that's not Marissa and me. And anyway I've done research," she added, looking around the table. "The first girl that died, I'm not sure about her. Couldn't find anything on her. But the two that died when Emma was there were supposedly a murder/suicide."

"Ryan didn't kill himself," said Emma.

Harley turned to her. "Actually, I think his name was Christopher. He's the one whose body was found in the lake."

"Who, now?" asked Jamie.

Harley was still looking at Emma, who wasn't answering. "Emma said he was one of the guys she knew."

Everyone turned their attention to Emma, who blinked several times and said, "Ryan was going to see me tomorrow, but he never did. He wanted to hang out. He had binoculars."

"Maybe he saw that girl on the ledge, Fern, through his binoculars," said Harley.

"He was nice about the people in the cult, but I think he liked me."

"Yeah, who wouldn't? You were hot," said Harley. "I've seen pictures."

"I wasn't hot. The fog came in."

"The fog came in?" Marissa repeated, her voice rising.

Emma turned to look at her. "Donovan said the fog knew things."

"What?" Harley snorted, but Marissa squeaked out a sound of fear and disbelief.

Jamie held up a hand. "Now, hold on. Where's this going? Let's stop talking about the fog."

"Who's Donovan?" asked Harley. "Was he at the camp?"

"He was there with Lanny and Owen and Ryan," said Emma.

Cooper drawled, "I think I'm losing track of this conversation."

"How could the fog 'know things'?" asked Marissa, completely ignoring Jamie's directive.

"It's sentient," said Emma.

All their heads swiveled her way again. "Now, *there's* a word," said Jamie, taken aback. Emma continually surprised them all with what she knew and didn't know.

"What do you mean?" demanded Harley. "Like the fog has *thoughts*?"

"The fog is *not* sentient," Jamie declared smartly, getting up from the bench around the picnic table. "Who's going to help me clean up?"

Emma said, "The fog and Twink know things that we can't."

"You are freaking me out," muttered Marissa, snatching up her plate.

"It's supposed to freak you out, but don't let it. It's just spooky camp stuff," said Harley as she grabbed her plate and her mom's. She and Marissa hurried ahead of the rest of them, up the back steps and into the kitchen. "Remember, we have to be careful not to say too much in front of the campers. Don't want to scare the kids," added Harley.

She nearly dropped her plate when Marissa suddenly grabbed her by the arm and hissed, "I don't want to go!"

Harley snatched her arm back. "We're packed and leaving. C'mon. Don't let that stuff get to you."

"I never wanted to go! This is your thing."

"This is our last summer together. This fall we go off to college. I'm not even sure where I'm going yet. It's still up in the air. But we gotta enjoy this while—"

"I'm not going away. I'm not leaving Cam. He'll find somebody else, if I'm gone. I need to be around here."

"Are you talking about community college?"

"I'm talking about this summer! I can't think about college! I don't want to leave Cam!"

"He's not going to find somebody else."

"Can't you talk my parents into letting me stay?" she urged anxiously.

"If you weren't coming with me to camp, you'd be doing something else, not hanging around all summer with Cam. They would never let you."

Marissa's plate slipped into the sink with a clatter but luckily didn't break.

"I just want you to go to camp with me. That's all," Harley pressed.

"We're not going to die out there, are we?"

"Seriously?"

"Well, you were asking Emma all about the camp. You're worried, too."

"I just want the inside scoop. You know that. I *want* to go to camp. And I want to be able to talk the talk. Shoot the shit about the fog and the suicides. That's why I've been grilling Emma, but she doesn't really remember much."

"I remember them dying," said Emma. She'd come in from outside and stopped short behind them, holding her plate and looking grim. But she always kind of looked that way. Even so, Harley felt the hair lift on her arms.

"Okay, you guys are freaking me out now, too," muttered Harley. "They killed themselves, okay? That's what they did. It's terrible, but it's not supernatural." Harley placed her plate in the sink and rinsed it off. She opened the dishwasher and set it inside along with her silverware.

"What about the ashes?" Marissa reminded.

"That part might be made up," said Harley.

Emma stated firmly, "The Three Amigos. They were best friends, but they were mean girls. I think they killed him."

Marissa stared at Emma in a kind of baffled horror and Harley said, "I'm almost afraid to ask who you're talking about, Emma. Mean girls? Not those guys you mentioned."

"Brooke, Rona, and Wendy. Rona didn't like me because she wanted Donovan and she knew I went with him behind the mirror, but I didn't like any of them kissing me. I had . . . standards."

"What mirror?" murmured Marissa.

Harley regarded Emma thoughtfully. "You were with Donovan . . . not this Christopher Ryan guy?"

"His name was Ryan."

"Yeah, okay, um . . . but you were with a guy named Donovan?"

"I didn't have sex with him."

"That's it. I'm out," said Marissa. She lifted up a hand to them and headed toward the back door again.

Emma called after her, "I'm coming to the camp, too!"

Harley couldn't imagine either her mother or her aunt at Camp Fog Lake with her. She said carefully, "Maybe we can rethink that."

"I only need to think once," said Emma, placing her plate carefully in the sink.

Harley let out a pent-up breath, unaware she'd been holding it in.

An hour later, Jamie was driving both Marissa and Harley to Camp Fog Lake. Nobody said much of anything during the trip, each lost in their own thoughts. They drove through Laurelton and then miles west to the foothills of the Coast Range and then north along a two-lane road, nearly missing the turnoff for the camp. A metal bar used as a gate was open, the only security to the twin ruts leading through the forest. Jamie had been warned that there was limited parking once at the camp, so she would need to drop the girls and then make her stay brief. There was a small camp bus used to pick up campers and other attendees, and a few other vehicles for camp maintenance, but otherwise there were no personal means of transportation on the premises.

"How will we get in touch with you?" worried Marissa. "They said the camp doesn't have Wi-Fi or cell service."

"I know. The camp's tucked in the hills and there are no cell towers nearby," said Jamie. "The camp director can reach us if necessary."

"I've got my phone anyway," said Harley.

"Me, too," Marissa responded quickly.

As her mom's Camry headed higher in elevation into the Coast Range, Harley suffered her first thrill of regret. Camp Fog Lake was isolated. Bad things had happened there. If

Greer weren't going to be there she would have a hard time being so eager. Maybe Marissa was right to have misgivings after all, though she just wanted to be with her boyfriend . . . same as Harley.

*He's not your boyfriend.*

"Wha'd you say?" Marissa asked her.

Harley hadn't realized she'd made a sound. "Nothing."

They bumped down the narrow, tree-canopied lane, the tires sinking into deep mudholes here and there. It felt darker and cooler, like descending into a deep well. Harley hid the shiver that came over her.

Marissa, clearly affected as well, said in a small voice, "It's like there's some kind of romantic sickness that overtakes people and they die."

"Don't be an idiot," Harley snapped back.

"Harley," Mom admonished.

And then they were pulling into a clearing where several cars were letting out other camp counselors and counselors-in-training. Harley glanced around quickly but there was no immediate sign of Greer. However, directly in front of her was Greer's Allie, her smile a bright, welcoming beacon. Harley would have liked to hate her on sight, but what she really felt was despair. The girl was just so perfect. Slim, blond, cute. Tan and muscular in that outdoorsy way, like she spent her afternoons hiking or canoeing. Her hair was pulled back in a loose ponytail with soft yellow strands framing her face.

"Oh, God," exhaled Harley.

"What?" asked Jamie, wedging the vehicle into a make-shift spot. "I'm not staying long," she added, as if Harley or Marissa had complained. "They don't allow it. I just want to talk to the director."

"What's wrong?" Marissa asked Harley as the car came to a full stop.

"Nothing," said Harley.

They opened the trunk of the Camry and hauled out their

overstuffed duffels and sleeping bags. Music was playing from somewhere inside the rows of cabins with their cedar-shake siding and peaked roofs; someone's cell phone playing tunes. The shutters were open on the screened windows and they caught glimpses of bunk beds lined up and ready for campers.

The three of them trudged toward the main lodge—more of an elongated cabin—which housed the kitchen, the camp director's apartment, and a large gathering room with tables and a river-rock fireplace that clearly had been there a while. The lodge looked as if it had recently been repaired and added on to, whereas some of the cabins appeared to be new, most mainly rebuilt. The air was heavy with the scent of pine and a mustier, muddier odor coming off the lake. Today there was no fog and the water riffled lightly, stirring under a soft breeze. The sun was still fairly high in the sky, the green water sparkling beneath it, nearly blinding.

Harley and Marissa dropped their gear in a pile beside the lodge, which had a wood plank with CAMP FOG LAKE in block letters written on its surface in forest green paint. An attached plank read: HOPE NEWELL.

The camp director herself stepped outside at that moment, calling back to someone named Warren as she stepped outside to come join her.

"Hi, there. Welcome! I'm Hope. Come on in," she said, waving them all forward. Her hair was in a ponytail, too, but the blond strands were streaked with silver. She wore no makeup and her face had a weathered look, tiny cracks along her upper cheekbones, like she spent a lot of time in the sun. She smiled tightly and her teeth were faintly crooked, but not in a bad way. There was something about her that suggested forced goodness that immediately put Harley on alert. Her mom had sent her to Sunday school once upon a time, when they were still living in Los Angeles, and her teacher had that same taut look about her, like she was holding herself in check. Underneath she'd been mean as a snake, her niceness a facade. She'd been cruel with her words, when no adults were around.

Mom introduced Harley and Marissa, and Hope pretended to be excited to see them, but she was really more interested in explaining all the changes that had come to the camp since the days before its closure.

"The last director wanted to make a lot of improvements, but she was hindered by the owners at that time."

"The Luft-Shawks," said Mom.

Hope faltered slightly. "That's right. Were you ever a camper here?"

"No, but my sister was." Mom left it at that, not explaining about Emma.

"Well, the Luft-Shawks sold the camp after all the difficulties, but the camp just sat here. It wasn't till I bought it and got it going again that it came back to this." She swept an arm around the room, encompassing the wooden table and chairs and the central river-rock fireplace. There was no fire today, but the firebox was black where many had clearly taken place before. The northern windows offered an expansive view of the lake.

"Who owned the camp in between?" asked Mom.

Now Hope really looked at her. "Pastor Rolff of Haven Commune sold it to me."

"Rolff Ulland?"

Harley nearly did a double take on Mom, surprised she knew so much. She glanced from her back to Hope.

The wattage on Hope's smile had dimmed a bit. "You obviously know about some of the troubles that happened before the camp closed," she said tightly.

"I know a little bit," admitted Mom.

"Yeah, like the suicide pact," Marissa chimed in.

Harley wanted to stamp on her foot. She didn't want to give anything away before they even tried to meet people.

Hope sized Marissa up before turning back to Mom. "It

was really an unfortunate drowning. The boy was drinking and got a cramp, they believe, and couldn't get back to shore. The girl . . . it was an overdose. She was from Haven, but she'd been a runaway who'd come to the commune. Rolff let her stay, but it was a mistake. She really used the camp as a hideout, but when she was found out she accidentally overdosed. The two deaths were unrelated except for unfortunate timing."

*What about the ashes?* thought Harley, throwing a glance at Marissa, who'd asked about them earlier.

"You sound like you know Haven Commune pretty well," said Mom. Harley narrowed her eyes at her mother. Mom was making polite responses, as if she wasn't really all that interested, but Harley knew her too well. She was actively listening.

"I always have to combat the fantastical lore," said Hope. Then, "Rolff has had some health issues."

"Did you grow up in the commune?"

This was from Marissa. Harley whipped around to give her a hard stare. Really? All of a sudden she had questions now?

"Yes," she admitted. "Joy is my older sister."

"Really?" Mom looked interested. "I'd love to see Haven. Would that be possible? Maybe when I come back for parents' weekend."

"Oh, you're coming. How wonderful." Hope smiled, but it didn't quite reach her eyes. She glanced at Mom's Camry and said, "You'll have to move your car soon, but we have a few minutes. Let me show you the kitchen and some of the cabins. They're named after wildflowers. Your names are on a list that's tacked to your cabin."

*Hope . . . Joy . . .* Harley wondered if everyone from the commune was named in the same fashion.

"The girls' cabins are nearest the lodge, and the latrine is located in between the girls' cabins and the boys' bunkhouses," Hope was explaining as she and Mom moved off. Marissa started to follow, then stopped when she realized Harley hadn't moved.

"I want to look around my own way," explained Harley. She'd seen where the maintenance buildings were on the south side of the camp and wanted to do some exploring.

"Okay, but I think I'll stick with your mom for now."

Harley watched them leave. Sunlight slanted down at her forearms, warming her. She could see various outbuildings crowded up against the hill at the back of the property that likely housed maintenance and other utility needs. There were a couple of trucks with minor dents and scrapes along with the school bus. Tomorrow the bus would be rounding up the campers from several sites around Laurelton and River Glen to bring their young charges for the week. Anyone coming from farther east into the city or generally outside the Greater Portland area would have to drive to a bus pickup site or the camp itself.

Harley had one day to orient herself before the campers arrived. She would have to grab her gear and find her cabin soon, but she might not have another chance to explore if she didn't take it now.

She headed straight for the main outbuilding, circumventing the field of dusty, fir-needle-carpeted ground and the main courtyard that filled the space between the maintenance building and the main camp, choosing instead a beaten dirt path along the west side of the lodge, which was screened by some shrubbery that in turn seemed about to be overtaken by blackberry bushes. It kept her out of view from the many cabin/ bunkhouse windows.

As she reached the board-and-batten-sided maintenance building, she circled to the back side, which butted up against a hillside with a narrow trail just wide enough for her to work her way along. The doors to the building were on the east side but there was a small overhead window about halfway down that was cracked open. She could hear what sounded like male voices and she edged closer, listening. Was that Greer?

". . . know what I need to do, and I'm doin' it. That's what the Maker wants. That's what I do."

Not Greer. Not by a long shot. An older man whose gravelly voice held a note of stubbornness.

The answering voice was male, but softer, almost whispering, and Harley couldn't make it out. Didn't sound like Greer, but maybe? She craned her neck closer toward the window, trying to discern.

"Gotta lot o' campers comin'. They need me," the older man said.

The other voice answered curtly, the words indistinguishable.

"I'm just workin'. That's all I'm doin'," was the older man's retort.

"Hullo?" A female voice made Harley jump. Pulse spiking, she whipped around, certain she'd been caught, wondering if she'd made some noise they might have heard when she'd shifted her feet. But no one was there. The voice was coming from the end of the building where Harley had seen the parked trucks and bus. Was the girl standing just outside the open garage doors?

"Are you the only one here?" she apparently asked the man whom Harley could hear, and Harley recognized her voice.

Allie.

"Yes, ma'am," he answered.

Where was the other guy? His voice was silent now. Had he left?

Harley didn't wait to find out. She backed up carefully on the trail. Her heart was racing. It wouldn't be good to get caught eavesdropping on her first day, before she'd even unpacked. When she reached the corner of the building she glanced around. Nothing but shrubbery. She quickly headed through the bushes to the sprawling main camp. A girl was standing outside the lodge, staring straight in Harley's direction. Harley nearly came to a screeching halt but managed to keep going after a little stutter-step. She would have liked to have passed unnoticed, but she decided to shrug off her exploration. The girl was about her age, maybe another CIT. She watched as Harley veered toward where she'd left her bags.

"What's over there?" the girl asked.

Harley glanced back. She was staring toward the bus and vehicles. "Oh, some trucks and buildings, I guess."

"What were you doing there?"

Harley gave her a long look. She had straight, dark brown hair that curled in under her chin, freckles across her nose, a smirking mouth, and greenish hazel eyes that already called Harley a liar, even though she hadn't answered her.

"I was snooping," Harley stated.

The girl smiled. "Yeah? What'd you find?"

Harley shrugged. "The maintenance guy's older and thinks his job's important." Might as well stick as much to the truth as possible.

"Oh, Marlon. Yeah, he's a little . . ." She pointed to her head. "Slow."

Harley always felt uncomfortable when people talked about others that way. She'd seen it a lot when she was with Emma. The stares. The calculations. The pity.

"How do you know Marlon?"

"You'll get introduced to him. When did you get here? I got here this morning. He's the maintenance guy. Kind of a grouch, but not somebody to be scared of."

"I'm not scared of him. I didn't even see him. I just heard him."

"Was he talking to that Greer guy?" she asked. "He's really cute."

Harley absorbed that. So, this girl already knew about Greer. "Hi, I'm Harley," she introduced herself.

"Harley? That your real name?"

"My dad was a motorcycle freak. That's how he died. On a motorcycle."

"Are you serious?"

Harley nodded.

"I'm Kiley McManus. My mom didn't want me to come to Camp Fog Lake, but I wanted to. She went here when she was young. That summer it closed."

"That last summer?" Harley repeated, brows raised. "That's when my aunt was here."

"Really? Maybe they know each other."

"Maybe." Harley didn't want to get into the fact that Emma was unlikely to remember if they did or didn't. Unless . . . "Was your mom Rona, Brooke, or Wendy?" she asked, reciting the names Emma had shot out.

Kiley stared at her as if she were speaking in tongues. "Rona," she said after a long moment.

"Really?" Harley hadn't really expected to hit pay dirt when she repeated the names, but there it was.

"How did you know?" Kiley asked suspiciously.

"I just heard their names from my aunt."

"What's your aunt's name?"

"Emma Whelan."

Kiley shrugged and shook her head.

Approaching voices broke the moment and Harley and Kiley both turned to see Allie and Greer walking side by side and heading in their general direction from the maintenance buildings. Allie was talking a mile a minute, her face turned toward Greer, her smile wide. It was definitely Allie's voice that had greeted the men inside with a "Hullo," Harley realized. Maybe the other man's voice had been Greer's after all. That made it worse.

"That's Greer," said Kiley with a sigh of envy.

"'Scuse me," muttered Harley, quickly turning away. She hefted her sleeping bag over her shoulder. Her pulse was thundering. She didn't want to face Greer until she was ready, and she for sure didn't want to face him with Allie.

She'd never really understood how girls could hate, hate, hate someone just because their ex was with them. Didn't the guy have any choice or blame in the matter? Harley would point out reasonably, if the subject ever came up. Now she had a taste of what it felt like and she understood more, though she also was pissed off at herself for falling so easily into that trap. Greer *did* have a choice, and he'd chosen Allie.

But it hurt like hell.

# Chapter 6

Harley hurriedly stowed her gear in her cabin beneath her cot, happy to learn that Marissa was a co-counselor-in-training with her in her cabin, not so happy to learn Allie was the head counselor assigned to them, as her name was written in large letters on a sign near her more substantial twin bed, built with drawers beneath it. Her bed was at the front of the room, near the main door, while Harley's and Marissa's cots guarded the back door, the only cabin with two points of entry, as far as she could tell. Foxglove, as their cabin was named, was long and narrow and accommodated six sets of bunk beds. From Harley's cursory glance around the area, it appeared to be the largest of the five girls' cabins, which probably accounted for why Harley and Marissa had been bunked together. Their cots flanked the back door, which was latched with a metal hook and eye.

Harley went in search of her mother and Marissa. Mom was standing by her Camry, getting ready. Other cars were dropping off counselors and it was getting to be a traffic jam. Hope had moved to greet the newcomers and was explaining how the machinery buildings were new, but that the cabins had been rebuilt to hang onto their original charm. That charm, as far as Harley was concerned, was in short supply. The knotty pine walls had been revarnished, and were striped with new boards amongst ones that had yellowed over the years, giving the rooms a patchwork look. The boys' and girls' bathrooms were between Foxglove and Snakeroot, the largest of the five boys' bunkhouses.

There was no cell service at the camp. Not a cell tower around, though Harley figured if you headed back toward civilization you would be able to connect somewhere. Certainly if you made it to the main road, right? But otherwise basically the camp was a dead zone. Hope hadn't asked them to relinquish their cell phones, as there was no need, but Harley planned to keep hers charged and ready in case there was an emergency.

Seeing Harley, Mom gave her the high sign and called, "Okay, I'm heading out. Have fun. Be safe. See you in a few weeks!"

Harley had a surprising moment of fear and said, "Wait a sec." She ran over to her mom, who looked at her askance. No wonder. Though the years of antipathy between them were long over, Harley rarely showed any real warmth. But now, for reasons she didn't want to examine too closely, she gave her mother an awkward hug, taking her by surprise.

"Did something happen?" Mom asked, worried.

"No. I just wanted to hug you. That okay?" Harley immediately stepped back.

"Perfectly okay," Mom said heartily.

"Okay, this is starting to feel weird."

Mom held up her hands. "If things don't work out, talk to Hope. She'll get in contact with us." Mom glanced over at Hope and then beyond her, over the lake that was now a dull pewter color, its surface restless in the stiff breeze.

"Things'll work out." Harley couldn't bear her mother thinking she was as unsettled as she actually was. She was mad at herself for feeling the heebie-jeebies at all. "Where's Marissa?"

"She said a few words to Hope, then . . . I don't know. Maybe she's in the cabin?"

"I'll check," said Harley. No reason to explain that Marissa hadn't been there when Harley had quickly stowed her stuff inside. She'd find her later.

She waved as Mom backed the Camry around and worked her way down the miles-long access dirt and gravel lane that led to the blacktopped road out of the mountains and away from Camp Fog Lake. Harley noted the other parents dropping off their kids who would be working as counselors and CITs and thought she saw one of the dads wandering along the periphery of the woods that pressed in on all sides of the camp except to the north, where the ground sloped down to the lake.

She took a deep breath. It smelled like leaves and fir needles and pine, a combination that reminded her faintly of some scented candles they had at Christmas time, only earthier. Hope was telling a man and a woman, whose son was holding his pack and sleeping bag and looking like he wanted his parents to just leave already, about the commune over the hill, waving in its direction. North, the same direction as the lake.

"We heard you grew up there," the man interrupted Hope.

She glanced toward the lake. Harley followed her gaze and made out the faint trail in the grasses that grew alongside the slope that rose quickly upward on the lake's east side, leading north. Harley realized with a quickening of her breath that somewhere up that trail was Suicide Ledge, where the dead girl had been found . . . both dead girls.

"Lovely place," said Hope, not really answering. "The produce the commune grows is sold all over the city and beyond. The gardens are organic. Incredible."

"They grow weed?" the older guy asked with a grin. The

woman with him looked pained and the boy stumbled away as if he couldn't take it anymore.

"Niles!" his dad called after him, at least Harley assumed it was his father.

"Bye," Niles called over his shoulder, practically running away.

The dad smiled tightly at Hope who wasn't paying that much attention as she'd bent to listen to something the mom was saying to her. "Yes, you can view the bunkhouse interiors," Hope answered. "There's still some daylight left and we can go through them right now. We don't have electricity. The lodge is run on a generator as are the hot water heaters in the latrines."

The dad was looking after Niles as he, Hope, and the mom started to walk toward the cabins. "Teenagers, huh? I don't know how you do it here."

"Our campers are younger," said Hope.

"Yeah, but you've got these guys." He gestured to Niles's retreating back.

"We just want Niles to be safe," the mom said as she hurried to keep up.

"The camp is very safe and Marlon, our handyman, lives off-property, but his place is near the gates and he watches out for the camp."

"Couldn't somebody come through the woods?" asked the mom.

"If they want to fight miles of underbrush, poison ivy, tough terrain, I suppose." Harley could tell Hope was getting tired of all the questions.

"Or from the commune?" the dad pointed out.

"Some of our counselors choose to go to the commune and join in Sunday service outside on the lawn. Pastor Rolff Ulland headed the service for years, which was very well received. Recently his health has deteriorated and his son has taken over, I believe."

"You don't know?" the man quizzed. He was interrogating Hope as if she were running a criminal enterprise. Even Harley felt an urge to step in and help her.

"Mr. Harwick, my interest is the camp," assured Hope as they reached the bunkhouses. The steel in her voice convinced Harley that Hope could hold her own as their voices faded off.

Harley determined she wasn't going back to Foxglove until the Harwicks had vamoosed. She already hoped they didn't show up to parents' weekend.

She found Marissa walking up the gravel lane toward the camp. Harley looked past her.

"Did you walk all the way to the road?" she asked in surprise.

"No way. It's way too far. I guess the handyman lives somewhere down by the gate to the camp. I only went partway."

"Marlon," said Harley. At Marissa's sharp look, she said, "The handyman. We'll all get introduced to everyone. I overheard Hope talking about him."

"Some of the CITs say he's weird."

"Maybe he's just kind of homespun religious. I think I overheard him talking, and he mentioned doing what 'his Maker' wanted him to do. What were you doing?"

"Just looking around. I gotta admit, I'm kind of freaked about this place. I know you're going to tell me to get over it, but I've got this bad feeling that I can't shake."

Harley didn't say anything. If she agreed with Marissa that would only make things worse and she needed to lessen her stepsister's anxiety, not add to it.

Fifteen minutes later, as they were arranging their living areas, they heard the loud clang of a dinner bell. They'd had their celebratory meal with the family earlier, but Harley realized how hungry she was . . . until she walked into the dining room and saw Allie sitting at a table, her arm linked through Greer's. Harley immediately turned around and headed toward the back of the room, making sure her head was down so he wouldn't be able to see her through the tables in between.

"There's Greer," Marissa said softly, seating herself beside Harley.

"Yep." Marissa had already known Greer was going to be at the camp, but Harley had purposely downplayed that fact so they hadn't really talked about it.

"Are you hiding from him?"

"No. I don't know. Maybe."

"You're going to run into him."

"I just need to pick my time, and both times I've seen him, he's been with Allie."

"Both times?"

"I saw him earlier with her."

Marissa glanced toward the front of the room and said carefully, "They look kind of tight."

"Stop looking at them or they'll see you."

Marissa immediately dropped her gaze to the table, but said out of the side of her mouth, "We should talk later."

"Nothing to talk about. If he's with her, that's it. I'm just here at the camp. I don't expect anything."

"Sure."

"What's that mean?" Harley demanded quietly.

"Nothing, I—"

Two guys sat down across from them, effectively blocking Harley's view of Greer and Allie. "You two up for some fun tonight?" the first one asked. "We're gonna have a campfire with s'mores and ghost stories."

"No ghost stories," said Marissa.

"Oh, yeah. Ghost stories," the second guy chimed in. Harley saw it was Niles Harwick. He and the first guy grinned like evil henchmen.

"Grab a tray," Hope called to the room at large from near the front. "Take it through the kitchen and Warren and Tina'll serve you up." She threw an arm to introduce a tall, solid-looking woman about Hope's same age, maybe late thirties, early forties, and a bony guy with a scraggly beard and longer brown hair about the same age. "And if you haven't met Marlon Kern yet, he's the reason our camp runs so smoothly. Anything goes wrong, call Marlon to fix it. Marlon, where are you? Stand up and say hello!" Hope began looking around the room.

Harley managed to peer around the guys who'd jumped up with their trays as one as soon as Hope gave them the okay to eat. She saw an older man rise reluctantly from a place at the nearest table to Hope's back rooms. He seemed slightly embarrassed as he raised a slow hand, his gaze fixed downward a bit as the counselors and CITs went for their food. Harley tagged him somewhere in his fifties or sixties. His shoulders were a little stooped and his hair was short and gray.

Harley and Marissa moved into the line at a slower pace. Harley wanted Allie and Greer to get ahead of them so she didn't have to face Greer yet. She needn't have worried. The two of them were so into each other that the rest of the camp was probably just a blur and hum.

"Do you want to go to the campfire tonight?" asked Marissa.

"Do you?"

"I want to go home, but since that's not going to happen, we might as well go."

"Okay," said Harley. She almost told Marissa that she wanted to go home, too. That seeing Greer with Allie was worse than she'd imagined. That whatever she'd thought she was doing at Camp Fog Lake, it wasn't what she'd hoped it would be. The whole thing tasted like ashes in her mouth. But what she said instead was, "Maybe their ghost stories will center on what happened at the camp all those years ago and we can finally learn something new."

Marissa made a face. "That's your thing, not mine."

"Whatever." Harley was through trying to jolly along her stepsister. So Camp Fog Lake wasn't what either of them had at least hoped for. Time to make the best of it.

Back from dropping the girls at camp, Jamie entered the house to hear Cooper on his cell phone, talking to his partner, Elena Verbena. They had a case with a woman who'd died by a fall down the stairs but both believed the husband, who'd taken out a hefty insurance policy on the wife just before her death, had maybe pushed her, though he swore he wasn't anywhere near the house when she died. They were still working through the possibilities and Jamie heard the word "poisoned" and pricked up her ears.

She waited in the living room, staring out the front window. Cooper had a tendency to pace when he was talking shop and was upstairs, probably wearing a trail through the bedroom carpet. Jamie could hear about one word out of three. Even though it was interesting, she really wanted his full attention to tell him about meeting Hope Newell and her connection to Haven Commune and how Jamie was definitely, definitely planning to go to the parents'/alumni weekend. In the back of her mind she had a nebulous plan to find her way to the commune, maybe using Hope as a liaison of sorts, and learn what she could about Mary Jo Kirshner.

*You're obsessed*, she told herself.

"Yeah, well, I need to know," she muttered under her breath.

Finally, Cooper was off the phone and she could hear him come down the stairs, though she didn't turn around from her contemplation of the front yard.

"Hey," he said, obviously seeing her and stopping short. He then came up behind her and put his arms around her waist.

"How's Verbena?"

"New theories on the Torres case."

"I thought Angela Torres died from the fall."

"Might be more to it than that. Toxicology found levels of arsenic. She had some gastrointestinal issues. Might have been slowly poisoned."

"So, he didn't push her?"

"He wasn't at home when she fell. But she was compromised. Now, we've just got to figure out if she was poisoned inadvertently, or if it was attempted murder."

"You think it was him."

"Leaning that way. You know Verbena. She thinks every man with questionable motives is a killer. What about you? How was the camp?"

Jamie turned into his arms and rested her head on his shoulder. "I'm going there for parents' weekend."

He nodded. She'd already basically said as much.

His voice rumbled beneath her ear: "You planning to check out Haven?"

He knew her so well.

"Well . . . I'd like to."

"You don't trust Mary Jo."

He spoke with finality and she slipped out of his arms. She wanted to confide her fears to him, but she hardly knew what those fears were. "I don't feel in control. Mary Jo is sweet and seemingly benign and I shouldn't make judgments on Haven Commune. So, she grew up there. So what? People say it's a wonderful place, and I'm sure it is. I just want to see for myself. I want to know that nothing bad happened there. That those deaths had nothing to do with the commune or the camp."

"You don't blame Mary Jo."

"No, no, no." Jamie shook her head. "I don't think that at all. But sometimes, she just seems too good to be true. She and Theo reconnected after years of not really talking to each other, and Theo mentioned us and said we were looking for a surrogate. Then Mary Jo chose us over supposedly other people."

"Supposedly?"

"I'm just rambling. Stream of consciousness. I just want to get it all out. Cooper, I know it sounds bad, but I don't think I like her. I don't get her. She's so beatific. Like she's empty behind that smile."

"It does sound bad," he said, smiling a little himself.

Jamie rolled her eyes. She'd known he wouldn't understand. She stalked past him toward the kitchen and he immediately followed her.

"She is having our baby," he pointed out.

"Believe me, I know. I should be thrilled and yet . . . I guess I resent her, a little. I'm so ungrateful."

"You're worried. It's okay."

'You think so?"

"Go to Haven Commune. See what it's like. Talk to people about Mary Jo. Why not? Make yourself feel better. Whatever it takes."

"You're not worried?" She'd been facing away, but now she turned back to look at him.

"Jamie, the baby is ours. This shit-eating grin? I didn't ever think I'd have a child of my own. Is this situation ideal? Well, no, I guess not, but it's pretty damn good. Mary Jo's been a surrogate before. I don't think she's going to turn on us. I just want the pregnancy to go well. And I want my wife to be happy and at ease."

"You think I'm a little crazy."

"I think you're processing." He put his arms around her.

"You think I'm a little crazy," she repeated. "I feel a little crazy."

"We're going to see Mary Jo tomorrow."

Jamie nodded against his chest. They were heading to Mary Jo and her husband Stephen's farm tomorrow. She hoped it would make her feel better. "I am happy that we're having a baby."

Cooper squeezed her tight and she squeezed him right back. It was all going to be fine. She was making mountains out of molehills. But she was going to see what she could learn about Haven Commune anyway. It had been a throwaway line during their interviews with her, that she'd spent her early years at the collective. Jamie hadn't known until Stephen had mentioned it, and when he did, Mary Jo had looked straight ahead with that fake smile on her face. "Mary Jo was part of Haven Commune," Stephen told them proudly. "Have you ever been there?" As Jamie and Cooper had shaken their heads, he'd added, "My family was part of the collective for some time, too. Everything homegrown with love. No additives, nothing to taint the food. You should go there sometime."

"I'd like to," Jamie had said and smiled at Mary Jo, whose own smile seemed to grow more and more rictus. That was when Jamie had gotten her first whiff of something that smelled funny. Just a passing moment, gone in an instant, but the words had eaten away at her self-confidence in the whole process ever since, though she really couldn't say why. Mary Jo's reaction—or, non-reaction, if you wanted to call it that—had been odd. It just felt to Jamie like something might have happened at Haven. And though Mary Jo's current life seemed picture-perfect . . . and maybe was . . . Jamie's radar had been engaged ever since that interview in a loop that wouldn't shut off. Had something happened to her there? Did it even matter to her being a surrogate?

Whatever the case, Jamie had an opportunity to find out and she was going to take it.

# Chapter 7

Harley sat close to Marissa around the campfire. They were outside the glow that swept across the courtyard from the generator-fed light on the roof of the maintenance building. It sent light pooling over the lodge, cabins, bathrooms, and bunkhouses, but it couldn't reach the campfire, which was sheltered from illumination by Snakeroot, the bunkhouse closest to the access road and away from the lodge. She didn't know what she'd do if Greer showed up. Feign surprise? Act nonchalant? Hug him like she was oh, so happy to see him and say how terrific Allie was?

She shivered a little and wished she'd brought her ski jacket with its thick layer of warmth. The short denim jacket she had on was hardly doing justice against the cold dip in temperature. She glanced past the sparks of orange being stirred up by Niles Harwick and flying up into the darkening skies. Below, the moving black surface of Fog Lake seemed forever restless. Soon it would be pitch black, but it would be near 10:00 p.m. at this time of year. At least there was no fog in the forecast, according to Hope, who had reluctantly condoned the guys' pleas for a campfire, but only after she'd inspected the area to make certain all was safe. "Only tonight," she'd warned them all. "No campfires after the campers get here."

Niles Harwick was flanked by the two guys who'd enlisted Harley and Marissa to join in. The one who'd spoken first was Austin. He possessed sandy, artfully mussed and moussed hair, and wore board shorts and a thin, long-sleeved gray pullover. The second said his name was Lendel. Austin was still giving Niles shit about being brought to camp by his parents as all of them were over eighteen and "adults," though Harley had her doubts about that label. They all seemed light-years younger than she was.

There was another guy named Esau. He was taller and darker and appeared a little more aloof from the others. There were a number of older girls, too, who were clearly counselors as they gave Harley, Marissa, and Kiley the cold shoulder after a very bored "Hello." Their leader was named Ella and they all acted like the CITs were down the scale a ways, apparently

The firepit itself was a large oval on the edge of the sandy beach that led down to the lake from the lodge. It was formed out of river rocks and far enough from the forest and other fuel sources to insure it wouldn't cause a forest fire.

A couple more girls drifted over and seated themselves on Harley's other side, closer to the forest. A couple more guys joined them as well.

Marissa leaned into Harley and whispered in an aside. "Where's Greer?"

"Where's Allie?" responded Harley.

As if she'd heard her, Allie suddenly appeared from the lakeside direction of the bunkhouses as the boys' buildings were closest to the firepit. She wore a thick coat and her hair was down around her ears for warmth. Harley sniffed to herself. Of course she knew the deal around here. Her aunt, or something, owned it. Maybe that was Hope?

Allie plunked herself down between the guys and girls, at

the end of the oval as if she were at the head of a table and they were seated for a board meeting. Well, she was the one who seemed to have the most experience, so yeah, Harley grudgingly could give her that. "Okay," Allie said, rubbing her hands and warming them over the fire. "Let's go around and tell all our names."

Immediately Harley was on edge. Her name might give her away to Allie, if Greer had mentioned her. Was she ready for that?

*Isn't that the point of you being here?* her inner voice remonstrated.

Well, yeah, but . . . already?

Niles said, "Niles Harwick," in a monotone, as if he were bored with everything already.

Lendel raised his hand and said, "Lendel. Here!" as if he were in school.

Allie said, "And your last name?"

"Why? You taking notes?"

She smiled at him. "Okay, forget it. Just trying to get to know you. Whatever you're comfortable with."

"Austin Norrie," Austin said, jumping up and giving a deep bow. "Pleased to make your acquaintance, Alison . . . ?"

"Allie Strasser," she responded.

"And you?" Austin asked Marissa, who gave her name, eyeing him warily.

Harley was next and she muttered her name, and when Austin repeated it as "Hayley," instead of Harley, she didn't correct him. He moved on to the other girls, one of whom was Kiley McManus, before going back to the guys who'd been forgotten when Austin had commandeered introductions.

"Anybody bring any booze?" asked Niles to which Allie said, "You better not have," while Lendel slowly lifted his hand and grinned slyly at her.

"Where's the guy you were with?" Marissa popped out to Allie.

Again, Harley wanted to elbow her in the ribs, but she just held her breath and waited for Allie's answer.

"Oh, Greer? He's not really part of the camp. I mean, he is working here, but he . . ." She half-laughed. "He doesn't want to be a part of our camp bonding."

"He your boyfriend?" asked the guy named Esau.

"He's a friend," said Allie, dimpling. "Let's leave it at that."

Marissa gave Harley the side eye, but Harley studiously turned to look at the fire. Yep. This was going to be torture. What a stupid move to come here. First day and she was already kicking herself.

Another counselor joined their group, staggering a bit. It was clear she was somewhat inebriated even before she burped, giggled, placed a hand on her sumptuous chest and murmured, "*Excusez-moi.*"

"Kendra," Allie warned in a tight voice.

"Sorry I'm late," Kendra responded breezily, plopping herself down beside Lendel. She either didn't catch Allie's tone or didn't care. Maybe a little of both.

"You didn't steal my stuff, did you?" Lendel asked her.

She pushed at him playfully. "What's happening?"

"We're playing Truth or Dare," Kiley spoke up.

"Let's wait on that. Let's get some background on each other first," Allie began, but the guys cut her off in a chorus of "Dare, dare!"

"I dare you to swing from that branch into the lake!" yelled Lendel to Austin, who was one of the loudest chanters.

"Nothing dangerous!" Allie snapped out sharply.

But Austin was already eyeing the tree in question, up the hill on the trek toward that cult. His eye landed on the tree closest to the lake with its limb that jutted over the water, judging it.

"I could do it," he said.

"Yeah, if you want to break your neck," said Esau.

"Do it," urged Lendel. "I will if you will."

"It's a long way down," Harley spoke up at the same time Allie declared loudly, "Not on your life! This is exactly what I mean by too dangerous!"

Niles gave Allie a studied look from between strands of long hair.

Kiley reminded, "We're supposed to ask each other questions, then you choose dare over truth if you don't want to answer."

"Dumb," Kendra expelled, leaning her head back as if she were going to fall asleep where she sat.

"Well, ask me a question, then," Austin drawled. He stood up and stretched his arms over his head. His shirt gapped from his pants, revealing hard abs.

Harley had a flash of recent memory. Emma. Giving her that serious look during one of their talks about the camp. "We sat around the campfire and had to tell the truth."

"Truth or Dare?" Harley had asked Emma, who'd replied, "Just truth. About when we were in trouble with our parents. I said mine was still coming because Mom didn't know."

As ever, Harley had tried to quiz her further, but Emma had been distracted and that was the end of it.

Now Allie cocked her head and asked Austin, "When did you first have sex?"

He grinned at her, surprised. "Fifteen."

"Bullshit," said Lendel, laughing. Then, "You were fifteen and a half." The two guys slapped high fives and laughed like hyenas. Harley wasn't certain it was true or not and didn't much care. Allie eyed them carefully.

"You guys go on ahead," said Kendra, stumbling to her feet. She wandered off toward the woods.

"Where're you going?" asked Esau sharply.

"Gotta pee. Don't peek . . ." She moved away from the campfire.

"The bathroom's that way," he said, pointing back to the camp.

She waved him off.

Allie muttered something under her breath that Harley couldn't catch.

"My turn to ask," Austin told Allie, ignoring Kendra. Harley braced herself for Allie getting the same question. If Allie admitted to having sex with Greer it wouldn't surprise Harley, she half expected it, but damn she didn't want to hear it.

But then he turned his attention on Harley, whose heartbeat began a hard tattoo in her chest.

"When did you first have sex, Hayley?"

Marissa swept in a breath beside her. Again, Harley was glad they got her name wrong, but she answered honestly enough. "Hasn't happened yet."

"Bullshit," Lendel said again.

"Let's get a different question going," Esau piped up. He was seated on the far end of the oval from the other guys, and his face was partially shadowed as night fell.

"Good idea," Austin broke in before Esau could ask. "When was the last time you were so scared you almost shit your pants?"

Marissa threw a glance at the dark woods. She'd been doing that all night, Harley realized, as if she expected someone or something to jump out at them. "You," Austin said, pointing at Marissa.

"Me?" Marissa squeaked. "How about right now! This is spooky out here. Is that fog gathering on the lake?"

They all turned to look and Marissa started chuckling. Harley was surprised at her boldness. Not Marissa's style, but then Marissa had definitely changed since she'd been going out with Cam, mostly not for the better. Who knew Marissa's first boyfriend would suck up so much of her time and energy? It was like zombies had overtaken her. All she thought about was Cam, Cam, Cam.

*Were you that bad with Greer when you were together?*
No. God no. She couldn't have been. Nope.

Lendel snorted and threw Marissa a look of appreciation for "getting" them.

Austin, not so much. He clearly didn't like losing the floor. He suddenly jumped up and stripped off his shirt, jacket, and sneakers. "Okay! I'm going for it!"

"Don't!" Allie warned.

Instead of listening to her, he whooped loudly and started running for the Douglas fir whose branches draped toward the water. Its lower limbs were thick with green needles and low to the ground and could easily be climbed. The branch that dipped closest to the lake was about fifteen feet off the ground, and the lake was a few feet lower than the camp so it was at a height of twenty feet or so, if he made the jump. But there were other hazards. Submerged rocks, maybe. And if he didn't get out far enough, he could miss the lake entirely, hitting the ground or the gently rising cliffside long before the water.

The other guys started running after him and after a frozen moment, Harley leapt up, too. Marissa was right on her heels, followed by the rest of them.

Austin quickly climbed the lower branches just as the sun dipped below the horizon, turning the sky into a gold and pink glow.

When he reached the branch in question he stood up and started sidling his feet along a lower limb, guiding himself hand over hand on the one above him. The branch bent, causing Harley, and all of them watching, to catch their collective breath.

"I don't like this," muttered Harley.

Kiley murmured in a kind of admiration, "What a moron. I could probably do that."

Allie yelled, "I'm going to tell Hope!" and stomped off toward the lodge.

Kendra had returned by this point and said, "This is bullshit," and wandered after Allie.

Austin kept on his endeavor. Harley sucked in another

breath as the branch quivered and dipped under his weight. She wanted to cover her eyes. Stop him. Do something. She looked to the guys for help, but they all seemed mesmerized.

"Wait!" Harley suddenly burst out.

At the same moment Austin leapt forward, holding one knee and cannonballing into the lake with a terrific splash.

Harley braced herself. *Be all right, be all right, be all right.*

They all ran down to the water's edge as Austin surfaced, flinging his hair from his eyes. "Fucking cold!" he hollered.

"You sick fuck!" yelled Lendel, laughing as, stripping off his shirt and kicking free of his shoes, he, too, ran for the tree.

"Don't!" screamed one of Ella's tribe, but she might as well have been mute. Only Esau stayed on the ground while the rest of them started climbing the fir tree.

One by one they jumped in after Austin, who'd made his way back to shore and started shivering. He hobbled over the small, sharp stones to get back to his place by the fire and grabbed up his shirt and jacket.

Pretty soon the rest of the leapers returned to the fire, cold but triumphant. About that same time Hope arrived, her face set, her eyes regarding the boys with cold fury. "You're supposed to be the adults here! Campers are coming tomorrow. What do you think you're doing?"

Allie stood by her, looking like she might want to cry. She threw a glance back toward the maintenance shed where candlelight glowed in one of the upper windows. Harley knew without being told that's where Greer stayed. Clearly, she wanted to alert Greer, or be with him, or something.

"Okay, I'll take the blame—" Austin started, but Hope cut him off.

"Go back to your bunkhouses and cabins. All of you. There won't be any more campfires."

"We won't do it again," said Esau, who hadn't been any part of the leaping into the lake. "Just a few more minutes."

Hope gave him a long look. Harley expected her to cut him off, too, but she waited a few moments, then lifted her chin and said, "If anyone jumps in the lake again, I'm alerting their parents and sending them home. We'll figure out how to take care of the campers without them. This is my only warning."

She turned back toward the lodge and Allie followed after her, still throwing glances to where Greer was bunked.

Lendel whistled softly as soon as Hope was out of earshot. "What the hell have you got going with her?" he asked Esau.

"Some kind of fucking superpower," said Austin.

"She needs this camp to work," he answered. "But she means what she says. She'll get rid of anyone who does it again. She'll bring in the cavalry." He hitched his chin in the direction of the trail.

"The commune?" asked Harley.

Esau didn't respond to her, just sat back down around the fire. The rest of the guys were wet, bedraggled, and shivering.

"I'm freezing my nuts off," muttered Lendel.

Austin threw some more wood on the fire. "Go dry off, pansy."

"Fuck you," Lendel said good-naturedly and headed in the direction of Snakeroot bunkhouse. Some of the other guys did the same, though others threw on their clothes and tried to tough it out, maybe trying to impress Austin, Niles being one of them.

"Where were we?" Austin asked. "Oh, yeah." He pointed at Kiley. "When did you first have sex?"

"The question was: When was I scared enough that I almost shit my pants?" Kiley reminded.

"Okay. Go with that one."

Marissa was staring at Austin. Harley couldn't get a bead on whether she liked him or was put off by him. She was on the fence herself. He was certainly good-looking, but he had that spoiled, need-to-be-the-center-of-attention thing that could bite you in the ass.

Kiley flipped back her hair and said, "I was sitting outside in a lawn chair in our backyard. The wind kicked up, but wasn't really terrible or anything. I got up to get a lemonade and this huge limb just crashed down and crushed the chair I'd been sitting in. My mom came out screaming, but I was okay. Scared me more afterward. I was crying and shaking."

Austin made a face. "Okay. What about you?" He pointed toward Harley.

"I already answered a question," said Harley.

"Not this one."

Lendel returned with some of the other guys, who shoved their way back into their seats around the fire. The flames had died down and now there were just orange coals throbbing in the darkness.

"Ask somebody else," said Niles, who'd tucked his knees into his chest and rested his chin on them. His hair had fallen forward, obscuring his eyes. Kiley had seated herself right beside him.

"No, I want her to answer," said Austin.

Harley wasn't quite sure why she was being singled out. Austin seemed focused on her, somehow. Everyone turned to her and she realized she was going to have to come up with something. Well, she did have something to say, something she rarely talked about, but considering how she wanted to know more about the history of the camp, it seemed like a good opening.

"Okay, but you won't believe me," Harley said.

"Why?" It was Esau who questioned her.

"You just won't."

"Try me," challenged Austin.

Harley shrugged and said, "A few years ago, my mom and I moved from Los Angeles to River Glen."

"You're right. I don't believe you," drawled Lendel. "Nobody would move from L.A. to River Glen."

"Shut up," said Austin.

Marissa was staring hard at Harley. She probably knew where this was going as Harley had finally told her stepsister what had brought her and her mom home, but Harley had been careful about telling anyone else.

"One night, I had this dream. In it, my grandmother, who I didn't know very well, told me to 'Come home.' It was kind of creepy. Turns out, my mom had the same exact dream at the same exact time. Then my Aunt Emma called and told Mom that Grandma had died. She died at the same exact time we had our dreams."

There was a moment of silence, then Austin laughed and Lendel sputtered, "Bullshit!" again. Niles and the other boys chuckled, too.

"Nice ghost story," drawled Austin. "I've got a few myself."

Harley had expected them to not believe her. She hadn't expected to feel so pissed off about it. "Well, mine is true."

"How do you know it was the exact moment she died?" demanded Lendel.

"I learned later. I can't explain it. That's just what happened."

"When my Grandma died, Grandpa ran into the street naked and screaming," Niles said, grinning like an idiot.

"Good one, Niles," said Austin.

"Harley's telling the truth," Marissa defended. "She's the last person to make stuff up like that!"

"How do you know?" demanded Esau.

"Harley?" queried Austin.

"Because I'm her sister. Her stepsister," Marissa corrected herself.

Austin was looking hard at Harley.

"Yes, it's Harley. I'm named after the motorcycle." At

least Allie had left so she didn't have to worry that she might recognize her name. She was going to have to meet with Greer and get it straight soon before it all went sideways.

"Cool name," said Niles.

"Well, that dream would freak me out and I'd never want to fall asleep again," muttered Kiley.

"You better keep one eye open the whole time you're here, then." Austin stood up again and walked around the oval to their side of the fire and squeezed in between Harley and Marissa. "I'm cold. You girls can warm me up. I'm not moving any closer to them." He gave a curt nod toward Lendel and Niles.

"Way to make your move, Norrie," said Niles.

"Yeah, tell 'em about the fog so you can huddle together," said Lendel, grabbing Niles and pretending to kiss and hug him. Niles shoved him forcefully away.

"We know about the fog," said Marissa.

"You don't know everything," warned Austin. Harley leaned to the side in order to see past the muscles in his legs and damp shorts, to his face.

"When the fog rolls in, it brings the souls of the unfairly dead with it," Austin said. "The suicide pact of the girl from the commune and the boy from the camp. The girl who was sacrificed and left on the ledge above the lake. The Indigenous people who died during the earthquake that collapsed the side of the mountain and shortened and deepened the lake. If the camp had been here then, it would have been buried as well."

Harley glanced around. Most of the guys were grinning. Lendel jumped up and threw his hand over his chest and started to wail like a banshee, but Austin ordered sharply for him to sit down, which he reluctantly did.

"Indigenous people?" Harley questioned. "That's one I didn't read about."

"Harley did research before we came," Marissa announced. She tried to ease a bit away from Austin but Ella's posse was on her other side. There wasn't a lot of extra space.

"So interesting," Ella said, bored.

"You clearly haven't talked to the right people. They'll tell you about it," Austin told Harley.

"Like who?" Harley challenged.

"Like Hope, the head of Camp Love Shack. Or, Joy, the old camp master. She's at the commune, if you want to see her."

"You talked to them?" Harley questioned. He just didn't seem like the type of guy to care.

"Ask Esau."

Harley turned toward the taller boy with the gangly arms. He wasn't bad-looking. He just seemed not completely put together yet.

"I've asked some questions," he admitted.

"How do you know 'em?" asked Marissa.

He shrugged and didn't answer.

"It wasn't a suicide pact," said Harley. "The boy who died was at the camp with my aunt. They were going to see each other, but he went missing. Later, his body was found in the lake."

"They're lucky they found it. The lake's deep and cold enough that bodies don't surface here," Esau said offhand-edly.

"That's not true," said Harley.

"Bodies are down there," he insisted. "Those souls Austin talked about? The fog does bring them to the surface from time to time."

"You're messing with us," said Kiley.

"Camp Fog Lake isn't that deep," Harley pointed out, feeling a prickle along her skin, even though she didn't be-lieve any of the rumors about the place. "It'd have to be really deep and really cold for bodies to stay put."

"Like Lake Tahoe," said Niles.

Everyone looked at him, then Lendel said, "You guys are fucking scaring me." He stood up and shook himself all over like a dog throwing off water. "Brrrr! I'm getting the hell away from that." He pointed to the lake, now a black surface, smooth as a mirror, no restless energy.

Harley thought about bodies in its depths, preserved indefinitely by temperatures cold enough to freeze. But that wasn't Fog Lake. It *wasn't* that deep. She was right about that.

Marissa had gotten to her feet, too, and Harley stood as well. Kiley's eyes seemed huge in the darkness, as were the other girls'. Harley would never admit it, but she wanted to scurry back to the cabin and make sure the doors were locked and pull shut all the wooden shutters instead of leaving them just with their screens.

"The camp's been closed for almost twenty years," she said, trying to keep her tone light. "Kind of a long-time dry spell for the undead."

"Maybe they've just been waiting for camp to reopen," said Austin.

Harley looked at him, trying to read his tone in the darkness. It was hard to say whether he was playing with them, or if he really meant what he'd said. Here she'd expected to be the expert on ghost stories about the camp, but he had a lot more information and was really doing a good job of putting everyone on edge.

Marissa took off for the cabins and Harley had to hurry to catch up to her. "I don't like it here," Marissa said for about the thousandth time.

At the cabin both she and Marissa went to their cots, Marissa on the north side toward the lake, Harley on the south side. They crawled into their respective sleeping bags and Marissa asked, "Where'd Kendra get the booze or whatever?"

"Don't know. But she was wasted."

"Yeah . . ."

Marissa fell asleep within a few minutes. Harley expected to do the same, but she was acutely aware that Allie was not in the room, and, well, she kept thinking of sightless bodies floating at the bottom of the lake. She forced her mind back to the girl who'd died on the ledge, the *first* girl left there. In her research she'd found precious little about her. It almost seemed like she was more myth than reality, and it was from this myth that the ash-covered arms crossed over the body had arisen. But maybe it was true. Harley had sifted through the internet, looking for articles, but she had no sense of a time frame and had given up finding more about girl number one.

*You should have pressed Cooper to check his police files, even though he doesn't like using his position with the department for personal business.*

Information about the second girl, the one who'd been with Christopher—Ryan, according to Emma—had been easier to find. Initially it had been assumed that she came from the camp, but that had been proven false. This was the year the camp closed . . . Emma's year, and there was no mention of a suicide pact, or murder/suicide. In fact, Harley had been hard-pressed to get much on the boy whose body had floated to the surface of the lake. His name was Christopher Stofsky and his family had lived at Haven Commune for about a decade. She was fairly convinced this was Emma's Ryan. Maybe he'd used his middle name? Or he'd lied about his name for some reason. In any case, other than the possible Haven Commune connection, there didn't seem to be any star-crossed-lover suicide or murder/suicide going on. One account said he'd been "difficult," but Harley wasn't sure what that meant.

The thing to do would be to check with the commune, she supposed, but she was fast losing interest in the whole endeavor. Her real purpose was to be close to Greer and that looked like it was turning into an exercise of self-torture.

He'd moved on and Allie was . . . fine. And probably making out with him right now . . . making love . . .

Harley pulled her pillow out from under her head and placed it over her face. This whole heart-aching misery was ridiculous. Nevertheless, she felt a few tears form in her eyes and track toward her ears before she pulled herself together and put the pillow back under her head. She fell asleep with a heavy heart and dreamed about chasing Greer or somebody down long hallways that never ended.

She awoke in the middle of the night, disoriented, before remembering where she was with a physical start. Camp Fog Lake. Something had woken her. The back door softly closing.

She glanced over at Marissa, who was stirring in her sleeping bag, and then toward Allie's bed at the front of the room. She quietly dug into her duffel until she found her small flashlight. She gave it a quick flash and determined that Allie was curled up and quiet. But was she faking it? Had she come through the back door instead of the front? Harley and Marissa had locked it tight, slipping the hook through the eye. Except the hook was hanging free now! A cold shiver skated down her back.

And Allie seemed tucked in and sound asleep, though it had only been a minute or so since the sound had awakened Harley.

Harley eased off the cot and tiptoed silently to the back door. She slipped the hook back into the eye with a tiny *clink, clink*. That wasn't the sound that had awakened her, Harley was pretty sure. Had the hook been left open just for that purpose? To avoid waking her?

Harley gazed at Marissa's back as her stepsister had turned toward the wall. Could Marissa have just come in from the latrine?

But Marissa was a scaredy-cat at the best of times. She would never leave the door unlocked after she returned. She

would rather wake the entire camp than leave the door unlocked.

So, the early morning creeper had to be Allie, but she was
at the far end of the room . . .

Harley climbed back into her sleeping bag and stared into
the darkness. Outside the shuttered window, she heard footsteps. Cautious ones, walking just beyond the cabin wall on
the side of her cot. She strained her ears to listen, heart
pounding.

Then the footsteps rapidly walked away, as if sensing
Harley's awareness. A stealthy exit.


It was 2:30 a.m. when Richard Jonas Everly—R.J. to
friends—raised bleary eyes from his beer to gaze across the
dimly lit bar. Billy Ray's was a dive by even R.J.'s low standards. He sat at the end of the bar and kept his eyes on the
slightly overweight fake-blond waitress cruising the last of
the occupied tables. Candy was, as ever, acting like she was
all that, which she was. Not in looks. Her nose was too big,
her belly too flaccid, though she did squeeze it into the tight-
est Spandex tops they made, pushing up a pair of bodacious
tits. She'd served him up some free French fries, apparently
feeling he could use some food. He'd paid them no attention
as he continued sipping his beer. This was the way it always
was when he stayed too late.

But Candy's greatest asset, as far as R.J. was concerned,
was her internet presence. A self-proclaimed influencer, she
said she had followers in the thousands, which was probably
a lie. She specialized in Diva Dietary Delights, which were
low-fat recipes with a touch of pizzazz that she found online
and then changed the recipe a bit, pretending it was her own.
Then she took pictures of herself, eating, or on the scales,
and kept a running commentary about her efforts to enjoy
food and lose weight. She said she had tons of subscribers to
her YouTube videos, but that was probably a lie, too. She'd

tried to quit Billy Ray's a time or two, but she always came back. She might use the internet to her advantage, but she was a piker compared to R.J., who could hack with the best of them. Lately he'd tried to tamp down his skills and go straight. He didn't want to go to jail again, but hell, there was money to be made.

Still . . . he may have screwed up this last one. A cold spot formed at the base of his spine as he thought about it. There were some people you just didn't fuck with and though he hadn't really messed up the job he'd taken on, things hadn't quite panned out the way he'd hoped.

When Candy cruised by he put a hand on her arm to stop her. She pulled her arm back and glared at him. She was not someone you could get too familiar with, no matter how friendly she might act. Like him, life was about making money.

He said, "Those girls that follow you on YouTube or TikTok or whatever . . . the ones who were pissed at the kid at Laurelton High who said they were ugly, or something?"

"He said they were fat," she declared icily. "They want his balls."

"You follow them back, too, right?" He knew perfectly well that's what she did, but it didn't pay to have Candy know the depth of his knowledge and skills. "And the kid . . . is he still saying the same stuff about Broo—uh, the woman in his dad's office?"

"No. My 'net girls shamed him right out of it," said Candy with satisfaction.

"Smart. Okay."

"That kid's shut down."

R.J. just nodded. The kid was off social media. Was that good or bad?

She leaned in and looked at him closely. "You haven't told me what you're doing with that information. Don't leave me out."

R.J. was a little surprised. He hadn't thought she paid attention to what he did or gave a crap about it. Maybe he'd talked a little too freely to her last week.

The cold feeling at the base of his spine spread. "This might not be anything you want to touch."

"Yeah? What have you gotten yourself into?"

He couldn't think of what to say. Maybe he was worrying too much, yet those tended to be the scams that resulted in jail time. He gave her a sick grin.

She read his expression and muttered, "Something real bad, huh? Keep me out of it."

"You just said not to leave you out."

"Fuck you." She sashayed away, giving him a nice view of her ample rear end.

R.J. finished his beer. He didn't really want to go home, but after the last few stragglers left the bar, he finally staggered out, more tired than drunk. It was the wee hours of the morning and he needed sleep, though his worries were multiplying and might keep him awake. His internet ploy hadn't worked all that well. Goddamn teenagers had merely snarked at the guy. R.J. had expected more of a major blowup. The kid's school jumping on the news that he was having an affair with an older woman. An arrest, maybe. A big, public *mess*.

He'd promised he would make trouble for a price . . .

He'd sure as hell stirred up Brody Daniels . . . who'd hired him to find out who was behind the rumors about his wife. Hah! Daniels never guessed it was R.J. himself, and for a while there R.J. was getting paid at both ends, from Daniels as well as from his original deal.

But it was all a big dud.

In the parking lot, R.J. realized he needed a whiz. Shoulda gone to the men's room while he was still inside.

He turned, thinking he might go back in, but they were already locking the door and turning off the lights.

Well . . . hell . . . There was no one about. He headed over to the dumpster behind the bar and pulled out his willy, letting fly a stream of urine through the chain-link fence to the empty lot behind the gas station, which was coldly glowing from the white outdoor lights above the pumps.

He was zipping himself back up when he heard "R.J."

He whipped around, banging his elbow on the edge of the dumpster. The shot of pain woke him up. He recognized the voice and drew a shocked breath. "Hey, what are you doing here? I thought—"

Gloved hands grabbed him by the throat. He had just enough time to cry, "What?" before his throat clamped shut.

"Sorry, man."

"But I did what you wanted," he squeezed out on a tortured breath. "I did what you wanted!"

He slapped at the man's hands, tried to push his attacker off and nearly did but then couldn't.

"It wasn't enough."

R.J. stared in fear at the face hidden inside the ski mask. He wanted to plead his case, but couldn't breathe. Weakness overtook him. He felt strong hands grab him and slowly lower him to the ground. Hands in rubber gloves. This had been planned, he realized.

R.J. fell into a dream world as his life flow ebbed. It wasn't enough to taint Brody's wife's reputation, he realized.

It wasn't enough because she needed to die.

# Chapter 8

Early on Sunday, Lucille's Café was only partially full, though the diner would likely pick up as soon as the after-church crowd arrived. Brooke fidgeted as she sat down on the red vinyl seat. If she had to wait much longer for Rona she was going to start biting her nails, one of those horrid habits from grade school she'd worked hard to outgrow. Lacquered nails had helped but now she wanted to just rip at her fingers with her teeth. Damn, but she was frustrated. What a nightmare. She didn't want to reconnect.

At that moment Rona burst in through the café's revolving door, looking totally the same . . . and completely foreign. Her hair was longer now, shoulder length like Brooke's own. There was hardly a line on her forehead so Brooke figured Botox was in order, or something like it. Hadn't they all done something by this age? But there were lines bracketing Rona's mouth and Brooke recognized the signs of discontent. She had them herself.

However, Rona still looked just as fit and hard-bodied as she'd been in high school. Probably a workout regimen that

Brooke kept fudging on herself. Ah, well. Life was hell sometimes.

Rona spied her and hurried over. She wore tight jeans and a cranberry-colored silk blouse. Her dark eyes swept over Brooke's white shirt and gray slacks as she sat down. "Thanks for meeting me. I want to scream. Not at you, but at everything and everyone else."

"Me, too," said Brooke.

"There. We can already agree on something." Rona smiled faintly. "I need a drink. Is it too early?"

"Yes. But they have mimosas," said Brooke.

"Oh, thank God. At least you haven't gone around the bend like Wendy, a total teetotaler. You look great, by the way. I love your hair."

"Thanks." Brooke had to admit she was pleased that Rona had noticed. She'd just had it lightened to a caramel, sun-streaked brown shade.

It was good to see Rona, she realized belatedly, letting some of the resentment and fear and overall bad feelings she'd been carrying around dissipate. She didn't have time or energy to keep fighting, though. When Rona had called the night before after taking her daughter to Camp Fog Lake, Brooke had suffered through crippling anxiety about the thought of going to that damn camp.

"I cried all the way home," Rona had admitted. "I don't know why. I don't think anything bad's going to happen to her. Not really. But maybe it is? Am I crazy? I don't want to wait till parents' weekend. I want to go back right now and yank her to me. Hug her and tell her to be careful and don't go out alone and don't make enemies and don't do *anything*." She'd sounded as undone as Brooke had ever heard her. "I don't want her there!"

"I don't blame you," Brooke had answered. She'd almost refused to pick up her cell when she'd seen who was calling. Nothing about that camp was good.

"That's probably why she chose Fog Lake in the first place! Because I went there and I don't talk about it. Maybe she thinks I'm weird about it. I *am* weird about it. God *damn* it. Why is she doing this? She's so rebellious!"

Brooke had made sympathetic noises, though her mind tripped back to what Rona had been like in high school. Rebellious didn't even cut it.

"And her father and Donovan are no help at all," she'd gone on. "Why did I marry Donovan? I can't even remember. You know, I resented you for not coming to the wedding, but I get it now. Everything's so clear in retrospect. I was trying to rewrite the past somehow. Make it better than it was. Make it *matter*. What a joke! Donovan hasn't matured one iota. I'd leave him if I thought I could survive on my own income. I almost can. Maybe not. And now he's going to the camp even though I told him I didn't want him there. I don't want him there! I want *you* there!"

"Does he know?" Brooke had asked as Rona gathered her breath for another go around.

That had stopped her for a moment. Then she'd said, "No," distinctly, and changed the subject. Somehow, during the rest of their conversation, Brooke had agreed to meet Rona for breakfast and so here she was.

Now Rona reached across the table and grabbed Brooke's hand. "Thanks for coming."

"No problem."

"Tell me you've changed your mind and you're going with me." Rona's doe eyes pleaded with her. "I *have* to go. I have to see my daughter and make sure she's okay. That no bogeyman is suddenly appearing out of the woods and attacking her. I just need you there with me."

"Oh, God, Rona. I've got problems of my own."

"Then this is good timing! You need to get away, too." She was momentarily distracted by the plasticized menu that

had been dropped on the table, but now she slid an eye upward to gauge Brooke's reaction. "I need to know Kiley's
safe. That's foremost, no matter what. All the other stuff that
happened . . . to us, I have to put that aside."

Brooke ignored the menu. "I can't go. Period. This thing
with Lukey . . . it's embarrassing, at the very least."

"How is the fifteen-year-old beau doing?" she asked, a
twinkle in her eye.

"Jesus, Rona."

"I'm kidding. I'm *kidding*. Too soon. I get it. It's just so
improbable that I can't take it seriously. Sorry."

"I have no sense of humor about it."

"I understand." But there was a faint amusement quirking
around the edges of her mouth that Brooke didn't appreciate, though Rona managed to contain her mirth while she ordered them both cranberry mimosas.

They were silent till the drinks arrived and then Brooke
drew a deep, calming breath. She supposed she might feel
the same if the situation were reversed and Rona was the one
dealing with rumors and innuendo about an affair with a
teenager. It was so ludicrous she almost wanted to laugh herself, except that no part of it was funny. Was Brody right?
Was someone targeting her? Maybe to get to him? Maybe
for some other reason she couldn't see yet? Or was it just
terrible and ridiculous teen bullying and she'd gotten caught
up in it? Who was the man who'd come to Brody with so-
called information of a dalliance between her and Lukey? It
was all so damaging and dangerous and *untrue*!

Rona consumed the pretty red drink in the champagne
flute in one swallow. Then she went on about her and Kiley's
fractured relationship as Brooke sipped her own mimosa.
Once upon a time she and Rona had been best friends. The
best. Though Rona and Wendy had been friends before Brooke
arrived at their grade school, it was Rona and Brooke who'd

bonded. In truth Wendy had always been a little step off. In high school Wendy had spent more time with her boyfriend, Caleb Hemphill, now her husband, so it was Brooke and Rona as the dynamic duo.

Now she remembered just how difficult Rona was. How she would blithely use anything you told her at any time if she thought it would further what she wanted.

But . . . Rona was also fun . . . and fun had been in short supply for a long, long time.

The waitress came and took their order and Rona ordered another mimosa. As soon as they were alone again, Rona asked, "So, what's the story with that? Any news?"

"I called Brody, but he really doesn't know anything more yet. Some girls in Lukey's school who post on social media all the time were teasing him, I guess, and they wouldn't give it up, so he came back that the hottest girl he knew worked for his dad. They wouldn't give it up. They wanted to know who this 'hot girl' was and he named me and it went from there."

"Girl?" Rona gave Brooke a skeptical once-over.

"His words, not mine. I don't really know how it became such a thing."

"Like it went viral?"

"I guess. Actually, I don't even know it *is* a thing, but Brody says it is. But then he's a liar."

Rona nodded. "A lot of shit over the internet is for shock value. It might not be as bad as you think."

"You agreed with me about Brody. You're not even going to ask me why I say that?"

"You know Brody better than I do," she said.

"You don't know him at all," said Brooke, but when Rona didn't answer, Brooke pressed, "Do you?"

"I know a little about him."

"You know he's a liar?"

"Should I have ordered the omelette? Lucille's is the kind

of place that probably cooks those eggs till they're concrete, kind of like Camp Love Shack, but what the hell."

"How well do you know Brody?" demanded Brooke.

"I don't. Just rumors."

"What rumors?"

"Brooke . . ." she said, exasperated.

"What rumors, Rona?"

"He's kind of crooked in his business dealings, okay? You said you're divorcing him. Good. Get out of it. You said he was contacted by some guy about the rumors between you and your boss's son, so maybe the whole thing is to get back at him somehow, not you."

"Then why use me? I'm not living with him anymore." She thought about Jacqui and Tom. "These people at the cocktail party the other night, at least this Jacqui woman, wanted Brody to join up with them. If he was really crooked, would they do that?"

"I don't know. I've just heard rumors about Brody. Donovan's more in that world than I am. You could ask him, I suppose."

"I don't know what to think," admitted Brooke. Then she said carefully, "You don't think it has anything to do with . . . the camp, do you? I mean, because of the timing of these rumors? The camp's been in the news lately and there's renewed interest. When I think about what we did—"

"How can it be? It can't," interrupted Rona.

"I'm just worried . . ."

"Don't conflate things that have no relation to each other."

"What if they *are* related, though? What if *someone knows*, Rona?"

"They don't! And why you, if that were true? Why not me? Why not Wendy?"

"How do you know something hasn't happened to Wendy? Have you talked to her?"

"Not yet."

"If the rumor about me doesn't have anything to do with the camp, and what happened there . . ." Brooke broke off as Rona stared her down. "It's just a pretty big coincidence, that's all."

"That's a pretty big leap, Brooke."

She shook her head. "You're right." Of course she was right. "It's just the only thing remarkable in my life. Forget it. You're worried about your daughter. I would be, too. I am, actually."

"Then go with me. Please." The waitress came back with their food and Rona's second mimosa.

"I'm good," Brooke said, when the waitress looked at her expectantly. Then to Rona, "I don't need another headache."

Rona stabbed into her omelette, which was, as predicted, rubbery and overly brown on the outside. "I almost want to get drunk," she said, making faces as she took several bites. "Ugh."

Brooke picked at her blueberry muffin. After a few minutes of silent eating, Brooke asked, "How is it going to help if I go to the camp?"

"It'll help *me*."

She heard the little bit of hysteria she was trying to tamp down. Rona wasn't nearly as sanguine about going to Camp Love Shack . . . Fog Lake, as she put on. "Call Wendy," Brooke told her. "Feel her out about the whole thing."

"I don't want her to go with me. I want you."

"Don't you want to know where she is on everything? Maybe you're right. Maybe the slander about me and Lukey is a sideways attack on Brody and it's not about me, and it's not about the camp. I just want it all to stop. To just . . . stop. So, if nothing's happened to Wendy, the timing's just coincidence."

"And it will all die down and you can go with me."

"Such a broken record," Brooke muttered, but she could feel herself weakening.

Rona finally dropped the subject. Maybe she realized she'd pushed as much as she could without alienating Brooke. She turned the conversation back to her relationship with Kiley, recounting a few humorous tales and painting a picture of her hardheaded daughter as someone who was definitely a chip off the old block.

Forty-five minutes later, Brooke was back at her apartment, literally pacing the floor. The breakfast with Rona had brought up questions she needed answered. Maybe she or Brody or both of them were being targeted. Maybe—

When the doorbell rang she jumped about a foot and then patted her chest. She slipped to the door and peered through the fish-eye peephole. Brody stood on the steps outside.

Well, good. Time to clear the air. She opened the door the length of the chain and stood in the aperture, blocking Brody's entry.

"Can I come in?" he asked when she didn't say anything.

He was tense and it made him brusque. "What's happened?" she queried.

"Brooke, open the door."

Gone was the self-confident, near-smirking man she'd seen just a few days before. Muttering to herself, she did as he ordered. He came in and waited while she shut the door behind them.

"What?" she demanded.

"I wasn't completely straight with you. I didn't have a PI checking into things. I thought I knew who was behind the smear against you, and I followed up on it on my own."

"Brody, I sure don't like the sound of that." Hadn't she said he was a liar? She could feel her anxiety turning to anger.

"I hired a guy who's basically a hacker. Has done some work for my company and Jacqui's as well."

"Did he get caught doing something illegal?" Brooke braced herself.

"I just know he gets around social media pretty well, and he finds out a lot of information."

"Maybe he's the one who . . . amplified the story about me and Lukey in the first place. Did you ask him that?"

"Lukey?"

"He's a *kid*, Brody. More a *kid* than most of them his age! It's so ridiculous and dangerous and harmful. I can't even think about it."

"All I know is when I got an email about you and *Lukey* I called up my guy right away and told him I wanted to find out who sent the email to me. He said he was on it. And then later he told me it looked like you were the main target, not me. Then he hung up and I haven't heard from him since."

"What does that mean?"

Brody shook his head. He was trying to hide it, but he seemed deeply concerned. "I thought I'd hear from him by now. I texted him but I haven't heard back. Called him, too. Got his voice mail. Didn't leave a message."

His tension was starting to infect her as well. That's all she needed. More to worry about. "So, no answers?"

"I know where he lives. I'm going over there. See what's what. Feels like he's ghosting me."

"You're really worried. You think *he's* involved?"

Brody didn't answer, but his silence convinced Brooke that yes, he did think so.

"Just stay here, okay? Until you hear from me, don't go to that camp."

"The camp? What? Why? What do you know that you're not telling me?"

"I'm just being cautious." He turned back to the door.

"You know something? About this guy? What is it, Brody?"

"I hate to think this might turn into a police matter," he muttered tensely, letting himself out.

*Police?* Brooke's heart squeezed as she closed the door behind him and slid the chain in place. She slid down the door and sat on the floor, working to get her galloping heart under control.

# Chapter 9

Jamie sat at the kitchen table. She'd gotten up early even though they weren't supposed to meet with Mary Jo and her husband, Stephen, until noon as the Kirshners were attending morning service at their church. Jamie could hardly sit still. She'd made a list of questions for Mary Jo. Questions she should have asked earlier. Ones that hadn't seemed as important then, but now felt imperative, even though they probably weren't.

*What is it about Mary Jo that is so wrong?* she asked herself for about the thousandth time. *You chose her as your surrogate. You had no problem, in the beginning.*

*Or, was it just that you didn't want to get Emma's hopes up and you jumped before you were ready?*

That was probably closer to the truth. Theo had vouched for Mary Jo, and she and Cooper were lucky to have her, but it was also a means to stop Emma's campaign to be her surrogate.

The back door opened and Cooper came in from an early morning run, breathing hard, a triangle of sweat around his neck sticking his shirt to his skin, his phone pressed to his ear. "They can't tell from the tox screen?"

He was clearly talking to his partner. She could hear Verbena answer but couldn't make out the words and after a few moments of listening, Cooper grunted an assent and clicked off.

"Do you still think you have a poisoning?" asked Jamie, referring to the case that seemed to be currently consuming them.

"Sometimes it takes a while to figure out what you're dealing with, especially with poisons. Might be accidental. Could be something that grows in the backyard, some common plant."

Jamie nodded as Cooper headed upstairs to change. She glanced at the clock. Still only 8:30 a.m.


Harley ate at one of the tables in the back of the camp's dining area, seated on a bench next to Marissa. She could barely taste her oatmeal with cinnamon and sugar, while Marissa was slowly working her way through two pancakes dripping in maple syrup. There were scrambled eggs cooked to within an inch of their life that both of them had passed on as they'd served themselves at the buffet. The plates and cups were institutional thick, beige plastic, and the flatware was thin enough to bend if you weren't careful. Hope had mentioned KP duty, and there was a chart that Harley had already examined. When the campers arrived later in the day, Harley and Marissa were to make sure they understood the rules and get them settled in their cabins. Currently Allie sat at a table with counselors from other cabins, while the CITs tended to group together. The guys stuck with the guys and they didn't seem to have many counselors-in-training. They'd all been here before, except maybe Esau, as far as Harley could tell.

Hope had rung the triangle to call them to the lodge, an old-timey touch that was surprisingly earsplitting. She'd already introduced Tina and Warren but today she'd touted the skills of the head cook, a woman in her late fifties, Harley calculated, named Sunny Dae. She was fairly stout with a mop of gray hair held in a tight hair net, but her smile was infectious. She wrangled the younger workers and had piqued Harley's interest when she'd mentioned that she came from Haven Commune every day to meal prep.

Even so, Harley's main attention was on Marissa, who was moving slowly, like she was dead on her feet, yawning and looking like she was still half asleep. What was going on here? Harley was beginning to suspect it wasn't just a trip to the latrine last night, that maybe she'd been out half the night instead. That would explain her tiredness today. But Harley hadn't had a chance to talk to her as Allie had chirped cheerfully at first light that it was time to get up—where the hell did she get her energy?—and while Harley had quickly taken a trip to the bathroom to wash her face and brush her teeth, Marissa had moved like a slug. Harley had tried to engage her in conversation, by saying, "The campfire was something, wasn't it?" but Marissa didn't even grunt an answer. As she'd made her way to the girls' bathroom Harley had decided to follow her, watching as she splashed water on her face to wake herself up.

"You seem pretty tired," Harley observed, to which Marissa said, "I am," and left it at that.

Now, they were seated with people on each side of them and across the table, so there would be no private conversation. Once the young campers arrived, they would be assigned tables, and Marissa's and Harley's days would be pretty full guiding them through their camp schedule until their week ended and the campers then left on Saturday with a new group arriving the next day.

And in about another week, the parents would be here.

* * *

Jamie went for a jog herself and then came back, took a shower and changed into a pair of jeans and a crisp, pink shirt. She pulled her hair in a ponytail, then yanked it back down, then ended up collecting it into a messy bun.

"You look nice," Cooper said, also in jeans teamed with a dark shirt, the sleeves rolled up his forearms.

"So do you."

He lifted a brow at her tense tone, but didn't say anything. She was still working on her positive attitude, but she already wanted their meeting with Mary Jo and Stephen to be over.

At eleven she could stand it no longer. "Let's get going."

"We're going to be early."

Though the Kirshners lived in a rural area southeast of River Glen in the foothills of the Cascade Mountains, on a Sunday morning, without traffic, they could probably be there in thirty or forty minutes.

"I don't care. I want to go."

"All right. Let's take my car."

"Okay." Jamie told herself to stop making mountains out of molehills as she headed outside to Cooper's SUV.

Forty minutes later, they arrived at the long gravel drive bordered on both sides by a black chain-link fence. The house was about a quarter mile from the two-lane road they'd turned from and dust rolled from beneath their tires as they crunched along. Hay grew on both sides of the lane, tawny stalks waving at them in a gentle breeze, looking near ready to bale. The rural aspect of the property was engaging, but Jamie was too uptight to appreciate it.

They pulled up next to a triple-car garage and a large shed that held farming equipment. A dog was already frantically barking as they stepped out of the car. The day was overcast and the air was cool and heavy, rain forecasted. Jamie walked beside Cooper to the front porch of the red, sort of ramshackle farmhouse. She'd been here once before, but never entered the house as Mary Jo and her husband and two freckle-faced youngsters, one redheaded, one dark brown, both looking out of central casting for a 1950s sit-com, had met with them outside.

This time Mary Jo herself came outside alone, beaming. "I love being pregnant," she said, hugging herself.

Jamie was encouraged, though Mary Jo's little-girl voice grated a bit. *Stop being such a bitch*, she warned herself. "So, do I," said Jamie, injecting such enthusiasm in her tone that Cooper slid her a look out of the side of his eye.

They all trooped inside. The furniture in the living room was a mismatch of Early American maple except for a modern couch and a dresser, which was currently being used as a TV stand, both of which Jamie recognized from Ikea. Incongruously, there was a crystal chandelier over the kitchen table, which stood in front of a sliding glass door.

"My mother's," Mary Jo explained when she saw Jaime looking at it. Some of the joy she'd expressed outside seemed to seep out of her. "She's gone now."

"I'm sorry," said Jamie, automatically.

Mary Jo seemed to pull herself together. "It was a long time ago." She turned to Cooper and apologized for her husband, Stephen, still being at church. Apparently he was an alternate pastor who was filling in for their regular one, who was suffering from a cold.

Jamie looked through the sliding glass door, her eye following a trail cut through a lawn of patchy grass to some smaller structures, several chicken coops and a rabbit hutch.

"Oh, you have bunnies!" exclaimed Jamie.

Mary Jo glanced Jamie's way. "We sure do. You want to see?"

"Love to."

Her two children had appeared and the redheaded boy held out a Lego construction of a rocket ship to Cooper, who immediately bent down and began listening intently to the boy's enthusiastic revisiting of the construction.

"I'll catch up to you," he told Jamie, who followed Mary Jo outside, listening politely as the surrogate expounded about what was coming up on the farm the next few months.

". . . the neighbors help out when we're baling," she was saying. "I do the cooking and Marjorie does the baking and we all get together. The Resnicks have five children and she's thinking about becoming a surrogate, too." She smiled prettily. Mary Jo had a pleasant, if slightly blank, face. Her dark hair was prematurely graying, silver strands shining in the light.

"That's nice," said Jamie. "Your children's names are . . . ?"

"Joseph and Constance. After Stephen's father and my mother."

They were walking along the trail and Jamie could see the chickens scratching and pecking through the dirt. The bunnies were in their hutches. A silvery gray one put its little nose against the wire mesh and Jamie pressed her fingers against it.

"Be careful. They can bite," Mary Jo said on a laugh.

Jamie withdrew her hand. "They're so cute."

"We used to have pigs, but we don't right now." Mary Jo led her around the back of the hutches to an empty sty. Jamie's gaze drifted back to the rabbits. A thick chunk of wood the size and shape of a stump had been placed behind the hutches. There was a hatchet stuck in its center. The blade was shiny except its edge, which was a rusty red color. The top of the stump was infused with red as well.

Bloodstains.

Jamie looked from the stumps to the rabbits and back again.

*Oh, no . . .*

She immediately felt ill.

"Excuse me," she whispered, breaking into Mary Jo's rambling dissertation on their lifestyle. "Do you eat them?"

She flicked a look at the rabbits and then at the chunk of wood. "We raise most of our own food. Chickens, rabbits . . . The garden's over here."

Jamie was still looking at the hutch. The bunnies' noses were turned their way, delicately sniffing through the wire mesh. Her stomach somersaulted and she closed her eyes and begged herself not to throw up. *Please, please, please . . .*

"Are you okay?" Mary Jo asked from far away.

"I just need to . . . uh . . ."

She opened her eyes and stumbled rapidly back toward the house, forcing herself to not break into a run. Cooper was just coming through the door and stopped short upon seeing her hurrying toward him.

"We have to go," she said.

"What happened?"

"Nothing. I just have to go."

Cooper said carefully, "Okay." He somehow managed to say his goodbyes to Mary Jo and the two children, who both seemed to have adopted Cooper as their new best friend. He gave his regrets that he and Jamie couldn't see Stephen on this trip, but that they would be in touch.

When they were safely in the car and heading back down the long drive, Jamie laid her head weakly against the head-rest.

"You're white as a sheet," observed Cooper, flicking her a look.

"I don't want her to carry my baby," Jamie stated flatly.

A long silence ensued. Cooper, God bless him, knew when to keep his mouth shut because Jamie really wanted to come unglued. She said unevenly, "They're killing and eating the bunnies."

He grimaced.

"I know what they're doing is probably normal. She grew up in that commune. They raise their own food. They eat rabbits. It's not unheard of. But, oh, God, Cooper."

He dropped his right hand over hers and she fought back tears.

"Don't ever take me there again," she whispered.

"We'll meet somewhere else, next time," he agreed.

Jamie pressed her forehead against the cool glass of the passenger window. "You'd think I'm the one who was pregnant, as nutty as I feel."

"I don't think you're nutty."

"I have this mental picture of her, cutting their heads off. Whack!" She gave her arm a chop.

"Can you put it out of your mind?" asked Cooper.

"I'll do my damnedest," Jamie muttered, but all the way home all she saw were those bunnies' inquisitive little noses, imagining them covered in red blood.


About 2:00 p.m., Marissa crawled back into her lower bunk and passed out. She and Harley had spent the past few hours going over what their campers' schedules would be and had checked out the outdoor activities: swimming, canoeing, archery, and badminton.

Harley had caught glimpses of Greer at breakfast, but had also learned as time went on that she was less and less eager to show herself to him. Where was her nerve? Where was her plan to meet up with him again, see how that went? She'd planned out this whole summer at Camp Fog Lake because of him and now all she wanted to do was hide?

*Coward.*

Irked at herself, she left Marissa and checked her cell phone's battery life. Still okay. The recent renovations hadn't included plug-ins inside the cabins; the only place to connect to power was the lodge, though she doubted there was a random electrical outlet for just anyone's use. Still, she could probably find one in a crisis if her battery pack should fail her. Hope had to be able to call for help, if necessary.

She walked outside into cool sunshine, staring across Fog Lake's dark green depths. Somewhere out there was the commune where those star-crossed lovers had supposedly come from. And that first girl who'd been left on the ledge. Unless those two stories had been jammed together in a mash-up of spooky camp lore.

Kiley was walking along the water's edge and she saw Harley and waved to her, then climbed up the small beach and across the uneven bed of river rocks and up the hill to where Harley stood. "The buses of campers should be here any minute," she said. "Then we're in trouble."

Harley had to admit she wasn't sure what she was going to do with her charges. She and Marissa were going to be bunking with eight- and nine-year-olds.

"Did Austin find you?" asked Kiley.

Harley shook her head.

"He had some question for you, I think."

They both started walking back toward the cabins. Harley was trying to figure out what that question might be when Allie and Greer appeared from the walkway between the latrines and the boys' bunkhouses, heading straight for them. Allie was looking at Greer, but Greer was staring straight ahead.

Kiley was saying something to Harley, but she had been looking in Greer's direction and there was no pretending she wasn't. He saw her and she saw him. Her heart started thumping irregularly, like it had fallen out of rhythm. Was this what it was like to have a heart attack? Was she going to collapse right on the spot? Maybe that's what caused all the death around the camp.

She saw him react as he recognized her. His head came up a bit and his focus sharpened. She slowly lifted a hand in

greeting and Allie, having been made aware that something
had caught his attention, swiveled her head until she saw
Harley and Kiley.

"Hi, guys," Allie called as they reached earshot.

Harley found her voice and managed a really breathy,"
Oh, hi."

Kiley, oblivious, saved the day. "Are the buses here yet?"

"Umm . . ." Allie glanced behind her, but the boys' bunkhouses obscured her view of the road and parking area. "I
don't hear them."

"Hi, Harley," Greer said.

His voice was the same as she remembered and it caused
gooseflesh to rise on her arms. He was smiling but there was
something quizzical in it.

*Yes, I came here because of you, Greer, but I'm sure not
going to act like it.*

"Hey, Greer," she responded. "I saw you at breakfast. So,
you're part of the maintenance team?"

Kiley gave her a look. Did she sound as lame as she
thought she did?

"Yeah. Allie just told me she had two CITs in her cabin,
Harley and Marissa."

"You must've known it was us." She managed a laugh
that didn't sound too fake, she hoped.

"You guys know each other?" asked Kiley.

Allie said, "I didn't know that, either." And she sounded
none too pleased about it.

"We were at River Glen High together for a year," explained Greer. He turned to Allie. "I told you about my dad
and all the stuff that went down."

She nodded and looked appropriately sad, then threw on
her megawatt smile as she said to Harley and Kiley, "Did
you test the lake water? Is it cold?"

"Freezing," said Kiley.

"We're going canoeing for a bit. Hope's meeting with

some of the counselors. You two might want to hurry up to
the lodge and go over last-minute protocol. Harley, you need
to wake your friend."

"Marissa?" asked Greer.

"Yeah, she couldn't sleep last night," said Harley.

"We'd better hurry." Allie leaned into Greer.

"See you around," Greer said, his dark eyes on Harley.

"Yeah, later."

As Harley walked the rest of the way up the incline to the
cabins, Kiley said, "He your ex-boyfriend, or something?"

"Why would you say that?"

"Because you're acting weird."

"No, I'm not."

"Yeah . . . you are . . . was it a bad breakup?"

"You're way off base."

"Sure." She smirked. "I've got my sights on Austin although Niles would be good. I was worried I might have to
fight you for them."

"Have at 'em."

Harley broke from her as soon as she could and then hurried toward the back door of Foxglove, which she learned
was now locked from the inside. She went to the front door
of the cabin, which was open. The front lock was a small
board that slid into a block of wood on the other side, so it
could only be manipulated from inside the cabin, like the
hook and eye.

When Harley glanced toward Marissa's bunk, she saw
that the sleeping bag was empty. She reversed her steps and
headed outside, aiming for the girls' bathroom. Austin came
out of the boys' as she passed and said, "Hey, Harley. I
wanted to talk to you."

"Kiley said you had a question for me."

"I saw your friend last night after the campfire."

Harley hesitated. "Marissa?"

"Ask her who she was meeting. Somebody in the woods."

He jerked his head in the direction of the forest behind the maintenance buildings.

Marissa? Really?

"I don't think so."

"Maybe you don't know her as well as you think you do."

Feeling defensive, she demanded, "What were you doing out last night?"

He smiled slowly. "Waiting for you . . ."

She rolled her eyes and brushed past him, but couldn't help looking back once. He stood in front of the sheet of metal "mirror" outside the boys' bathroom door, his image watery and indistinct and looming.

Harley pushed into the girls' bathroom. She could hear a shower running and yelled above the rushing water, "Marissa?"

"Yeah?" came the muffled reply.

"Let me know when you're out! I want to talk!"

The taps shut off and Marissa appeared a few moments later dressed in jeans and a sweatshirt with a towel around her head. She still looked sleepy.

"It's Cam, isn't it?" Harley accused in a harsh whisper. "You met Cam last night."

"What?" She reached for indignation but Harley didn't buy it.

"Austin saw you with a guy." A bit of a lie, but Harley knew she was on the right track. "Is that why you finally decided to come to camp? Because Cam said he'd meet you here?"

Marissa paused, and it was clear she was debating whether to come clean or not. Finally, she drew a heavy breath. "You're going to tell them, aren't you?"

"Who? Cooper and Mom? Our cell phones don't work. I can't tell anyone except people at the camp, not like I would anyway, but, good God, Marissa! You could get kicked out or worse!"

"I probably won't see him while the campers are here."

"*Probably?*"

"He's got work. He's only free on the weekends."

"Well, great. That's okay, then."

"You don't have to be so mad."

"You plan to see him again next weekend?"

"I don't know. Maybe. It's a bitch for him to park and walk down the lane and into the woods. I don't know if he wants to do it again."

So sad for him.

"How will you know if he shows up again?"

"He'll flash the light about a minute apart about midnight," she admitted reluctantly.

"Marissa . . ." Harley wanted to tell her what a waste of space she thought Cam was but she knew, deep in her heart, that if Greer and she had cooked up the same scheme, she would go to him.

She sank against the wall, seeing words, graffiti, that had been painted over but still showed through the thin layer of latrine-green paint: *Donovan is a . . .* She couldn't make out the rest, but it looked like a picture of a fox.

"I love him, Harley," Marissa said earnestly.

Harley closed her eyes. She wanted to argue with her, tell her, like a parent would, that there would be other guys, but she was no shining example of relationship maturity herself.

"Just don't get caught," Harley finally snapped. It was all she could do not to lecture her on her poor choices.

"You're not going to tell anyone?"

"Have you met me?"

Marissa smiled and gave Harley a big hug. A more robust sign of friendship than they usually indulged in.

"Yeah, yeah." Harley moved out of the embrace. She was still mad at Marissa for being out all night, but trying to get over it.

Marissa yawned. "When are those campers supposed to get here? I have got to get more sleep."

At that moment they heard the rumble of the first buses. Marissa swore softly as Harley said, "Looks like right about now."

As they headed out, Harley admitted, "I just ran into Greer."

Marissa gave her a sharp look. "How was it?"

"He was with Allie."

"Oh."

Harley nodded. Nothing much else to say about that.

# Chapter 10

Monday morning, Brooke had barely sat down at her desk when she was called into Franklin Lerner's office. Her heart galumphed. That was unusual in itself. He wasn't her immediate boss. He owned the landscaping business and was hardly ever at the office, leaving the day-to-day operations to people who worked for him.

Things got worse as soon as Brooke was seated in the chair opposite Franklin's desk and his wife came into the room behind Brooke and crossed behind her husband to stare down at her. Valerie Lerner wasn't a tall woman. She was barely five-two, but she had a hard eye that surveyed Brooke over a set of rather massive breasts.

*So they heard.*

Brooke's pulse turned to a gallop before a word was uttered. She forced herself to remain quiet even while her body felt like it had flipped into hyperdrive.

Franklin cleared his throat. "Brooke . . ." he said, then didn't seem to know how to quite continue.

Brooke pressed her fingernails into her palms and looked at him expectantly.

Valerie Lerner had no such qualms. "My son is only *fif-teen*," she snarled. "You're going to jail!"

"Val, let me handle this," Franklin snapped.

"Oh, like you handle everything so well," she spat back.

"Luke says—" he started.

"I don't care what Luke says!" she cut him off. "He would lie to protect her. I want to hear what *she* has to say!"

Brooke's pulse was thundering in her ears. She could feel her face drain of color. How in the hell was she supposed to defend herself? Would it have been better to be blindsided? She couldn't disavow knowledge of the discussion without lying.

"What are you accusing me of?" she finally managed.

"You know what you did!" Val looked like she wanted to jump over Franklin's desk and attack her.

"If it's something to do with your son, I don't know what it is. I don't know Luke that well."

She sputtered. "Oh, you *know* him!"

"Val, shut up." Franklin's face had turned beet red, whether through embarrassment or anger, Brooke couldn't tell. Maybe a little of both.

Valerie turned on him. "You probably think it's funny. Lukey being sexually *groomed* by an older woman! Like it's every boy's dream."

"I haven't done anything with Luke!" Brooke protested, getting to her feet in spite of herself.

"You were seen," Val shot back, her hands clenching and unclenching.

"Val!" Franklin snapped.

"It's a lie. I've been nowhere near him!" snapped Brooke.

"I saw the pictures!"

Brooke was growing angry herself. Infuriated, actually. She almost wanted to grab Valerie's dyed red hair and yank it out by the roots. But she hung onto her reason with an ef-fort. "Where? The internet? Whatever you saw wasn't real.

If you even saw anything. Luke's a child. Check with his friends. And leave me out of it!"

"You know about it. I can tell you know about it," she accused.

"I heard about it," admitted Brooke. "Before you accuse me of something, you should check your sources."

"Lukey admitted it!" she bleated in fury.

Franklin swept in a breath. "Val, shut your mouth!"

"He did not," said Brooke. "You just said he would lie about it. I don't know exactly what I'm being accused of, but if it has to do with Lukey it isn't true."

"Lukey!" she screamed, pointing at Brooke, her eyes bugging with an "I got you!" expression.

"We all call him that," Brooke reminded, though her head was buzzing. She hated emotional encounters. Hated controversy of any kind.

But she could rise to the occasion when necessary. She had a strong flight response, but fight was in there, too . . .

"Brooke, we think it would be a good idea if you didn't come to work for the next few weeks," said Franklin.

She whipped back to look at him, astounded and disappointed, too. "You seriously believe this?" she asked him.

"Stay away from us," Val ground out. She was having a helluva time getting control of her own emotions. "Franklin's afraid of lawsuits, but I'm not. You had sex with my fifteen-year-old son! You're not getting away with that!"

"We don't know what happened," Franklin cut in quickly before Brooke could respond. "We're giving you two paid weeks, and then we'll see where we are."

"I didn't have sex with your son," Brooke said again. "And you should be careful of lawsuits. Slander me and find out."

Val actually shot around the desk. Brooke braced herself, but Franklin, showing surprising spryness for a man of his age, leapt after his wife and grabbed her arms from behind.

Brooke stood her ground in front of her chair but there was a tremor ripping through her. She remembered that other time. Vividly. Could almost see herself quaking from head to foot. *SMASH!* The rock came down on his head.

When neither Valerie nor Franklin said anything more, she turned on her heel and left the room. Picking up her purse and mug from her desk, she left Greenscape without a backward glance. She would sue the hell out of them. She needed an attorney. She needed Brody.

She plucked her phone from her purse and before she left Greenscape for the last time, she punched in Brody's number. The line rang and rang and she was forced to eventually click off, angry and somewhat scared.

Before she could pull out of the lot, her phone buzzed back. *Brody.* Finally! She had a moment of annoyance when she considered he might have just been letting the phone ring when she called.

"What the hell?" she launched in as soon as he answered. "I just came from work and I was *fired* because they think I had an affair with their son!" She then gave him a quick recap of her meeting with Franklin and Valerie, but at his continued silence, she snapped, "Are you there? Brody. Say something." She just managed not to add *Asshole* to her demand, as she felt it was his fault somehow.

"Brooke . . ."

The seriousness of his tone caught her unaware. "Oh, God. What now?"

"He's dead. The man who tried to blackmail me with the information."

"*What?* . . . Blackmail?"

"The police contacted me this morning. He was strangled and found behind a dumpster early Sunday. They got my contact information from his phone and asked me how I knew him."

Brooke collapsed against the back of the driver's seat, her body limp. She hadn't put the car in gear yet, which was just as well.

"Don't worry. I'm not going to tell them about you. I'd had him do work for me before, so I'll lean on that."

He spoke slowly, sounding out the words as if listening to them himself to see if they sounded credible.

"Oh, my God, oh, my God . . ." she murmured. "Strangled? *Murdered?* What did you mean by blackmail?"

"I'll keep you out of it," he said with more determination.

"Well, don't lie, for God's sake! They always find out and then everything's worse."

"Omitting's not the same as lying," he said. "I've got to go. I've got a meeting and this thing has thrown off my morning."

Brooke was left staring into space, her heart pounding, sweat forming on her brow, her autonomic responses on overdrive.

Her mind tripped backward. To that night at the camp. Wendy shrieking. Rona whispering for her to calm down. Brooke moving as if in a dream, slack and unfocused and barely able to put cohesive thoughts together. She felt like that now, too.

Her phone was still in her hand.

She pressed in a number and Rona answered right away.

"You're going!"

"No . . . I don't know . . . I don't know."

Rona hesitated, then said, "You're not at work?"

"I'm home. I got . . . fired."

"Ah . . . oh, shit. I'll be right over."

And she hung up.


Detective September Rafferty pushed through the heavy wooden door into Billy Ray's, a Laurelton sports bar she'd never had the pleasure of patronizing until now. She looked around at the huge televisions mounted all around the room and the dusty pennants and photos and other paraphernalia that labeled the place a sports bar. The TVs were set to different stations depicting a variety of sports programs with panels of men dissecting games, plays, and scores. In the moment she glanced at them, one set moved to a commercial for Taco Bell, another for Carl's Jr.

The place had just opened for the day and the only person she saw was a bartender in a white-and-navy-blue pinstriped baseball shirt with a fabric patch on his left chest, embroidered with ED in navy script.

"Hi, Ed," she said with a faint smile.

His eyes ran up and down her lithe frame. She'd been working out, shedding the five pounds she'd gained since she'd been married, weight that had jumped onto her as if just lying gleefully in wait. It had taken a lot longer to take off the pounds, but now she was generally better about what she ate. Not that the fire burger from Carl's Jr., or whatever the hell it was, on the screen didn't look good. Fast food was likely on the menu today.

She was in black slacks and a dark gray jacket that covered the firearm at her hip, but she saw Ed's eyes stray to the bulge anyway.

"You a cop?" he questioned.

"I'm Detective Rafferty. I think you talked to Officer Crowley about the male body found in your parking lot yesterday."

"Yeah, I did. And he asked a lot of questions. You're gonna ask 'em now, too?"

"I'm following up."

He was pulling beer glasses from a dishwasher and stacking them on the bar. "I don't have a lot of time. You see anybody else, here? No. Cuz they all can't come in on time. Sick, traffic, appointments . . . same old horseshit."

"You're the manager?" she said.

"I'm everything, lady . . . er, Detective."

September had been handed the case after the victim, Richard Everly, had been found. The file had been on her desk this morning with the initial report from Crowley, who'd been on duty yesterday when Everly's body was discovered. Crowley had called Tech and the body had been processed. Everly's body had been left near the dumpster behind Billy Ray's. His cell phone had been recovered from a line of vicious blackberries that ran behind the dumpster. It may have been flung from his hand when he was attacked. If the killer had wanted to keep the phone, he might have been unable to sift through the thorny brambles in the dark. Everly's body was currently at the morgue in the basement of Laurelton General Hospital.

"You told Officer Crowley that the victim, Richard Everly, was talking to one of the waitresses Saturday night," September said, cutting through Ed's grievances.

He snorted. "Candy."

"What's Candy's last name?"

"Rundell." He stacked the glasses with enough force that September half-expected one to break. "She'll be here later on today, if she shows up. About three."

Crowley had asked about Candy but she hadn't been at work on Sunday, either. September had put in a call to the listed owner of the bar, but it was under an LLC with a number that reached a voice mail and no one had gotten back to her yet.

"Was Everly a regular here?"

"I told Crowley this already." When September just waited, he shook his head and rolled his eyes. "Yeah, we saw R.J. a lot. He was full of shit, you know? Said he's an internet salesman. What is that? I call it 'scammer.'"

Privately, September thought Ed was probably right. She

asked a few more questions and the whining that he'd "already told them that" continued. Finally, she gave up. She would come back when Candy's shift started.

She walked out of the dark and dingy, rectangular building and drew in a long breath of clear air. A strand of auburn hair escaped the hasty bun she'd tossed together this morning and she blew it out of her face. She'd been with the Laurelton P.D. long enough now, in two separate stints, to stop being considered a newbie. She'd been let go during hiring cuts, but had been rehired when the regime had changed. Her old boss, Lieutenant Aubrey D'Annibal, had been replaced by Captain Dana Calvetti, who'd brought September back. Calvetti ran the department with a firmer hand on the rudder than D'Annibal—maybe a little too firm, according to September's ex-partner, Gretchen Sandler, who'd since left the department and the state, a huge loss in September's opinion. Acerbic pain in the ass though Sandler may have been, she was tough and irreverent and September had learned to count on her. But she'd taken off and moved to the L.A.P.D., having fallen for a detective from the area whom she'd dubbed "Beverly Hills Cop." But then Gretchen had never really clicked with Captain Calvetti, who was hard and somewhat mercurial. Now September was teamed with Detective George Thompkins, who'd been with the department for years and was known for riding his chair and never doing much, if any, fieldwork. In that, things had not changed. September was the legs. George was the man on the computer.

"Tech got into his phone from facial recognition," George had told her, handing her a list when she'd asked him what he knew about Everly so far. "Most recent at the top."

She'd scanned the document. "Called any yet?"

"Checkmarked 'em." He pointed to the list in her hands without lifting his eyes from the computer.

"What about family?" George might ride his chair more than September liked, but he certainly did thorough background checks.

"Parents are dead. No siblings. The guy's been in and out of jail, a two-bit grifter who passes information back and forth to whoever'll bite. Sometimes legit companies use him. He fashions himself a private investigator, but no chance. Grew up around Portland. Dropped out of Lincoln High School. Parents put him in some private pseudo-Christian academy . . . Glory to God . . . which didn't take, either."

"Pseudo-Christian?" she repeated.

George shrugged. "The school's one of those that's supposedly built on Christian tenets, but there was a scandal of some kind . . . inappropriate relations between students and faculty that's never been proven. The next year after Everly attended, Glory to God was gone."

"Does he have a girlfriend? Partner?"

"He seemed to be a loner. House he rented is in the county. Been there a while. Maybe the sheriff's department knows him."

"I'll check with them."

September had yet to do that. Now, as she left Billy Ray's, she put through a call to the Winslow County Sheriff's Department and was connected to a detective named Barb Gillette. After introducing herself, she asked if the detective knew anything about one Richard Everly.

"R.J." Detective Gillette made a disparaging sound in her throat. "One of those guys who can't stay away from the lure of a quick buck. We keep hauling him in, and he keeps getting out and doing it again. What's happened now?"

"Looks like he's a victim of homicide. He was strangled and left behind a dumpster Saturday night."

"Holy shi . . . Toledo," she said, editing herself from what she clearly wanted to say. "Where? How?"

September then explained about his body being found behind Billy Ray's Bar in Laurelton, adding, "I understand his address is outside the Laurelton city limits."

"He's up on Carmine Ridge. Unincorporated county. Still a lot of land up there. Neighbors don't live close to each other. Good meth-lab land," she added ironically.

"Was he a meth manufacturer? Bartender at Billy Ray's said he was an 'internet salesman.'"

"No meth that we know of. I just meant there's a lot of space up there. But internet scams are exactly the kind of thing that would appeal to him. Everly is—was—a career lawbreaker. He had no compunction about stealing your last dime if he could winkle it out of you."

"Mind if I take a look at his property?" Everly's home was outside September's jurisdiction, but since the man had been killed in Laurelton it was her case.

"Come by the station. We'll get you in there. Jim Carrus can go with you."

"Okay, thanks."

September determined she would check in with the Winslow County Sheriff's Department after she talked to Candy. For now she motored through the drive-thru at Burgerville, an Oregon fast-food burger joint, checked in with her husband, Jake, who had sold his investment business only to be dragged back into it, a situation he said he still wasn't certain he liked but September was fairly certain he did, then she stopped at a local park and ate her burger in her car in relative quiet. As she finished up, she pulled out the sheet she had from George and checked the phone list. Everly had a string of messages that had been sent to his personal email address. The last one was to bdaniels@centuryprime.com, which September recognized as an investment firm. George had also listed a phone number, which he'd called earlier this morning and connected to the man. She smiled as she read George's notation on bdaniels: *Kind of a dick. Went dead quiet when I told him about Everly, then tried to say he didn't know him.*

Could be nothing, September thought as she wadded up the paper wrapper of her burger and tossed it into a waste can. Could be the shock of having the police call and alert you that someone you knew was dead.

Or, could be something. Time would tell.

# Chapter 11

Brooke was blankly changing the channel on the TV when the doorbell rang. Her mind was full of dread. She was being set up. This was no accident by vengeful teenagers who wanted to get back at Lukey. Not to Brooke's way of thinking. All of the rocks had fallen on her, not Luke, and she didn't see what this had to do with Brody, no matter what he said, unless someone thought attacking her would give them leverage on him, which seemed preposterous.

*More preposterous than thinking it has something to do with the camp?*

She dropped the remote and went to the door, looked through the peephole.

Rona was holding the twine handles of two grocery bags from a nearby upscale grocery store. She lifted the bags higher.

Brooke opened the door and Rona said, "I have wine and snacks. You sounded like you're about to have a breakdown. Not that I blame you. Those assholes, whoever it is who's shitting on you . . . it's time to take charge."

Rona swept past her and into Brooke's kitchen, dropping the bags on her counter and pulling out several bottles of white wine, condensation having formed on the recently refrigerated bottles. Rona then hauled out crackers, smoked salmon, cream cheese, and a small vegetable tray, which she pointed to and said, "In case guilt overtakes us and we decide to get healthy."

"Heaven forbid."

"Donovan's at work. I'm pissed off at him. Why did you allow me to marry him?"

Rona's breezy, take-charge attitude helped, somehow. Brooke managed to parry, "So it's my fault?"

"Well, it can't be mine."

"Of course not." Brooke hadn't attended Rona's wedding, nor had Rona attended hers.

"We shouldn't have let our friendship lapse," said Rona, the statement surprisingly heartfelt.

Brooke felt the pull of Rona's personality and wanted to be drawn in. But it was Rona who'd made them row the body to the far end of the lake that dreadful night. Brooke's arms hurt just remembering. "I shouldn't have called you this morning. I was just . . . at a loss."

"Are you kidding? We need to get to the bottom of this attack on you." She shook her short dark hair. "By the way, you look dreadful."

"Thanks."

"I'm not trying to be mean. You just look like you feel like shit."

"I *do* feel like shit. I feel this weight on me."

Rona was already rummaging around in Brooke's drawers for a corkscrew. Brooke moved to the correct drawer and found it for her, handed it over. Rona pulled out the cork with a muscular twist as Brooke opened another cupboard and retrieved two stemmed glasses—strictly utilitarian from Target as she'd left everything she and Brody had amassed together with him.

Rona poured them each a healthy glass of sauvignon blanc. "Okay, what happened?"

"I told you on the phone about the Lerners and getting fired."

"Yes, you did, and that's a pisser. But now tell me about Brody."

"What specifically?"

She gazed at Brooke over the rim of her glass. "You know I've never liked him."

"Really. How well do you know him?"

"Just through rumor, mostly, like I said."

Brooke watched Rona belt down half her glass. "What are you, an alcoholic?"

She was pouring herself a second glass and stopped in the act. "Did we always insult each other this way?"

"That was more of a query than an insult."

Rona resumed her pour. "I do drink too much," she admitted, "but I'm not stopping today."

"If I drink like this, I'll get a killer headache."

"We've all learned to cope with what happened in our own way. I sometimes drink too much and you reverted to marriage to a wealthy man who only sees you as arm candy. A wife as jewelry." She lifted her glass in an imaginary toast to Brody. "Bet it made him insane when you left. You shoulda called me right then."

"Brody does well, but I don't know if I'd call him wealthy."

"You're hedging."

"I don't really care, Rona. This whole thing is horrible and I just feel awful."

For a moment she looked concerned. "Do you think there's any chance he's lying to you about the online attack?"

"The Lerners *fired me*!"

"I know, I know. But Brooke, I haven't been completely honest with you."

"Oh, great. What a surprise." She lifted her glass to her lips.

"I know Brody Daniels is a narcissistic asshole who's cheated on you from the get-go."

Brooke choked on her drink of wine and had to cough for a while before she was back in control.

"Donovan may be an ass, but he's strictly junior varsity compared to Brody. He's worked with Brody some, did you know that? No. Because Brody never tells you anything."

"I worked in finance, too. That's how we met," she argued defensively.

"He steals from people, Brooke. An investment guy? He's taking money out of his clients' accounts and moving it around. Bernie Madoff's got nothing on him, except how much money he swindled. Brody might've been legit when you first met him—although I doubt it—and anyway, that's been a while. He got you out of the business, made you a glorified bookkeeper for some rinky-dink landscape company, meanwhile he's been robbing his clients blind."

"Where do you get this? I thought Donovan was in real estate."

"We both know people in finance, as do you, I know. You should do a deep dive into his business practices. Check with some of your old business buddies. See what they think about Brody."

"You're wrong, Rona." As ever, she was making mountains out of molehills. "Just the other night he was being financially wooed by this woman, Jacqui, from—"

"The function he had you go to with him?"

"Yes!"

"He's making a play. Not for her, necessarily, for whatever money she can tap into. Bet he's got serious money trouble."

"He's in demand, Rona."

"I'm not arguing. It's just that at some point it's all going to come crashing down. You're lucky you left him. Keep it that way."

"Why are you saying all this now?" Brooke demanded.

"Because you need to know. Have some more." She indicated Brooke's barely touched glass. "I've heard whispers for a while. I've wanted to tell you. But we've all left each other alone all these years because of what happened."

"What happened is, we committed a crime," reminded Brooke.

"We saved Wendy," she came right back with.

*Did we, though?* Brooke took a healthy swallow of her drink. Rona was making her feel mad and anxious. She didn't need this, especially from Rona, yet . . . hadn't she thought some of these same things about Brody? Hadn't she wondered sometimes about what he was really doing? Why he'd been so insistent she give up her job in the industry when they'd gotten married. Why sometimes he seemed to care about her and other times acted like she was as off-putting as bad breath? His interest in her seemed to wax and wane depending on her interest in him, maybe. The more aloof she became, the more he showed her attention. Arm candy? Wife jewelry . . . ? Maybe. His inconsistency was why she'd finally left. She recalled his shock and fury when he'd realized she'd opened her own checking account and moved enough money to rent her apartment and live for about a year. He'd then changed tactics and said he understood. She'd thought they were quietly heading for divorce, but Rona's accusations made her question her assessment of his motives.

"We saved Wendy," repeated Rona with more emphasis when Brooke went quiet.

Brooke picked up the smoked salmon and cut it from its shrink-wrapped plastic, then arranged it on a plate along with the cream cheese and crackers. She then opened the pack of vegetables and picked up a watermelon radish, dipping it in the accompanying ranch dressing and biting into the crunch.

They looked at each other.

"Brody keeps saying he wants to know my secret," Brooke revealed after a long moment. "He blames that for the marriage failing." She hadn't really planned to tell Rona, but it just came out.

"I think that's bullshit. What have you told him?"

"That there is no secret."

"And he doesn't believe you?"

"No, he doesn't," she admitted.

"If he finds out, he'll use it against you."

"He's not going to find out. Give me some credit, Rona. I've held it together for damn near twenty years. What about Donovan?"

"He doesn't know anything," she said, a trifle too quickly.

"Have you told him—"

"No. Nothing. He can't know anything. But you . . . Don't trust Brody too much. He's going to look out for his own neck, and that might not mean that he'll protect yours."

Brooke lapsed into irked silence. She knew he wasn't the man she'd made him out to be in her mind. She knew she'd jumped into the marriage. She even knew that Rona might be right about his being a narcissist. Still, she felt almost compelled to defend him. He was her husband.

She picked up a small celery stick, shoved it in the cream cheese, then munched away, her chewing short and angry sounding even to her own ears.

Rona selected a cracker and turned it over and back, as if looking for flaws. She took the tiniest of bites, then asked, "You met Brody through work?"

"Yep. He came up to me at a work function and we started talking and he was charming. It just went from there."

"When did you know it wasn't going to work out?"

Brooke took a large drink of the crisp wine, thinking that over. She tried to put aside her annoyance, recognizing she was half mad at herself for falling for him. She set the glass back down and looked into Rona's dark eyes. "Truth?"

"No dares . . ." Rona smiled faintly.

Her comment sent Brooke back to that night around the campfire at Camp Love Shack. If she'd known what was going to happen. If she'd listened to the warnings about the insidious, evil fog and the deaths that surrounded the camp . . .

She shook her head. That was then, this was now. "I almost backed out of the wedding," she admitted. "I would've, but it just felt like we were so far down that rabbit hole that I had to go through with it. I kept thinking it would all be okay. I just . . . I've always wanted a normal life and I thought that's what Brody offered."

Rona's gaze slipped from Brooke's. "None of us gets a normal life."

"No, I guess we don't. We killed a man."

She slowly shook her head, not wanting to hear it. "You say Brody keeps asking you about your secret? Maybe he does know and he's waiting for you to say something."

"How could he know?"

"Someone told him, maybe?"

"Well, I didn't."

"And I didn't. And I just don't see Wendy running in the same circles as Brody. She's . . . well, she's not like us. But Brody knows something. He interviewed me a while back."

"*What?*"

"He was fishing, but he knew something. I acted like I didn't know what he was talking about, but Donovan's brought up the camp several times since then. I think he overheard."

"Where? When?"

"Just like you said. At a financial real estate event."

"You sure Donovan doesn't know?" Brooke moaned.

"He knows something went down at the camp, but he's not sure what. He knows we three quit being friends for some reason, but when he brings it up I remind him that he slept with half the girls at camp and he shuts up. I can't believe he even wants to go with me now, but whatever." She took another deep swallow, emptying half of her second glass. "But the last time I met Brody he said something to me, one of those offhand comments."

Brooke took her glass and moved blindly toward the couch, sinking into it.

Rona picked up the tray of salmon, cream cheese, and crackers, and followed her, setting the tray down on the side table then seating herself beside Brooke. "I called you when I learned you were seeing Brody, but I didn't leave a message. I should've. I was . . . I don't know. Afraid you'd tell me to butt out, I guess. I should've left the message."

"Brody doesn't know what happened. He's pressured me about my 'secret' over and over again. He's still pressuring me, but he doesn't know."

Rona didn't respond.

"Why do you think he knows? What do you mean he interviewed you? Where did you see him?"

"It was a real estate thing in Portland. Lot of people there with a lot of money. Brody was cruising for new clients. He has a reputation for getting people really good returns on their investments. He came over to Donovan and me. Donovan was his usual charming self, flirting with the women. I thought Brody wanted to talk to him, but he started chatting with me instead. I confess I was kind of glad for the attention. But I could see he was a player. There's an edge to him. You know what I mean."

Yes, she did. She'd known Brody was untrustworthy, even while he was professing his love for her. She'd felt it, but had pushed it aside.

"I'd had a lot to drink and he kept refilling my glass, not

that I stopped him. I flirted right back. Outrageously. I even thought about having an affair, but he wasn't interested in me that way. And then he said to Donovan, 'She's a killer, you know.' Just like that. We all laughed but I saw it in his eyes that he meant it. I told myself later I was wrong. I was just drunk and mistaken. But then he met you and then he married you." She paused to take a drink.

"We've been married for three years. You could have checked in at any time."

Rona broke off a tiny piece of salmon and nibbled at it. "I don't know how much Brody knows, but he knows something. Same for Donovan, though I have to admit I've thought about telling him. What happened was self-defense."

"I'm having trouble remembering it that way, Rona." The low-level dread she'd been feeling was growing, expanding in her chest so she could scarcely breathe.

"Just don't trust Brody."

"Don't trust *Donovan*," she shot back. Donovan . . . the guy Rona just *had to have* back in their Camp Love Shack days! "Don't tell him anything."

"I won't. I'm telling you, I never have." Rona held up a hand as if to ward her off. "We can't trust either of them."

"Have you talked to Wendy yet?" demanded Brooke.

"No."

Brooke curled her fingers into her palms. She felt light-headed and at the same time like her limbs were being dragged down, down, down with ten-ton weights.

"What if he's not dead?" whispered Rona.

So, there it was. What was really eating her. Brooke met her gaze. For all her big talk, Rona wasn't half as certain about everything as she made out to be.

"He's dead," stated Brooke firmly.

"But they never found the body."

"That we know of."

"We would know. I've checked reports. I've circled back

and reread everything about Camp Love Shack. Everything and anything I could find. Ryan's body was found, and so was that of the girl on the ledge, Fern Galbraith."

"You remember her name?"

"I memorized it. It's been with me since it happened. After Zach left me, I tracked down Donovan. I wanted to go back . . . make it all turn out differently. I don't know." She drained her second glass of wine and set the stem down. "Be careful what you wish for."

"Neither one of us really got what we wanted," observed Brooke. She, too, finished the wine in her glass. "Brody's 'killer' comment? Sounds like it was just a compliment to you."

She shook her head. "There was a message there."

"It could be just coincidence that I met him shortly after you did."

"I'm not saying anything you haven't already thought. He could be the one setting you up. Maybe he made all that other stuff up about the PI. Maybe he's the one who sent a message to your boss."

"Brody knows it's all a lie. Hell, *Lukey* knows it's all a lie!"

"Come with me to Camp Fog Lake," Rona pressed again. "Don't talk to Brody, or anyone. I'm looking out for all of us, Brooke. Don't trust anyone but me."

"What about Wendy? Are you including her in 'all of us'?"

Her hesitation was barely perceptible. "Of course . . . since she's the reason all this happened."

Brooke was leaning her way despite her arguments to the contrary. Did she trust Rona? Not on her life. But what she said held a lot of truth. Brooke had always felt a little off base with Brody. Maybe that's what had made the sex so good, the edge of danger that always flickered around their relationship. She had always wanted children, but had never been able to really broach the subject with Brody other than lightly joking. *Someday when we have children . . . when we look back on this with our kids . . . it'll be strange to see ourselves in them, won't it . . . ?*

But he'd ignored every overture she made. And if he responded at all, it was with that little half smile she'd grown to hate, the smile that said she was oh, so faintly amusing.

"The camp's in, like, ten days," said Brooke.

"You'll be completely out of Brody's range for a few days. Might be a good thing."

"I want this resolved before that."

"Of course you do. But will it be?" she asked.

Brooke returned to the kitchen and poured herself another glass of wine. "You're going to make me paranoid."

"You're already paranoid. We all are."

"You think Wendy is?"

Wendy was happily married to Caleb, as far as Brooke knew. After camp, she'd reunited with him, the two of them had found each other again and grew more intensely in love. They'd gotten married within weeks of the camp's closing.

"I don't know," admitted Rona.

"When you talk to her, you can ask her."

"I don't suppose you want to call her with me?"

"Hell, no. This is your party," said Brooke. "I'm just a wallflower."

Rona looked at the near-empty bottle and said, "Good thing I bought two."

"Good thing," Brooke said, feeling slightly more relaxed. Yes, alcohol wasn't going to help either of them, but right now she almost wanted to embrace the oblivion.

"I might have to spend the night rather than face Donovan," Rona admitted.

"Fine with me." A faint bubble of hysteria floated upward. "I only have one bed, so I'll have to tell Lukey he can't come over!"

Rona gave a short bark of laughter. "So, you *do* have a sense of humor."

"Yeah, well . . . not much of one." She was already sorry she'd made a joke.

"I can always take the couch." So saying, Rona moved back into the living room and threw herself onto the sofa. "We've got a lot of hours yet."

"Days," said Rona. "Before the camp weekend."

Brook felt a slight buzz from the wine. "I didn't say I was going."

"Uh-huh."

"You don't always get your way anymore, Rona," warned Brooke.

"I never get my way. But I'm always hopeful." She picked up the remote and switched the television back on. "Can I give you some advice?"

"Like you haven't already?"

"It might be better if you stopped calling that kid *Lukey*. Just sayin' . . ."

She thought about the morning with the Lerners and that terrible dread descended again. She glanced over at Rona. In some ways, it already felt like they'd never been apart. But being with her brought the trouble to her door. The trouble she'd been trying to avoid—and deny—for most of her adult life.

Could she be right about Brody?

"Thank you for calling me back, Mr. Daniels," September said politely into the telephone.

"I'm sorry. What is it you want again? I'm between phone calls and I don't have a lot of time," was his brusque response.

September had left several messages at Brody Daniels's

office and he'd finally deigned to call her back, but his impatience was clear.

"I'm interested in your relationship with a Mr. Richard Everly."

"As I told your partner, I don't have a relationship with Everly. I barely know his name. And excuse me, I checked with your superiors after I got your messages. They said your name was Westerly, but you call yourself Rafferty?"

It was a conundrum September had faced over changing her name to Jake's. Initially she'd dropped Rafferty in place of Jake's surname, Westerly, but she'd forged so many relationships using her maiden name that she'd now reverted to Rafferty. She found it interesting that Daniels had called the department on her. "It's Rafferty. You received a number of phone calls from Mr. Everly over the last three or four weeks. Can you tell me what those are about?"

"I'm sorry, no. Client confidentiality."

"So Mr. Everly was a client of yours? You said you didn't have a relationship with him."

"Well, in a manner of speaking. Our company has used his services in the past."

"What kind of services?" September chafed a little at making this interview on the phone, but Brody Daniels's office was a single room on the first floor within a larger office building guarded by a receptionist who wasn't interested in anyone getting past her, even the police. September had shown up at Daniels Century Prime in person this morning and had been refused entry. The receptionist was a woman in her fifties, solid and stone-faced and surrounded by black-and-white television screens depicting the parking structure, hallways, and a number of rooms within the building. She clearly took her job very seriously. She'd called Daniels's office and been told he was unable to see her right then. As a police detective, September maybe could've pushed the point, but had decided to place a few calls instead. She had no wish to antagonize Daniels before she could take his measure, thus she was now in an unsatisfying telephone wrangle with him.

"R.J.'s a private investigator, Detective," Daniels said smoothly. "He does background work for us."

There was something about his tone that suggested he was both bored and maybe faintly amused at talking to a police detective. In her experience, this kind of game-playing was often a smoke screen, a delaying tactic used to hide something else. Maybe he was just the super-private type who didn't trust the police as a matter of course, but she sensed he was purposely parrying with her . . . Maybe it was because she was a woman? That had happened more than a few times during the course of her work.

"Our company provides its clients full protection," he went on. "I can't just give out information to anyone who asks."

She was hardly just "anyone," but she let it pass. "You keep saying 'our' company. I understood you're the principal and only owner of Brody Century Prime Investments."

"It's just a manner of speaking."

"How recent was your last dealing with Mr. Everly?"

"I think I spoke to him sometime earlier in the month."

"You hired him?"

"We just talked about the possibility. Nothing formal."

"And you've hired him in the past."

"As I said, R.J.'s done background work for me . . . for my company, once or twice. That's about all I can tell you, Detective."

September tried a few more questions, but Brody didn't have any more time for her. He hustled her off the phone after intimating she would be well served searching for answers in some other direction.

She had several other names to call from Everly's phone records and she dutifully spent the afternoon tracking them down. Two of the people were clearly stunned to hear Everly was dead, especially the violent nature of his death, even though they knew his profession as an investigator came with risks. September felt their reactions were more genuine, and though she was going to dive deeper into Richard Everly's contacts and movements over the past few weeks, it was Brody Daniels who'd caused her antennae to raise the most.

# Chapter 12

*Oh . . . boy . . .*

Harley looked around at the cabin filled with chattering, exuberant nine-year-old girls. An only child herself, Harley found herself a little overwhelmed by all the commotion, but they'd made it through their first night. Marissa, also an only, and suffering from lack of sleep, was in the same boat. By the time they got the girls corralled and into the dining hall—after claiming their beds and racing around the camp, exploring all its ins and outs—Marissa wasn't the only one who wanted to crawl back under the covers. Luckily, Allie was enough of a natural drill sergeant to keep the campers in line. She even had a whistle that she blasted in sharp, staccato blasts when things got out of hand. As much as Harley wanted to dislike Allie, she was glad for the help. Kiley McManus was the only other CIT in her cabin and Kendra, her cabin counselor, as Harley already knew, was kind of flaky and not above breaking some rules.

Harley and Marissa took their time heading to the dining room themselves. They'd been assigned a table near their campers, but since Allie had marched in with the group of nine-year-olds, they had a few minutes alone.

"When are you gonna tell me about Cam?" Harley asked in an undertone.

"I told you."

"I mean, what happened? You were alone out there together damn near all night."

"You want me to break it all down for you?" snapped Marissa.

"Yes," Harley retorted.

"Well, I'm not going to. I—"

At that moment, Kiley flew out of her cabin, aiming for the lodge, but upon seeing Marissa and Harley, veered their way.

"Thought I was late," she said breathlessly.

"Are your campers at dinner?" asked Marissa.

"Yeah, Kendra took 'em. Get this. She's got some guy she's seeing while she's here. She snuck out last night to be with him!"

*Oh, really . . .*

Harley sent a sideways look to Marissa, who pretended not to notice.

"Her guy's older, but she's really hot for him."

Niles Harwick came out of his bunkhouse and hurried toward the door to the dining hall. He flicked a look at the three of them as he passed and said, "I hate that triangle."

"I'm with you," said Harley. Hope rang it and rang it until it made your head hurt.

Kiley's eyes followed his passage, and she muttered under her breath, "Gimme some of that."

"I know. Niles is cute," said Marissa.

Kiley whipped her gaze to her. "You like him?"

"No, I just thought maybe you did. I've got a boyfriend."

Kiley took that in, then said, "Austin likes Harley."

"No, he doesn't," Harley denied, when Marissa regarded with raised brows.

"He's been asking all about you." Kiley watched Niles till he opened the door to the dining area. A blast of noisy voices heralded his entry.

Marissa said, "Harley's not interested in him."

"Why? Is there someone else?" Kiley looked at Harley.

"Come on." Harley headed for the door.

The decibel level in the hall had climbed with all the young campers, who were hooting and hollering and only half interested in the "manners" game the counselors were trying to teach at their tables.

Raising her voice to be heard above the din, Kiley said, "My parents are coming next weekend. At least my mom is. I don't want her, but I can't stop her. She's a pit bull. What about you guys?"

"Nope," said Marissa.

"My mom and my aunt, maybe," said Harley.

"Your aunt?"

Harley wasn't sure she wanted to explain about Emma, but Marissa had no qualms. She clued Kiley in that Emma was an alumna from the last year of Camp Love Shack, but that her life had irrevocably changed a few months afterward when she was attacked and suffered a head injury.

"You think it had something to do with the camp?" Kiley asked with a swift intake of breath.

"No," Harley and Marissa quashed in tandem. Marissa added, "But Harley's been talking to her, and she kind of remembers things that happened."

"Like what things?" Kiley turned her brown eyes on Harley.

"Impressions. That's all." Harley wanted to throttle Marissa once more. She was doing all this on purpose, she realized. A payback for her finding out about Marissa's meeting with Cam.

"That boy and girl who died were from the commune,"

said Kiley. "They were running away to get married, but someone stopped them and killed them. There was no suicide. They just made that up to protect the commune."

"That boy, Christopher, or Ryan, whatever, was at Camp Love Shack," Harley pointed out.

"Nah, I don't think so . . ."

"My Aunt Emma said he was. He was going to see her the next day, so I don't know about that supposed love thing with the girl."

Kiley looked at Harley as if just discovering her.

Harley and Marissa took seats next to their campers and Kiley hung with them.

Kendra came over at that moment and barked at Kiley to get in and help. Kiley hurried to comply and Harley and Marissa headed toward the plastic trays that were stacked at the head of the buffet line. By the time they'd selected their green salad, chili, cornbread and honey butter, and found their way back to their table, their campers were chanting, "Stella, Stella, strong and able. Get your elbows off the table. This is not a horse's stable, but a first-class dining table!" Poor Stella, shy and always on the verge of tears, did just that, tucking her head and crying. She wanted to go home and Harley hoped she would pull herself together soon, or she was going to have a miserable time.

"I'll take her back to the cabin," said Marissa.

"No, no. I will."

Harley touched the girl on the back and said, "You want to head out? I can get that cornbread for you and—"

Stella beelined out of the lodge before Harley finished speaking. Harley grabbed up cornbread and some honey butter and a glass of water and headed after her. At the cabin, she tried to lure Stella down from her top bunk with food, so she could maybe have a heart-to-heart with her or something, but the girl just lay atop her sleeping bag and cried.

There was a knock on the door and Harley went to open it, to find Greer standing outside alone.

"I saw you following a camper out of the lodge. She looked upset."

"Yeah, she's having a tough time." Harley stepped outside and eased the door shut behind her. She explained about the manners game and how Stella had inadvertently had her elbows on the table and been shamed.

He nodded. His hair was wet and he smelled of soap and she realized he'd just taken a shower.

"Think she'll make it the week?" he asked.

Harley shrugged and by mutual unspoken consent they moved away from the cabin and out of earshot of the homesick girl. "She didn't come here with a friend, so she feels alone, and then when they played that game and chided her at the table . . . I wouldn't blame her if she left."

"Allie wants her to stay."

"Ah . . . well . . ." She didn't want to bring Allie into their conversation. "Were you at dinner?" She hadn't seen him there.

"Heading there now. What are we featuring?"

"Chili, cornbread, cole slaw, a square of chocolate cake."

"A lot better than canned ravioli." He smiled and she looked at his teeth and remembered kissing him.

"College fare?" asked Harley.

"Thought I told you that. In some of our texts."

He had. She just hadn't wanted him to think she'd pored over all those minor missives and could practically recite them back to him verbatim. "I think you did," she said now. He looked at her and she could feel her heart beat deepen in response. Mouth dry, she added, "Allie's nice."

"Yeah, she is."

Something about his tone brightened Harley's hopes. It didn't sound like he really meant it . . . but maybe he did? It was so damn hard to tell.

"Well, I guess I'd better get some of that chili before it's all gone." He started to walk toward the lodge and then stopped and looked at her. "Did you get to eat?"

"Yeah, it's fine."

He peered at her more closely, a trait she recalled with a rush of emotion she hardly knew what to do with. "Want me to bring you back something?"

"Oh, no. I'm good. I'm . . . fine."

"I'll bring you something," he said, then gave her a quick smile as he headed toward the lodge.

*Holy crap . . .*

She went back into the cabin and sat down on her cot, reliving every word, every moment. Stella lifted her head from her pillow and looked at Harley, then at the cornbread on the plate Harley'd set on the counter by Allie's bed.

"Can I have some of that?" the girl asked in a small voice.

"Sure. Come on down."

Stella climbed down the end of the bunk as Harley got her the cornbread and honey butter. "Wasn't there chocolate cake?"

Harley, still in a romantic daze, surfaced for a moment. "A friend's bringing some by. I'll give you my piece, if he remembers it."

"Is he your boyfriend?"

"Umm. No. No, he's just a friend." Then realizing Stella might know who Greer was because of Allie, she added, "He's Allie's boyfriend." Somehow, even saying the words felt like a betrayal, especially when Stella said in her nine-year-old way, "I know him. He's nice. I think they're getting married."

Harley swallowed, unable to say anything more.


Jamie walked down the halls of Ridge Pointe Independent and Assisted Living toward Emma's room, toting the cat carrier Emma had requested. She wasn't certain trying to relocate Twink was going to work for any of them, but she wanted to keep Emma's anxiety level from spiraling.

She knocked on Emma's door and said, "Emma? I'm here."

No response except a long whine from Duchess, who was clearly just inside the room.

Jamie tried the handle but the door was locked. "Be right back," she said to the dog, dropping the cat carrier outside the door and retracing her footsteps to the main reception area with its dining room and tiny bar. She caught sight of Emma seated at the bar next to a woman Jamie recognized as Jewell, Twink's next would-be "target for death." Emma's back was toward Jamie and she didn't see her enter. Jewell was talking, complaining and remonstrating to Emma, apparently, for being friends with the cat.

"It's a menace," Jewell declared for about the third time in the few minutes that Jamie was able to hear the conversation. "Bob's finally recognized that. No one wants that kind of publicity for a group living situation! The cat scares everyone here."

"I'm not scared," said Emma.

"Well, that's because you're young," Jewell snapped. "Most of us can't say that around here, but when Twinkletoes climbs in your bed you might say differently."

"Twink," Emma corrected her.

"That cat's up to all kinds of skullduggery. I swear I'm going to kick it the next time it starts hovering around."

"No, no. You can't hurt her."

"Then get the miserable beast out of Ridge Pointe!"

"Hey," Jamie said, walking into Emma's field of vision.

Emma regarded her sister in her blank way. "Hi, Jamie."

"I brought the cat carrier. Left it by your door."

"I was just talking to Jewell," she said.

Jewell was having a cup of coffee and Emma looked to be having water. Or maybe it was straight vodka. Hah. Unlikely, as Emma didn't drink.

Jamie didn't drink much, either, but ever since seeing the bloody blade of the axe outside the rabbit hutch she thought tossing back a few shots might be in order. She wanted to block the image any way she could.

Emma slid off her stool and started walking back toward her room without saying goodbye to Jewell, whose lips were pursed into a frown. Jamie told her it was nice seeing her again, which netted her a tight smile before she headed after Emma.

They met in her room and Duchess gave a happy bark to see them and went to stand beneath the drawer where Emma kept treats. The dog waggled her eyebrows, an effective ruse as Jamie invariably broke down and gave her something, but Emma was a sterner mistress.

"Not now," she told Duchess.

She stooped to pick up the carrier, placing it on her small table. "I'll have to catch Twink," she said.

"How hard's that going to be?" asked Jamie.

"Hard."

"Maybe you might want to rethink trying to relocate the cat . . . ?"

Emma thought that over, frowning. Finally, she asked, "Do you think I have 'resting bitch face'?"

"What? Well, that's a mean comment. Where'd you hear that?"

"Laurie's granddaughter said it to her mom at lunch about me. They were visiting."

"Who's Laurie?"

"She has red hair but it's fake. She's really gray."

"Well, her granddaughter has a lot to learn," Jamie said tightly.

"Jewell says she's a mean girl."

"For once I agree with Jewell."

"Is Harley okay?" asked Emma.

Jamie easily moved with the change of subject. "I'm sure she is. It's kind of hard to communicate right now. You have to get outside the camp to get a cell signal, but if there was a problem we'd know."

"I don't like her there."

"Yes, I know. But she wants to be there."

"We leave in ten days."

Jamie forced a smile. She glanced down at Duchess, who was still patiently waiting to be told it was treat time. "If we move Twink, I think someone needs to stay with Cooper and help the cat adjust, if that's what we're doing."

"Jewell thinks she's going to die, but Twink hasn't slept in her bed. She goes into the dining room and sits by her."

"You said that was new, right? Twink doesn't usually go into the dining room."

"She knows better."

"So, why do you think she goes in there now?" asked Jamie, gazing at the cat carrier. What she'd seen of the black-and-white cat didn't fill her with confidence that Twink was going to go along with Emma's plan.

Emma cocked her head and looked across at the paper towel holder that was hanging beneath one of her cabinets. The edge of the next square was crumpled and she smoothed it out between her fingers. "Twink likes Jewell."

"Doesn't sound like it's mutual."

"Jewell has stinky feet and Twink wants to grab them with her claws."

"Hmmm."

"Jewell and Mr. Atkinson are trying to turn us against Twink," confided Emma.

"Well, that's bad for Twink, but Duchess doesn't like the cat, either."

"I like Twink. A lot."

"We'll do what we can," Jamie assured her. Then added, "I haven't seen the cat around since I got here."

"She's outside. Mr. Atkinson got really mad at her and chased her around because she sat in his office chair."

"Sounds like Twink has a death wish."

Emma had been sternly eyeing Duchess but now turned

her blue eyes on Jamie. "She doesn't wish them dead. She just knows they're going to die."

"I didn't mean . . . well, never mind. Are we going to try to find Twink now, or . . . what?"

"She will show up at dinner."

"I don't know if I can stay that long. Cooper and I have plans tonight."

"I will catch her."

"Okay."

Jamie headed out of the room and Emma followed after her, leaving Duchess inside. When they reached the reception area and sliding glass doors, Emma stopped short, letting the sliding doors open and then slowly slide back together again.

"*Jamie,*" she said.

Jamie looked sharply at her sister, arrested by the odd sound to Emma's voice. Normally Emma spoke in a monotone, but there was a tension that thrummed in that one word.

"I was bad at the camp. Harley kept asking me about the camp, but I didn't tell her I was bad."

Jamie glanced around but they were out of earshot of anyone else. "Well, that's all right, Emma. It was a long time ago." She wasn't sure where this was going and kind of felt maybe she didn't want to know.

Emma moved in closer. "I thought I liked him. I think I saw his ghost hand on the tree. I didn't tell them about him."

Jamie looked at her sister and considered questioning Emma about this reveal, but once again thought better of it. She'd been down this road many times, expecting answers from the convoluted encyclopedia inside her sister's subconscious, but had learned it didn't pay to ask too many questions. "Like I said, it was a long time ago."

Emma whispered, "I think they were bad with him."

*Who are "they"?* Jamie wondered, but before she could ask Emma stepped on the pad for the glass doors, which had kissed shut again. As soon as the door opened Twink raced inside, a black streak with white front paws rotating in a blur of motion as she shot through reception.

Emma turned quickly, moving faster than usual in an ungainly trot in her bid to catch the cat. "Goodbye," she told Jamie.

Jamie would have stuck around to help catch the cat if she hadn't had the date with Cooper, but as it was, she left Twink to Emma. She moved through the opened glass doors, causing them to catch in mid-close and slide back. Her mind was already tripping ahead. Ten days until the camp. Cooper had told her he would go with her to Haven Commune, if she really wanted to see the place ahead of the camp, but Jamie was reluctant to take him with her. This was her own weirdness and she wanted to deal with it alone.

Briefly she wondered what Emma meant about a "ghost hand," then shook her head.

# Chapter 13

Even though she'd just been to Billy Ray's a few hours before, September was hit again with the smells of stale beer and popcorn and burned oil, and thought the bar was the kind of place you wouldn't want to examine too closely when the lights were up. She'd waited till twenty minutes after three to see if she could intercept Candy. When she entered the bar, Ed inclined his head toward one of the muted wide-screen TVs on the wall across from the bar and the jukebox below it with its bubbling green lights and bright primary colors. An ample blond woman was loading a tray with used glasses from one of the empty tables and hefting it onto fleshy arms. She turned around and spied September, hesitated briefly, then carried her load to the café doors on the far side of the bar that presumably led to the kitchen.

She returned a few moments later and said, "You must be the lady cop who was asking about me."

"I'm Detective Rafferty," September introduced herself. "I understand you knew Richard Everly. I'm looking into his homicide."

"R.J." Her tone was somewhere between a sneer and a

sigh as she shook her head. "I don't know anything about him. He bragged about his hacking skills. I thought it was bullshit."

"You didn't take him seriously?"

"He was always talking about making money, but he was blowing smoke."

She flicked a look at Ed, who was trying to act as if he were cleaning some of the dusty glassware but was really leaning in to eavesdrop. Candy glared at him and he straightened up.

"Did I hope R.J. could make me a ton of money?" she went on. "Sure. He was just good enough. But he was scamming people and I . . . Okay, I didn't really care how he went about it, but I didn't want it to be illegal." Ed made a noise that sounded like a constrained laugh. "The point is, I wanted it to be legit enough that I could keep whatever money came my way. R.J. was such a doofus. Smart and stupid, at the same time. He knew people, or so he said, and he always had money. Bet now that he's dead they'll probably find millions in some off-shore account or plastered in the walls of his house."

"He lived in one of those apartments off J Street," said Ed, joining the conversation. "Doubt he'd put his money in the walls there."

"It was a figure of speech," Candy sniffed.

"I thought he lived in the county, outside Laurelton city limits," said September.

Ed frowned. "Nah. He stumbled over to the apartment lots of times. That's why he was a regular here. We're the closest bar."

September had wondered why Everly had chosen Billy Ray's bar as his hangout when he lived so far away. Now maybe she had her answer.

"He mentioned something about his place in the boonies," said Candy, thinking about it. "Wanted me to go there once. Like that was gonna happen."

"Do you think he moved from there closer into town?"

Candy shrugged. "He coulda."

"Do you know anyone who had something against him?"

She half laughed. "Probably all those people he scammed."

"You know any of them?"

"Oh, hell no, honey. I didn't want to know."

"Did he ever meet anyone here?"

"No. He'd just stop in for a drink and to schmooze a little." She looked to Ed for corroboration.

Ed said, "He was mostly on the phone."

"Ever hear those conversations?"

Both Ed and Candy slowly shook their heads, then Ed said, "Well, somebody was sure giving him an earful last week. 'Member that?"

"No." Candy straightened up, certain. Something about her body language alerted September.

"Just blistering him. R.J. held the phone away and pointed at it, silently laughing. You were there. You remember," insisted Ed.

"He was always joking around." She looked across the room and added, "I gotta get to work."

Since there was hardly anyone in the place at this time of day, September guessed she was trying to end the conversation. Ed either wasn't paying attention to her body language or deliberately making her uncomfortable. He went on, "R.J.'d done something. Put up something on the internet that got him in trouble with some guy. Though R.J. was laughing about it, I think it got him. The guy on the phone said to leave her alone no matter what the devil said."

"The devil?" September repeated. "He used that word?" Ed was a lot chattier this time around, though it appeared his motivation was needling Candy. Either way, it worked for September.

"Yup. Candy heard it, too."

"I just said I didn't," she reminded icily.

"Well, then you're deaf, girl."

"Did R.J. have any kind of partner? Someone he worked with, or for . . . ?"

"No." Candy was adamant. "But Ed, if you know something I don't, be my guest." She swept her arms out and bent down in invitation, then flipped him the bird and sashayed off to the far side of the bar.

As soon as she was gone Ed grew less animated. "R.J. didn't have friends that I know of. If he lived somewhere else, I didn't know that, either."

"How often did he come in?"

"He'd come in for a bunch of days, then we wouldn't see him. Kinda hit and miss. He had a thing for Candy but she treated him like dogshit, mostly." He thought about it a minute. "Seemed like he'd come in when he was feeling flush."

"What's the name of the apartment complex on J Street?"

"Shangri-la, or something. Keeps changing. You can rent by the week. You can't miss it, though. It's right behind the Goodyear Tire store."

September, who'd grown up in Laurelton, knew where the Goodyear Tire store was. She figured J Street must be the little alley behind it, and the Shangri-la had been the Safari Inn, last she'd checked.

She left to check it out and sure enough the Safari Inn had changed its name to Shangri-la and its paint colors from sand and taupe to light blue and puce, not an improvement. September headed to the manager's apartment and explained about Richard Everly's death. She was informed that Everly paid by the week and his current week's rental was up. A notice had been posted on his door. They trooped up the stairs together to his second-story apartment and the manager—a woman in her early forties with straw-like hair from numerous bleach jobs, and a smoker's cough—opened the door.

The place was fairly neat but it smelled musty. Currently, the bed was unmade and a small overnight bag with a change of clothes sat on the one chair.

"That's his," the manager said, nodding toward the overnight bag. "Saw him walk in with it last week."

"How many weeks has he been here?"

"Lots. Off and on. Lots. He sometimes goes away, but he always comes back." She heard herself, coughed, and added, "Guess not anymore."

By his meager belongings it looked as if the Shangri-la was a crash pad. September thanked the woman for her time and asked that she not touch anything. She would send the tech crew over to go through the room. Meanwhile, she hoped to hear soon from Jim Carrus of the Winslow County Sheriff's Department to check out R.J.'s home on Carmine Ridge.

"I'm calling Wendy," said Rona. "Right now."

They'd made it through the afternoon and now Brooke was nursing a headache while Rona thought they ought to go out to dinner. When Brooke had said no, Rona had made a face and reached for her cell phone. At first Brooke had thought she planned to order in, but then she'd just said she was calling Wendy and was already scrolling through her contact list and stabbing numbers on her keypad.

"You have Wendy's number?" asked Brooke.

"You know Caleb works for his father's company. They have that nursery that sells plants to Carvella Homes and all the other big builders around."

Brooke nodded. She'd driven by the nursery with its neat lines of trees and plants and garden sheds more times than she could count, and had known it was owned by the Hemphills.

"Well, I've stopped in there a few times and talked to Caleb. He tried to lecture me on the Lord and all that, but I cut him off. I don't know what his job is exactly. Waiting for the old man to die, probably, so he can take over. His sisters were passed over. Girls don't count in Hemphill Land. So,

Caleb's the only son, so . . . Anyway, I asked him for Wendy's number and he gave me their home phone. I don't know if he didn't trust me with Wendy's cell number, or if she even has one."

"She's bound to have one."

Rona shrugged. "Time to find out."

She placed the call as Brooke went to get herself a glass of water.

"Oh, hi, Caleb," Rona said sweetly, her gaze searching for Brooke as she lifted her brows. "Is Wendy there? It's Rona." A pause, and then she said with lazy amusement, "Rona *Keegan*." Another pause. "Yes, that Rona. Didn't know you knew so many." She mouthed, *What an asshole*.

Brooke almost smiled. Rona had never trusted Caleb's religious bent, which she equated with his being an uptight prick. What Wendy had ever seen in him remained a mystery, though Rona had rubbed her fingers together, indicating it was all about money. Brooke hadn't seen it that way. Wendy had always been somewhat needy. The two of them had dated throughout high school but had broken up right before graduation. After the events at the camp, Wendy had found her way back to Caleb again, and since Brooke hadn't been any part of her life again, she'd never learned the particulars.

"Wendy!" Rona's voice was full of happiness—probably faked, Brooke thought cynically. "How're you doin', girl? It's been way too long." Brooke couldn't hear Wendy's response, but remembering her, she expected it was something along the lines of cautious agreement. She would be wondering why Rona was suddenly calling, and Rona didn't make her wait. "Hey, you saw that Camp Love Shack is reopening? Well, Camp Fog Lake now, I guess, which was always a boring name, but apt. My daughter, Kiley, is at the camp already." That elicited a surprised response. Brooke heard the louder uptick in Wendy's response even if she couldn't make out the words. "No, kidding. You're a parent, too. You must know what I'm talking about. I'm going to the alumni weekend, actually, with Brooke. We wondered if you were going." Rona made a face toward Brooke, who hadn't completely agreed and shrugged her shoulders. "Oh, you *are* going? That's great! I gotta say, I'm a little surprised, really, that any of us are going, but Kiley kind of made that decision for me." A pause and then, "Well, you can see for yourself. Kiley should be able to clue us all in." Wendy said something else and Rona responded slowly, "I don't know about Emma Whelan. I mean, you heard what happened to her . . ." Wendy went on for a bit and Rona started nodding. "Bad things happen. We've certainly all had our share." Brooke heard Wendy's voice rise again and she thought she heard "Goodbye," and was proven right when Rona said, "Oh. Goodbye, then. See you at camp!"

"I never said I was going," Brooke reminded her as she clicked off.

"She didn't want to talk about what happened."

"*I* don't want to talk about what happened and it's all because of Wendy. I just want it to . . . go away, and going to the camp is not going to help." Brooke opened her own phone. "I'm ordering food from somewhere."

"We could drive through Goldie's," said Rona, mentioning a local burger joint.

"Done," said Brooke, clicking off. "I'll drive. You drank more than I did."

"Hours ago."

"One hour ago . . . maybe."

"Let's stop and get some more wine, too."

"Hell, no," muttered Brooke. She wasn't sure she could stand being with Rona overnight—overnight, after all this time! She was hoping she would be fit to drive. Rona just couldn't seem to stop scraping close to truths Brooke didn't want to face.

"Why is Wendy going?" she asked as she pulled out of the apartment parking lot.

"I don't know," admitted Rona, looking out the window. "How did she sound, after all this time?"

"Well . . . strained, actually. But she was always that way, careful and worried. Really worried about her reputation." Rona snorted. "She sure knew how to play that good-girl role. She never wanted Caleb to know anything, that's for sure."

"None of us wanted anyone to know," Brooke reminded her firmly.

Rona didn't respond, which worried Brooke. Maybe she hadn't seen Rona in a lot of years, but one thing she remembered that clearly hadn't changed was Rona's willingness to do what it took to get what she wanted, even if it hurt others.


"Wendy?" Caleb asked, watching her as she hung up the receiver on their landline.

Wendy swallowed and carefully arranged her expression as she turned to face her husband. "Well, that was certainly a surprise," she said, giving him a smile. "Rona, my gosh. She's going to be at Camp Fog Lake, too. She's going with Brooke!"

Wendy could feel her cheeks flush like they always did when she was nervous or upset or trying to hide the truth. It was this telltale flag—more like a flashing neon light—that telegraphed her emotions, and Caleb was keenly aware of it. She could never get away with anything. Well, almost never . . .

Caleb's own face was set and he was blinking in that way that meant he was having trouble knowing quite how to react. He didn't trust Rona, or Brooke, or anyone from Laurelton High whom she'd been friends with. He'd thought they were too fast a crowd and maybe they were. Caleb had a deep commitment to his faith and the Lord, and Wendy felt the same.

*You're a whore.*

The voice inside her head always spoke harshly when she tried to put herself on the same spiritual plane as her husband. It reminded her to keep her humility.

*Not a whore*, she told herself. *Just a flawed human being who's made a terrible mistake . . . or two.*

Caleb settled on tight-lipped acceptance. "I'm assuming they'll both be with their husbands."

"I didn't ask." She didn't know anything about Rona's and Brooke's lives. Were they good friends with each other again now? Had the rift between them been healed? She felt a tiny bit of jealousy . . . and a whole lot of fear.

Caleb ran a hand through his short, blondish hair. He still was so good-looking. Not a trace of gray, while she had to pluck the silver strands from her own head. You weren't supposed to. You could thin your hair until your scalp showed, but she couldn't help herself. Every silver strand represented a transgression, a sin. Luckily her hair was still mostly light brown and brushed her shoulders in a thick curtain. People commented on it, and her youthful looks. Both she and Caleb were approaching the forties with their bodies slim and strong and their faces unlined. "Pure living," Caleb would say with a smile, while he clasped arms with the good people from the church. His piety shamed Wendy sometimes, but she strove for goodness.

*You're a cheater.*

She could feel her face heat even more and she turned away, but Caleb, ever watchful, said sharply, "What else did she say?"

"That was about it."

He grabbed her arm and turned her around to look at him. She kept her eyes downcast. "What else did she say?"

*Bad things happen. We've all certainly had our share.*

Unbidden, the memory of hands stripping off her clothes came again, his body covering hers, penetrating her, his mouth smashed on her lips, swallowing her screams . . .

"I asked her about Emma Whelan," she said, clearing her

throat against the faint tremor that had invaded her voice, knowing Caleb would hear it.

"The girl who was attacked. Such a tragedy."

"I just think about her sometimes."

*You think about his cock inside her, too. You do. You know you do. You thought he was only with you, could save you, but he was the devil . . .*

"Emma won't be able to go," he predicted.

"And I think about how the fog came in and those people died." Wendy's hands were suddenly slick with perspiration and she could feel her heart rate accelerate. To pull herself together she thought of her and Caleb's son, Esau, who was truly good.

"Come here," said Caleb. He walked over to one of the wooden chairs around their kitchen table and seated himself. He spread his legs apart and patted his thighs.

Wendy froze. Esau was at the camp. She and Caleb were alone.

He didn't like it when things from her past arose.

"I need to take a bath. It's been a long day," she said.

He had that light in his eye. A dangerous flicker. It had been doused for a long time, but since their monthlong retreat, it had returned with a vengeance. "Come here."

"Caleb, I'm tired. Please . . ." She hated the begging tone of her voice.

"Come . . . here."

She had to obey or there would be hell to pay.

*You're a fucking whore. You deserve this.*

She came to him and he bent her over his knees. She was wearing a dress, as he preferred, and he pulled up the skirt and ran his hands over her buttocks. She stared at the floor. She had on the "granny panties" that spoke of chasteness. He hooked the fingers of his right hand in them and pulled them down to her knees. He bent down and kissed one cheek and then the other. She quivered with fear, though the chuckle deep in his throat said he believed she was hot and filled with desire.

When the first slap hit, she reacted as if goosed.

"Shhh," he crooned and she could feel his cock grow hard beneath her chest.

When the spanking began in earnest she sent her mind far, far away as his own breathing grew harder and faster and he couldn't help the groans of pleasure issuing from his own throat.


He stared through the binoculars at the camp. Ever since he'd learned they were coming back, he'd been planning.

After a few moments, he stuffed the binoculars back in his pack and returned to the site of the pit. He was digging a grave. A big grave, enough for three. It wasn't quite finished yet, but it was close. In his mind, he was already laying the fir boughs over its top. Maybe a thin wire mesh to hold the boughs in place. Something weak enough to drop them into the hole when he was ready for them.

With a determined smile, he picked up the shovel and began digging in earnest.

# Chapter 14

Saturday night, Harley kept herself awake till after midnight.

The weekly campers had been sent home, though little Stella hadn't made it the full week. Greer, true to his word, had brought some extra food for Harley the night she'd comforted Stella, but the little girl had lasted only one more night. Harley had hoped Greer would stick around, but it hadn't happened that way.

Now, Harley was worried about Marissa sneaking out to see Cam again. She'd already dozed off once or twice, jerking guiltily to consciousness, only to find Marissa still in her bed.

Until about 1:00 a.m. Then Harley heard the *tink, tink* of the back door opening and Marissa slipping out. Noiselessly, she followed Marissa into the night, but Marissa was only standing just outside the cabin, staring toward the woods.

"What are you doing?" Harley whispered, causing Marissa to squeak and jump a foot.

"I want to see Cam."

"*No.*"

"Well, don't worry about it. No lights tonight. He's not there." She turned back to the cabin, her disappointment real.

Harley let out a pent-up breath and followed her back inside, carefully slipping the hook through the eye and tucking herself back into her sleeping bag. Luckily, no one else woke up.

Harley managed to catch a few hours of sleep, but then had to haul herself up at dawn with an effort. A new batch of campers was on their way and she needed to be ready.

As the Parents/Alumni Weekend approached, Jamie began to waffle about her decision to go. She'd spent the last week and a half making plans to attend, but now that it was almost here, she was starting to lose energy over the idea. Her burning desire to see Haven Commune and dig into Mary Jo's past had been nearly snuffed out as she'd gotten used to the idea that Mary Jo, for better or worse, was the woman who was carrying her child. A cowardly part of herself just wanted to bury her head in the sand, cross her fingers, and hope for the best.

And Emma was still hell-bent on bringing Twink from Ridge Pointe, though she had yet to catch the wily feline. The cat seemed to have a sixth sense about Emma's intentions, as she'd been avoiding her for the past week and a half, according to Emma.

"Twink doesn't like me anymore," Emma revealed in her toneless way.

"I don't think that's true," said Jamie. "But we know she doesn't like Duchess."

"Duchess has been in my room."

"Well, maybe the cat doesn't like the smell of the dog. It's not the greatest idea to put them together. Bringing the cat to the house keeps them in closer contact than either of them might like."

"She hasn't been near Jewell."

"She's given up her interest in Jewell's stinky feet?"

"She's a ghost."

That didn't sound like Emma talking, so Jamie questioned her about who else had noticed Twink's disappearance. "The cat was gone for a while once before and came back," Jamie reminded Emma.

"Twink isn't gone. She just knows Mr. Atkinson wants to get rid of her."

"So, the cat's avoiding you . . . and Jewell?"

"I don't think I can catch her."

There was a hint of regret in Emma's voice, more emotion than she could normally project, so Jamie realized how traumatic it was for Emma to be unable to save the cat from the dreaded Mr. Atkinson. "We'll come up with some plan," Jamie had assured her, which hadn't seemed to assuage Emma's worry even while Jamie was glad not to have the headache of the cat foisted on them, at least for now.

On the night before she and Emma were slated to head out for the four-day extended weekend at Camp Fog Lake that ran through the Fourth of July, Jamie drove over to Ridge Pointe to see if she could dissuade Emma from going. She didn't want to disappoint her sister, but she thought maybe she could plead a case for staying since Emma felt she was Twink's protector against Bob Atkinson. If Emma wasn't around, Twink could be at Atkinson's mercy and therefore maybe Emma should stay at Ridge Pointe . . . at least that was Jamie's rationale.

When Jamie got to Ridge Pointe, an ambulance was just pulling away. She felt a moment of worry for Emma, though ambulances at the independent and assisted living facility were fairly common.

She hurried inside and found a group of people, mostly administrators, huddled in the main reception area. Through one of the adjoining room's glass walls she saw Faye, who was Bob Atkinson's second-in-command. She stood with her arms crossed over her chest and was speaking to the dark-haired woman Jamie normally saw at the reception desk, Talia.

"What happened?" Jamie asked one of the older, female residents who was gripped onto her walker.

"There was an accident. They just took Bob Atkinson to the hospital."

"Mr. Atkinson?"

"He collapsed."

The group in reception was all atwitter. Jamie listened in to their accounts of how Bob had been at his desk and fallen out of his chair. His skin was chalky and his eyes were blank. "Heart attack" was the overall conclusion.

Faye left Talia and entered the reception area. Her spiky blondish hair was standing straight on end and she looked shell-shocked. "Hey, let's all move to the dining room," she suggested. "Bob's in good hands."

"We're all praying for him," the woman Jamie had spoken to said.

Faye gently herded them forward. She shot a look toward Jamie, who asked, "Does Emma know?"

"I haven't seen her."

"I'll check in her room."

Jamie headed down the hall and was surprised to see Twink camped outside Emma's door, her tail curled around her feet while she languidly licked one white paw. Was it her imagination or was there a self-satisfied look on the cat's face?

*Maybe she* does *wish them dead.*

Jamie knocked on Emma's door. The sound seemed to disturb Twink, who got to her feet and trotted away at the same moment Duchess gave one loud "Woof!" from behind the panels.

Emma opened the door. "Jamie," she said blankly. "I didn't know you were coming."

"Yeah, I know. I just wanted to talk about the camp, but, uh . . . did you hear what happened to Mr. Atkinson? That he was taken away by ambulance? They think it was a heart attack."

Emma swung her head to just catch sight of Twink rounding the corner at the far end of the hall. "Twink sat in his chair."

"I don't think this is the same thing as when the cat senses one of the older residents is going to die." Jamie heard how uncertain she sounded and cursed being infected by all the *woo-woo* ascribed to the cat. "She's just a cat," she stated firmly, wondering who she was trying to convince as Emma swung the door wider and Jamie entered her apartment.

"Twink doesn't like Mr. Atkinson," said Emma, shutting the door.

"I'm sorry Mr. Atkinson is ill, but I don't think the cat had anything to do with it. But speaking of Twink, since you can't catch her, I was thinking you might want to stick around Ridge Pointe and make sure she's okay. I'm not sure I want to go to the camp anymore. I think Harley's just fine."

Emma turned her blue eyes on Jamie. "Twink is safe now. Mr. Atkinson is not here. We have to go save Harley. He comes with the fog."

"He?" The hairs on Jamie's arms lifted for reasons she couldn't quite explain. "Who are we talking about?"

"Cain."

"Cain?"

"I didn't have sex with Cain, but he told me he was able," she said, as if she were quoting.

Jamie smiled, at a loss. "Cain and Abel?"

"I thought about it, but I don't think it happened. I went behind the mirror with Donovan."

"Is that a metaphor?"

A line formed between Emma's brows and she went to a cupboard, opening it and centering the row of small dinner plates inside even though they appeared already perfectly placed. "We have to go to the camp, Jamie," she said with more urgency than normal. "We have to make sure the fog doesn't take Harley."

Jamie thought about making another attempt to change her mind. And then she thought about her daughter and her heart gallumphed, and she wondered how she would feel if any part of what Emma feared came true and something terrible happened to Harley.

"Okay. We'll go. I'll pick you up early tomorrow. Pack your clothes. I'll take care of everything else."


Brooke looked at the clothes she'd laid out on her bed: shorts, army green cotton pants, tees, and a lightweight jacket. Rona's tenaciousness had gotten to her and though she'd seesawed back and forth about heading back to Camp Love Shack/Fog Lake, she'd finally been worn down enough to agree. Since losing her job she'd had a lot of time to think . . . and she still didn't know what she was going to do. Her threats about suing were just that: threats. She was just waiting for the other shoe to drop. Like she'd been waiting for nearly twenty years.

This morning she'd almost gone back to Greenscape and demanded that Franklin and Valerie bring Lukey in to make it clear that their accusations were libelous and just plain wrong. But another part of her, the tired part, just wanted it all to go away, and that was the part that had prevailed this last week and a half since her termination. She wasn't even sure she really wanted the job back. It had just been a stopgap while she figured out her relationship with Brody. He was the one who had found the job for her in the first place and now . . . ? Well, to hell with them all.

Meanwhile, Rona had made all the arrangements for her to join in the fun and festivities at Camp Fog Lake. Brooke still didn't want to go. Maybe she could find a way to back out.

She thought about calling Brody and seeing what progress he was making on the PI/hacker dude who'd brought the allegations about her and Lukey to him.

*Don't call him Lukey*, she reminded herself, which kind of pissed her off anew. Why shouldn't she be able to call him whatever she wanted? He was a kid. Nothing about him was all that interesting. She didn't even know which high school he attended, although if she were really interested she could probably look him up on social media. But she had no intention of doing that because SHE DIDN'T CARE. She didn't know why this was happening. She just wanted it to stop.

Picking up her phone, she punched in Brody's number, walking from her bedroom down to the kitchen. An automated recording told her his voice mail was full, and she hung up. What the hell was he doing? He'd been out of touch for days. The last time she'd spoken with him, he'd told her he was too busy to talk. She suspected half the time it was just to get her off the phone. He professed to love her, want her, need her in his life when it suited him; Rona was right about that. The rest of the time he was on the edge of annoyance.

She thought about the camp, wondering who might be there. She thought about Owen Paulsen and how they'd fumbled around behind the mirror, having sex in a rush, which she'd regretted immediately, feeling like a fool for going along with the whole Camp Love Shack "ya gotta do it" vibe. She'd never seen Owen again and by some quirk of fate he'd died in a car crash caused by a thick blanket of fog.

Her thoughts moved to Ryan, whom she'd barely paid any attention to. Had he even been there the whole time? And the girl who'd been laid out like a sacrifice . . . and the fog.

The fog . . .

Though she was perfectly aware that fog was just fog, an atmospheric condition, nothing more, it had crept in and wrapped itself around them, thick and suffocating, and ever since that dreadful night she'd been leery and a little afraid of it. It had seemed malevolent. Okay, not malevolent, but bad things happened when it rolled in. Beneath its cover, she could see his white face and the black blood that ran down his head as he lay in the bottom of the canoe. She could still hear Wendy crying and begging Rona not to kill him.

"He's already dead," Rona had hissed and when Wendy wailed, Brooke had wanted to slap her, but she was too busy working the oars. Wendy had tried to help but she was damn near useless. Even now Brooke felt a mixture of anger and fear when she thought of her and that night. She should feel sorry for her, she supposed, but she never really had, not the way—

*Ding-dong!*

Brooke jumped at the sound and glanced quickly toward the front door. She couldn't see who was on the other side. Rona? Likely. Or maybe Brody, finally

She moved quickly to answer it, pausing to look through the peephole.

*Oh . . . shit . . .*

Cautiously, she removed the chain and opened the door. Luke Lerner stood on the other side. Fifteen years old and slouching, dark hair a mat over his face, he looked up at her sideways, from beneath his hair and smiled uneasily. "Hi, Brooke."

"Lukey. *Luke.* What are you doing here?" Her voice sounded unnaturally high.

He wore faded denim jeans that hung on his lean hips. It looked like one good tug would send them shimmying to his ankles. His sweatshirt was light blue and a nod to the coolish June weather. His Nikes had seen better days, but maybe that was the style.

"I'm really sorry about what happened. I yelled at my mom. She's such a *bitch*! They need to give you your job back."

"It doesn't matter. I'm fine," she said quickly, darting a glance around the parking lot. God, she felt like a criminal!

"I told them how unfair it was."

"How did you get here?" she asked tensely.

"A friend dropped me off. Can I come in?"

"No. God, no. Lukey . . . *Luke!* I can't . . . we can't be seen together. This is not a joke. You and I aren't friends. How did this happen? No, never mind. I don't need to know. You have to go."

He looked crestfallen. "I said I was sorry." He sounded the tiniest bit put out. "Those girls . . . they're drama queens. They love to stir stuff up. Nobody listens to them."

"Your parents listened to them."

"They didn't really put that stuff out. They're bitches, yeah. But they didn't mean for that stuff to go all over. That just happened."

"You all should be careful what you put online, then," snapped Brooke.

"I was really mad at 'em."

"Well, great."

"Are you mad at *me*?"

Brooke wanted to slap her forehead. Luke was just a dorky kid who'd hung around the Greenscape offices. Brooke had always been nice to him. She'd felt a little sorry for him because his parents had so clearly ignored him. It always seemed like Luke was an annoyance to Valerie in particular, as she'd ordered him around like a drill sergeant, barely concealing her impatience.

"Who's picking you up?" she demanded. "How're you getting home?"

"Can I come in?"

"No! This is a problem for me!"

"Just for a few minutes."

"NO!" How many of the neighbors had cameras? Probably Mrs. Engle with the parakeet in unit twelve, for sure.

"I didn't say that, you know . . . about you and me in your bedroom . . ." He smiled sheepishly.

"Oh, my God . . . oh, my God. You can't come in. You have to go away. We can't give your parents any further ammunition against me. Lukey, you gotta go. Sorry. I'll call you an Uber or a Lyft."

He gazed at her through hurt brown eyes. "What am I supposed to do?"

"Go home. Make your parents understand that it's all lies about us."

"I'll call my friend Sean to come get me." His shoulders were slumped.

"Do that. I'm sorry. Goodbye."

She closed the door, her heart pounding. She snatched up her phone from the counter and called Brody. Once more the call went to voice mail. She hung up.

"Brody, for God's sakes, where are you?" she yelled.

She felt ill. This was no good. No good. There was absolutely no proof because nothing had happened between her and Lukey, but she felt guilty anyway!

She peered through the peephole and watched Lukey head down the stairs to the parking lot. He was loitering by the manager's office. Her heart squeezed in fear. Jesus. What a mess. A *stupid* mess that was not her fault!

Her phone rang in her hand. *Brody!*

But it wasn't Brody, it was Rona. "Hey, friend," said Rona when Brooke clicked on. "We're going tomorrow, right? You haven't started waffling, have you?"

"We could go tonight, for all I care."

"Really?"

"Really."

"Well, hold that thought till tomorrow. Donovan's going to take us. I told him he couldn't stay, but he's such an asshole. He'll drop us and then park at the end of the lane or something. I wish he wasn't going, but he'll have to sleep in one of the boys' bunkhouses, so fine. You and I are to-gether."

"Okay," she said tersely.

Rona hesitated. "Did something happen?"

"I'm just ready to get out of town. What time will you be here?"

"About ten a.m. That work?"

"I'll be ready," she said grimly. She called Brody one more time after they hung up. When she heard again that his voice mail was full, she swore a blistering string of swear words, then returned to her packing.


Shirley, the receptionist for the Monterey Building, so named for its blatant copying of a building on California's Monterey Peninsula, left her row of black-and-white moni-tors to tap on Daniels Century Prime's door, which was just down the hall from her command post on the first floor. She hadn't seen him come in but there was the possibility he'd slipped in when she wasn't at her desk, she supposed. He wasn't answering his phone and she'd had to turn away sev-eral of his clients because she didn't know where he was.

"Mr. Daniels?" she asked softly, rapping on the wooden panels.

No response.

She returned to the front desk. "I don't think he's here," she told the current client waiting at her desk, a nicely dressed woman named Jacqui Dortland from Tumwater Financial. Ms. Dortland was glaring at Shirley and impa-tiently tapping her toe. Well, she could just tap that toe till it fell off, Shirley decided as she checked all the monitors. Nothing.

"I was supposed to meet him today," Jacqui said through tight lips. She was sick and tired of getting the runaround from Brody, who was supposed to have met her on Tuesday and now it was Thursday and where the hell was he? She had the distinct feeling that he'd chosen some other company to work with and she was not pleased.

"Sorry, ma'am," Shirley told her. A few days ago she'd seemed smug when she'd turned Jacqui away. Now she was clearly a bit baffled. Well, screw her. And screw Brody!

She left the building and tip-tapped angrily across the parking lot to her brand-new Mercedes-EQ. She called Tom and asked him to meet her for a drink, but he couldn't make it. She didn't believe the rumors that Brody was running a Ponzi scheme, though she'd definitely heard them. Half the people she knew were accused of the same thing and nothing ever came of it. Hell, hadn't she done a little of that herself? Not seriously, but there was that time she had to move funds around to pay off an investor who suddenly wanted to move his money to some other company. She was still about a million off, but she could fix that in a jiffy if Brody would just fucking get back to her!

Where *was* the man?

She called him again to learn that his voice mail was full. Well, shit. That wife of his had probably talked him out of the deal. She looked just the type to screw things up for her husband. Bitch.

"I hope you die," she said aloud, and instantly felt better.

One of the best affirmations in life was wishing someone dead.


Though Jacqui didn't know it, she wasn't the only one wondering what had happened to Brody Daniels. September sat at her desk, waggling a pen back and forth in her fingers, thinking about the investor who'd put her off with excuse after excuse. He hadn't returned her last three calls and now his voice mail was full. The man was ghosting her.

She looked down at her notes on the Richard Everly homicide. No solid leads. She'd gone to his house on Carmine Ridge in the company of Jim Carrus, the Winslow County deputy that Detective Barb Gillette had told her about. Carrus was a heavyset officer with bad feet who nevertheless was an entertaining partner as they drove into the western hills of the county.

"This here county's where I was born and raised. My old man had a farm about six or seven miles thataway." He'd pointed to the northeast. "You say he's got a place in town, too?"

"In Laurelton," said September.

"Huh."

They'd reached Everly's home, an old barn converted into a house by some DIY-er somewhere along the line. It had different sections added on in a haphazard manner that gave it a dilapidated look. Everly's landlord had allowed the sheriff's department in and they'd done a cursory look, but hadn't turned up anything. The place was fairly empty of furniture, but filled with clutter. Several kitchen drawers were open and there were boxes on the floor filled with cereal boxes, plastic receptacles, and canned goods. Had Everly been in the process of leaving, or was this just the way he lived?

They poked around through all the rooms of the cavernous, one-story unit. At one point something fluttered past the corner of September's eye and she thought maybe there were literally bats living in the ceiling, one of which they'd disturbed. His lifestyle appeared to be a little like camping, if this was the way it generally went. She suspected he'd been based out of the house on Carmine Ridge, but spent most of his time at the Shangri-la.

She'd come away with precious little in the way of real evidence relating to Everly's homicide. She had found a metal box filled with papers, apparently R.J.'s filing system of sorts, but it was mainly filled with old bills and notices. She knew there'd been an older desktop computer with an ethernet connection that had been picked up by the techs, but there had been no sign of a laptop or iPad or any other newer electronic device, which was a surprise given that R.J., according to Candy, was a gifted hacker. September expected he would have some way to access data other than his phone, but maybe not.

But she *had* run across a few items of possible interest. One was a scratched-out phone number that she'd learned belonged to a cell phone belonging to someone named Deena Royner. She'd tried the number, which had rung to a voice mail. She'd left a message with her name and number, but Deena had not called back.

The other piece of information was an old clipping from a newspaper that R.J. had apparently cherished. It showed a group of teenagers helping out at a soup kitchen in Portland called Helping Hands. September hadn't recognized the shelter and wondered if it was still around. Her twin brother, August Rafferty, a Portland police detective, knew the city far better than she did, so she'd put in a call to him and was waiting for a call back. August, nicknamed Auggie, and September, nicknamed Nine, were twins born on either side of midnight August thirty-first and September first. Her father had the quirky desire to christen his children in the month they were born and had probably been in a quandary when he'd learned he was having twins. Fate intervened and September had been born in the ninth month, while Auggie was born in the last few minutes of August. September also had a brother, March, a living sister, July, and a deceased one, May. In the past few years the Rafferty family had also grown with the addition of her half sister, January—her father and stepmother's child—and her niece, Junie, who was July's daughter, the name eccentricity having been passed on to the next generation, apparently. Neither she nor Auggie had fallen into this trap, but as yet neither of them had children, though September had no plans to keep up with that particular insanity.

An hour later, she called Auggie again and this time she reached him. At his "Hey, Nine," she asked, "Do you know anything about a soup kitchen named Helping Hands?"

"What about it?" He sounded distracted.

"Is it still around? I couldn't find a number for it."

"You didn't look too hard." He snorted, giving her a hard time like always. "It's called The Daily Bread now. What's up?"

"I found a newspaper article and picture from about twenty years ago," she guessed, based on R.J.'s age, "taken at Holding Hands. Found it at Everly's house, maybe a keepsake. Looks like he was a teenager." She'd talked over the case with Auggie earlier, as a matter of course. They might not work for the same departments, but they picked each other's brains when they could.

"It used to be near Burnside, around Eleventh, before the Pearl District took off. Now it's farther north."

"There was a school right around there, too. Glory to God," September realized.

"Don't know it."

"It's long gone. I only know it because that's where R.J. went. I'll let you go. You sound busy. Thanks."

"Just picked up one of the heads of a catalytic converter thieving ring. Wealthy kid from the West Hills. Looks like he's going to jail."

"Messy," September commiserated.

"Very."

"Talk later."

"Bye." And he was gone.

She'd had no luck connecting with anyone associated with the Glory to God school and had back-burnered that avenue of investigation, focusing more on R.J.'s current associates. But the man had held on to that newspaper article for a reason.

She decided to head to The Daily Bread. She would stop

by Daniels Century Prime on the way and try again to catch
Brody Daniels at work.


Harley's eyes flew open at the creaking of the cabin's
back door. She knew none of the campers had gone out because they were told never to go out alone and to wake either her or Marissa for a nighttime bathroom trip. They
complied because they were terrified of the dark. But it
couldn't be Marissa. The campers were here until tomorrow
and it wasn't a weekend.

But sure enough, it was Marissa returning from somewhere, slipping the hook back into the eye. The teeny,
metallic sound had caught Harley's ears, though not apparently when Marissa left.

Before she could snuggle back into her sleeping bag,
Harley climbed out of hers, jumped up, and grabbed
Marissa's arm. She squeaked but didn't scream and Harley
whispered in her ear, "Outside." As silently as they could,
they reopened the back door and closed it behind them.
Holding Marissa's arm, Harley walked her away from the
cabins, past the bunkhouses, and to the edge of the woods,
though Marissa's steps grew more reluctant.

Finally Marissa hissed, "Where are we going?"

"Out of earshot!"

"I'm not going back there." In the faintest moonlight
Harley could see her nod her head toward the forest.

Harley whispered urgently, "You were in the woods?
With Cam? It's Thursday! The campers aren't leaving till tomorrow."

"Cam's leaving. He's been hanging around for two weeks
and we've hardly seen each other."

It sounded like she was blaming Harley. Harley opened
her mouth to protest, but Marissa broke in on a half sob,
"This was my last night with him!"

Harley peered at her, unable to make out her features clearly. She glanced back at the camp. The one central light on the pole illuminated the clearing and the edges of the cabins and bunkhouses. Everything was quiet and still. Harley's eyes automatically turned to the two windows on the upper floor of the maintenance building that were part of Greer's living space, but they were dark.

"What happened?" asked Harley.

"Nothing!"

"Shhh. Damn it, Marissa. Be quiet." When she realized Marissa was sniffling, she whispered, "Something happened. He didn't . . . do something that—"

"*No*. We were . . . just fooling around, you know. I thought maybe this would be it."

"Where were you?"

She jerked her head toward the woods. "Cam has a spot. There's like an old, broken-down log cabin way, way back there. We didn't go that far. But Cam says there's a pocket of cell service there. We were in his pup tent and we were . . . kissing and then there was this noise." She shivered. "It was kind of a shriek. I thought it was a bear! I started kind of freaking out and Cam went out of the tent for a while. He said there was nothing there but I was scared. I couldn't get back to kissing and stuff. I just couldn't."

"That's not a crime. That would creep me out, too."

"Harley . . . He broke up with me!" She started crying in earnest. "He said he had to get back and this was our last night and I ruined it!"

Harley bristled. "He said you ruined it?"

"No. *I* ruined it. We had kind of a fight and he walked me back a ways and then told me we couldn't see each other anymore."

"He didn't walk you back all the way to camp?"

"You're not listening!"

"Marissa, I know you can't hear it now, but he's an asshole. He only cares about himself."

"Just because you don't like him, you don't have to be mean." She turned back toward the bunkhouses and cabins.

Harley hurried to catch up to her. "I'm sorry," she whispered. "I doubt it's over. You just had a fight."

"You don't know anything."

Marissa finally slowed down when she got to Foxglove. She carefully reentered the cabin with Harley on her heels. Harley carefully relocked the door and they both returned to their respective cots. Harley wanted to mention that the parents were coming the next day, but Marissa turned her back to her and she probably didn't need to be reminded anyway.

She was just drifting off to sleep when she heard stumbling footsteps outside their shuttered window. She would have liked to look out but she would have to climb up the back of the nearest bunkbed to do so and that would risk waking the campers. The top bunk belonged to the most freaked out of the current girls.

She let it go and fell into a fretful sleep where the woods themselves, the whole of the trees and undergrowth, bulged in and out toward the camp like some mega-monster breathing heavily.

# Chapter 15

Though it was only Friday, the second-week's campers were packing up their belongings and getting ready for the bus that would take them home for the Fourth of July weekend. Harley and Marissa got up early to help get their charges organized, and Allie went to the lodge to check in with Hope. Luckily, they hadn't lost any of the campers to homesickness this week like they had Stella.

Marissa and Harley had yet to speak more about the events of the night before. A light rain was falling but was supposed to ease off by the time the parents/alumni arrived.

"I'm glad my mom isn't coming," Marissa muttered, hearing the ringing triangle and sending the campers to breakfast for their final camp meal: Happy Face pancakes with Nutella and whipped cream and fresh strawberries from the Haven Commune gardens, courtesy of Sunny Dae, their cook, who lived at the commune and dragged a squeaky cart full of fruits and vegetables back and forth most mornings and evenings.

When the campers were all inside the lodge, their belongings stuffed into their bags, their sleeping bags rolled up, everything placed under the cabin eaves to keep from getting soaked, Marissa and Harley began sweeping and dusting and cleaning Foxglove Cabin into readiness. They could have gone to breakfast, but in unspoken agreement, both decided to grab one of the breakfast sandwiches made up daily and wrapped in plastic for later.

"I never wanted to come here. You know that," Marissa said, opening the conversation.

"But what if you got caught? If he's left, it's better this way. You can make it up with Cam later."

"You're happy it's over," she accused, her nose turning red and her eyes filling with tears.

"It isn't necessarily over."

"Yes, it is. He's breaking up with me," Marissa moaned. "There's no getting back together. I want to leave and find him and tell him I love him."

"Don't do that. Give him a chance to regret."

"He'll find someone new."

"Well, then you're lucky you didn't sleep with him." She paused. "You didn't, did you?"

"I didn't have a chance! That shriek sounded. Like an animal in a trap. That's what Cam said. And then it was just over."

Harley was sweeping, but it felt like she was just shoving dust from one part of the cabin to another. Marissa had a rag and was climbing atop the bunks and wiping down the shutters and windows. She peered out between the slats and said, "Here comes Kiley. Don't say anything to her."

"Like I would."

Kiley rapped on their door, then flung it open without being invited.

"Hey," said Harley. "We could be dressing."

Kiley threw back the hood of her windbreaker. "Kendra's missing. She didn't come back last night. She met that guy. I know she met that guy again, but she's not here!" She took a breath. "Nobody knows yet. Campers at our cabin thought she was at the bathroom, but she's not. And she's not at breakfast! She's nowhere!"

"Have you told Hope?" asked Harley.

She vehemently shook her head. "I just said nobody knows."

"Maybe you should tell her," suggested Marissa. She was atop the nearest bunk to the front door.

"They're gonna grill me like it's my fault. I'll have to tell 'em that she's been sneaking out the whole time."

Harley glanced at Marissa, who was studiously avoiding returning her gaze. She asked Kiley, "Has she ever returned this late before?"

"No! Something's happened to her. I'm scared shitless and my mom's coming today . . . ugh . . . I don't want to see anybody." She chewed on her lip. "I—I wasn't there the whole time, either."

"You left the campers alone?" Marissa asked tentatively.

"Just for a little while. I just . . ."

"What? Where were you?" asked Harley. Then, "With one of the guys?"

"I don't want to get anyone in trouble. The campers were all fine when I got back."

"Well, that makes it okay." Harley rolled her eyes. "Which guy was it? Niles? Austin . . . Lendel? Seems to have been a night when everyone was out."

Kiley shook her head.

"Esau?" asked Marissa.

"No, he has a girlfriend. But he might've been out, too. She's from the commune."

"Esau has a commune girlfriend?" asked Harley.

"You have to tell Hope," Marissa encouraged. "If something's happened to Kendra . . ." She left the thought unfinished, glancing at Harley, worried.

The scream she'd heard in the woods . . .

At that moment hard, pounding steps sounded outside the cabin, running. Uh-oh. Harley darted out the front door, Kiley behind her, Marissa scrambling down from her bunk. Lendel was racing for the lodge. Behind him came Esau and Niles, carrying Kendra between them.

"Jesus," Harley breathed, hurrying up to them. "What happened?"

"She just collapsed," Niles gritted out.

Kendra was awake but her face was pale and she was struggling to breathe. Her eyes found Harley's. She said, "Marlon," and then her eyes rolled back into her head.

"What'd she say?" Esau gritted out as he and Niles hurried as best they could under Kendra's dead weight.

Kiley moaned, "Is she dying?"

"No." Niles picked up the pace and Harley tried to offer help. She put her hands beneath Kendra's head, which lopped over. She drooled on Harley's arm.

"What'd she say?" Esau repeated at the same moment Marlon appeared from the maintenance shed, head down, as if in serious thought. He spied them at that moment and his head snapped up.

Harley said, "Marlon . . ."

"What did you do to her?" the older man demanded of the boys.

"Nothing. She just came out of the woods and fell down," said Niles, whom Marlon muscled out of the way, his eyes fierce. He practically shoved them apart, tenderly pulling Kendra into his arms.

"Back door," Marlon snapped. He was a lot stronger than he looked, burdened by Kendra's dead weight and practically running for the lodge's back door. Esau tripped and struggled to stay up with him while Harley barreled into him and fell.

She picked herself up as Marlon headed down the alley between the lodge and Bird's Foot bunkhouse to the back door. "She said, 'Marlon,'" she chattered to Kiley and Marissa. "She said, 'Marlon.'"

"What? What?" Marissa cried.

"Oh, shit. Oh, shit. Oh, shit." Kiley wrung her hands.

Harley was closest to the front of the lodge. She threw open the door and was nearly run over by a bunch of campers who were exuberantly exiting en masse. Pushing past them, she frantically looked for the other counselors. Her gaze fell on Allie and Greer and she stumbled to them. "Where's Hope? Kendra's unconscious. Marlon's taking her to the back of the lodge. She said his name before she passed out."

"Marlon?" Allie asked. She and Greer had been sitting, but now Greer was on his feet and heading toward the back of the lodge and the doors to the kitchen and Hope's apartment, while Allie was still slowly rising.

"He hurt her!" Kiley declared.

"Marlon?" Allie asked again.

Harley was already following after Greer. At the door to Hope's apartment they ran into Tina and Warren, who blocked their passage, but Greer practically pushed them aside and Harley followed in his wake.

Kendra was on Hope's sofa, her breathing sporadic, her eyes open again in mute terror. Hope had a glass of water and was trying to get her to drink it. Through a door that led to the lodge kitchen she could see Marlon. She screamed at him, "Get the truck!" Greer pushed past Marlon and both of them tore out the kitchen back door. Lendel, Niles, and Esau were standing there and quickly followed after them. Sunny Dae had a walkie-talkie to her ear and was yelling at someone on the other end to pick up.

"Kendra, honey, drink this," Hope commanded as Kendra tried to feebly push her away.

Harley asked, "Did Marlon do this?"

Hope swung her head around to glare at Harley. "Of course not. What are you doing here?"

"What's happened to her?" asked Harley.

"Pick up, Joy!" Sunny Dae snapped into the walkie. "Joy. Pick up!"

*Joy?* Harley wondered.

"Go back out with the rest of them," Hope ordered. "Keep everyone calm."

"Tell me something I can tell them," said Harley.

A crackle from the walkie-talkie. "Joy's not here. We're at prayer," a perturbed male voice answered.

Sunny Dae straightened abruptly, clearly surprised.

"Josh, we have a girl here who needs an ambulance."

"What's wrong?"

"Don't know . . . um . . . alcohol poisoning, maybe. Or something . . ."

"It's alcohol poisoning!" Hope snapped.

"What? Who?" asked Josh.

"One of the counselors," said Sunny Dae. "Kendra?"

"Is she conscious?"

"Barely."

"Keep her quiet. Don't cause stress. Calling 911 now. Over and out." He clicked off.

"Roger," Sunny responded a little weakly, now that she'd transferred responsibility.

Hope blurted, "There're pockets of transmissibility in the woods. But Josh'll take care of it."

"Yes, he will," said Sunny.

Kendra was breathing shallowly, her eyes closed but fluttering. Hope said, "Kendra, we need you to keep drinking water. We need to flush your system. That's what we need to do."

"Came . . . my mouth," she whispered.

Hope shot a look of horror toward Sunny Dae, who shook her head. They both looked at Harley, and Sunny Dae motioned Harley out of Hope's quarters and into the kitchen, closing off the kitchen door. Harley returned to where Marissa and Kiley were standing anxiously in the lodge by Hope's apartment door with Tina and Warren standing side by side in front of it, as stoic as Secret Service agents.

Kiley grabbed Harley by the arm and dragged her away. "What happened? Is she all right? Oh, my God, is she okay?"

Marissa was right there. "We heard someone say poison."

Harley said, "They're calling 911." Then she explained about the walkie-talkie. "I think Sunny reached the commune because it's closest to us and she was calling someone named Joy, like the old camp director, but she got someone named Josh instead. He's on it."

"Is Kendra going to die?" Kiley whispered.

Other counselors, seeing them, started coming over. Austin was with them, as was Ella. The two of them seemed like they'd grown rather close. "Where are the other guys?" Austin demanded.

"Heading for the trucks," Harley told him, and he did an about-face and went out the front door, after them. Allie did the same, practically running over Austin in her haste, while Ella moved to the side of the room with her friends, arms crossed over her chest. Maybe she was wrong, but Harley thought Ella didn't know what to do if she wasn't the center of attention.

Everyone started peppering Harley with questions until Sunny Dae stepped out from the kitchen and told them all to go about the business of getting the camp ready. She then immediately returned to Hope's quarters, and Tina and Warren started barking orders.

"What happened in there? Did she say anything else? Was it Marlon? Did you tell them where Kendra was?" Kiley asked Harley.

"I didn't really have a chance."

"Did she say anything else?" Kiley demanded.

They were walking back to Foxglove. Kiley was near tears and Marissa was white. Harley inhaled a breath and said, "Do you think she could have been with Marlon?"

Kiley recoiled. "*No.* She said her guy was hot. Marlon's

not hot. You think he did this? Like, maybe he was jealous, or something?"

"I don't know. No." It just didn't feel right.

"I hope she's okay," said Marissa.

"Sunny Dae said alcohol poisoning."

"She was that drunk?" asked Marissa in disbelief.

Kiley was shaking her head. "She didn't have that much stuff left. She and I drank it before I met . . . Niles."

"Niles. Okay." Harley nodded.

"Kiley!"

They all turned to see Warren bearing down on them. "You all need to get to your cabins and make sure your campers are packed up."

"Who's gonna help me?" Kiley said tearfully. "Kendra's my counselor."

"Tina's on her way over. We'll get them on their way."

Kiley shot them a beseeching look as she left. Harley turned to Marissa, who was shaking. Before she could say anything Marissa declared, "We have to tell them about Marlon. He could have given her more stuff. There's something not right about him. You know it, too!"

"Marlon seems fine. I'll talk to Greer. He knows him," Harley snapped, annoyed. She regretted mentioning his name in those first moments of fear.

"Okay . . ."

Harley wanted to be irked that Marissa had fallen into the trap like everyone else, so quick to blame Marlon because he was different, but she'd been the one to repeat what Kendra had said. She didn't want to accuse anyone of anything until she knew more, but she wanted her stepsister's opinion. "Marissa, Kendra said something else. It sounded like 'came in my mouth.'"

"Oh . . ." Marissa made a face.

"As soon as she said that Hope and Sunny wanted me out of there. They did anyway, but that sealed it."

"She and Marlon were having . . . sex?"

"It's not Marlon. It's probably this other guy."

"Why would she name Marlon, then?"

"I don't know. But he isn't what Kendra would go for. And he's a lot older. A *lot* older. Like a grandpa, almost."

"Well, who, then?"

"I don't know. Why would she say that? Of all things?"

"God, I hope she's okay," breathed Marissa.

"Me, too."

From inside Foxglove, Harley saw Greer wheel the truck to the back of the lodge, where he conferred with Hope, who obviously told him an ambulance was on its way as no one brought Kendra out. It wasn't long after that they heard the scream of the ambulance siren, and she and Marissa both headed outside to witness Kendra, bundled onto a gurney and attached to a portable respirator, as she was placed in the back. Her eyes were open and she feebly waved to them before the doors were slammed shut and the ambulance headed out, sirens wailing once again.

Hope came outside and Harley went over to her. "Is she going to be all right?" Harley asked.

"We're praying for her." Hope regarded Harley with hard eyes. "She said she and others were leaving their cabins at night. That's dangerous and I won't tolerate it."

Harley felt like she'd been slapped in the face. She'd wanted to talk to her about Kendra, but she couldn't find the words and, well, she didn't want to rat out Marissa. "Maybe she was meeting someone?" she tried.

"That's none of your business."

"Marlon?" Harley pressed. "I thought I heard Kendra say his name."

"Definitely not. No. And if I hear you spreading false and demeaning rumors, I will kick you out and report your behavior to your parents. Do you understand?"

She walked away before Harley could answer. She could

feel her face flush in embarrassment. Marissa, who'd been several feet away, came up to her.

"I'm sorry. I'll go tell her that it was me."

"Hell, no. Then we'll both be on her bad side. C'mon, let's get ready for Mom and Emma. I can't believe they're coming. Jesus, what a cluster. God, I hope Kendra's all right. Maybe I can talk to Mom later . . ."

What happened to Kendra in the woods? She longed to talk to Greer about everything. And she really needed to talk to the rest of the guys, she decided, her eye traveling over Niles, Lendel, and Austin, who were huddled close to one another in a small group outside Snakeroot, Austin and Lendel's bunkhouse, the one that backed up to the bathrooms.

Cooper's Trailblazer bumped hard along the lane that led from the road to the camp.

"This is bad for the car," said Emma, seated in the middle of the back seat.

Jamie was in the front beside Cooper, who was behind the wheel. She twisted to look back at Emma. Duchess rode in the seat beside her and whined a bit, as if agreeing with the sentiment.

"It gets better. There's a clearing at the end. You'll probably have to dump us and scoot," she told Cooper. "They need to move the cars through as there's limited parking."

"Not a lot of room for two cars on this lane, either," observed Cooper.

His suspected homicide case with Elena Verbena had appeared to have wrapped up. No mysterious poisoning. The victim had made herself sick on a cocktail of over-the-counter medicines and then fallen down a flight of stairs. Maybe she'd meant to commit suicide, or maybe she'd meant to blame it on her husband. In any case, he did not appear to be the culprit. Cooper was meeting with Verbena after dropping off Jamie and Emma at Camp Fog Lake to write up a final report.

It was just after noon when they arrived, and there were already two vehicles at the camp dropping off other parents and alumni.

Emma said in her toneless way, "Rona and Brooke," as they watched a Mercedes SUV nose out of the area, a man at the wheel, leaving off two women and their bags. A girl with shoulder-length dark hair greeted them.

"Who are Rona and Brooke?" asked Jamie.

"The Three Amigos."

"I only see two," said Jamie. "And I think they're 'amigas.'"

"That's Donovan," Emma said, watching the driver of the Mercedes as it passed them and headed back down the lane.

"Is he the third?" asked Cooper.

"Wendy is the third."

The other vehicle had a Lyft sign in the back window, and a man and a woman were exiting. "That's Wendy," said Emma, leaning forward to get a better look. "She was crying hard."

Jamie threw her a look. "She's not crying."

"She hid behind Brooke at the campfire, but she sneaked around a lot. Rona said she wasn't that nice."

"I take it this was when you were at camp."

"You take it right," said Emma.

The Lyft pivoted in a tight circle and then it was Cooper's turn to let them out. Duchess tried to follow Emma, then barked in protest when Emma told her to stay and closed the door.

Marissa and Harley greeted them, both rather subdued. "Hey," Cooper called to his stepdaughter from the driver's seat, and Marissa went to him and reached in the open window to give him a big hug.

Harley looked at Jamie and gave her an awkward hug as well. When she'd been dropped off, she'd hugged Jamie without reservation, but that was then and this was now, apparently. It gave Jamie a pang. She was close to Harley in ways, but not physically. She thought of the new baby on the way and her gut fluttered.

"Our campers just left. We've got the cabin cleaned," said Harley. She then lifted up a hand to fist-bump Emma. As a rule Emma didn't like to be touched at all, but she allowed this brief contact, though only with Harley. She lifted her own fist and punched Harley's.

Marissa circled back to them as Cooper eased the SUV around, letting another car slip in to discharge its passengers. A steady stream of vehicles was carefully negotiating the lane, avoiding one another's bumpers by inches.

"What's up?" Jamie asked when she recognized that Harley and Marissa were being extraordinarily quiet.

"One of the counselors was taken out by ambulance this morning," said Marissa, who'd looked to Harley to answer but Harley had remained silent.

"Uh-oh. What happened?" Jamie looked from one girl to the next.

"We don't know yet." Marissa was still staring at Harley.

Harley said, "Maybe alcohol poisoning."

Emma said, "Poison hemlock grows along roadsides and ditches and abandoned fields. It can be anywhere."

They all looked at her. Harley said, "Where'd you get that?"

"Someone died of it at camp."

"Camp? This camp?" questioned Jamie. "It sounds like you're quoting someone."

"Joy said it looks like a flower but don't touch it."

"Man, I wish I could access the internet," Harley muttered. "We need access to information."

"What cabin are we?" asked Emma, looking past them

toward the bunkhouses, which were closer to where they stood. "There are more of them than before."

"Foxglove," said Harley. She and Marissa helped grab up Jamie's and Emma's bags and led them to the cabin.

Emma said as they walked, "Foxglove is a poison, too. There are a lot of poisons."

# Chapter 16

September found a parking spot on the street, though it took a few turns around the Portland blocks before she discovered the empty space. She walked back to The Daily Bread and tried the door. It opened into a vestibule, which in turn faced a large meeting room with rows of tables. She could smell canned corn and onions as she stepped inside.

Yesterday she'd asked George to dig deeper into the Glory to God school, seeking information specifically on when R.J. was there. She'd then looked up what she could on The Daily Bread after failing to connect with Brody Daniels. The man seemed to have disappeared. Had he just taken off? That was suspicious in itself. Or had something happened to him?

She'd also asked George to search out more information on Deena Royner, the name she'd found on a scrap of paper among R.J.'s belongings. So far he hadn't gotten back to her with anything.

"May I help you?" a middle-aged Black woman with steel-gray cornrows and a ball-like shape asked pleasantly.

She wore what looked like surgical scrubs over a pair of blue jeans.

September smiled and said, "I hope so. I'm looking for the director, Annie Manderly?"

"You found her."

"I'm Detective September Rafferty with Laurelton P.D. I heard you've been associated with The Daily Bread even before the name was changed."

She crossed her arms over her chest. "What do you want, Detective?"

September suspected she was already bristly because she didn't want to share information with the cops about the men and women who came and went through The Daily Bread's doors. "Is there somewhere we could talk?"

She gestured to a door at the back of the room and September followed after her to a small cubicle with an oversized desk and wooden chair. A cup of coffee was growing cold on the wooden desktop. There were dozens of rings where others had been placed in approximately the same spot.

There was no second chair and Annie kicked her own back under the desk, choosing to stand for this meeting along with September.

September pulled out the newspaper clipping, handed it to her, and explained that she was looking for any kind of information she could find on R. J. Everly. She pointed him out among the others in the picture and related that R.J. had been a victim of homicide and that she was looking for his killer.

Annie Manderly gazed at the picture a long, long time before she handed the clipping back to September. Once again she crossed her arms.

"Were you around at that time?" September prompted when she didn't seem inclined to offer anything further. "Do you recognize him?"

"Oh, I remember R.J."

"He was memorable, then."

"Only because he was a sweet kid. Most of 'em weren't, especially in that group." She inclined her head to the photo.

"So, you know them all?"

"I recognize one of them. There was a third one, but his name escapes me."

"Which one do you recognize?"

"This one." She pointed to one of the boys whose back was to the camera, his face half turned.

"Really."

"You think I can't tell, but I grabbed the collar of that jacket enough times to see it in my dreams. That's Brody Daniels. A proper little devil. Would smile at you and lie through his teeth and you'd believe him."

Brody Daniels. A proper little devil. September tried to hide how surprised she was. "You believed him?"

"Not for a minute. But others did. He was used to getting his way. That church would bring them through on a regular basis. Those kids would go hungry if we didn't feed 'em now and again."

"Glory to God."

She snorted. "Yeah, that's what it was called. But they were using the Lord's name in vain. Nothing godly about them. They took money and spent it on themselves, yes, they did. One day they were operational, the next there was a handwritten notice that the school was closed. That was it."

"Do you know when that was?"

"Not long after that, I'd say." She nodded to the newspaper clipping again. "That class was already gone, but it wasn't long afterward, I don't think."

"Any idea why they left?"

"IRS? Somebody doing what they shouldn't with the students?" She shrugged. "Wasn't because they just wanted a change of scenery."

September asked a few more questions but Annie Manderly didn't have much more to offer. September thanked her and gave her a number to call if she thought of anything else.

She called George and said, "Get me as much as you can on whoever was running Glory to God school and also a deeper background on Brody Daniels of Daniels Century Prime. I just learned that he was at Glory to God when Everly was."

"Huh. See what I can find," he said.

"Do it fast," September pushed, to which George snorted and made some comment beneath his breath she couldn't quite catch.

She felt like she was getting somewhere now that the meeting with Annie Manderly had netted her Brody Daniels's name, placing a connection between Richard Everly and the head of Daniels Century Prime, but it made reaching Daniels again even more imperative.

Where the hell *was* the man?


Jamie leaned over her upper bunk, tucking her sleeping bag tightly into the corners. There was a window by the head of her bed and she looked through the partially closed slats to where Harley and Marissa were having a confab with several other girls. Hope, the camp director, was going to meet with all of them—counselors, CITs, parents and alumni alike—later today with more information on the girl who'd succumbed to alcohol poisoning.

Directly below her, Emma was tidying up her bunk and stowing her belongings beneath the bed. Their bunk bed set was in front of Harley's cot and across from Marissa's. Two of the other bunk bed sets had rolled-up sleeping bags and duffels tossed onto the bottom beds. Emma was staring at them hard.

"What are you thinking?" asked Jamie, climbing down the end of the bunk. She knew Emma's obsessive penchant for placing items in order, and was afraid she was going to tackle someone else's belongings.

"It smells the same," she answered.

Jamie inhaled. The cabin smelled like cut fir and pine and dust and an earthy scent that probably came off the lake. "I wonder who those bags belong to," she said, hoping to dig into Emma's thoughts.

"Brooke and Rona."

"You know whose they are?"

"Wendy isn't here."

"The Three Amigos?"

Emma turned to look at her. "The Three Amigos are boys."

"I thought you said it was three girls."

Emma blinked. "It was Donovan and Owen and . . ." She trailed off, frowning.

"So you had three amigos and three amigas?" Jamie said lightly.

"There was Ryan, too. He had binoculars and saw the girl on Suicide Ledge. And then the Three Amigos killed him . . ."

"Mom?"

Jamie jumped about a foot as Harley burst into the cabin. "What?" she asked, a bit sharply.

"Are you done getting ready? I want to show you around. Emma, too."

"I know this place," said Emma. "It's not a good place."

"Yeah, well, I might agree," said Harley. "But we're here together, so come on. I'll show you the lodge and we can go down by the lake."

The three of them headed out and ran into two women, one with shoulder-length brown hair and green eyes and one with short, dark hair and a pugnacious chin. That one stopped short and said, "Emma? Hi, it's Rona."

"I know," said Emma.

"And this is Brooke."

The green-eyed woman said, "Hi, Emma."

"Hi." Emma's gaze was somewhere past them. She rarely made eye contact. "You need to make up your beds," she told them, sidestepping their blockade and aiming in the direction of the main lodge, Harley right behind her.

"I'm Jamie, Emma's sister. Harley's mother," Jamie introduced herself. "Looks like we'll be bunkmates for the weekend." Jamie shook hands with both Rona and Brooke.

"We heard about what happened to Emma. It's really good to see her again," Rona said and Brooke murmured an agreement.

Jamie centered her gaze on Rona. Out of the corner of her eye she saw Emma and Harley stop and wait for her. Before she could respond, Rona asked in a lowered voice, "Is there anything we should know? To make sure she's . . . comfortable?"

"Emma's fine. Just treat her normally." It got under Jamie's skin, the way people wanted to talk in hushed tones about Emma. She had to remind herself that they were uncomfortable themselves and just trying to figure out how to act.

"She remembers us," said Brooke.

Was there a thread of worry in her tone? Jamie told herself she was imagining it.

"She remembers a lot about the camp. She insisted on coming. Nice to meet both of you. See you at the cabin later."

"She remembers a lot about the camp?" Rona repeated as she and Brooke entered Foxglove.

"She never saw us," said Brooke. But she had . . . she had . . . Brooke remembered the light.

"You sure?"

Brooke felt slightly dazed. This wasn't the cabin she'd stayed in. This one had been rebuilt and was half again as large as the ones from twenty years ago. But it might as well have been the same, as she had a suffocating feeling of déjà vu that made her plop down on her bunk, her knees weak.

Rona climbed half of the back of the bunk that had been made up.

"What are you doing?" Brooke hissed. Rona's bed was on Brooke's side of the room, butting up to hers.

Her motive became clear when she looked through the window that faced the main clearing.

"Wendy's here," she said, her voice oddly strained.

Brooke drew a breath and thought, *Here we go . . .*

Caleb had his hand tight around Wendy's upper right arm, as if he were planning to march her to the director's office. He'd just been directed to his camp room, which was in the Hawk's Beard bunkhouse, while Wendy was told she'd been assigned to one named Foxglove.

"My wife and I are staying together," he snapped imperatively to the tall younger woman with the shaved side of her head. Wendy watched with a kind of intrigued horror as her husband faced off with her. Caleb did not approve of anything avant-garde, especially if it smacked of non-gender vibes. This girl, Tina, had that in spades.

"I'm sorry, sir, we aren't designed for co-ed sleeping arrangements. For the few days you are here, we have separate living quarters."

"That's unacceptable." His grip tightened. She could tell he was working himself up to one of his fits.

"You can take it up with our director, Hope Newell." Tina pointed toward the rooms at the back of the main lodge, which, though it had been cleaned up and renovated from twenty years earlier, apparently served as Hope's apartment, the same as it had for Joy.

"Or you can sleep outside together," Tina added. There was amusement lurking in her eyes that Wendy hoped Caleb missed, because if he thought she was laughing at him, there would be hell to pay with a capital "H."

Caleb didn't bother responding, just kept marching Wendy forward. She thought back to when they'd dated in high school. She'd been so smitten. While Rona and Brooke had gazed lasciviously at all the jocks, practically moaning over their muscled chests, arms, and legs, Wendy had found herself enfolded in Caleb's goodness. The Lord was his polestar. He was guided by faith in God. She'd joined an after-school club devoted to Christianity and though the lessons learned were valuable and the get-togethers with pizza and punch were enjoyable, she just wanted to be with Caleb. He'd had his eye on another girl then, a sweet-faced, vapid moron with a killer body, but luckily her family had moved away. On the Rolodex of attractive females in the group, Wendy had popped up next. She was thrilled when he came to her, tentatively touching her hand. For an answer she'd slipped her fingers through his and squeezed. He took the message and before long they were steaming up the windows in his Ford Fiesta every chance they got. She learned a lot of innovative ways to pleasure him, but it took a while before they had actual sex. Her own body was wickedly ready. She didn't understand Rona's complaint about never reaching a climax. She could do it with barely any rubbing. The fact that Caleb disapproved of her sexual enjoyment only made it better.

The mistake she'd made was telling Rona. One of those late-night overnights where they'd confessed their deepest, darkest secrets. Wendy had admitted that all she thought about was sex with Caleb, and Rona had teased her about it in little sideways comments that scared Wendy because if Caleb ever found out, it would be over. She knew it.

And then a guy named Dean came to one of their meetings. He wasn't a Christian. He didn't even believe in God. He was the devil dressed up in tan chinos and black T-shirts that showed off his biceps. He had dark hair and a wicked smile and when he turned his attention on Wendy it was like being blasted by a nuclear ray gun. Wendy melted. Reduced to molecules and atoms. One evening, when everyone else was gone, she let him ride her up against the bole of that tree behind the meeting room. He went down on her—something Caleb never even thought of—and she climaxed several times over. They were both still clothed but he'd pulled her underpants down and stuck his head under her skirt. When he surfaced she'd dragged him as close as she could get him, and when he unzipped his pants and bent her head to his cock she just went for it.

They never got to actual intercourse because, as it turned out, everyone else wasn't gone from the meeting. There was one girl waiting to be picked up by her parents and she wandered outside and caught them in the act. She screamed and ran for the youth pastor, who kicked Dean out of their group. He then had a talk with Wendy, scaring her with his threats of damnation and the prediction that she would end up selling herself on the street if she didn't beg the Lord's forgiveness and make a vow of chastity. She absolutely agreed and did as he'd ordered. Dean, who'd tasted her against the tree, was sent away and she now could scarcely remember his name. It didn't matter. She was relieved he was gone, and she didn't have to see him again. All was well except, taking the youth pastor's advice to heart, she'd told Caleb they could no longer pleasure each other, that it was a sin . . . and he dumped her flat.

That was all at the end of senior year. She tried to tell Rona and Brooke that sex was bad, that it could turn them into whores, but Brooke had rolled her eyes and Rona had laughed out loud. In a strange way, that had made Wendy feel better. She wanted to believe that she wasn't ruined, as the youth pastor had implied. She got back with Caleb and tried to explain how much she loved him and that he was the only one for her, and maybe they could do a few things together without God damning them, but he was still angry. When Wendy learned she was pregnant, suddenly everything was good again between them. Caleb said he would marry her and they made plans, but first he had that Christian sabbatical to a village in Chile, so Wendy went off to Camp Fog Lake with Rona and Wendy. She didn't tell anyone of her pregnancy . . . or that she miscarried the day after graduation.

"Miss Newell?" Caleb demanded as soon as he marched Wendy into the lodge and saw the director, who was talking to an older man who slid a look at them, then took a few steps away as they approached.

"Yes." She was clearly distracted.

"My wife and I need to sleep together in the same cabin."

"We aren't set up for—"

He interrupted, more loudly, "My wife and I need to sleep together in the same cabin."

Hope stopped whatever else she was going to say and really focused on Caleb. Her gaze flicked to Wendy and then back to Caleb. "This is a weekend for fun and remembrance. It isn't like Haven Commune, where you have your own private rooms while you stay."

Wendy felt a tingle of uneasiness. Hope knew that their family had just spent several weeks at Haven? It had been Caleb's idea. Wendy had resisted. But their marriage had been showing some cracks and, well, she'd thought it might be a respite from some of the more unpleasant parts of their wedded life. It was while she was at Haven that she determined she was going to the parent/alumni reunion at the camp. Their son was there already and she wanted to make sure he was okay. She hadn't counted on Caleb joining her, but she should've. He rarely let her out of his sight.

"That's not acceptable," answered Caleb.

"You're in the same bunkhouse as your son," Hope said reasonably.

"It'll be okay," Wendy spoke up. Caleb's head whipped around in surprise. She never argued with him. Never. "We can be apart for a few nights," she went on, surprising herself as well. She smiled into Caleb's stormy eyes, marveling at her own backbone. "It'll make being back together that much more fun after the Fourth. And it'll be a good bonding time for you two men. I'll be thinking of both of you."

"Good enough," said Hope. "We're kind of in a turmoil here, with one of our counselors in the hospital. I'll bring everyone up to the moment about that at dinner. Nice to meet you both. I'll tell Joy I saw you."

"This is unacceptable," Caleb said again, but Hope had headed to the back of the lodge and her rooms, closing the door behind her with a perfunctory slam. "What's gotten into you?" he asked, rounding on her.

Out of the corner of her eye, she realized the older man had hesitated by the main door to the lodge and was within earshot. She thought he might be actively listening to them. She lifted her eyebrows at Caleb and inclined her head. He whipped around immediately and the older man let himself back outside.

"He was eavesdropping?" Caleb demanded.

"I don't know. I just didn't want to talk in front of him."

"You sure were talkative with Miss Newell."

She put her hands over his and held them tightly. "Let's not make a fuss. It is only for a few nights. Sometimes a split can be beneficial. I promise I'll make it up to you."

*You're a devious whore.*

She saw herself as if she were looking down from above. A sneaky, lying, smiling woman who wanted to smack her husband in the face even while she looked up at him with false adoration.

# Chapter 17

Harley had made an excuse to her mom, Emma, and Marissa, who were currently strolling along the lake, because she'd seen Marlon walking back to the maintenance shed and wanted to catch up with him. She fell in behind him. His gaze was centered on the ground in front of him and his shoulders were hunched. She wanted to talk to him. She'd gotten over her initial spurt of fear where he was concerned. She just couldn't see how he'd been responsible for what happened to Kendra in any way.

But she did want to know why Kendra had mentioned his name.

He went inside the maintenance shed through the open garage doors. Harley followed, past a large mower and some smaller tools that were on hand to keep the grounds tidy. She spied him trudging up a set of wooden steps to the floor above, his head disappearing as he reached the second level. She followed him up, trying to mask the clatter of her steps on the boards, but failing. In the end she reached the top and found him waiting, unsmiling, holding open a door to a long attic room. Another door to her right was closed and she thought that must be Greer's room.

"Hi, Marlon," she said, swallowing against a dry throat.

"Why're you here, girl?"

"I wanted to talk to you."

"Me? Or him?" He inclined his head to the closed door.

"Well . . . you," she said, as Greer's door suddenly opened and Greer stood in the aperture. "Hi," she said lamely.

Greer flicked a look at Marlon and said, "I got this."

The older man nodded and went into the attic, shutting the door and locking it with what sounded like some kind of wooden latch.

Greer stepped back into his room and motioned her inside. Harley's heart was thumping hard. As soon as she was through the door, he closed it with a sliding piece of wood, exactly as she'd imagined Marlon's door had.

"I thought he lived down by the main road," said Harley.

Greer walked to the far corner of the room and she realized he was getting as far away from Marlon's earshot as possible. "He does," he said softly, as soon as Harley walked closer. They were under the slanted roofline and Greer had to bend his head toward her. "What the hell are you doing?" he whispered.

Though it was a whisper, she could hear the repressed anger. "Nothing. I wanted to talk to Marlon."

"Why?"

"Because Kendra said his name this morning."

"And what? You thought he'd hurt her somehow?"

"Well, no. I don't know. That's why I wanted to talk to him."

"You think he's responsible for her drunk on her ass? That's on her."

"Agreed, she doesn't make the best choices. We all kind of go through that, though, don't we?"

Greer had had his moments in high school that had gotten him in hot water. Those days seemed far, far away right now.

His gray eyes bored into hers. Harley's breath caught a little. She glanced away, afraid she would focus on his lips. Her head was full of memories and it made it hard to concentrate.

"He's scary . . . not quite there . . . I've heard the talk. But Harley, you, of all people . . . I didn't think you'd be one to blame someone who's different."

"I don't! That's not it. I just want some answers!"

"Sure."

"Yes, *Greer*," she said, feeling righteous anger herself.

They stared at each other. Harley broke eye contact first and Greer said, "Hope's going to have a meeting with everyone tonight and she'll tell all of you that Marlon isn't to blame for whatever Kendra does. Not that you'll believe it. Easier to point blame."

"Hey. When did you get so high and mighty? Don't tell me how I feel. I love my aunt, and I've seen a ton of shitty looks and heard a lot of shitty comments directed at her. So, keep your judgment to yourself. All I was looking for were some answers, which you've given me. Thanks very much."

She stomped toward the door. Before she could open it, Greer was behind her, grabbing her arm and keeping her from removing the slide bar.

"Wait . . . wait . . ." he muttered.

"Let go of me," she said through her teeth.

He immediately dropped her arm and took a step back. "Please, wait," he said.

"Give me one goddamned good reason."

Harley could feel her nose burning. Her pulse was beating, and if she wasn't careful she was going to cry. *Damn.* She hated caring so much.

"I'm sorry," he said. "I've already had one argument about Marlon, I didn't expect another, especially from you."

"Is that an apology? It doesn't sound like an apology."

"You're still so testy."

Harley wasn't sure how she felt about that. Though, yeah, she was testy. She slowly turned around to face him. "I call it self-protective."

"Against me?"

"Against everyone."

Harley didn't want to meet his eyes again, so she looked around his room and noticed the array of small, crudely carved animals, several bears, and maybe a wolf.

"Marlon whittles," he explained, his gaze following hers.

"They're cool," said Harley, meaning it. She was starting to realize that Marlon and Greer's friendship was closer than she'd expected.

Footsteps sounded on the outside steps. Rapid ones. And then a pounding on his door and an attempt to open it. "Greer!" Allie called through the panels.

Harley's heart leapt to her throat, but Greer slid the bar back without compunction. Allie threw herself against him and said, "Sorry, sorry, sorry. I don't want to fight any-more!"

"Harley's here," Greer said stiffly and Allie pulled away from him as if burned. "She came here to see Marlon," he went on. "You're not the only one who suspected him."

"I didn't suspect him, not really," Allie protested before Harley, whose own denial had leapt to her lips but was left unuttered, had a chance.

"I just wanted to talk to him," Harley murmured, edging for the still open door.

"How did you end up *here*?" she asked.

"I intercepted her," he said.

Harley circled around them as Allie pulled back a bit but didn't leave Greer's embrace.

"See you later," she mumbled, then clattered down the stairs. When she reached the bottom steps she made a beeline toward the open garage door, and nearly ran into Marlon, who reached out a gnarled hand to steady her as she tripped.

"Sorry," she said.

"You be careful, miss," he said seriously. "The Lord only helps us when we help ourselves."

She nodded. She just wanted to get away and assess her encounter with Greer in more detail. Clearly he and Allie had had an earlier fight over her assumptions about Marlon. It made Harley feel doubly bad that she'd fallen into the same trap.

Marlon had dropped his hand from her shoulder, but now he held out the palm of his other one. A tiny wooden deer with surprisingly delicate features lay in his palm. "For you," he said.

"Oh, no, I couldn't take it." Harley felt like a complete fraud.

For an answer he clasped her wrist, gently twisted her hand upward, placed the deer against her palm. He smiled, kind of crookedly and sadly, then headed away from her, toward where the school bus was parked.


"Oh, my God, she's coming in here," said Rona, looking out the window.

"Who?" asked Brooke. Then, "Wendy?"

"Yes, but . . . well, she's trying to come in. She and Caleb are having a tense conversation, I believe." Rona peered closer, then climbed down from the top bunk. "Come on." She then threw open the door and headed outside. "Wendy!" she cried exuberantly.

Brooke followed more sedately and realized this was her role with Rona: Stay in the background. The only time she'd seen Rona completely at a loss was when she and Kiley reconnected and Kiley stared blankly over Rona's head, as if bored out of her mind, while Rona tried to wedge information about the camp out of her.

"Hi," Wendy said and then Rona gushed, "Caleb. My God, you look just the same. Maybe a teensy bit grayer here." She swirled her pointer finger around her temple. "But man, you look good."

Caleb's stiff demeanor didn't really change, but it did seem like he loosened a bit under the compliment. Brooke, picking up on the vibes, said to Wendy, "Well, come on in and pick a bunk. Rona and I are on bottom ones. You remember Emma Whelan? She's with us, too, along with her sister and her sister's kid and another girl."

"Where's Rona's daughter?" Wendy asked as Brooke led her inside while Rona remained with Caleb.

"Kiley's a CIT, counselor-in-training, and the counselor in her cabin is the one who was taken to the hospital by ambulance," answered Brooke. "You heard about that? Each cabin has a counselor, but now there isn't one at Bird's Foot."

"Why isn't Rona with Kiley?"

"I don't know. There didn't seem to be room." Brooke suspected, as did Rona, that Kiley had put the kibosh on her mom staying with her, but she didn't need to tell Wendy that.

"My son's a counselor at Snakeroot."

"Really." Brooke's brows lifted. "I didn't know your son was here."

Wendy nodded. She'd grayed a tiny bit, too, though her hair was still thick and lush. She wore little to no makeup, less now than in high school, and Brooke privately thought a little color might do her good as her complexion was wan and washed out. Her big, brown doe eyes were still filled with a naivete that Brooke knew was largely faked, but that fakeness was part of her personality.

Wendy took the upper bunk above Rona, climbing to the top across from Emma's sister Jamie's bed. She closed her eyes. "I could just go to sleep." But then she suddenly opened them. "Except I see . . . him."

Brooke drew a deep breath as her skin turned clammy. She'd always managed to push their misdeeds to the back of her mind until someone, like Wendy, boldly brought it out.

*Misdeeds . . . who are you kidding?*

When Brooke didn't immediately respond, she said urgently, "What are we doing here, Brooke? I don't want to be here. We should be back in our homes. Safe."

"Why did *you* come? I came because of Rona . . . she talked me into it. But why did *you* come? And why with *Caleb*?"

"It was his idea. I tried to talk him out of it, but that only made it worse. He wanted to see where Esau was spending his summers—last summer and this summer. We just got back from nearly a month at Haven Commune. Esau was with us. Caleb didn't want him to come to the camp, but Esau's over eighteen and he was already at Camp Fog Lake, so here we all are."

Brooke had a strong memory of Caleb Hemphill. Though she hadn't been as vocal as Rona about objecting to him, she'd certainly felt the same way. He'd always been controlling, humorless, and judgmental, and she doubted he'd changed significantly over the years, either.

But she didn't say that to Wendy, who surprised her by saying a bit dryly, "You and Rona are still looking out for me."

"What do you mean?"

"You separated me from Caleb and Rona's out there schmoozing him."

Brooke, who'd been wound up and tense ever since Lukey had shown up at her door—and coming to the camp hadn't helped that; she'd only traded one kind of anxiety for another—did feel a moment of lessening tension. "Why, Wendy, whatever do you mean?"

Wendy smiled faintly, but the smile quickly fell off her

face. "I've been afraid he'll find out," she said so softly Brooke could scarcely hear her. "Though sometimes I think about telling him, just to get it out there. When we were at Haven, and I was praying, I thought about those girls who died on the ledge. I thought maybe I'd go there, make a pilgrimage. There were two of them, you know. They don't talk about it much, but they were both from Haven. And so was Christopher. He told us his name was Ryan, remember him?"

"Oh, yeah. Of course."

"Christopher Ryan Stofsky. I talked to this woman who didn't want me to repeat what she said, but Ryan's family and several others left the commune years ago. Pastor Rolff was very strict in those days and he would hardly let them go, but they did. Ryan was friends with Fern Galbraith. They weren't lovers, but she knew he was at the camp. Pastor Rolff tried to make them say that Ryan was a problem. I don't know if he was or not, but he seemed fine when he was at camp with us. I hardly noticed him."

"Donovan sucked up all the air, along with Lanny and others."

"Owen," Wendy reminded her, looking hard at Brooke.

She nodded. "Another tragedy. And in the fog, of all things."

Wendy sighed. "Everything feels so far away and yet it's like yesterday."

Brooke could relate. "What happened between Ryan and Fern? Did they say anything about that at the commune?"

"I think they think Ryan killed her and tried to make it look like suicide. That he was at the camp just so he could see her." She shivered and rubbed her arms down.

"What about that other girl? The first one? Did they say anything about her?"

"They said she was sick. Or actually Pastor Rolff said she was sick, when he was pastor. But he has a little dementia himself now, so I don't know what that means. He did say

her name was Arianna, and I heard him say she was a runaway, but he was kind of hustled away."

"That's a lot more than I ever heard."

"I got it in bits and pieces. Almost like secret messages."
She smiled wanly. "But we were there to reach another spiritual plane. I wasn't supposed to be gossiping. I think Esau
was bored to death. I didn't see a lot of him. But Caleb was
in his element."

"Hmmm."

After a long moment, Wendy asked, "You haven't found
the Lord, have you?"

"Not in the way you have."

"How are you going to be saved from what we did?"

Brooke shook her head. She had no answer for that.


Rona pretended to listen politely while she closed her
ears to Caleb's droning. She'd done Wendy a favor by cutting her loose from him; she'd read their relationship in two
seconds flat, although she did have the benefit of knowing
Caleb from high school.

". . . the ascension isn't something you can take for
granted. Reaching a new spiritual plane with the Lord takes
an effort. You don't get there by eating processed foods and
watching television. When you get in that rut, of course it's
hard to get out of, and I'm ashamed to say Wendy and I were
falling into the abyss. That's why I suggested Haven. They
have a program there for the whole family and while we
were there, the message came from Camp Fog Lake. I knew
Wendy needed to go and I should go with her, so—"

"The whole family?" Rona could feel a scream building
in her head. If she had to stand here much longer with the
man, she thought she might claw her own face and shriek
like a banshee. Thank God she'd smuggled the vodka in her
bag. She'd expected she might want to get drunk.

She saw Donovan over Caleb's left shoulder, talking to

Kiley. Oh, so she'd talk to him? Why? She despised him. And that Tina person was standing by as well, hovering somewhat protectively. Was she a lesbian? Was that the direction Kiley was taking? The idea made Rona feel better. Maybe that's why it was so difficult between them. Kiley didn't feel she could confide in her mother, but . . . *her step-father*? More likely she was just being polite to Donovan, like Rona herself was being to Caleb.

". . . didn't want to go with us, but Haven changed his mind. He had a direct meeting with former Pastor Rolff and he was transformed. You could see it in his face."

"This is your son. What's his name?" Rona's eyes were still on Kiley and Donovan, but she was trying to keep up with the man's boring narrative.

"Esau. After my father. He was born the same year my father died. I made a vow to the Lord to raise him as my father raised me and now Esau is planning to go into the ministry this fall. He wanted to come to this camp. Neither Wendy nor I agreed at first, but Pastor Josh said Esau deserved the time with people his age. Pastor Josh is former pastor Rolff's son."

Rona straightened. Donovan had split from Kiley and Tina and was heading their way.

Caleb sighed. "I would like you to send Wendy out of that cabin now. I know you've been humoring me. It's time she was with me again."

Rona's attention shifted back to him. "Well, I think you're going to have to wait till after camp, Caleb."

His smile was cold. "Do you think I will really trust her with you and Brooke? I know what you did."

Rona's pulse spiked but she kept her expression neutral. "If you've got a problem with me and Brooke, I suggest you go take it up with God. But step a foot inside Foxglove and I'll make you wish you hadn't."

He blinked rapidly and his face went bright pink. "God hears everything!"

"Yeah? Maybe you need to take a lesson from Him because I'm not sure you're hearing me. Let me make myself clear: If you step a foot inside Foxglove to grab your bride, I will hurt you."

With that she headed over to Kiley, Donovan, and Tina.

Emma didn't like the lake, the camp, or the lodge. She wanted to go back to Foxglove and, finally, when Harley caught up with them again, they trooped to the cabin together. Emma tried to push the door, but it wouldn't budge. She turned to Harley, Jamie, and Marissa and said, "It's locked."

"Well, then someone's in there," stated Harley, who rapped loudly against the wood panels.

Brooke opened the door and peeked out. Seeing them, she threw it wider and stepped back. As soon as they were inside she slid the bolt again.

"Sorry," Rona said. She was sitting on the bottom bunk. She waved at the door. "We thought it was Wendy's jailor."

Emma looked at the woman sitting on the top bunk, the one across from Emma's. Wendy.

Wendy said, "She means my husband, Caleb. We're not really trying to keep him out."

"Aren't we?" Rona said, arching her brows.

Emma said, "You're drunk."

"I wish," Rona responded.

Brooke looked at Harley and Marissa. "You must be the counselors. I'm Brooke, and that's Rona and Wendy." She pointed to the women on the beds, then to Jamie. "We met earlier. And we went to camp with Emma, years ago." She gave Emma a big smile, like they were all friends, but Emma thought she was lying.

\* \* \*

Wendy said, "Hi, Emma. How are you? I'm so sorry about your disability."

Harley immediately wanted to jump in and defend her aunt, but Emma got there before her: "Why don't you like your husband?"

'Oh, I like my husband . . . a lot. I *love* my husband."

Rona laughed. She was sitting on a lower bunk and drinking from a blue cup with a plastic straw attached. At Emma's accusation, she'd set the cup down and hadn't picked it up again.

Brooke said, by way of explanation, apparently, "We haven't seen each other in years. It's really like celebrating."

There was renewed banging on the door and Mom opened it. Allie stood outside and she entered the room and looked around.

Harley informed them, "Allie's Foxglove's counselor. Marissa and I are CITs."

"How is everyone doing?" Allie asked, her smile a bit tense.

"So, alcohol poisoning," asked Rona. "The girl okay?"

"Kendra's in the hospital and I just talked to our director and it looks like she's going to be fine." Everyone murmured their relief. "We would normally be a little more organized, but now we're getting together down by the lake. It's overcast, but good canoeing weather. Maybe a little chilly out on the lake. And we have badminton and archery . . . we use rubber-tipped arrows, to be safe. You'll hear the dinner triangle. Dinner's at five but there are snacks. Normally we don't have snacks for the campers, but since this is a special weekend with all of you here, we even have red, white, and blue Popsicles. Let me tell you some things about our particular cabin. As you can see, there's a back door, and the bathrooms are behind it. There's a path that circles to the women's side . . ."

Harley tuned out. Though Allie was going through her

welcoming routine, she wasn't at full enthusiastic power.
Her eyes were red and though she'd clearly added makeup,
she couldn't quite hide that she'd been crying. Was she lying
about Kendra's condition, or did this have something to do
with her fight with Greer? Maybe a little of both. Harley
wasn't much for prayers, but she did wish for Kendra's recovery.

When Allie finished, she made a quick retreat, heading
outside. Harley looked outside the door and saw Allie cir-
cling around to the bathroom. She toyed with the idea of
following her, but Marissa stepped in front of her and whispered, "She's drinking."

"She's legal."

"Yeah, but they're at camp. And with Kendra?"

Harley shrugged.

"I have something to confess." Marissa gave Harley a
somewhat pleading look.

"Oh, no. Don't tell me. Cam's still around."

"No." She sighed heavily. "I just overheard two of the
women talking earlier. Not the one drinking, the others."

"Brooke and Wendy."

"Yes. The one on the top bunk, Wendy, is Esau's mother.
They were all just at Haven Commune; Esau, too. And they
were talking about those two girls that died on Suicide
Ledge when they were at camp."

"Only one died while they were at the camp. Fern
Galbraith."

"I know. And the guy's name is Christopher Ryan something. So, you guessed right. He went by his middle name.
They said the name of the other girl, the one that died before, too. Arianna."

Arianna. Huh. Harley hadn't picked up that from her research.

"What else did they say?"

"I don't know. Umm, some other stuff about the commune."

Harley pushed Marissa for more, but she was about tapped out. She knew Mom wanted to know more about the commune, but Marissa just said, "Maybe your mom should talk to them about it."

"I'll tell her."


Harley had to work to drag Mom away from the klatch of women inside Foxglove and when she finally managed it, Emma tagged along. She wasn't sure how much she wanted Emma to overhear, so she had to keep what she said truncated, but Mom got the message anyway and nodded at Harley that they would talk later.

Harley then headed with Emma toward the latrines while everyone else prepared to join the festivities down by the lake. As they walked beside a full-length mirror made of sheet metal, Emma stopped short and said, "I was with Donovan behind the mirror."

"In the boys' bathroom?" Harley lifted her brows.

"No."

"Well, that's what's behind this mirror," Harley pointed out.

"Inside it."

Harley regarded Emma for a moment, then looked at the mirror closely. She realized there were nails every two inches around its perimeter. A lot of hardware used to hang the thing up.

"It was a real mirror then," said Emma. "I didn't have sex with Cain but he said he was able."

"What?" Harley laughed.

"That's what he said."

"That's, like, a joke, Emma. Cain and Abel. From the Bible?"

"I know."

She walked on past the mirror and around to the girls'

bathroom. Harley followed after her but her gaze drifted back to the mirror.

Jamie stood near the lake and watched as several of the men tried out the canoes. The three women from Foxglove were by the archery set along with another man who hovered by Wendy. Caleb, she figured. He seemed to be arguing in her ear while Rona swung around with a bow and arrow and aimed it at him, losing her footing a bit. His arm darted out like a striking snake and grabbed the bow from her.

One of the men down by the lake was watching the group closely. He seemed to sense Jamie's interest because he glanced her way.

"Oh, no," she murmured to herself as he started up the hill from the water to where she was standing. She didn't feel like making small talk, but she pasted a smile of greeting on her face.

"Hi, there, I'm Donovan Keegan, Rona's husband." He pointed to where Rona was getting an earful from Caleb. She was clearly pissing him off. "You must be Emma's sister. You look just like her."

"So I've heard. Brown eyes, not blue, though."

Donovan was a nice-looking man who'd clearly put on a few pounds over the years. "You're here with Emma. She seems . . . okay."

"A lot different from when she was here," Jamie allowed. "You knew her?"

He threw an arm in the direction of several men by the canoes. One, lanky and tall, was seating himself inside a two-man canoe with a younger man who had the same build. "Sure, we knew Emma. That's Lanny Zenke and his son, Lendel. Lanny was my bunkmate, then and now."

"And Ryan?" Jamie asked. She'd done a little research of her own about the camp when she'd dived into learning about Haven Commune, and Harley had made Camp Love Shack a project, a lot of which she'd shared.

"He was in a bunkhouse with Owen." He made a face. "I don't know what happened to him. He liked Emma, though. That's what Owen said. He's gone now, too. Multicar accident outside of Fresno—in the fog, ironically."

"I heard about the fog."

"Big part of the lore out here," said Donovan. "When we were all here before, I tried to scare everyone with it. Emma called me out, though."

"She was like that," Jamie said with a faint smile.

"Yeah."

She changed the subject. "I thought Ryan was supposedly in love with the girl who died on the ledge?"

He shrugged. "I don't even know if they really knew each other, but Ryan sure defended the cult every time it was mentioned."

"The 'cult' being the commune."

"Maybe he killed her, maybe he didn't. Maybe somebody killed him. I tried to look into it after camp was over. Checked with the sheriff's department. First they said the cause of death was unknown. Eventually they said strangulation."

"But . . . ?" Jamie asked, sensing something more.

"Those ashes that were on that girl, Fern, were of poison hemlock."

Jamie got a jolt. Poison hemlock? Like Emma had mentioned? "Seriously?"

"It can cause serious blistering and skin irritation in some people. But it'll kill you if you swallow it. Not always. Depends on the amount, but you don't need a lot. Used to be used for medicinal purposes, but it's a fine line between herbal medication and death."

"You know a lot about it."

"Years of research and still not enough." He smiled and

shook his head. "Does Emma know any more of what happened back then?"

"I don't think so."

"She wouldn't remember anyway, right?"

It was Jamie's turn to shrug. She felt the conversation was getting away from her somehow, that she might be getting manipulated.

"I had a thing for her, too," he said. "Wonder if she remembers us making out."

Jamie didn't respond. Now she knew she wanted out of this conversation.

"She cut it off before we got down to it. I got the feeling she was seeing someone else."

"At the camp?"

"All of us wanted her. She was beautiful and smart and kind of a bitch. If she hooked up with someone, it was a solid secret, which I don't believe. Everybody talked. I would know . . ." He trailed off, his eye snagged by a couple of female counselors or CITs who were likely wearing swimsuits covered by sweatshirts, their long legs bare.

With his attention taken up, Jamie moved away from him.

# Chapter 18

September tried the number for Deena Royner one more time and was so surprised when she answered that she nearly drew a blank; her mind was so far down the path with Brody Daniels. She was actually just walking down the front steps of Daniels's house after another fruitless attempt to reach him and was thinking of requesting being allowed forcible entry, which she would likely be denied at this juncture, when a woman's cautious voice, said, "Hello?" on the other end of the line.

"Ms. Royner?" September asked.

"You've called me a bunch. Take my number off your list," she ordered flatly.

She sounded young. Maybe a little scared. "I'm Detective September Rafferty of the Laurelton Police Department and I found your number among the belongings of Richard Everly." When there was no response to that, she went on: "Mr. Everly was a victim of homicide. His body was discovered behind a Laurelton bar."

"I saw it on the news," she remarked flatly.

"Could you tell me anything about your relationship with him?"

"How do I know you're who you say you are?"

"Could we meet?" September suggested.

"I just worked with him, some, that's all," she said, avoiding the question.

"Were you a client of his? I understand he did private investigation work . . . and internet . . ." She almost said "trolling," but then let herself just fade out and see what Deena had to say.

"He was no private investigator. He was just . . . a guy."

September tried to read her tone. If called upon in court, she would say she thought it sounded a little sad, maybe a little frustrated. She took a chance that Deena considered the victim a friend of sorts. "Deena, I want to find out who killed R.J. I want to put him away. If you could help in any way, I'd appreciate it."

There was a long pause and then she said, "I have a friend who's a PI, a real one. His name's Taft. Jesse Taft."

"I know Taft," September said on a note of surprise.

"Talk to him about me," she said and clicked off.

September checked with George again and asked him to find Taft's number for her. She didn't know Jesse James Taft well, but she knew of him. He was an ex-cop whose rogue nature hadn't been a good fit with Portland P.D., though he still maintained some good relationships there, according to Auggie. Taft had recently been involved in a couple of high-profile cases centered in River Glen, the town next door to Laurelton. George secured the number, gave it to September, and she placed the call.

He answered on the third ring. "Taft."

"Hello, Mr. Taft. I'm Detective September Rafferty with Laurelton P.D. A woman named Deena Royner suggested I call you for a . . . uh . . . reference, I guess I'd call it."

"Ah, September, the twin . . . How's your brother?" he asked. "Haven't seen him in a while."

"Doing fine, last I heard. Busy. Haven't seen him in a while myself."

"He's one of the good ones."

"Yes, he is," she agreed.

"What does Deena want?" he asked, shifting gears.

"It's more what I want." She then gave him the rough outlines of Richard Everly's homicide and how she'd found Royner's name. "She suggested I call you."

"She did, huh? Let me talk to her and then I'll call you back."

"What is this?" asked September. "The runaround?"

"Nah. I'll call you back."

Fifteen minutes later, September's phone buzzed and it was Taft's number. Before she could even say hello, he was talking. "Deena doesn't want to get in trouble. She came across Everly in the course of her work. They . . . uh . . . share an interest in the internet."

"She's a hacker," concluded September.

"Your word, not mine," he said, sounding vaguely amused. "She would like to help you find R.J.'s killer, but she won't testify in court. She won't make herself public."

"I can't guarantee anything, but I'll do what I can."

"Call her back. See what she says."

She did just that, but the phone rang on and on and on again. Frustrated, September clicked off, only to have her phone ring in her hand. Deena Royner.

"Can we meet?" September asked her again, but Deena demurred. She was willing to talk, however.

"R.J. could get places on the 'net but he was messy. I knew he'd run into trouble. He just . . ." She sucked air through her teeth. September thought she might be fighting emotion. "He had bad friends and he couldn't say no to them. He couldn't leave things alone."

"Who were his friends?"

"I don't know their names. I mean, I never wanted to

know their names," she corrected herself. "When he stayed away from them, he was okay."

"Brody Daniels?"

"I don't know, ma'am . . . Detective. I made a point of not knowing."

"Someone he went to school with, maybe."

"Maybe," she said cautiously, which led September to think she knew more than she was saying. She had a mental picture of Deena hacking R.J. for information on him.

"I'm following up on his years at Glory to God, a Christian school in Portland."

"Year," she said. "Singular. And there was nothing Christian about it."

And then she was gone.

The lodge was crowded with older adults and Harley— seated on a bench with her mother on one side, Emma and Marissa on the other—felt like she was at some kind of job rather than a summer camp. Hope stood at the front of the group. She was on the young side, compared to the parents and alumni, and she seemed a bit intimidated as she related that Kendra's parents were with her at the hospital, and that though Kendra was still unconscious, she was still alive.

"I know there have been rumors about what happened to Kendra, but it looks mostly like alcohol poisoning," Hope told them.

There was a stir among the counselors and CITs. Austin raised his hand and Hope somewhat reluctantly, it seemed, nodded toward him.

"We heard it was poison hemlock," he said. "I know what that stuff is. I read about it. It can kill you."

A loud wave of gasps and "oh, no"s ran through the crowd. Hope lifted her arms and raised her hands up and down, asking for quiet.

"That's what you were talking about," Harley whispered to Emma.

Her mom had stiffened beside her and added, "Donovan mentioned it, too."

"That's not what happened to Kendra," Hope was going on. "Yes, poison hemlock does grow around here. It grows all over Oregon and lots of the U.S. in fields and ditches and roadways, and it blossoms at this time of year. However, just touching it generally won't hurt you."

"Yeah, but if particles get in the air, or you accidentally eat it, you're a goner," Austin argued.

"What's the antidote?" a balding guy asked, one of the alumni.

"There is no antidote," Austin stated before Hope could answer.

"If you ingest poison hemlock, you need to flush fluids. Stomach pump. This is what the EMTs did, for her alcohol poisoning as well."

"You need to pray," said a woman's voice.

Harley looked over and saw Sunny Dae, her arms crossed over her rounded belly.

Hope said, "Let me say it again. That's not what's going on here."

Marlon was seated in the front row. Harley, two rows back, could nevertheless see him well as he was on a diagonal from her seat. He kept rubbing his hands together. She saw he was whittling and she wondered if whittling was an anxiety reliever for him.

"Is there some around here? Poison hemlock? Could any of us get it?" a woman asked. She had short blond locks in a bob and a turned-down mouth that looked as if it could be perpetual.

Emma, beside Harley, looked at the woman and asked, "Do I look like her?"

Mom shot Emma a questioning look, as did Harley.

"Resting bitch face," Emma explained.

"No," Mom whispered vehemently.

"There's some by the maintenance shed," Marlon rasped. "And some in the woods."

"We need to clear it out!" the balding guy said.

"It's not the problem here," Hope insisted. "But we should still get rid of it." A chorus of voices echoed their agreement. "It needs to be dug up carefully. No hacking," Hope added quickly, as a restlessness gripped the room.

"What does it look like?" the woman with the down-turned mouth asked.

"I don't have a picture, but it's similar to Queen Anne's lace, if you're familiar with the plant." Hope held up her hands again, trying to keep the crowd in their seats. "Marlon will take care of any poison hemlock around the camp. But again, that's just an unfortunate rumor. Kendra is sick with *alcohol* poisoning."

More questions were asked, but Hope tried to instill a feeling of security and safety. Someone asked how Hope had contacted the hospital and she explained about the walkie-talkies whose range reached the commune, and also the pockets of transmissibility found in areas of the woods.

Harley determined she was going to have to find one of those pockets. But where to charge her phone? Her battery chargers were only going to last so long. Hope's quarters and the kitchen were hooked up to a generator, but no one there was going to allow Harley to charge up.

The maintenance building.

Her eyes drifted around the room. She didn't see Greer, but she suspected he was somewhere behind her.

Soon after Hope finished her explanations, she invited people to enjoy dinner, which was grilled burgers with all the fixings: sliced tomatoes, onions, pickles, relish, cheddar cheese, buns, and condiments, the fresh vegetables brought in from Haven Commune.

Harley saw her mom chatting with Sunny Dae, who lived

at Haven. It caused her a jolt of remembrance. Mary Jo was pregnant. She was going to have a sibling!

"Hey," she said, reseating herself next to her mother after they'd gotten their burgers. Emma sat across from them. She had every piece of her burger laid out across the top of her dinner tray. Emma was very precise in her eating habits and wasn't much of a burger eater, as far as Harley knew. "You okay with that?" she asked her.

"They have burgers at Ridge Pointe."

"I'm going to go over to Haven tomorrow," Mom said, spreading mustard over her bun. She'd added some french fries into one of the divided squares of her tray. "The camp's cook, Sunny Dae, invited me and told me to talk to Joy."

"How'd you wrangle that?" asked Harley.

"I showed an interest."

"I'm going, too," said Emma.

Mom stopped in mid-spread. "Why don't you stay here and join in the activities? I'm kind of doing some research."

"I don't want them to poison you."

"Emma, that's not what happened to that . . . counselor . . ." She trailed off.

"Kendra," Harley supplied, realizing her mother couldn't come up with the name.

"Yes, Kendra." Mom nodded. "She drank too much. No one actually poisoned her."

"Joy knows about poison hemlock," said Emma.

"I'll ask her about it when I see her."

Marissa, who'd stayed out of the conversation thus far, said, "What if Kendra . . . like, fell into the plant? She'd been drinking."

"Rona was drunk," said Emma.

"A lot of that going around," said Harley, throwing a look toward the three women—well, two, as the one named Wendy wasn't with them. She was seated beside a man with a tight jaw. Harley looked him over. He wasn't actually gripping his wife, but there was the looming sense that he wanted to. Her head was turned to look at Hope. As if feeling Harley's eyes on her, she glanced her way. Harley played it off that she was looking past her and then she slid her gaze back to Rona and Brooke. As she watched, Rona brought her cup up, the one she'd set down so carefully at the cabin, and drew the straw to her lips. Brooke was still focused on Hope.

They broke up soon afterward. There was a talk of a campfire, but the adults didn't seem like they were getting it together. There were still hours before the sun went down, but Harley, Marissa, Mom, and Emma headed back to Foxglove.

Emma lay on her bed, waiting, but Rona and Brooke didn't come back for a long time.

"You're right. Emma knows," Rona said to Brooke. She'd sobered up from her high, but was still fueling herself with alcohol. She wasn't drunk, per se, but she wasn't tracking all that well, either.

Brooke looked out over the lake, the surface rippling lightly beneath a westerly breeze. Had Emma seen everything? If so, how much did she remember?

"Fucking row!" Rona hissed at her that night as she and Wendy struggled with the oars. Wendy's soft crying was the sound track for their midnight voyage. She could smell the musty and mucky scent of the lake, but also the faintly metallic odor of blood.

The fog was thick. She lost all sense of direction. Maybe they were rowing back toward camp. But no, a faint break in the wall of gray. Water all around. Maybe a shoreline in the distance? Not the camp.

"Help me," Rona whispered tensely. There was barely constrained panic beneath the anger. "You, too, Wendy!"

Awkwardly, the canoe rocking as if it were ready to capsize, they got his shoulders up. His head was a mass of blood. Brooke's stomach revolted. She managed to hold it in until they slipped him into the water, Wendy letting out a small shriek as she jumped to the other side of the craft to counteract the weight all on one side. Brooke moved with her and vomited over the side.

She didn't remember rowing back. Rona told her later that they were lost for a bit before going in the right direction; no one had brought a compass. They beached the canoe and turned it upside down on the shore, next to the ones already lined up for the next day's activities.

As they hurried up the bank, Brooke looked up and stopped short. Someone was standing in the shadows. Rona and Wendy paused when she did. Neither said a word but Brooke wasn't sure she would have heard them over the pounding of her heart.

Brooke blinked and the person was gone. She almost thought she'd imagined it, but someone had been there when they rowed out, and that someone was still there when they returned: Emma.

The following day, when it was time for the canoe races that were scheduled, Brooke held her breath as they turned over the large one that they'd taken to drop the body in the lake. There were bound to be bloodstains. She just hoped the water that had splashed in had taken care of most of it. What if there were rusty lines of blood, from what had pooled in the bottom hull dripping down once the canoe was upended?

But to her immense relief there was no trace, once the canoe was righted. Relief gave way to puzzlement, and puzzlement to fear.

Someone had cleaned out the canoe, and it wasn't Rona, Wendy, or herself . . .

\* \* \*

Now, in the softening daylight of their first night back at camp, Rona said again, a bit more belligerently, "She saw us."

"She doesn't remember. Maybe it wasn't even her."

Rona paused. "Maybe we should ask her."

"Are you crazy? What, do you want to go to prison? Self-defense isn't going to work when it was all three of us rowing *him* out to the middle of the goddamn lake!"

Brooke headed back toward the cabin and nearly ran into a tall, lanky man with a thick head of hair. "Sorry," she said.

"Hey, Brooke, you look just the same."

She felt a sizzle of fear as she squinted up at him. "Oh? Hi." Then, "Lanny?"

"Got it in one. I look a little different. But you . . . Rona, too, really," he added, though he didn't sound as sure.

"How are you?"

He wore board shorts and a sweatshirt. His legs were tan and muscled, his feet in a pair of tan Vans. There was something relaxed about him that Brooke felt herself respond to. "Doing great. Yourself?"

"I'm okay," she lied. She wasn't okay. She didn't feel okay.

"Sad stuff about Owen, huh? Did you guys keep in contact after camp? I always thought you would."

"No, we didn't."

"But you and Rona"—he hitched a lightly bearded chin toward Rona—"you're still like this." He crossed his fingers. Brooke noticed there was no wedding ring.

"We reconnected recently."

"You're married, right, huh? Husband here?"

"Nope."

He assessed her. She'd never noticed the interesting shade of hazel in his eyes. Kind of a dark green, darker than her own, with specks of brown and blue. He leaned into her and said, "You ever tell him what went on around here?"

Brooke's heart flipped painfully. "Those deaths didn't have anything to do with the camp."

"I wasn't talking about that."

"We were just dumb kids, going to camp." She eased away from him. "Good to see you again. Are you a parent, or just an alumnus like me?"

"Both."

"Oh, who's your kid?"

"Name's Lendel. I didn't want him to come here, but his buddy Austin talked him into it. So, okay. I'm here. Just kind of wanted to put it all behind me, you know, but . . ."

*Oh, she knew.* "Mmm-hmm."

"Why'd you show up? You don't have any kids."

"How do you know?"

"I mighta known a few things about you before I came. You and your husband are separated, maybe divorced? Not sure about that. Wasn't on the internet."

"You got information about me from the internet?"

"Don't look so worried. I know you're not banging some underage kid."

"Thanks," she said, turning away, her mouth dry.

She'd never even looked at Lanny. It was Donovan she'd wanted, just like Rona, just like Wendy, but it was Emma who got him, or at least he'd wanted her. Emma had been too aloof to know what she wanted. When Donovan's right-hand man, Owen, had decided to romance Brooke, she'd let him. She'd even squeezed into that closet space behind the mirror with him. They all knew about it. Took turns, basically. Standing up, squeezed together. She remembered Owen pushing excitedly against her and her own hands dropped lightly on his hips, encouraging him, sort of. But her mind had been on Donovan. She pretended it was his mouth ravaging her lips and neck and breasts as he thrust against her, his fingers yanking down her shorts as he sought to stick his cock between her thighs.

*Brooke, Brooke, you're the one I want . . .* Fantasy Donovan had groaned. *I can't live without you . . . I want to come inside you, let me come inside you . . .* All the while Owen was humping against her, rattling the mirrored door.

She hadn't been able to keep up the fantasy, what with his fumbling and the fact that Owen's breath still carried a little pungent scent left over from the garlic bread served with spaghetti.

"Sorry," she'd mumbled, grabbing her shorts and pushing him off enough to get out of the mirror closet. It was late night when she emerged.

And Owen was out behind her in an instant. "You fucking tease!" he hissed.

"Shhh!" She'd hurried toward her cabin.

A man was standing right in front of her in the dark! She shrieked bloody murder!

*SMASH!*

She'd nearly leapt from her skin when Owen kicked in the mirror, whipping around. When she turned back, the man was gone. Maybe he was a figment of her imagination. She ran into the cabin and buried her head beneath her pillow, shaking all over.

The camp had replaced the mirror with sheet metal almost immediately, and Brooke stopped speaking to Owen.

# Chapter 19

Early Saturday morning, Jamie lay awake in the dark, watching as dawn lifted the darkness and began to sneak in around the edges of the window shutters while the birds awakened, twittering and whistling in the first light of day.

She sat up in her bunk in the sweats she'd worn to sleep in. No one else was moving. Gathering up her personal belongings, she headed toward the girls' bathroom, passing the sheet-metal mirror that dulled and distorted her image a bit.

She quickly took a shower and dressed in jeans and a long-sleeved blue tee, shivering a bit. She'd brought a sweatshirt and planned to put it on over her shirt as soon as she got back to the cabin. Early mornings in June could be really cold.

As she was pulling her sweatshirt over her head, she heard Emma stir. She poked her head through the neck hole and saw that Emma was sitting on her bunk, her blue eyes on Jamie. Jamie signaled for her to get dressed and meet her outside.

Ten minutes later, Emma stepped out in her usual loose

pants and top. She couldn't handle anything too tight or constrictive. Her day wear was very similar to her nightwear.

"I have to pee," Emma said.

"Follow me to the bathroom."

"I know where it is."

Nevertheless, Jamie started to walk with her sister when Emma stopped at the sheet-metal mirror. "I told Harley I didn't have sex with Cain, but he said he was able."

"You told her, too, huh?"

"I almost had sex with Donovan, but we didn't go all the way. I thought about sex with Cain, too, but I didn't go all the way."

"Donovan . . . and Cain," Jamie repeated. She determined Emma must be talking about Rona's husband, Donovan.

"They both went all the way with other girls."

Jamie absorbed that information with a nod of her head. "Camp Love Shack."

"I was going to get married, but I never did." She cocked her head. "I could still have your baby."

Jamie didn't respond, just started walking again toward the bathroom. Sometimes it was best not to ask too many questions. After a few moments, Emma followed her.


Harley and Marissa had KP duties at breakfast and helped clean up along with Kiley and a couple of the guys, including Lendel and Esau. Almost immediately after breakfast duties were over, Harley went to look at that mirror again, wondering if she could ask Greer about a way to remove all the nails and see what was behind it, when she saw Esau, Wendy, and the man she realized was his father, Caleb, outside Hawk's Beard bunkhouse.

"We're going to have our own cabin. That one the girl in the hospital was in doesn't have many people to move. I've talked to Hope," the dad said.

"Have you?" asked Esau. "What about Kiley?"

"Caleb, it's only for a few nights," Wendy said in a sooth-ing voice.

Caleb's face suffused with color. "You want to argue with me?" He glared at his wife in a challenge, then glanced up and noticed Harley, who'd stopped short by the mirror. "Miss?" he demanded coldly.

"Excuse me," she said, lifting her hands as if warding him off. She changed her plans and headed past the mirror toward the girls' bathroom. What a dick.

Brooke met up with Donovan at the archery range, where three large targets with colorful concentric circles were ar-ranged on sturdy easels. Other adults were hovering around, waiting for some instruction. Warren showed up and began arranging for them to shoot.

"Don't tell me, Rona went back to bed." Donovan looked over the rubber-tipped arrows, their fletched ends sticking out of a barrel. Bows were lined up against a low, uneven rock wall.

"She'll be here," Brooke automatically defended, which elicited a snort out of Donovan. They'd signed up for archery and then canoeing. At Wendy's insistence, she and Caleb had chosen pottery in one of the rooms off the main maintenance shed, but then Caleb had decided on bad-minton, so that's where they were.

"Did Wendy tell you about their monthlong stay at Haven?" Donovan asked, selecting an arrow and examining the tip. "Think this thing'll actually stick to the target?"

"I don't know. Yeah, she mentioned the commune."

"Caleb told us all about it in excruciating detail. I stopped listening when he got into the steps to reach the next spiritual plane. Esau wanted him to shut up, I could tell. I did, too. What a bunch of shit. I think their marriage is breaking up."

Brooke didn't respond to that. Rona had acted like their

marriage was also on life support and hers was basically dead. "Rona said that Brody's business is tanking and that you felt the same way."

He looked up at her. "Tanking? It's fucking criminal, Brooke."

"That's quite an accusation."

"Do you really not know? I thought you might be in on it with him. I can see how tempting it would be to use other people's money."

"Never." Brooke was affronted.

"Okay. You're innocent. Whatever you say."

Brooke could feel herself fuming and had to remind herself she was mad at Brody, not Donovan. "I'm going to talk to him about it."

"Yeah, have a good friendly talk. That'll do it."

"You're an ass, Donovan."

He laughed. "You sure wanted me back then, though, didn't you? Had to settle for Owen. Poor son of a bitch. Ironic, huh? The fog got him."

They heard a shout and laughter from the lake, where one of the female counselors in a white bikini was bending over, trying to help guide a canoe into the lake. Donovan's eyes lingered long on the girl and a smile played on his lips.

"Think you can tap that?" Brooke asked.

"I don't see why not," he drawled.

As they watched, Esau joined her and they helped another adult couple climb into a canoe.

"Esau found some girl at Haven that he's hot for, but Caleb's got him set for the ministry." Donovan shook his head, still smiling. "I tried to talk to Caleb when Esau was out of the room. Told him Esau was just humoring him and that he would sneak out and head over Suicide Ledge to the commune as soon as it got dark. Caleb practically ran after Esau before I was finished talking. I saw 'em in a wrangle down by the water."

"You're stirring the pot, Donovan."

"Just tellin' it like it is. You know Kiley's fucking that boy, Niles."

"You're so crude."

"Oh, your tender ears. Think I should tell Rona?"

"Leave me out of it." Brooke should have known better than to talk to Donovan. He still had to be that obnoxious alpha male.

"So, when are you and me going behind the mirror?" He lifted his brows.

Brooke didn't deign to answer. She left the archery grounds and headed back to the cabin.

"Ever ask yourself who cleaned out the canoe?" he called after her.

Sunny Dae bustled out of the kitchen with a small picnic basket, which she handed to Jamie and Emma to take with them to Haven, though they hadn't asked her to. "You didn't need to do that, but thank you," Jamie told her.

"They'll invite you for lunch, but it can be kind of . . . healthy . . . if you're not used to it. I'm sorry I can't go with you, but we've got a crowd here." She looked behind her where Tina, Warren, and several other counselors were helping prepare food for later in the day. "Ask for Joy. She can tell you all about Haven."

"Thank you." Jamie had let Sunny Dae in on the fact Mary Jo was her surrogate and that she was curious about the commune. Sunny had been surprised at first. She'd even tried to dissuade Jamie from dropping in on the commune, but when Jamie hadn't budged in her resolve, she'd done a complete turnabout and now was helping them.

"I know Joy," said Emma.

"Oh, that's right. You were at the camp when she was director."

"How long was she camp director?" Jamie asked.

"About six years? Seven? She wanted it to be her career.

She even spent winters at the lodge here, but then Mrs. Luft-Shawk got pneumonia and was down for a long time . . . and then everything that happened at the camp later shut it down."

"Joy ran the camp for the Luft-Shawks in those days?"

"Yes, but the camp was really Pastor Rolff's. He'd granted it to Georgia and Jedidiah for several decades, but it was his. He'd bought up all this property around here and when the Luft-Shawks wanted to buy the camp from him, he turned them down, but he did strike a deal and he rented to them. They lived in Laurelton, and Joy stayed on the property."

"Are they still in Laurelton?" Jamie asked.

"I think they moved to Portland. I'm sorry to say I lost track of them."

Jamie had half-turned to leave, wanting to get on their way, but she was also gleaning information from Sunny Dae that she hadn't gotten before. "Were they part of Haven Commune? The Luft-Shawks?"

"They were connected to our community at one time," she allowed. She looked away for a moment, as if thinking, and then said, "Joy'll tell you all about it if you ask her, I'm sure. She . . . um . . . she grew close to the Luft-Shawks' daughter, Arianna, in those days."

Emma repeated, "Arianna," as if turning it over in her mind.

"I don't want to speak ill of the dead, but Arianna was a bit of a problem. She kept running away," Sunny Dae explained. "She even showed up at the commune a time or two but Pastor Rolff wouldn't let her stay. I have to get back, but since you're seeing Joy, I should tell you—Arianna was the girl killed and left on Suicide Ledge with ashes poured over her. The first one."

"Oh." Jamie blinked, surprised.

Emma leaned in. "It was not a suicide."

"She just said that, Emma."

"You know who killed her?" Emma asked Sunny Dae.

"Oh, heavens no. I wish I did."

Jamie hustled Emma away after that, clutching the small basket firmly to her side.

"She lied to us," said Emma when they were barely out of earshot.

"I don't know if that's true. She was just trying to warn us that if we talk to Joy it might be a difficult subject."

"She knows who killed her."

Jamie let that one go as they headed up the trail that led away from the camp.

When they reached the crest, Emma's steps slowed and she stopped by the slab of rock where the two girls' bodies had been found. The lake glowered below them, dark green and rippling.

"Ryan could see to here," said Emma.

Jamie looked down at the slab of rock and felt a cold knot form at the base of her spine.

"You can't see it without binoculars. They rolled him into the canoe." Emma looked over the lake and then back the way they'd come, toward the camp.

"Who rolled who into the canoe?" Jamie asked, hearing herself and thinking it sounded like the beginning of a children's rhyme.

Emma cocked her head, Emma style, a sure sign she was searching her brain for an answer. "I'm going to ask them."

"Who?"

"The people that killed Cain."

Jamie regarded Emma carefully. Sometimes Emma got things completely turned around backward, and sometimes she was so dead on it was mind-blowing. She wasn't entirely sure this Cain was even real, but Emma had gotten that phrase from somewhere. "And who would those people be?" she asked, turning back to the trail, stepping carefully as there were exposed roots that she didn't want to trip on.

"I couldn't see them very well."

"See them? You saw someone roll Cain into a canoe?" queried Jamie.

"The Three Amigos."

"The women in our cabin?"

"I heard Wendy. She's a screamer."

"Emma, are you really remembering something?"

"Nobody liked each other after that."

Jamie didn't know what to make of that, but when Emma added, "I'll talk to them about it," she put in quickly, "Emma, don't do that." Was her sister's memory true? False? Even a real memory? Whatever the case, the cold feeling in her lower back had intensified. "Let's think about this some more before you bring it up to Wendy."

"We can ask Joy," Emma said suddenly. "She was there."

"Joy was one of the people?"

"She was smoking under the eaves. But that was . . . because of Ryan. He was dead." She paused. "That was a different time."

"Okay, let's table this for now and I don't think it's a good idea to bring it up to Joy, either." Joy of the poison hemlock . . .

"I don't have to give her my whole life story."

"That's absolutely right," Jamie said. She'd given that advice to Emma once and Emma, who had a tendency to repeat things, had grabbed onto it and turned it into a mantra.

September carried her coffee cup outside onto the back patio, curling into a chair, feet tucked beneath her, in her bathrobe, and reviewed yesterday's actions. She'd called Daniels's wife, Brooke Daniels, but it had gone directly to voice mail. She'd tried a couple more times with no success, then got her address and visited her apartment complex. No go. The lady wasn't home, and when she'd cruised by a second time, same thing. She had her license plate number and found her BMW in the lot amongst the Nissan, Ford, and

Chevy sedans in the outdoor parking lot. Not much of a place for the wealthy, maybe soon-to-be divorcee, but maybe that was the point. Brody Daniels could've kicked her out and left her with a shoestring budget. Or, maybe there was a prenup . . . or maybe she just got the hell out of a toxic marriage.

Or, maybe they were together now, she mused, tentatively sipping the hot, dark liquid, testing it with her tongue. Mrs. Daniels had gone off somewhere without her car. His wasn't at his house or at work, as far as September could determine, so maybe they'd taken Uber or Lyft to the airport? Or called on a friend or neighbor to take them?

Was that why Daniels hadn't answered any of her calls? Could he, or they, be out of range?

Today was Saturday, and George wasn't behind his desk. Neither was she going to the station, but she was on call. Jake was already golfing with a business associate who was also a good friend, so she was alone. She'd taken her time getting up and was debating whether to head out for a late breakfast or fall back on cereal, or if she delayed much longer on nourishment, maybe wait for lunch.

She finished her coffee and moseyed into the bedroom, where she decided on a run first, changing into a black Athleta long-sleeved tee and leggings. She threw her hair into a ponytail, slipped her cell into the thin side pocket, then grabbed her Nikes and headed out the door. She jogged for several miles, breaking into a run for a short sprint, then back to a jog, then a fast walk as she turned for home. Her route took her past a pop-up fireworks stand that she glanced at as she went by. She and Jake had no plans for celebrating the Fourth other than a meal from the local Presbyterian church of barbequed chicken and potato salad.

She thought about the Glory to God school as she let herself back in the house and down the hall to the en suite bathroom and shower. George had given her a printout yesterday of what he'd found and she'd glanced through it but it needed a deeper look. Since understanding that Deena Royner and R.J. had apparently shared a "professional hacker" relationship, she'd toyed with the idea of asking Deena to follow R.J.'s electronic footprints. The techs hadn't given her anything much off his phone, and though she'd asked for a deeper dive, she knew no one was going out of their way until after the holiday weekend.

Out of the shower, she combed her wet hair down straight, threw on a pair of jeans and an army-green collared shirt, then sat down at the kitchen table with a bowl of cornflakes topped with milk, sugar, and banana slices. Her cell phone lay beside her right hand and she kept looking at it. If she asked Deena to help her, it would likely be asking her to commit a crime.

She finished her cereal, rinsed her bowl and spoon and put them in the dishwasher, then grabbed up the stapled printout George had given her.

The Glory to God school had been started in the mid-nineties and closed up shop rather abruptly in the early 2000s. It was a charter school for junior high and high schoolers that seemed to be a way station for teens who'd fallen out, or been kicked out, of public and/or other private schools. The curriculum was heavily into the teachings of Christian religion and the founders' mission was to instill faith, hope, and yes, charity, into their troubled student body. September didn't have class lists, but she did have the names of a few teachers and the founders. George had gone so far as to write down some current phone numbers and addresses for members of the defunct school that he could easily find, which was saying a lot.

She picked up her cell phone, wondering who, if anyone, she would connect with on Fourth of July weekend.

The cell suddenly rang in her hand and she nearly dropped it. The number on the screen was Deena Royner's. She answered quickly, "September Rafferty."

"R.J. lurked on social media and he could break into the admin on accounts if he wanted to," she said without preamble. "He didn't do it much, because that usually didn't pay off, but he did it recently. He blew up this story on this woman and a teen having sex. Pretty sure it's all fake. If I had to guess, someone paid him to do it."

September took that in. "You think someone hired R.J. to set this woman up?"

"Or maybe it's true and R.J. just made it public."

She could hear the skepticism in Deena's voice. "Do you have a name for her?"

"Brooke. She works for the teen's parents at Greenscape Landscaping."

"Brooke *Daniels*?"

"Yeah." Deena's voice lifted with some surprise as well. "That mean something to you?"

"Yes . . . thank you."

"We never talked," Deena told her and clicked off.

September sat still for a moment, her mind racing. She glanced down at the printout with the names of Glory to God's founders, but her mind was elsewhere, wondering if Greenscape Landscaping was open the Saturday of Fourth of July weekend.

She glanced down at the printout. For now she set aside calling Georgia Luft and Jedidiah Shawk, who had started Glory to God school, in their "dedication and love for Jesus Christ."

# Chapter 20

Harley stood by the badminton net where she'd been assigned by Hope. Niles's parents were taking on Esau, Caleb and Wendy Hemphill. Caleb had stopped complaining about not sleeping with his wife as he'd turned his attention to the competition, which was fierce for a badminton game, Harley thought, but she didn't think Caleb had given up his crusade to pull Wendy out of Foxglove. After her run-in with him she'd written him off as a complete asshole and felt sorry for Esau. If she had a parent like that, she didn't know what she'd do.

The day was cool and the lake was calm as the breeze that had been with them most of the time was missing. In fact, the air felt closer than it had. The badminton players were beginning to sweat.

Marissa was with a group of counselors and CITs by the canoes and it looked like she was flirting a little . . . with Austin. Good, Harley thought. Anyone but Cam. But she was worried about whether she should come clean to someone—maybe Mom—about Marissa's sneaking out to meet him. It would be a betrayal, for sure, but with what happened to Kendra, could she remain quiet?

Harley shook her head, pushing that aside for now. She'd think about it later.

Allie and Warren were with some of the parents and alumni, including Brooke and Rona, at the archery grounds. There were others at the arts-and-crafts room and still others sitting around the lodge swapping old camp stories. Harley, just in passing, had heard one guy's twice already. Apparently he'd been sweet on Joy, when she was the camp's director.

Harley was getting tired of being relegated to her post. Hope had made it clear that she was to stay right where she was, available in case any of the parents or alumni needed her. Could it be that Allie was behind this? She'd seen Harley inside Greer's room and even though she'd seemed fine with it at the time—too upset to really care, Harley had thought—it might be that she did care a teensy-weensy bit and wanted to get Harley out of range. Harley doubted Greer had told her about their past relationship, so maybe she was making too much of it . . . but maybe he had?

As if just thinking about them had conjured them up, Allie and Greer appeared on the lakeside of the cabins where the outdoor activities were, Allie's arm wrapped around his. Harley straightened. She saw Allie scan the crowd. When her eyes came to rest on Harley she stared for a moment, then looked in the same direction as Greer, who was watching a woman struggle with the oars. The woman was in the canoe and just shoving off when one oar dropped in the water.

Greer leaned as if to help, but Allie was still clamped onto him. It was Lendel who splashed through the shallow end of the lake and grabbed the oar, stretching it toward the woman's outstretched hand. Couldn't quite make it. Lendel stepped forward and went under.

Well, yeah. The gradual slope at the shore only went out so far and then it dropped off. Lendel's dad—Lanny?—jumped in and swam out to the drifting canoe, grabbing the floating oar on the way. He swam back and by then Lendel was on the shore. Harley regarded Greer, who looked tense, and Harley knew if that had been his dad and him, there would be harsh words.

"You almost had it before you dunked yourself!" Lanny called out.

"I meant to do that!" Lendel yelled back, and they both laughed.

Harley hadn't realized she'd been holding her breath until then. Greer's shoulders relaxed a bit, too, and to Harley's delight, he pulled his arm away from Allie and joined the others by the lake. Allie followed after him slowly. She played a little with her hair and sent another glance Harley's way.

*Okay, she does know. Shit.*

"Hey, you. Girl?"

Harley realized Caleb was talking to her.

"We need some cold drinks here."

"It's Harley," she said. She wasn't supposed to leave her post but this was a direct request.

He bent his head to his wife and asked in a stage whisper, "Did she say Harley?"

"She's Emma's niece," Wendy answered, and Harley could practically feel his eyes boring into her back as she headed toward the back door of the kitchen.

She shivered involuntarily.

Sunny Dae was overseeing several counselors helping to clean the kitchen, and Tina and Warren and several others were starting prep for lunch. Seeing Harley, Sunny Dae came to the back door and invited her inside the kitchen as she pulled down a tray and sturdy plastic glasses that looked like they'd been around for years.

It had been a little over a day since Kendra had been taken away by ambulance and the parents and alumni had arrived. With the whirlwind of activity that came with all the adults, Harley had hardly had time to process that Kendra had drunk so much alcohol she'd poisoned herself. Probably most everyone felt the same. There seemed to be an underlying fake and frenetic enjoyment thing going. Like everyone was trying a little too hard to have a good time. Well, except for Mr. Hemphill. Meanwhile, Harley had seen Marlon with a hoe, bucket, goggles, long-sleeved shirt, and pants head behind the school buses into the tall grass at the edge of the forest. She assumed he was on a mission to find poison hemlock and she'd wanted to follow and get a good look at the plant herself, but Hope had been barking orders and she had to let it go. Some of the guys had ignored Hope and gone after Marlon, though. Harley had managed to ask Austin about it; he'd told her there was really nothing to see. The ground had been dug up and he thought Marlon had already taken care of the plants near the camp. Marlon had headed farther toward the woods, some of the guys following, so Hope had rung the dinner triangle in an effort to get them to return.

For all Kiley's comments on Austin being sweet on Harley, he didn't have a lot of time for her. He'd defected to Ella's posse and was currently hanging out with them, whatever his assigned job was.

Sunny Dae handed Harley the tray with three glasses of ice water and three of lemonade, the ice cubes tinkling merrily in the plastic glasses. Harley balanced the tray carefully as she turned back toward the lake, stepping carefully between the lodge and Bird's Foot cabin on her way toward the water. Suddenly, Esau came barreling around the corner.

"Whoa!" he said, reaching a hand to steady the wobbling tray.

"Whoa!" she gasped at the same time.

When the drinks were secured, they both breathed a sigh of relief. He shot her a sheepish look and said, "My dad's an ass, sometimes."

*Sometimes?*

"Let me take that." He leaned in and took the tray from her hands.

"I was taking these to the badminton players and whoever else wants some."

"We might need more when people see these."

"I'll head back and tell Sunny Dae. I saw you and some of the guys head out to see the poison hemlock. Austin said there wasn't any."

"Marlon had already taken care of it."

"Did he say he had? He didn't mention it when it came up at the lodge."

"He doesn't talk a lot, but he did stop and give a good hard look at the ground, like it wasn't what he expected. Then he told us all to go back. Shooed us. And went on toward the woods. The way he was dressed, we all decided we weren't prepared so we went back to the lodge rather than risk it."

"Smart move. Oh, I heard you spent some time at the commune with your family. My mom and aunt are checking it out right now."

His eyes flicked her way, assessing. "Why?"

Harley wasn't going to go into the whole surrogate thing, but here was someone who'd actually been there. "Mom just wanted to see it. Why were you there?"

"We went as a family. You stay in a yurt and join in prayer and live a simpler life for about a month. I didn't like being with my folks," he admitted. "It was a little close, so I slept in a smaller tent. My dad wanted to meet Pastor Rolff, who used to run the camp, but he's compromised now and his son's taken over. I think there used to be a lot more people living there, but now it's just . . ." He trailed off, smiling slightly.

"What?" she asked,

He glanced back toward the badminton group, then said, "I met someone there. It's why my parents came to the camp now. They're checking on me. I wanted to see her again and my dad wasn't going to let me. He thinks I'm going into the ministry."

"Thinks?"

"Thinks," he repeated firmly. "Lark knows my parents are here this weekend, but we're going to meet anyway. She needs to get away. Don't tell anyone," he added, a bit alarmed.

Harley held up her hands. "Never."

"It's just that if my dad found out—"

"I won't tell anyone. It's your thing. Go for it."

He gave her a big smile and Harley realized how careful and closed off he'd been at the camp.

"Have you seen her at all these past few weeks?" she asked.

"Once. Right at the start. I had to sneak out. We don't have great communication. Even though my parents are here, it's looser on her end with all the people from the commune helping out Hope with the camp. Not as much oversight at Haven."

"You make it sound like a prison."

"It is," he said.

They'd stopped at the edge of the lodge while the badminton players were in a tight back and forth. Finally, Esau's dad slammed the birdie at one of the alumni, who managed to whack it back where it sailed over Wendy's head. Caleb turned toward his wife, racquet raised.

"Dad!" Esau shouted in alarm.

Caleb held back, tossing the racquet to the ground. He came over to Esau, throwing Harley a look. "Finally," he said, grabbing a glass. "I see you got someone to help you."

"I offered, Dad."

When the others saw that there were drinks, groups of

people started heading their way. Harley turned back toward the kitchen and so did Esau, and with the help of Tina made sure everyone had their thirst quenched.


Jamie stepped off the trail into Haven Commune after walking several miles or so. It seemed like a long way. She felt beads of sweat on her forehead even though she'd walked fairly slowly so that Emma wouldn't have to hustle.

Emma waved a hand in front of her face and said, "I'm hot."

"Sticky weather. Supposed to get colder though."

"I'm still hot."

"Give it a few minutes." The trail melded into a dirt road that ran toward the commune one way and led to the main road outside both the camp and the commune the other. A split-rail fence rife with a clinging plant with purple flowers was a welcoming touch as they turned toward the commune. At least that's how Jamie took it.

There were no sidewalks in the central area between buildings, just dirt trails winding around old barn-like buildings and a collection of yurts on platforms that looked over the commune like sentinels. Beyond the dozen or so squat structures, which were centered around a rambling, two-story log lodge, were fields of vegetables, the plants in neat green rows. She saw raspberry vines on a trellis line that stretched toward the Coast Range. Lines of blueberry bushes marched beside them, filled with green to bluish-purple berries. There were also rows of fruit trees, and, at a glance, Jamie saw pear, apple, and plum. Her gaze slipped past the fields, and she stiffened as she saw the rabbit hutches. There were also brown and white and tan goats chewing straw and watching them.

"They have square eyes," said Emma, looking at the goats.

"Yeah, they have rectangular pupils," agreed Jamie, knowing what she meant.

A tan goat with tiny horns baaed at them. Emma walked up to it and they stared at each other, the goat inside a wire-fence enclosure. It cocked its head in much the same way Emma sometimes cocked hers.

"Hello."

They both looked over as a woman somewhere in her fifties moved toward them. She carried weight in her stomach and her hair was long and gray. She looked at Emma, then Jamie, then her eyes lingered back on Emma.

"Do I know you?" she asked Emma.

Jamie spoke up. "I'm Jamie Whelan—er, Haynes, now, actually—and this is my sister—"

"Emma," the woman said. "Emma Whelan."

Emma frowned at her.

Jamie said, "Are you Joy? Sunny Dae told us we should talk to you."

"You don't look like Joy," said Emma.

"I'm sure I don't. I'm older and rounder." She glanced behind herself, her welcoming smile tightening a bit. "Sunny Dae mentioned you might come by. Let's go to my place." She headed for one of the buildings near the vegetable garden. Jamie and Emma followed, climbing up the three wooden steps into a room with rough hardwood floors and a smattering of small carpets in bright colors. Jamie saw a bathroom and a bedroom off the main room. There was a sideboard with a microwave and an under-counter refrigerator. She estimated the space was about 400 square feet in total.

"Find a place to sit," Joy invited, pointing to a butterfly chair and a wooden, maple one that looked as if it might have belonged to a set at one time. "You're at the camp," she said lightly. "Did Hope know you were coming here?"

"I didn't check with her, exactly. She might have heard," said Jamie.

"Then we'd better get right to the point. My sister is very protective of us."

"Hope is your sister?" Jamie was surprised.

"My half sister. Our father is Rolff Ulland. I don't know how much you know about us, but he was our pastor for many years. I still think of him that way, but he only preaches occasionally now that he's . . . older."

"You were at Camp Love Shack?" asked Emma, still frowning. She clearly was having trouble with connecting the Joy of then, with the Joy of now.

"I was the director. I wanted it to be . . . a good camp." Jamie thought she'd been going to say something else and changed her mind.

"You smoked cigarettes," Emma said.

"I did a lot of things, once upon a time, but no more. Sunny Dae said you wanted to talk about something," Joy said to Jamie, as she glanced sideways out a pane glass window to the front clearing.

There was a strange feeling in the air. Something dangerous. Jamie tried to put her finger on it and failed. The place was bucolic, beautifully rustic, like a walk into a simpler past. Theo had said it was a great place to grow up and so had Mary Jo. Jamie had expected to feel the same, after she saw it. Instead, the hairs on the back of her neck had risen.

Emma regarded Joy in her unblinking way, which made the woman uncomfortable.

Jamie asked, "Do you remember a woman named Mary Jo . . . ? Um, I'm not sure about her maiden name, but her married is Kirshner."

Joy gave her a look. "Mary Jo left a long time ago."

"She's having Jamie and Cooper's baby," Emma put in.

"She's a surrogate for us," Jamie explained. She would have rather talked a bit more before offering up that nugget of information, but Emma didn't work that way.

"She's a lovely person," said Joy.

Through the window Jamie saw people moving into the central area of the community. "They're coming from lunch," Joy explained, seeing Jamie's interest.

"Mary Jo is a lovely person," Jamie agreed. "When I heard she grew up at Haven, I just wanted to know more."

Emma looked at Jamie hard. Jamie could feel herself start to sweat. She was bullshitting a little, looking for a way to ask more personal questions. Emma had picked up on her tone.

"Mary Jo left when she was betrothed to Stephen Kirshner. She always helped out a lot."

"Are her parents here?" asked Jamie.

"No, they both passed on. Would you like to see the gardens?"

"Sure. Yes," said Jamie. She wanted to get out of Joy's small abode as a sense of claustrophobia was overcoming her.

They walked across the main square, which was mostly a dusty wide street like in an old western movie. No saloon, though. Just gray-boarded buildings that had maybe been erected in the forties or fifties and then had been "dressed up" to look like they were older and with more character.

Jamie smiled at some of the other commune members as they followed Joy toward the farm. She saw young children with their mothers. One young woman was holding a six-month-old baby who smiled and gurgled as they went by. It tugged at Jamie's heartstrings.

*You're having a baby*, she reminded herself. There was still something so surreal about it, it brought her up short sometimes.

"I smell it," said Emma, sniffing.

"Smell what?" asked Jamie.

"The lake."

"The lake's right over there." Joy pointed toward the south, the direction in which they'd come. "Haven is hidden from it behind that narrow stretch of woods."

"Where's Cain?" Emma questioned.

Joy's reaction was remarkable. She stumbled around, trying to find words, but never really did. She looked sharply toward the lodge, blinking several times before she finally found her voice and rasped out, "Do you like blueberries? There are riper ones farther down the row." Then she stumbled forward toward the bushes, grabbing up a green plastic pail lying on the ground. Emma and Jamie followed suit.

*I didn't have sex with Cain but he was able . . .*

"Cain came from Haven?" Jamie whispered to Emma when Joy was way ahead of them.

She nodded.

"He told you that?"

She leaned in to whisper in Jamie's ear. "He came with the fog . . ."

"Do you know where your mother and aunt are?" Hope demanded.

Harley had moved down to the lake to help Marissa while Kiley had been relegated to badminton along with Niles. Or maybe she'd chosen it. Niles's mother and father—the man who still asked all kinds of questions, mercilessly embarrassing his son—and another couple had taken over badminton doubles.

Hope was barreling her way. Harley did a quick assessment and decided she would lie. "Nope," she answered.

Hope's eyes scanned the surrounding area. "They're not in the camp. I just came from the arts-and-crafts room."

Marissa, overhearing, suggested, "Maybe they went for a walk."

"I hope they listened to me to leave poison hemlock alone. I don't need another emergency," she snapped back, and then, as raucous laughter from the group of adults at the archery area filled the air, she glowered and headed in their direction.

"A lot of the weekenders aren't here. Maybe they're in their rooms," observed Marissa to Harley.

"Thanks for not saying where they are."

"Hope just seemed so worked up."

"Yeah. I don't know what that's about. I hope Mom and Aunt Emma get back soon."

Ten minutes later, Esau came over to Harley and said, "Just overheard Hope and Sunny Dae getting into it about your mom and Haven. Did your mom go there?"

"Sunny Dae told Mom it was no big deal."

"Hope's on her way there now."

Harley felt a flash of worry. She couldn't see why it would matter, but there were connections between Camp Fog Lake and Haven Commune she didn't quite understand.

"Lark's meeting me tonight. I don't want anything to screw that up."

"Where?"

He shook his head and put a finger to his lips as he backed away.

"What was that about?" Marissa asked. She'd seen Esau come over to Harley and now watched him hurry back up the hill toward the lodge.

"You're not going to try to meet Cam tonight, are you?" Harley was beginning to think she was the only one not sneaking out for a hookup.

"I told you he broke up with me!"

"But if you see that flash? Your signal? Whatever? Don't go."

Marissa just rolled her eyes and moved off, which Harley did not take as a good sign.


Jamie was still ruminating on Emma's comment about the fog as they finished picking the blueberries and returned from the garden with a half-full bucket. They'd dropped their lunch baskets at Joy's apartment and now were back there, and Joy was inviting them to forget their lunches and share a meal with the other members of the commune in the lodge instead.

"You can meet everyone. Mary Jo is well remembered here. Then you can go back to the camp."

It seemed like Joy wanted to get rid of them now. So much for Sunny Dae's assurances that Joy was the one to connect with.

Emma headed outside and toward the lodge, making the decision for both of them, even though Jamie was as eager to leave as much as Joy wanted them to go.

Haven Commune's central lodge was a log cabin inside and out. Whereas the camp's lodge had retained its old-timey style after refurbishment, Haven Commune's main building was rustic to the extreme with a rough-hewn plank table surrounded by benches that looked as if they would leave slivers in your legs. Even the bowls, plates, and flat-ware were carved from wood. Jamie's stomach seized as they served up a stew. If it had rabbit meat in it . . .

Emma gave the steaming bowl a hard look. "What is it?" she asked the woman across from her, who was flanked by a young twenty-ish woman and a boy of about ten.

"It's stew!" the boy said.

"What kind of stew?" asked Jamie cautiously.

The boy looked at his mother who said, "Pork."

Not much was said after that as everyone at the table went back to their meal. There were five rows of tables, about forty people all told. An older man was leaning heav-ily on the arm of a young woman with dark blond hair. Was that Rolff Ulland? Jamie wondered. She suspected so. She realized then that there were very few younger men in the group. It was mostly women and children. All the boys looked younger than eighteen.

Jamie dipped her wooden spoon into the stew heavy with vegetables, as did Emma, who'd stared at the utensils, bowls, and drinking cups with her frown that spoke of her confused thoughts, before following Jamie's example. Jamie managed to eat through about a quarter of her bowl. The stew was good, but she was still tense. Something felt wrong in Whoville.

*Or is that just because you want it to be? Like that will vindicate you somehow?*

Emma said loudly, "Where's Cain?"

Jamie sucked in a breath and glanced around quickly, but no one seemed to react. The older man asked crankily, "What did she say?"

It was Joy who answered him. She turned her head and said loudly, "Pastor Rolff. We have guests. Emma and Jamie. They are sisters, staying at Camp Fog Lake."

"Eh?"

The young woman who'd helped him to his seat quietly repeated Joy's words. He looked around the room and focused on Emma, then Jamie. He was white-haired and had startling blue eyes beneath thick, gray, bushy brows. His chin was pugnacious but he was thin to the point of emaciation.

"Camp Fog Lake." He gave a derisive snort, then asked peevishly, "Where's Josh?"

The girl leaned down again, but this time Jamie could make out what she said: "He's readying our rooms."

"Eh?"

"For our wedding."

"Where's your mother? Where's Rebecca?"

"Pastor Rolff, Rebecca is Josh's mother. She's gone to heaven, remember?" She lowered her voice more, as if aware Jamie could overhear her and said a few more things.

"My son is at school," said Rolff.

"No, sir. Josh is here. He's—"

Joy, her eyes on Jamie, purposely broke into her eavesdropping. "There's a wedding tomorrow. Pastor Josh is finally getting married. We're all looking forward to the celebration." Seeing that Emma had pushed aside her bowl, she added, "Now, if there isn't anything else, I should help with the preparations . . ."


Austin was flirting outrageously with one of the other counselors, who looked as if she hadn't decided to bite or not, as Harley made her way back to Foxglove to grab a thin sweater. It wasn't cold, but the gray skies almost made you feel that it was. "Fog tonight," someone had said, and the warning ran like wildfire through the counselors and CITs.

Harley stepped back out of the cabin's door, shrugging into her gray sweater. Spying her, Austin gave up his flirtation and hurried to intercept her path to the bathroom. She stopped short in front of the sheet-metal mirror.

"Hey," he said. "You see Moron checking the ground behind the buses? No deadly, poisonous plants." He brought his fingers to his lips as if he were chewing his nails. "Oh, my, oh, my."

"*Marlon* went into the woods to see if there was more. Somebody had already dug up the ground by the buses."

"You believe that bullshit? C'mon . . ."

She'd been half inclined to tell him about the mirror, as it was on her mind, but luckily she didn't. She wanted to tell Greer anyway. See what he thought of it.

"Hey, did you see Hope tear outta here? Had a walkie with her and headed up to Suicide Ledge."

Harley had an uneasy feeling about Hope's intentions. "Maybe going to the commune."

"And leaving us here all on our lonesome?" His eyes danced and she regarded him intently.

"You on something?" she asked.

"If only. One of the 'adults' did leave on a booze run. I heard 'em talking. I'm just in a party mood now that Hope's gone."

"She'll be back."

"Like she's any kind of chaperone." He snorted.

"Kendra was drunk on her ass and coulda killed herself. We all know she was going out to the woods and meeting some guy. We followed her, me and Niles. Way back there." He swept an arm toward the dense woods behind the maintenance buildings and in the general direction of the main road. It was the same area that Marissa had said Cam had pitched his tent.

"She was about as stealthy as a herd of buffaloes," he went on. "But then *he* popped up and stared at us like he could see us, even though it was really dark and we were way back."

"Kendra's guy? How do you know he was staring at you, then?" Harley had decided he was making it up. If he'd been following Kendra, he might just as well have seen Marissa, but he didn't act like it.

"It was a vibe. This whole area's haunted. Niles almost shit himself. We didn't even try to hide. We just turned on our flashlights and ran. Kendra stumbles out in the morning and passes out, and Esau and Lendel go nuts, and so we all act like something's happened to her, but it's just alcohol poisoning."

"Alcohol poisoning is serious."

"Not as serious as poison hemlock," he rejoined, lifting his brows.

Harley dismissed him. He was one of those people who always had to have the juicy gossip and the last word. Even so, Emma's recitation about poison hemlock came to mind. And she'd said Joy was the one who'd told her about the weed.

# Chapter 21

Emma decided she'd had enough. She swung her legs over the bench and said, "I'm going. Bad things happen at the camp. I don't want bad things to happen to Harley."

"Wait. Emma. Please wait," said Jamie.

"I will be outside," she told her.

Joy's voice followed her outside. "Hope will make sure nothing bad happens to anyone. She's very capable."

Emma didn't like being at Haven Commune. She needed to be with Harley.

She walked back to Joy's place and stood by the front porch, waiting for Jamie.

She could almost remember being with Cain behind the mirror.

*I love you, Emma.*

He'd been ripping down her pants.

*I love you, Emma.*

"He was lying," she said aloud. Donovan had lied, too, but he wasn't like Cain. Cain was . . .

She couldn't think of the right word, but she remembered

the feeling. She'd been a little scared. She'd pushed him away, but he wasn't like Donovan. Cain was . . .

"Mean. A mean boy."

"Excuse me . . ."

Emma looked up and saw the girl who had been with the old guy, hurrying up to her. She was looking behind herself. Running forward, but looking behind.

"You could run into something," Emma warned her.

"You're going back to the camp?" She was breathless. "Can I give you something?"

"What?"

"A note. For Esau. Do you know who he is? He's one of the counselors."

"Eee-saw . . ."

"That's right."

"Is he a friend of Harley's?"

"I don't know Harley." She pulled a note from a hidden pocket in her dress and held it out to Emma. "Please take it. Don't tell anyone. *Don't read it.* Don't let anyone see it but Esau. Please."

Emma accepted the note.

"*Hurry*," she whispered, then ran away without saying anything more. She glanced over her shoulder and changed from a run to a fast walk. Joy and Jamie came out of the lodge as the girl passed by them. She waved and smiled.

Emma looked at the folded piece of paper. She tucked it into her pants pocket.

Jamie was glad to see Emma had waited for her outside Joy's apartment. They collected their lunch baskets.

Joy asked Emma sharply, "Were you speaking to Lark?"

"Lark?" Emma repeated.

Jamie had seen Emma slip a folded piece of paper into her pocket. Where had she gotten that? Her eyes followed the young woman who'd been helping Pastor Rolff as she disappeared into another building. Her big smile and wave had seemed to catch Joy's attention. Had something transpired between the young woman and Emma? Something slightly secretive? Whatever it was, Emma was a truth teller, and she would confess to Joy unless there was some distraction . . .

"Joy, excuse me. I meant to ask. Is Josh your brother? You said Rolff was your father."

"Half brother," she said, her eyes still on Emma.

"So, he's Hope's full brother."

"Yes."

"And he's the pastor for the community. Having taken over from his father?"

Joy finally swung her full attention back to Jamie. "Pastor Rolff is still considered the man in charge of us."

"Where are the men?" asked Emma.

"Pardon me?"

"There are no men."

Joy paused for a moment, clearly searching for words. Jamie realized Emma was right. She'd seen no males at all except for the children and a few teens. "Most of the men move on and find jobs in the outside world."

"The outside world?" repeated Emma, frowning.

"I think she means where the rest of us live," Jamie explained.

"There's Hope," Emma said.

Jamie almost questioned what she meant, but then she saw that Hope was walking briskly their way from the direction of the trail.

Spying Jamie, Emma, and Joy, Hope's lips tightened and she aimed for them. Jamie looked between the two sisters as Joy, who was a good fifteen years older, gave her sister a tight nod. There was a resemblance in the shape of their faces and right now they both looked slightly pissed.

"You could have told me you were leaving," Hope scolded Jamie.

"I thought you knew. Is there a schedule for us? I didn't see one."

Joy said, "We just finished lunch."

Hope looked surprised. "Was everyone . . . there?"

"Lark sat with our father."

"I heard there's a wedding here tomorrow," Jamie said to Hope. "Your brother and . . . Lark?" Jamie was doing some estimating in her head and thought there could be a decade or two between the girl and Hope's brother.

As if reading her mind, Hope said, "We've been waiting for Josh to marry. It's taken a long time."

"Why?" asked Emma.

"Sometimes it just does," Hope practically snapped. Hearing herself, she added, "He was in love with someone, but it didn't work out. She . . . died."

Emma said, "Was it Fern?"

Joy's head swiveled her way. "You know her name?"

Emma looked back at her. "I was at the camp."

"Oh. Yes, that's right . . ." Joy murmured.

Jamie regarded her sister with misgivings. There was tension here that she didn't think was good for any of them.

Joy looked back toward the lodge, but her dreamy gaze said she was seeing something internal. "Yes, the wedding's tomorrow night, unless something happens."

"Nothing's going to happen," Hope assured her. To Jamie and Emma, she said, "Let's head back. Lots of stuff going on at the camp, and I don't want to be away too long. I hope Joy showed you around. Haven is such a wonderful retreat. A place for people to reset their lives."

"Uh-huh," Jamie murmured.

"We need our lunch baskets," said Emma.

"I'll get them." Joy headed inside her rooms.

"Why are you tense?" Emma asked Hope.

Hope choked a bit and Jamie swallowed a smile. Emma's forthrightness took some getting used to. "I'm not tense, I'm out of breath from that long, fast walk. We'd better go. People will be looking for me. Sunny Dae's taken care of lunch, but there's lots to do."

"Did you come to Haven just to get us?" asked Jamie.

"Well, yes." She hesitated a few moments, as if unsure whether to add more. Eventually, she said, "I know you came to Haven looking for answers about Mary Jo Kirshner."

"How did you know?" asked Jamie, a bit surprised.

"I know Mary Jo. We keep in contact."

"She's Jamie and Cooper's surrogate," said Emma.

Hope nodded. "She told me. She's a wonderful choice."

Joy returned and gave them back their baskets. She said goodbye, her gaze lingering on Emma, and Hope hustled them back toward the trail.

"I don't like to talk a lot about Haven," Hope admitted as they began walking along the lake, the trail heading inexorably upward as it rimmed the water, running along the top of the long cliff that separated the commune from the camp. "It's a beautiful place. A wonderful place. But our family has had some issues, as every family does. I'm sure Mary Jo has filled you in."

*Not at all*, Jamie thought, but offered a noncommittal "mmmm," hoping Hope would continue as she really wanted to hear where this was going.

Emma, as ever, had no such reservations. "What issues?" she asked.

"My father was married to Cornelia, Joy's mother, and Cornelia developed early dementia. She's gone now, but she was diagnosed with Huntington's, which is a fatal, genetic disease that affects the mind and motor skills . . . just about everything. Cornelia suffered terribly; it's a blessing she's gone now. Before my father's own mental deterioration, he believed Joy had inherited the disease from her mother, though Joy has never shown any signs of it. But my father became . . . obsessed, I guess you'd say. God's will and all that, but he didn't want it in his family. He married my mother and had me and Josh . . . and Adam.

"Joy lost a daughter. My father thought it was because of the disease. As a means to take that sting away, he put Joy in charge of Camp Fog Lake. The Luft-Shawks had started Haven Commune with my father, back in the late sixties. They're about ten years older than my father and they were happy to transfer management to Joy, and Joy managed the camp very well. I think my father would have given the camp to her. He'd already bought out the Luft-Shawks, but you know the rest. The 'alleged' murder/suicide closed the camp down, so Joy came home to Haven."

"Why did the baby die?" asked Emma.

Hope was thrown off stride for moment, then said, "Just one of those terrible things at birth. I know Sunny Dae told you to talk to Joy, but you're better off talking to me."

Jamie wasn't so sure, but all she really wanted was more background on Mary Jo. "When did Mary Jo leave Haven?"

"Years ago. She and Stephen were both young . . . and in love. Mary Jo was betrothed to my brother, first," she admitted, "but she fell in love with Stephen and Pastor Rolff, my father, blessed the union."

"Stephen's family is part of the commune as well?"

"We knew them. They left shortly after Stephen and Mary Jo."

Jamie sensed there was more to that story as well.

"A lot of names," said Emma.

"Yes, well, we're a close-knit group," Hope responded, kind of a non sequitur. "And you heard that Josh and Lark are getting married, praise the Lord."

Jamie thought that last part sounded a bit sardonic. Though her father was the elder pastor, Hope seemed anything but devout. Her tone was brittle and tight.

"Your last name's Newell," said Emma.

"I kept my mother's name."

Jamie wondered if that was to hide her connection with Ulland, a name inextricably bonded to Haven Commune.

They'd reached Suicide Ledge and, of unspoken accord, stopped short, gazing over the dark green water far below. The cliff's edge broke off abruptly along a natural stone slab that knifed downward to the lake.

It was Emma who broke the brief silence that had descended. "Fern died here, but Ryan didn't kill her."

"The sheriff's department concluded it was a murder/suicide," Hope corrected her. "Christopher apparently covered her with ashes as some kind of homage before he killed himself, too."

"Ryan didn't kill anyone."

"If you're trying to keep the lurid folklore surrounding the camp and commune alive, that's the way to do it," Hope answered tartly before resuming their hike toward Camp Fog Lake.

Jamie shared a look with Emma, whose face was a deep frown as they followed after her, away from the crest of the trail.

Donovan tramped along the lane toward the camp, sweating, his arms tiring under the weight of the two bags of liquor. Jesus. Couldn't they park a little closer? This rutted piece of shit road went on forever. It was hell carrying the bags. But nobody else had jumped up to join him in bringing in the booze. If he and Rona were going to make it through the rest of the weekend, they sure as hell needed refreshments, libations of the kind the camp wouldn't supply, so he'd volunteered.

He saw movement at the periphery of the woods. Was that a guy? Long pants?

"Hey," he called out. "You wanna help me here?"

For an answer the dude melted into the shadows.

"Guess not," Donovan said in disgust. He kept looking to where the guy had disappeared as he trudged along. Something familiar about him.

"I know you," he called into the forest. "C'mon pal. Lend a hand."

No answer.

Ah, fuck him.


"Let's go down to the shore," Rona announced, tipping back her water bottle, nearly missing her mouth on the first attempt.

Brooke felt the beginnings of a headache. She and Rona were in the archery area, neither one of them trying to shoot at the target since Donovan had returned with three large bottles of Grey Goose vodka and one of Captain Morgan's rum. The "stash" was behind the target in a shallow hole and covered by small pine limbs. Not exactly a secret, especially the way Donovan and Rona were swilling it, but so far they hadn't been caught out. For all Rona's worries about Kiley she was leaving her daughter alone. Or maybe that was productive parenting. Rona was here, she could see Kiley was all right, everything was cool.

Brooke had refused most of the liquor Donovan had smuggled in after an apparently long and exhausting walk to and from his vehicle, to hear him tell it, and a drive to the liquor store. It was like being back in high school, trying to hide their drinking, but Hope wasn't around to give them detention and Tina and Warren were with other groups. Maybe the counselors or CITs would tell on them, but so far, their misdeeds seemed to still be under wraps.

"I'm not going to the lake," said Brooke. Her repulsion to Fog Lake had only intensified since she'd arrived. She'd thought she could handle it, but as the hours wore on the anxiety she'd tamped down had risen up again.

Had Donovan really cleaned out the canoe? He must've.

How else would he know? She was furious at his attempts to dig, dig, *dig* at them. She'd told Rona about what he'd said and she'd just thrown up her hands and snarled, "I knew he saw us!"

Ugh. She needed to get all of this out of her head. She'd taken a sleeping pill last night. Nothing too major, but as the sky had darkened she'd felt full-blown paranoia just outside her focus. If she let it, it would take her over. She'd listened to Rona probe Wendy with questions and Wendy deflect them until the pill took effect. She slept like the dead and woke with a slight dullness. She'd eaten very little breakfast. Lunch had been an array of sandwiches set out for the taking: egg salad, pressed turkey, or, for the vegetarians and vegans, peanut butter, which she'd yet to partake of. She'd made the mistake of drinking some of Donovan's smuggled vodka supply, mainly to be part of the group, and now was suffering the consequences and condemning herself for being such a follower.

Wendy and Caleb were nowhere to be seen. Brooke had realized Caleb had been trying to hustle her away all day, so maybe he'd finally gotten his wish. In an aside to Brooke, Rona had said that Wendy had alluded to Caleb needing his "fix" every day, which apparently was sex with Wendy. "I bet it's kinky sex," Rona had added. "Whips and chains, maybe a hair shirt."

"You're bad," Brooke had told her.

"You're thinking it, too," she shot back, which, well, maybe was a little bit true. Caleb had been serious and humorless in high school, but he was nearly unbearable now. His only saving grace was he'd hung on to his good looks, but hell, that only got you so far and then it was over.

"I'm going to lie down." Brooke left them and returned to Foxglove. Luckily, she was alone. She thought about another sleeping pill but it was pretty early still. She stretched out on her bunk and dozed, but her traitorous mind had been fully awakened since she'd returned to Camp Love Shack . . .

* * *

She, Rona, and Wendy had left the cabin together after everyone was asleep and sneaked to the edge of the woods. Brooke had actually snagged a joint from Owen before their fumbling exploits behind the mirror, and they all planned to indulge that night.

But Wendy had other plans. "I'll be back," she told them.

"You're not going to meet that guy, are you?" demanded Rona.

"Of course not. I'm back with Caleb. I just need to pee."

"Yeah. Sure . . ." Rona waved her away.

Brooke was totally stoned and so was Rona. They stretched out on the ground outside the cabins on the dusty rise above the lake, staring into a black sky with a sliver of a moon that was playing tag with dark clouds.

"Donovan and I had sex," said Rona. "Did you and Owen?"

"Sort of."

Brooke fell asleep and woke up cold, alone, and sober. Well, she thought she was alone, but Rona wasn't far away, as it turned out, leaning over Donovan, his hands in her hair and pushing her head down, trying to get her to go down on him. Rona wasn't going for it, and there was a sharp bark of anger from him before he jumped to his feet, and stalked naked away, holding his shorts.

"Fucker," Rona spat after him, then stumbled back toward Brooke.

Sometime afterward she realized that tendrils of fog seemed to be wisping off the lake, moving toward them.

"I'm going back in," Brooke said, staggering to her feet.

Rona was still muttering what an asshole Donovan was, half crying. "I'm going to the lake," she declared.

"The fog's coming. I'm not going down there."

Rona didn't listen and was swallowed up so fast Brooke thought she'd blinked and missed it. But no . . . she was just gone.

*"Hhhheeeellllppp!"*

A shriek of terror whispered through the fog. Wendy. Not from the woods. From the lake. Brooke stumbled blindly toward the water arms out in front of her, unable to see.

*The sentient fog.*

It was bullshit, for sure, but it felt almost real. Panic took hold. *Where were her friends?*

And then suddenly Wendy was there. Right in front of her. At the lake's lapping shore. Beneath some guy who was pumping away at her even while she was flailing her arms and legs. Raping her. His hands around her neck and squeezing.

The fog descended. One moment they were there. The next they were enveloped in the dense gray curtain.

Brooke ran blindly forward. She could hear them.

And then the fog drifted and Rona was there, her hands in his hair, yanking with all her strength.

Wendy's palms were pressed on the man's chest, pushing hard against him. His teeth were bared and he was thrusting with force. He reached around and grabbed at Rona, throwing her onto the rocky shore.

Rona struggled to her feet, but he was suddenly up, naked and wild-eyed. He charged Rona and tackled her and she went down hard, the man atop her.

Brooke didn't think. She jumped onto his back. Dug her nails into his thick neck. Wanted to kick and maim and kill.

He flipped over, smashing her beneath him into the dirt and rocks and mud at the water's edge. The lake water came up and Brooke swallowed a mouthful, spitting and choking. Rona was atop him now. Her hands clawed for his neck and she squeezed and squeezed while Brooke struggled to get out from underneath him.

*SMASH!*

Brooke felt the impact through his body to hers. Her head was underwater. She couldn't *breathe*!

*SMASH!*

His whole body shuddered. She pushed him aside, her head surfacing, gasping for air. Rona was still astride him, her hands losing their grip on his neck as his hands clamped around her throat. Her fingers pried at his, but her eyes were filled with terror.

*SMASH!*

The rock hit him in the face one last time and he finally collapsed. Wendy reared back to hit him again but she lost her footing and went down. Brooke, soaked to the skin, wriggled out from under him and crab-walked away from his inert body, half in, half out of the lake. Rona, on her knees, held her own throat and dragged in whistling gasps of air.

The three of them stood, shaking, freezing, crying.

"Is he dead?" Brooke whispered. He was lying still, faceup, staring toward the sky, his legs in the dark, lapping water.

Rona whispered, "Get the canoe." Cleared her throat, ordered: "We have to get rid of the body . . ."

"Noooo . . ." moaned Wendy.

But they all did as Rona suggested. And when they were rowing out across the lake, Brooke thought she saw a flashlight beam outside their cabin. A figure. Emma?

"She knows," said Rona, but they kept on their task anyway.


Now, all these years later, Brooke pressed the heels of her hands to her eyes and wished the memory back into its cage at the back of her mind. They should have told Joy what they'd done, or the police, or somebody. Did Emma remember? Even if she did, her faulty thinking could be their saving grace. But did she want that? To keep this secret that Brody so desperately wanted her to tell him about?

Brody . . . Lukey . . . her life was a mess. Maybe they were legitimate in killing him. He'd attacked and raped Wendy and he'd attacked her and Rona, too, though that was in self-defense.

"Who is he?" Rona had whispered through her teeth that night to Wendy, who was uncontrollably crying and shaking as they rowed the body to the center of the lake. "*Who is he?*"

"Cain," she'd whispered back. "Cain . . ."


He stalked silently through the thick woods, backpack on his shoulders along with a quiver of arrows. His shoes were moccasins with thick rubber soles. He wore forest-green pants and a tan shirt from Under Armour. Thought about camo, but that would be remembered and standing still, his clothes blended in, were just about as good and unremarkable.

His ears were alert for all sounds. It was dangerous to be out in the daylight, but it gave his whole body a buzz of anticipation. He'd had to hold back with all the tramping around yesterday after the drunken slut had escaped—luckily they hadn't found anything. He'd thought he'd taken care of her, but she'd spit out half the poison hemlock he'd had her take. She hadn't been quite as drunk as she'd maintained. It had been a sly act on her part. She'd wanted sex so badly that she'd pretended not to know what she was doing, but it was all an act.

Shame coursed through him and he bared his teeth. He'd underestimated her. When she started to feel the poison she'd cracked a stick on his head and shrieked and stumbled away. He'd momentarily seen stars and would have gone after her, but she was heading straight for that damn pup tent that idiot had erected. He'd worried she would stumble into the pit and it wasn't meant for her. Or run into the idiot who'd set up shop in the woods to see his girlfriend.

The camp was his hunting ground. No one else's.

He hadn't expected the drunken slut to live as long as she had, but she would die soon enough.

The thought that she might live through the poison sent an icy chill through him, settling in his scrotum. He flexed his hands, encased in thin plastic gloves, and automatically touched the pocket where the chopped-up pieces of poison hemlock were wrapped in several layers of Ziploc bags. She didn't know who he was. She thought she did, but she didn't. But if she survived and told what she knew?

The plastic bags made a little scritching sound as he navigated slowly through the underbrush. The noise was problematic, but he couldn't afford the slight chance that he might inhale some of the chopped poison's dust. He also had a vial of its boiled-down essence.

Now, as he drew closer to the pit, he could feel adrenaline course through him, replacing the icy chill. It stirred his cock like it always did. Adrenaline fed him. Adrenaline and sex.

He threw a glance in the direction of the camp, though it was screened by the dense woods. A smile split his lips. He'd already walked among the parents and alumni at the camp, hiding in plain sight. The danger of it heated his blood. This gathering was a godsend.

*Not a godsend,* he corrected himself. *God is no part of this. This is war. And opportunity . . . and retribution . . .*

He moved unerringly to the tree with the poison ivy wrapped lovingly around its bole and carefully moved the shiny green leaves at the trees' base aside. He lightly brushed back the dirt and small sticks he'd covered the urn with, making sure it was still there, untouched. He felt the top of the lid and was reassured. He covered it back up and then moved to the pit. Almost done . . .

His gaze tracked once more toward the camp as if pulled

by a magnet. There were girls there, and women. They'd come to him and he was ready for them.

One by one he would make them pay. One by one he would makė love to them and slip the poison in their mouths. While they resisted and tried to scream he would squeeze their windpipes shut and watch their eyes silently plead and beg until the light went out of them.

Then he would pick up the urn and pour hemlock ashes over them.

# Chapter 22

It was about 2:00 p.m. before September could connect with the owner of Greenscape Landscaping, Franklin Lerner. The business was open on Saturday, sort of, but the offices were closed and only workmen were coming and going from a large warehouse full of equipment for their residential and commercial landscaping jobs. September could certainly wait until Monday to follow up on Deena's information about Brooke Daniels and Luke Lerner, the supposedly underage boyfriend, but she didn't want to wait. Brody Daniels was nowhere to be found and Brooke hadn't been back to her apartment, and September wanted to know why R. J. Everly had stooped to amplifying dirt on Brooke, whether credible or not.

She'd gone into the station to research their home address and phone number as George was off for the weekend as well, both of them on call if something happened over the weekend that required a detective. At work, she'd guiltily remembered a report she needed to finish, so she worked on that a while, then Jake had called and wanted to know when she was coming home and she'd dropped everything to be with him for a few hours.

Now she was making a house call on the Lerners. She could have phoned, but nothing took the place of a face-to-face. She didn't know what she expected to learn . . . maybe nothing . . . but she wanted to meet Luke's parents and maybe him as well.

The Lerners lived in a nice, two-story traditional home with a jungle of trees, bushes, and flowers in their front yard. She walked up a path that was flanked by rhododendrons, their flowers just losing their petals, the ground beneath her feet a carpet of red, orange, and fuchsia. Towering laurels encroached the nearer she approached, making her automatically hunch in her shoulders.

She pushed the bell, the button the center of a copper daisy. A trill of notes sounded inside, followed by the yapping of a small dog. There were three glass panels in the country-style door, and September watched the little white fluff ball run down the stairs and to the door, barking its head off.

A woman came from the back of the house. "Stop, Bijou. Stop!" She flapped a hand at it, then opened the door the length of a chain. Bijou tried to stick her head in the gap and was pushed back by a firm foot. "Yes?" the woman asked a bit impatiently.

"Hello, I'm Detective Rafferty with the Laurelton Police Department. I was wondering if you—"

"I told Franklin to call you, but I didn't think he did. This is about Brooke Daniels." She didn't wait for clarification, just scooped up the still barking dog, shut the door, and released the chain. Bijou was clambering to get out of her arms but she must've been used to the dog because she held it in a death grip. "Come in, come in."

"Are you Valerie?"

"Yes, I am."

"Your husband didn't call me, but I am here about the internet claims against Mrs. Daniels."

"Internet claims," she repeated with a sneer. "She's a sexual predator. Luke!" she suddenly yelled, looking toward the ceiling. "I'll get him downstairs. *Luke!* Franklin's out in the back. Just a moment."

She turned and huffed back the way she'd come, toward the kitchen, September believed. She heard a door open and then Valerie yelled, "*Franklin! Get back in here! The police are here!*"

A teenaged boy moved reluctantly down the stairs. His face was all sharp angles that would probably smooth out as he grew older. Like his mother, his hair was dark and he had nice hazel eyes with thick lashes. He was currently working on a major zit on his chin, which sort of spoiled the effect.

He threw a glance toward the kitchen and said, "Nothing happened between me and Mrs. Daniels . . . Brooke. I know everybody says that, but it's not true. Nothing happened. That'd be *too weird*."

Valerie Lerner steamed back. Whereas her son was lean, she was rounded and her dark hair flatly absorbed all the light, clearly dyed.

Franklin Lerner appeared a few moments later, wearing jeans with dark smudges at the knees and a wrinkled work shirt. "Gotta do some watering. Hasn't rained enough," he said by way of introduction. He spent a moment or two deciding whether to shake hands and then gave up and wiped them on his jeans.

Valerie said to September, "Have you seen what's being said?" Her chin wobbled a bit.

"I'm not here to adjudicate the internet accusations. I'm looking for Mrs. Daniels and I haven't been able to find her. I thought maybe she left a message at work."

"She's fired. We fired her," Valerie stated flatly.

"She was home on Thursday," Luke piped up.

Both of his parents stared at him in disbelief. "You talked to her?" his mother managed to spit out.

"I went to see her," he said belligerently. "Gavin took me."

"*You went to see her?*"

September stepped forward automatically to shield Luke, who shrank back at his mother's shriek.

"Val," Franklin admonished.

"I don't know where she is, though," Luke said, a tad regretfully.

Valerie turned on September. "You have to arrest her! She's a menace. A sick, spoiled *predator*. I can't believe this. Luke, go to your room. And Gavin's not welcome in this house anymore!"

As Luke ran up the stairs, Franklin said, "Luke says nothing happened, so I don't know why we wouldn't believe him."

"You don't see he's covering for her?" Valerie snapped.

"We've both known Brooke a while. She's not like that."

"You men. You're so gullible," she fumed.

September saw that she'd stepped into an ongoing battle. The Lerners clearly didn't know anything about Brooke Daniels's current whereabouts, and she also sensed the two men were telling the truth while Valerie Lerner was only intent on sticking to her version of the narrative, whether fact or fiction. Maybe jealousy was a factor here? It was hard to tell.

What she did know was that she was going to redirect her attention back to the Glory to God school and see where that led. It was likely Brooke and Brody would be home at the end of the holiday weekend.

Jamie touched her sister's arm before Emma could open the door to Foxglove cabin. Emma immediately turned to stare at her, as Jamie rarely touched her sister without warning her first.

"Did Lark give you a note?" she asked, her eyes following Hope's progress to the lodge.

"How did you know?"

"I saw you put it in your pocket."

"I can't read it. I have to give it to Eee-saw."

"Esau?" Emma had a way of dragging out the syllables as she committed things to memory. "Maybe we should look at the note because—"

"No."

"But Lark's getting married tomorrow. It might be important." A secret missive, Jamie thought.

"It will be important to Eee-saw. He will read it." She paused, then asked, "Which one is he?"

"I'm not sure. Talk to Harley," Jamie suggested.

"Okay." The matter was settled as far as Emma was concerned.

Harley helped push a canoe into the lake, steadying the older couple inside as they awkwardly thrust their oars in the water. She'd already helped fish out one woman who'd swallowed enough lake water to send her to Sunny Dae and the area they used as an infirmary near the arts-and-crafts room.

Straightening up, she pressed a hand to her lower back. She'd been bent over so long her muscles were aching. She'd been aiding people in and out of the canoes for several hours, having been relieved at badminton by Kiley. Marissa had also helped load up canoes for a while, but now she was hanging around by the shoreline with Niles. Their togetherness had caught the attention of Kiley, whose eyes were not on the people playing badminton but on Marissa and Niles, who were now walking the edge of the lake, lost in conversation. Harley knew Marissa had just found a willing ear; she'd overheard her telling Niles how she'd been broken up with, and he'd told her how much that sucked. But their bonding was worrisome, nevertheless. You just never knew where these things could lead, and if Kiley felt threatened, if that's what this was really about, then anything—

"Hey."

Harley startled at the sound of Greer's voice behind her. She turned slowly and he was standing a few feet away, looking at her.

"Hey, yourself. What are you doing?"

"Taking a break from poison-hemlock hunting. Actually, Marlon sent me back and told me to help out with the alumni."

"And parents," said Harley.

"And parents," he agreed.

"Did you find any poison hemlock?"

"Not near the camp."

They stood staring at each other for a long minute. Harley was the first to turn away and she could feel her face heat. "There was something I wanted to show you," she said. "You know that mirror by the entrance to the boys' bathroom?"

"The sheet-metal one."

"Have you ever noticed how it's nailed all around it? Maybe it's just the way it's hung, but my Aunt Emma said something about being behind it, so I don't know. Think there's something there?"

"She said she was behind the mirror?"

"That's what it sounded like. She'd didn't mean the boys' bathroom. She acted like it was a hook-up space, or something." The conversation was heading into uncomfortable territory, at least for Harley, who was remembering several places they'd hooked up for some intense making out themselves.

"I'll take a look at it." He started to turn.

"Wait. Maybe later? I kinda don't want everybody to see."

"I won't open it up without you," he said lightly. "I'm just going to look."

Harley automatically started to protest that that wasn't what she meant, but actually it was, so she clamped her mouth shut.

"Meet me there when everyone else is at dinner?" He lifted his brows as he moved off.

"Sure."

Now, what was that all about? If she didn't know better, she might think she'd given him the excuse he'd been looking for to be alone with her.

Marissa appeared a few moments later sans Niles. "What are you smiling about?" she asked.

"Nothing." But the smile still stayed on her lips even while she tried to hide it.

*Oh, girl, you've got it bad.*

Emma was on her way to find Harley when the Three Amigos got in her way. They were standing outside Foxglove, deep in conversation. Emma couldn't reach the door without getting them to move, so she stopped short.

"I don't give a flying fuck," Rona was saying. "He wants to screw every underage girl in this camp, be my guest. I'll just call the police . . . the sheriff, whoever . . . and he can explain it to them."

"Rona, you've just had too much to drink," said Wendy.

"Donovan isn't going after underage girls." Brooke's voice was angry, Emma thought. She didn't remember Brooke getting angry when she was at the camp before.

"Oh, so now you're the expert?" Rona glared at her. "Did you tell Wendy? Of course not." She put a finger to her lips and said, "Shhh."

"You're drunk," said Wendy.

"You're sure handling this well," Rona snapped back at

her. "We aided and abetted, but *you* killed him. And Donovan cleaned the canoe!"

"Shut up, Rona!" That was from Brooke, but Wendy said something similar. They all looked around and saw Emma.

"Sorry," said Brooke. Her face looked kind of white. Wendy murmured something, too. Rona stood by, silent. She stared hard at Emma.

"Do you remember that night?" Rona demanded.

Emma thought Rona might be getting mad. "I have to go inside."

"You do, don't you? When the fog came in, and Wendy was screaming, you were watching us."

"You don't have to tell your whole life story," said Emma.

"Rona, stop." That was from Wendy and she really sounded mad. Her face was red and blotchy. Maybe she was going to cry.

"Leave her alone," ordered Brooke.

"Sometimes you *do* have to tell your life story," Rona argued. "What happened to you, Emma? You got hit in the head? Somebody hurt you? And now you can't remember?"

"Stop!" cried Brooke.

"*Excuse me.*"

The hard voice was Harley's and as Emma turned, her niece stepped forward. She was mad, too. The maddest. In a mean voice, she said, "Emma was attacked, but she's fine now. Better than fine."

Emma said, "My head hit the mantel and—"

"I got this, Emma," Harley interrupted. She stepped between Emma and the Three Amigos. "My aunt doesn't need to talk to you about a traumatic incident that changed the course of her life."

"Of course not," said Brooke, looking at the ground.

"Absolutely," said Wendy. She sniffed, but those tears were in her eyes.

Rona lifted her hands. "Okay, I'm sorry. I'm sorry."

"Glad to hear it." Harley clamped her mouth shut. Emma thought she wanted to say a lot more.

The Three Amigos moved off and Emma heard Brooke angrily ask Rona, "What the hell is wrong with you?" before she couldn't hear them anymore.

"What the hell?" muttered Harley. "Where's Mom?" Emma pointed to the lodge where Jamie had gone to talk to Hope some more. "I don't know what those three women were after, but it *really* pisses me off."

Emma decided against saying "No swearing." Instead she told Harley, "Rona knows I heard them. But the fog was in the way. Something happened and they weren't friends anymore."

Harley was leading the way to Foxglove cabin now that the Three Amigos were gone. "They're just amazingly rude."

"Try not to be mad."

"Impossible, Em. I am so, so mad."

"I need to find Eee-saw."

Harley looked at her. "Why? I didn't know you knew him. Did you ask Wendy?"

"I have a message for him."

"For *Esau*?"

Emma pulled the note out of her pocket, but didn't hand it to Harley. She thought Harley might want to read it like Jamie had. "I can't read it and neither can you."

"Where did you get it? Oh. The commune?" She sucked in a breath. "Is it from Lark?"

"How did you know?" Emma marveled.

"Esau said she was his girlfriend."

Emma frowned. "She's getting married tomorrow to Josh. There's a wedding."

"Are you sure? Esau met her when his family was at the commune for a retreat of some kind."

"It's a wonderful place to reset and it has a good reputation."

"Did you hear that somewhere?"

"It's kind of confusing." Emma was starting to feel unsure and that made her chest tight.

"I'll ask Mom. I don't know where Esau is, but we could look for him." Harley was staring at the note in Emma's hand. "For his eyes only, huh? Okay. C'mon. We've got some time before dinner."

Jamie stood outside the back door of the lodge kitchen, thinking. She wanted to talk to Sunny Dae again. Hope was prickly and lying to her, or at least omitting information, and Joy had been . . . what? Careful and anxious? For a place that was supposed to be a respite from the troubles of the world, Haven Commune sure wasn't filling the bill.

Sunny Dae and her helpers would be preparing dinner. Jamie was pretty sure she wouldn't be welcomed, but maybe she could make a date with her out from under Hope's eagle eye, possibly after the meal was finished and the kitchen cleaned. Sunny Dae would likely be heading back down the trail toward the commune, but Jamie thought she might be able to walk with her partway. Feel her out about Haven. She knew she was being somewhat obsessive in her quest to know more about Mary Jo, but there were buried secrets. She could feel it.

She was almost to the edge of the cabin closest to the lodge, Bird's Foot, when she heard Hope's voice filter from the kitchen; the back door wasn't completely closed. Jamie stopped short.

". . . directed them to Joy. I don't know what you're doing. I could tell Joy was freaked out. I don't know what she said to them!"

"Do you really think Kendra's just sick with alcohol poisoning?" Sunny Dae's voice calmly replied.

"Yes!"

"Hope, darling, I love him, too. You know how much. But we can't keep protecting him."

"Nothing's happening. It's not like . . . before. You know that. And if we don't protect him, who will?"

"We have nothing to hide."

"I know we have nothing to hide, Mom!"

*Mom?*

There was the faintest edge of hysteria in Hope's voice as she added, "Kendra is sick with alcohol poisoning. She broke all the rules. I want this camp to work. It's my ticket out. I'm not going back like Joy did."

"Then run the camp, Hope. And answer Jamie Whelan's questions about Haven. Her husband's a police detective. You say you know we have nothing to hide, then act like it."

Jamie heard the creak of the opening door and quickly backed up, heart pounding. She didn't want Hope to catch her eavesdropping. When Hope came striding into the main court-yard, Jamie was strolling toward the lodge's front porch.

It was Hope's turn to stop short. She looked behind Jamie. "Where's Emma?"

"At the cabin, I think. Just thought I'd get some water. Are you heading into the lodge?" Was her voice squeaky? It sounded squeaky to her ears. She cleared her throat.

"No. I've got some things to do. Please don't bother the kitchen staff. They're busy preparing dinner."

"I'll just get the waters and leave."

She hesitated, then said, "I have a couple of minutes. I'll come with you."

Jamie pasted on a smile and managed to ask innocuous questions about the running of the camp, purposely staying away from discussion of Haven. There was an icy feeling running through her veins at the warning she'd heard.

*Her husband's a police detective.*

\* \* \*

Rona lay on her bunk, her arm thrown over her face. She was sober enough to already know how badly she'd acted.

*Why are you such a bitch?*

And her stomach was roiling. She'd begged off going to dinner, making Brooke even angrier.

Was it her fault Donovan had chosen this trip to come clean about cleaning out the canoe? She'd known he knew something! But how much did he know, really? He'd mumbled something today about seeing a guy who looked familiar. Someone from their old camp days. Was he trying to poke them about Cain? It would be just like him!

She needed to get to the bottom of that, but she was sick of Donovan.

Caleb had collected Wendy and marched her off somewhere, and Brooke had gone to dinner alone, though Lanny had tried to engage her. Rona snorted. Brooke would never be interested in him, like she never was with Owen. She'd fallen for the wiles of Brody Daniels, who was good-looking and magnetic, and Rona could admit all her nerve endings had gone on alert when she'd met him, but the man was a crook. She suspected he was as hollow inside as Donovan was . . . as she was . . . as Wendy was.

She knew Wendy better than Wendy knew herself. She'd been screwing that guy in high school when she was supposed to be with Caleb, then had cried herself sick trying to get back with Caleb.

Dean, that was his name. He'd already gotten a girl pregnant from some Portland school, and his family yanked him out of Laurelton and moved back to California, Rona had subsequently learned. He was the polar opposite of Caleb, and Wendy's experience with Dean seemed to have cured her of bad boys. She'd managed to win Caleb back—what a prize—but then . . . that night . . .

"He'll blame me . . . he'll blame me . . ." she'd burbled as they rowed Cain's body into the lake. "He can't know. Caleb can't know."

"No one can know!" Rona had hissed at her. She'd wanted to slap her. And she'd wanted to slap Brooke, too. They both seemed to be in some kind of delusional shock. Somehow believing everything was going to be all right.

They'd gotten lost in the fog. Once they'd tossed Cain overboard they'd tried to turn the canoe around, but they'd bumped up underneath the cliff that led to Suicide Ledge. It had taken what felt like hours to follow that shoreline back to the camp. Rona had insisted they first turn the canoe on its side, letting enough water flow into it to mix with the blood, before setting it on the shore upside down. As the sun came up the next day, Rona had gone down to look inside the canoe. There'd been no evidence of lingering fog. And no evidence of blood in the canoe.

So, both Donovan and Emma had seen their "secret mission." She shook her head. She and Wendy and Brooke hadn't been able to look at one another after that night.

*Maybe you should have left it that way.*

Rona groaned aloud. She was fully aware she'd pushed for this. Fully aware she had some romanticized view of their friendship. Fully aware that she'd unloaded on Emma because she wanted to blame someone, and all she'd accomplished was to make everyone hate her, but no more than she hated herself.

Her stomach quivered. *Oh, fuck.*

She ran outside, almost barreling into that Greer kid as she raced around the boys' bathroom to the girls'. She made it to the first stall and puked and puked.

Greer saw the woman rushing toward the girls' bathroom and waited to pull out his claw hammer, then began extracting the nails that held the mirror against the wall.

\* \* \*

Harley powered through her mashed potatoes and mystery meat . . . well, eating the potatoes anyway. There was a rumor going around that the meat for the camp was from game killed by the cult people. She didn't know what it was and she toyed with being a vegetarian and vegan sometimes. Didn't matter. She hadn't been able to blow off dinner entirely without giving away what she was up to. But she made sure she was the first one finished so she could hurry away, lying to Marissa that she wasn't sure she felt all that well.

She met up with Greer, who was standing by the full-length mirror. All the nails had been pulled out and there were several broken shingles on the ground from the damaged siding.

"Look," he said. He pointed to hinges on one side that had obviously been covered by the shingles. He swung open a door to reveal a recess behind it. The space was tall enough for them to step inside, wide enough for about two bodies. "Looks like this sheet metal was placed over a real mirror." He entered the space and ran his hand along the rough-hewn wall. "Backs up to the guys' bathroom. Must've been for storage at one time."

"Wow," said Harley. She gingerly stepped in beside him. The door swung shut of its own accord and they stood in the dark. It was impossible not to touch bodies, though Harley kept her back pressed against the wall.

Neither said anything for a moment or two. It had seemed natural to step behind the mirror. She hadn't really even thought about it. But now, body to body, she could feel her heartbeat accelerate and she was having trouble breathing normally. She could smell him, a spicy scent that was familiar enough to make her knees weak.

"You said your aunt told you about this?" His lips were close enough to her ear that he only had to whisper to be heard.

"Yes."

"Ah."

Harley's eyes were adjusting to the dark. She could make out the line of his jaw. She realized he was looking at her and she was looking at him. An eternity of stretched silence passed, then he leaned down, lightly brushing her lips with his. Her own lips quivered slightly. It wasn't the first time she'd kissed him, far from it, but it sure felt like it. Her heart was thrumming, damn near deafening her.

A voice suddenly sounded through the wall to the boys' bathroom. An argument, it sounded like. She and Greer jerked apart as if burned.

"I—" she started to say, but he pressed a finger to her lips. The argument was between two men, the voices too indistinct to recognize. Both she and Greer leaned closer to the wall, listening hard.

*SLAM!*

It sounded like the door to one of the stalls.

There was a scream of fury, then the sound of a scuffle, then pounding footsteps.

Greer squeezed around Harley to push open the mirror door a crack.

"See anyone?" Harley whispered.

"No."

He pushed the door open farther and trotted into the clearing, stopping and looking in all directions. Harley carefully stepped out and closed the mirror behind her, obscuring that it was a door. Greer came charging back and straight into the boys' bathroom. Harley was right on his heels.

"Shit," he declared, worried.

Someone was on the ground. She could see jean-clad legs sticking out from under the cubicle door.

She recognized Marlon's work boots. Greer opened the door.

Marlon was half in, half out of the only stall. Blood ran down his head from a nasty cut above his forehead.

Greer leaned over him. "Marlon. Hey, man."

He didn't respond. His glassy eyes were focused on some

point beyond her. Then his eyes rolled back into his head. Greer put his ear to Marlon's mouth. "He's not breathing! Help me pull him out."

Harley leapt forward, grabbing Marlon's legs as Greer tucked his hands beneath his head and arm and brought him to the floor of the bathroom.

The bathroom door opened and Rona stared down at them. "What the fuck?" she said, alarmed.

"Get help!" ordered Greer. He was already rhythmically compressing Marlon's chest. "You know CPR if I need you to take over?" he demanded of Harley.

"Yes, yes. I think so. Yes. I can."

"Go get Hope!" he yelled at Rona, who stood in shock, her face sickly white.

She turned around, bumping her shoulder into the door-jamb in her haste to leave.

# Chapter 23

Greer said through his teeth, "Hope can bring up somebody at the commune on the walkie. We need to get to the hut, deeper in the woods, between camp and the road. There's cell service there sometimes. Don't know how much charge my phone has right now."

Harley said, "My phone's charged. I've got a battery. I'll go."

"Hope'll call on the walkie," he said again.

"I want to do something. I want cell service anyway."

"I don't want you to go. I should go."

She was watching him pressing Marlon's chest. "You're stronger than I am. You'll last longer. I'll take Marissa. Maybe Esau, or Austin, one of the guys . . ." She didn't really want any of the guys, but this was an emergency. "Tell me where this place is."

He gave her directions reluctantly, explaining landmarks that would take her to a faint trail through the dense trees. "It's not all that far from Suicide Ledge, but sloped down toward the main road. But Harley . . ." His eyes met hers. "I don't want anything to happen to you."

"I'm cool," she said.

"Don't go in the woods alone. And be on the lookout for whoever did this. I can't believe it's someone from the camp, but . . . No, I think you need to take over for me. Here. I'll show you how."

"No, Greer. I'm not going to argue with you." She'd been on her knees, ready to help take over if necessary. Now she jumped to her feet. "I'm grabbing my phone and going."

"No, Harley! I don't want anything to happen to you!"

"I'll be okay . . ."

Before she could leave, however, Hope was there with the walkie. She took one look at Marlon and snapped out orders to whoever answered on the other end. Josh, as it turned out. Once again he would call for an ambulance using the commune's cell service.

"What happened?" Hope asked as soon as she'd cut the call.

"There was an argument," said Rona.

Both Harley and Greer looked over at her.

"I could hear it through the bathroom walls. I was . . . next door." She waved a hand in the direction of the girls' bathroom. "It was two men, I think."

Allie suddenly appeared, squeezing into the room around Hope. "What happened?" She looked with horror at Marlon, then swept her eyes to Greer, who was still working on Marlon. She threw a sharp look Harley's way. Another time Harley might have felt a little bad about kissing Allie's boyfriend—or more accurately, him kissing her—but the fraught moments didn't allow room for anything but worry and fear for Marlon.

"Want me to take over?" Harley asked.

"Not yet. I'm good."

"I know CPR," said Allie, moving forward. She practically shouldered Harley out of the way.

At the same moment, Emma stepped around Hope, who unfortunately put her hands on Emma's shoulders, trying to push her back out of the room. Emma jerked away at her touch and bumped past her into the room. For some reason, Harley's eyes filled with tears as she watched her aunt. Emma, in many ways, was her rock.

Emma looked down at Marlon and Greer. "He's dead," she said in her toneless way. "They die a lot at Ridge Pointe."


Brooke shivered, hugging herself and rubbing her arms as she stood in the main clearing with everyone and watched the ambulance take Marlon away. Two ambulances in two days. Not an auspicious beginning for Camp Fog Lake's reincarnation.

She thought about leaving. Asking someone to drive her home. Not Donovan . . . she didn't trust him at all! Maybe, she could just walk out to the road and hail an Uber, as soon as she picked up cell service, that is. Hell, maybe she'd just hitchhike! Would the danger be any greater than staying at this place?

But the thought of returning to her regular life was depressing. Regular life? There was nothing there. Just a messy divorce from a man who was a cardboard character of someone she'd imagined him to be. And she'd known it. She'd known it right from the start. Some deeper part of her subconscious had recognized Brody wasn't who she'd thought he was, who she wanted him to be.

But here . . . here at *Camp Love Shack* . . . here the memories were worse. The girl, Kendra, was in the hospital and Marlon was dead. What the hell was going to happen by tomorrow?

Several of the counselors and CITs were huddled together. She heard various whispered comments.

". . . never seen a dead person before. Wanna puke . . ."

". . . sure he's dead? Just looked tired to me . . ."

". . . always was weird, though. Can't believe Kendra was with him . . ."

". . . are you stupid? She wasn't with *him*!"

". . . hooked up with everyone *but him* . . ."

". . . had one of those creepy, carved animals in her stuff. *He* gave it to her."

". . . in love with her. She laughed about it. Maybe it wasn't alcohol poisoning . . ."

Brooke tried to see who was talking, but the group of girls was tightly packed. How quickly horror turned to salacious gossip. Now Brooke felt like puking, much as apparently Rona had earlier.

She went back into Foxglove. Rona was lying on her bed, staring upward. She turned slowly toward Brooke. "How's it going out there?"

"The ambulance came and picked up Marlon, but he's clearly dead."

"Jesus."

"Yeah."

"Some of the counselors think Marlon was involved with Kendra."

Rona snorted. "Never overestimate the intelligence of teenagers." She rose to a sitting position. A bit of color had come into her cheeks, which was a good sign as she'd looked like the walking dead when she'd burst into Foxglove and announced that Marlon was receiving CPR in the boys' bathroom. They'd emptied out of the cabin as one and had practically run into Hope and her entourage, whom Rona had alerted first. Brooke had hung back, but Emma Whelan had followed Hope inside the bathroom and announced Marlon was dead. She'd turned out to be right.

Rona rubbed her face and grimaced. "Was it an accident? Did he slip and fall?"

"Hope speculated that it was some kind of cardiac problem."

"A heart attack?"

Brooke shrugged. "Emma's niece, Harley, said she overheard an argument between two men but there was no one around, so I don't know."

Rona gazed past Brooke, frowning. "Didn't somebody say Kendra was seeing someone older? Not Marlon," she clarified. "I think Kiley was talking to somebody about it."

"Well, all the counselors are about the same age, so . . . not any of them."

"And then we got here . . . Do you know all the parents and alumni by sight?"

"Um, yeah. I guess."

"I feel like I saw somebody who didn't belong . . . maybe. Maybe Donovan was right. I heard this slam in the boys' bathroom and I got myself up off the floor and moving. When I was coming back out I glimpsed him over by archery. He was practically running. Kinda had it in my head he was, too. Like he'd heard and was helping, too. But he was going the wrong way, toward the forest. I wasn't really thinking straight."

"Who was the guy?"

"I just said I don't know," Rona reminded her, peeved. Then she tossed up a hand and added, "Sorry. I just feel like dogshit."

Brooke almost said "You should stop drinking," but knew it would not be received well and wouldn't have any effect anyway.

"I was really mean to Emma," Rona said regretfully.

"Maybe that guy was one of the parents."

"Don't think so. He was in pants and a long-sleeved shirt. All the guys are in shorts around here except . . . Marlon . . ."

"You think this guy had something to do with Marlon's accident?" asked Brooke.

"I don't know what I'm thinking." She collapsed back on the bed. "Any chance you could find me a soda of some kind? Don't think they have anything around here besides water, milk, and lemonade."

* * *

Harley, Emma, and Jamie sat at one of the tables in the lodge. Others were huddled in groups, too, but Harley had made sure they were in a quiet corner where they couldn't be overheard. Marissa was outside with Niles; Harley had seen her on the way to the lodge. Kiley was near them, looking pissed off.

Emma said, "I haven't found Eee-saw."

"Give me the note and I'll get it to him," said Harley.

"He was not at Snakeroot bunkhouse. He was supposed to be."

"We'll find him," Harley assured her. She looked at her mother. "Okay, I gotta tell you some stuff, but don't get mad."

"Uh-oh," Jamie said, worried.

"Uh-oh," Emma repeated.

They both regarded her seriously. She drew a breath and exhaled, hating being a rat, knowing it was time to bare all. Marlon's death had shaken her to the core and she could feel tears burning at the back of her eyes.

She told them about Marissa and Cam and sneaking out, and about Marissa hearing a scream in the woods—maybe an animal, maybe not—the night before Kendra staggered out drunk on her ass and collapsed. She then explained that Cam had broken up with Marissa and she seemed to be consoling herself with Niles . . . and that Kendra had been seeing some "older guy." She also confessed that she and Greer had been "behind the mirror" when Marlon had been arguing with someone and that she would have gone into the woods to find this place where there was cell service except that Hope had shown up with the walkie-talkie.

There were long, long moments of silence as Mom processed all she'd heard. Finally, she drew a breath and asked, "Marissa's not sneaking out any longer?" She shot Harley a hard look.

"No. That's over." She hoped . . .

"Okay. Good . . . good. Then, Cooper can talk to her . . ."

Emma said, "You had sex with Greer behind the mirror."

"Absolutely not. We just . . ." *Kissed.*

"Isn't he with Allie?" asked Mom, but she was distracted, still processing. "Holy mother of God . . . We need to tell Hope about all this."

"Do we have to?" asked Harley, anxiously. "Greer's on it."

"Well, yes. We need to know who was arguing with Marlon, and who Kendra was seeing. Maybe he supplied her with the alcohol." She threw a glance over at Rona and Brooke's table. Rona's husband was seated beside his wife but they were turned away from each other. Wendy was seated on Brooke's other side with her husband, who'd scooted close enough to practically overwhelm her. It didn't look like they were getting along, either.

"Oh . . . God . . ." Mom said again, pushing her barely touched plate away. "We have to talk to her. But I don't entirely trust Hope," she admitted with a grimace. "It was weird at the commune."

"Tell me," Harley urged.

She waved it away. "But this information about Marlon is imperative. If this other person was involved in his death, somehow, we need to tell someone."

"Hope knows. Kiley's mom told her that she heard Marlon and a guy arguing."

"Okay, but—"

"Let's find the cell service place. We can call Cooper and you can tell him."

"Cooper's a policeman," Emma offered.

"Maybe I could talk to Sunny Dae," Mom mused. "Did you know she's Hope's mother?" She touched a hand to her forehead as if she felt faint.

"Are you all right?" Harley asked.

"I'm fine. Just shaken up. Like everybody."

"Sunny Dae's Hope's mother?" Harley repeated.

"I heard Hope call her 'Mom.' She wanted to protect

someone at the commune, but Sunny Dae thought he should face the music. I don't know."

Emma said on a note of discovery, "Sunny Dae is Josh and Adam's mother, too!"

"Who?" asked Harley.

Mom said, "Hope's brothers. I'll fill you in." She then gave Harley a concise account of what she had learned about Haven Commune on her trip there and from talking to Hope. She said with finality, "Maybe I will talk to Sunny Dae."

"What if she and Hope are in it together?" asked Emma.

Both of them looked at her and Harley asked cautiously, "Into what?"

Emma thought a moment, then said in a low voice, "Skullduggery."

The dining tables had been cleaned and the benches tucked beneath them post dinner as Hope called another meeting. It was still light out, not many days past summer solstice, sunlight slanting over the heads of all the counselors, CITs, parents, and alumni. Everyone was quiet.

Hope was grimmer than Jamie had ever seen her. She looked over the crowd and said, "I know we're all in shock. I know I am. Marlon had been like family to me. But I wanted to assure you that this tragedy was an accident. Nothing sinister, as I've heard some of you suggest. There's been no foul play. One of the EMTs who came to collect Marlon suggested he possibly had an aortic aneurysm and was likely already dead when he fell into the bathroom stall. I've asked for an autopsy to be sure, but I'm inclined to believe the EMT."

Someone raised their hand from the back of the room, a man Jamie had seen around but didn't know his name. "What about the poison hemlock you mentioned . . . ?"

Annoyance crossed her face. "That's not in effect here. This was strictly a case of Marlon having a cardiac episode of some kind."

"But could the poison have brought that on?"

"I also asked toxicology for tests," she said tightly. "We'll know more later. I'm sorry this happened while you were all here. It's unfortunate, and I would say go out and still have a good time, but I know it's hard."

Rona's daughter, Kiley, raised her hand.

"Yes, Kiley," Hope said, pointing at her.

"I didn't know Marlon all that well, but he carved those little animals. Kendra had one. I have one. He kinda gave them out sometimes. He was a really nice man . . ." She shot a meaningful glance toward a group of female counselors who suddenly seemed to be looking anywhere other than at her. "I was wondering if we could have a candlelight vigil tomorrow night for him? I'm happy to try and get it going."

Harley, seated to Jamie's right, whispered, "Ella and her posse all just thought Marlon was weird, but I bet they get on board with the candlelight vigil."

Marissa, on Harley's right, didn't say anything, but her cheeks pinkened.

Sure enough, as the meeting broke up a crowd of mostly female counselors joined up with Kiley and wanted to help. Ella, her bright, blond ponytail bobbing, a smile pasted on her face, corralled Kiley, clearly working to usurp her position in charge.

Harley snorted as they left the lodge and headed back to Foxglove.

Emma said, "I haven't found Eee-saw."

"He wasn't at dinner," Marissa pointed out.

"You're probably going to have to give him the message tomorrow. Do you think it's time sensitive?" Jamie asked.

"It's for Eee-saw's eyes only."

"Then you can give it to him tomorrow."

They all retired to their beds and if it was representative of the whole of them, it took nearly forever to wind down and fall asleep.

Sunday morning, September was up early and took another run to stretch her muscles and get a handle on the day. She passed several houses with red, white, and blue bunting in preparation for the holiday. Lucille's Café was offering up waffles with blueberries, strawberries, and whipped cream as a Fourth of July treat, and she and Jake were going to head over later this morning.

She'd tried reaching numbers listed within the sparse information she had on the Glory to God school and its owners, Georgia and Jedidiah Luft-Shawk, with only fair to middling success. One call she'd made had connected, however. The woman had been a teacher at Glory to God for about a year. She pooh-poohed the rumors of financial misappropriation, assuring September that the Luft-Shawks were decent, honest, God-fearing people. What she recalled was a particular group of boys, troublemakers, who'd all been kicked out of the school because of their disruptive behavior. She couldn't say if Richard Everly was one of those boys, but had offered up the opinion, "I don't know what school would take them afterward, where they would go unless it was straight to jail. They didn't take the Lord into their hearts the way they should. Pushed themselves on the girls, if you know what I mean."

"Sexual abuse?" September had asked.

"I have no word on that, but . . . you might check with Georgia and Jedidiah. They both go by Luft-Shawk, though God made man in his image, not woman, so I don't understand what that was all about, if you know what I mean."

She was coming through loud and clear. September asked, "What was the camp?"

"The one that was closed about twenty years ago after those kids killed themselves." She snorted. "Camp Fog Lake."

Ah, yes. Camp Love Shack. September remembered hearing about the camp, though she'd never attended. Her older brother March had, she believed, which was hard to imagine as March was a stuffed shirt among stuffed shirts, nearly as bad as their father. She couldn't see him at any camp for any reason. He would undoubtedly complain about everything and balk at doing any kind of camp work.

September had then found a phone number for Jedidiah Luft-Shawk and had been put through to the Luft-Shawks. A quivery male voice had answered, "Who is this?" and when September had tried to explain, he'd repeated the question, only louder, "*Who is this?* I can't hear you!" several times. She'd tried to explain and failed miserably, although he'd seemed to finally focus on the word "police" with a gasp of fear, and hung up on her.

September had then determined she would try the Luft-Shawks in person the next day, maybe pay another visit to Brody Daniels and see if he would answer his door. If Everly had any other friends, she hadn't found them. He was a hacker and a barfly and very little else. No ex-girlfriend had popped up in the course of her research. Hardly any ex–guy friends.

After her run, a shower, and a plate of red, white, and blue waffles, she would see what she could tackle.


Breakfast at Camp Fog Lake was a subdued affair: the usual pancakes, syrup, eggs, and sausage or bacon, and a selection of sliced fruit, apples, pears, watermelon, and cantaloupe. Also, you could order "bird in a nest" today, which was a fried piece of toast with an egg in the center. Emma went for pancakes, but Jamie and Harley tried the egg dish. Marissa defaulted to cereal.

Harley was gung-ho to find cell service and Jamie was with her. She definitely wanted to talk to Cooper. But she also wanted to talk to Sunny Dae, if possible, away from Hope. She hoped to learn who was being protected. Was it Hope's brothers? Josh? Maybe Adam? Or someone else at the commune?

Ella, the clear ringleader of the counselors, was definitely working on Kiley to become committee head of the candle-light vigil, as Harley had predicted. But Kiley wasn't one to push around. There appeared to be a power struggle going on there. The rest of Ella's group seemed to be milling around, wondering what their roles were.

"Hypocrisy," Harley said aloud, watching them from across the tables. "Ella called Marlon a skeezy creep."

"And worse," said Marissa.

Emma said, "Allie is mad at her boyfriend."

Jamie turned to look in the same direction Emma was. Yes, Allie Strasser was in an argument with Greer Douglas. She then glanced at Harley, who'd switched her attention to that scene as well. Something was going on between Harley and Greer. Though Harley hadn't copped to it, she clearly knew that Greer had planned to be at Camp Fog Lake, and Jamie saw that this then had been the major draw for her daughter to become a CIT here.

Allie stated loudly, "Ella just wants to help Kiley. Is that a problem for you?"

Greer was having none of it. He turned and left without another word and Allie rejoined Ella's group.

"Cru-Ella," said Harley.

Emma looked from Allie to Harley and then back at the posse of female counselors as they all left the lodge together. "Mean girls."

"No shit," muttered Harley and looked at Emma, who opened her mouth but didn't say "No swearing," for once.

"Are you ready to go?" Harley asked Jamie as they pushed

their chairs in. They picked up their plates and glasses to take to the window to the kitchen.

"Let's head out later, after lunch. I've got some things to do and Hope wants you and Marissa on deck."

"We both have arts and crafts," groaned Harley. "This is far more important."

Jamie assured her, "I want to talk to Cooper, but I want more than innuendo. I'm going to try to check with Sunny Dae."

"Pull me out of arts and crafts when you're ready to go," said Harley.

"Me, too," echoed Marissa.

"Don't forget us."

Jamie headed in the direction of the trail, thinking to head Sunny Dae off at the pass. Jamie had learned that normally the cook stayed at the commune for Sunday service, but Hope had roped her into the alumni/parent weekend breakfast, apparently, even though there was a wedding planned for later in the day—a wedding where Sunny Dae's son, Josh, was the groom, no less. Jamie wondered about the dynamics of all of that, but needed to catch Sunny Dae first.

# Chapter 24

Brooke wandered into the arts-and-crafts room. It was a large space with several tables in the center and a credenza of sorts at the end of the room with all manner of woodsy items: pine and fir cones, tiny branches, acorns, ferns, and wildflowers, some pressed between the pages of large tomes with blank pages, held together with screws through leather strips. There were cans of metallic paint so you could spray down your items, gilding them with gold or silver. A woman was working hard on a collection of fern leaves and white wildflowers. Brooke did a double take, wondering if those plants were Queen Anne's lace or poison hemlock . . .

"That's yarrow," one of the young women overseeing the project told her.

Brooke looked up and realized it was Marissa, one of her Foxglove bunkmates. Marissa pointed to a poster with a list of Oregon wildflowers that was hanging on the wall.

"Ah," said Brooke, realizing Emma's niece, Harley, was also at the arts-and-crafts station.

She wandered back out. She didn't want to run into Rona,

Donovan, Wendy, or, God forbid, Caleb. Rona and Donovan were at odds, and Brooke didn't want to see him, and she wasn't interested in drinking anymore while she was at camp. Caleb was all over Wendy, as if expecting her to somehow escape his clutches. Wendy was harder to read, but where Brooke would have told the overbearing Caleb to get the hell away from her, Wendy was apparently still dialed into the marriage. Maybe she couldn't leave for financial reasons, or maybe she wanted to stay for her son, Esau—who, from what Brooke had seen, was pretty well-adjusted—or maybe she stayed because of her enduring love for Caleb himself . . . which Brooke couldn't imagine.

It was impossible to guess what really went on inside a marriage.

*You really should sit down and decide what you're going to do with yours when you get back.*

As luck would have it, she ran directly into Wendy and Caleb as she crossed the courtyard on the way out.

Wendy asked, "Is Esau in there?," pointing back to arts and crafts.

"No. None of the kids," answered Brooke.

"He's here somewhere," Caleb said curtly.

"Have you tried down by the lake?"

He regarded Brooke pityingly. "Of course we have."

Wendy revealed, "He stuffed a bunch of blankets in his sleeping bag and Caleb thought he was still in his bunk, but he wasn't." Her face was pinched with worry.

"I told you he was there last night! It was only after breakfast that I noticed what he'd done," Caleb denied.

"But you didn't see him last night," corrected Wendy. "None of us did. Did you?" she asked Brooke.

Brooke shook her head.

"Do you think he went back to . . . her?" Wendy asked in a small voice, to which Caleb boomed, "*NO!*"

"He had a girlfriend; he met her at the commune," Wendy said, ignoring Caleb, whose face had turned a dusky red. "But she was engaged to someone there. He just fell for her, though. We were supposed to be there a month but—"

"Enough!" Caleb hissed.

"—when that all came to light, we were asked to leave." Wendy's jaw was tight.

"We left on our own accord!" Caleb refuted.

Brooke was inclined to believe Wendy. "Who asked you to leave?"

"Josh," said Wendy.

"We'd been there three weeks already," Caleb insisted at the same time.

"Esau fell for Josh's fiancée, Lark."

For a moment, Brooke feared Caleb was going to strike his wife. He just had that look about him. Wendy turned her eyes on him and practically dared him to. When he managed to keep from exploding, she said to Brooke, "Maybe he went to be with her."

"That's not what happened!"

Brooke suggested, "Maybe you should take it up with Hope. She has walkie-talkies. She can call the commune and find out if he's there."

Caleb's eyes were hot as they turned on her. "He's not there. Esau is not involved with Lark. It was just a flirtation. Lark is marrying Josh Ulland, and Esau's going into the ministry this fall."

Brooke left them, pretty sure Caleb's recap was a blue-print of what he wanted, but was not necessarily reality.

"Sunny Dae!" Jamie called out, as the older woman walked briskly toward the trail, toting several empty baskets to take back to the commune.

She stutter-stopped. She'd been so lost in thought she hadn't looked up to see that Jamie was waiting for her. "Well, hi. I'm sorry. I can't talk right now. I need to get back."

"Of course. For the wedding. Your son's getting married." Jamie smiled and nodded.

"Where did you hear that?" Sunny Dae asked slowly.

"Joy and Hope both mentioned the wedding yesterday."

"I meant that Josh is my son."

Jamie couldn't quite cop to eavesdropping on her and Hope, so she said, "At the camp, I think. I believe it was mentioned that Hope, Josh, and, I believe, Adam are your children?"

"Joy told you that?"

Jamie shrugged. "I'm not sure. But that's wonderful news about the wedding. I just got married a few months ago."

"Congratulations," she said. She seemed unsure how to rid herself of Jamie.

"Mind if I walk with you a ways? I'd sure like to talk to you."

"Oh?"

Jamie fell in beside Sunny Dae whether she wanted her to accompany her or not. "I'm so terribly sorry about Marlon. Harley overheard him and someone arguing right before it happened. Hope knows that."

Sunny Dae gave a long deep nod.

"I heard Marlon was very connected with the commune," Jamie went on. She hoped she didn't sound like she was fishing, when in reality she was. "I mean, we all know that he had a place at the end of the Camp Fog Lake access road, but he'd always been a member of Haven."

"We don't really have members . . . it's just a way of life. Not a lot of people want to live without all the modern conveniences, though we do have several generators and water tanks and septic tanks. However, like Camp Fog Lake, most of our toilets are communal. Cell service is outside of our grounds. Not far, but not at hand."

Jamie had seen or heard that for herself. She thought Sunny Dae was detailing the commune's shortfalls as a way to keep her from following her. "Oh, I thought you had cell service."

"It's more accessible than at Camp Fog Lake," she allowed.

"Did Marlon grow up on the Haven campus?"

"What is your interest, if I may ask? His death is certainly terrible. My heart is heavy. But it was an unfortunate tragedy, not a mystery."

"I think we're all just processing. It's so hard. He gave my daughter a small carved deer."

"He was always whittling," she acknowledged, thawing a bit.

"Was he friends with . . . Pastor Ulland, er, Pastor Rolff? Hope said he was her father . . ." *And you're her mother.* She trailed off, hoping Sunny Dae would be more forthcoming as she'd seemed to be in the beginning.

"Rolff and Marlon have known each other for years. Marlon had some problems in his youth and Rolff helped him through them. They helped each other." She exhaled heavily. "I sent you to Joy. I thought she might be able to introduce you to Haven and ease your concerns about us, and Mary Jo, but I don't think that happened."

"Joy clearly loves living at Haven."

Sunny Dae regarded Jamie with skepticism. Maybe she'd overplayed her enthusiasm.

But then Sunny Dae seemed to mentally shrug, her tone more companionable, as she said, "You're probably wondering about my relationship with Rolff. We don't believe in divorce. I'm his second wife. He couldn't marry me because Cornelia was sick, but he made an exception. We were married down by the lake after I had Hope. Later, I had Josh . . . and Adam. Adam drowned when he was sixteen."

"Oh, I'm sorry."

"He was a good swimmer. It was unfortunate. I have a love/hate relationship with Fog Lake."

Jamie was struggling to understand. "Pastor Rolff made an exception? What does that mean?"

Sunny Dae smiled faintly. "In your world, I guess you'd call it bigamy."

"Oh."

"It took Cornelia a while to accept me, but she did."

"I thought . . . Hope said she had . . ."

"An incurable disease? Huntington's?"

"Well, yeah."

"Rolff has always believed Cornelia's dementia—which is far less severe than his own now, mind you—was caused by Huntington's. She was misdiagnosed by a quack. At least that's my opinion. Hope chooses to believe her father, but Cornelia and Joy and Ari . . ." She cut herself off, then said, "You've met Joy. She's not mentally or physically incapacitated. Rolff is the one who's mentally failed, but since he decreed that Cornelia has Huntington's, Cornelia has Huntington's . . . and so does Joy, and so did Arianna."

"Was Arianna related to them?"

"Joy didn't tell you she was her daughter?"

"No."

"It's a difficult subject. She was raised by the Luft-Shawks."

"Oh." No, Joy hadn't mentioned that the first girl found on Suicide Ledge had been her own daughter. "Isn't there a test for Huntington's?"

Sunny Dae pulled herself together. "Yes, but Rolff can't be wrong. That would go against everything he's preached all these years. Don't misunderstand me. I love Rolff, as I love the Lord. And I love my daughter and son, too. I just don't have any illusions about the truth."

"But this would be easy to prove."

"Pastor Rolff is our guide. We follow him."

Jamie was slightly taken aback. She'd thought Sunny Dae was somehow different from others at Haven Commune, and yes, she kind of was, but it sounded like if everyone else was drinking the Kool-Aid, she would, too. Or, at least pretend to.

Jamie said slowly, wanting to know, but feeling like she was pressing a tender sore, "Arianna was killed by persons unknown. And then Fern was killed the same way, or at least left at Suicide Ledge the same way."

Sunny Dae didn't respond for a long time, then said, "Hope mentioned your sister doesn't believe Fern's death was a murder."

"Emma knew Ryan . . . Christopher."

"I don't think that's really true. She didn't even know his real name because he hid it from her." She sighed. "Christopher had relations with Fern while she was betrothed to Josh. Rolff couldn't abide it, and he sent Christopher and his family away. Banished them. But then Christopher became a counselor at Camp Fog Lake. Joy let him and he used it as a way to be near Fern again, but she never loved him. She told him over and over again that it was not to be, but he ended up killing her and himself. Don't look so surprised. The sheriff's department knows this. We just don't like to talk about it. It broke Josh's heart. He blamed himself and he was so destroyed that he lost his faith. Marlon tried to help him, but Rolff sent him away. It was years before he came back to us."

"You're saying it's a fact that Christopher killed Fern and himself?" Jamie hadn't realized until this minute that she'd believed Emma so completely.

"My son, Josh, has been betrayed by two women already: Fern . . . and Mary Jo. Fern Galbraith was killed by her lover, and Mary Jo chose Stephen Kirshner and left Haven.

Josh and Lark are getting married today. Lark's a lovely girl who takes care of Rolff and whose own parents' addictions to drugs and alcohol caused their early deaths. She was an orphan when she came to us, and Rolff and I took her in, and though we never believed Josh's heart could be mended, he's fallen in love with her. It's something of a miracle. There is no other mystery to Haven Commune. It feels like everything is going to be all right now."

They had reached Suicide Ledge. Sunny Dae glanced across the lake and said, "Looks like the fog is coming."

Jamie could not see any changes. The lake was dark green and glimmering dully under a sun obscured by clouds. Sunny Dae hesitated only briefly, then kept heading toward Haven.

Jamie fell a few steps behind her. She wondered if she was reaching the end of Sunny Dae's tolerance.

But then Sunny Dae asked, "Are you coming?"

"I should get back. I really need to talk to my husband. My daughter and I have a 'date' to find cell service."

*Her husband's a police detective . . .*

She wondered what Sunny Dae had meant by that. It had sounded like a warning. And who was it she'd told Hope she could no longer protect?

"You can use the cell service at Haven," Sunny Dae suggested. "The northernmost yurt gets the best signal. Would you like to try calling from there?"

"Absolutely," Jamie answered promptly. She had her cell phone with her. She felt a little guilty that she was finding cell service on her own after she'd promised Harley, but the aim was to make contact and finally that's what she would be doing.

Harley heard the *ring-ring-ring-ring* of the "dinner triangle" and hurried to the window and peered out. Marissa joined her.

"What is that?" asked Marissa. They both knew it wasn't time for lunch.

"Hope's ringing it."

They turned to look back around the arts-and-crafts room. Several other parents/alumni had entered and desultorily picked up items to create their Camp Fog Lake projects, but their energy had devolved into a coffee klatch with no one really attempting to finish a project.

"They're calling us," Harley announced to them.

"What for?" one of the women asked.

Another got up from her chair and left the wooden frame she'd half-constructed from small sticks. "I need a cigarette," she said.

"You can't smoke here," another responded as they got up en masse.

"You can't drink, either," the would-be cigarette smoker said with a smile and they all laughed. Harley and Marissa followed them out. They would have to clean up the space later, but for now they wanted to know why Hope was calling them.

"We're having canoe races. Everyone down to the lake!" Hope yelled as people converged in the main courtyard.

"That's it?" asked Marissa.

Harley, too, was underwhelmed, but then said, "Maybe this is a chance to go find that hut."

"We have to wait for your mom."

"I know. But if I could find it first, I'd just go. I'm going to find Greer."

"Harley, he's with Allie. Things are getting tense."

"I know! But if you go down to the canoe races they might not miss me, and Greer doesn't have to show for them at all. That's not his job. He and I could go now."

"Harley." Marissa stood in her way, as she would have peeled off and headed toward the maintenance building instead of with the group moving down to the shore.

"Don't make it worse. Wait for your mom."

Harley saw Emma step outside Foxglove. "Okay. I'll make sure Emma knows what's going on."

"I'll come with you."

"No, Marissa. Get down there and represent for us. We'll be right there. Find Niles."

"What does that mean?"

"*Nothing.* Just *go!*"

Marissa gave her a *look*, but Harley's comment about Niles had penetrated and she headed down to the shore with everyone else. Why Hope was basically calling them all down to the water was anyone's guess, but Harley didn't have time to worry about it.

She met up with Emma, who stood stiffly outside their cabin door and said, "I don't want to get into a canoe."

"You don't have to," Harley assured her. "Do what you want. I'm going to look for cell service." She entered Foxglove and dug through her belongings, grabbing up her phone, happy to see it was charged. When she headed back outside, she saw Emma had wandered to the sheet-metal mirror.

"The nails are almost gone," said Emma.

"The nails *are* gone," Harley rejoined. "Greer took them out yesterday. We were inside there when Marlon was hurt. I told you that."

"There's one." Emma pointed to a screw at the shoulder level of the outside frame.

Harley put her hand at the same area, which was where she would automatically grab to open the door. It was screwed down tight. There were a few more back in place.

"Greer must have closed it."

"There's Austin," said Emma.

Out of the side of her eye, Harley saw that Austin was moseying their way. She had a feeling the "moseying" was a put-on. "Can you distract him? I'm going to find Greer."

She pretended she didn't see him coming their way and headed across the clearing toward the maintenance shed.

Austin watched her leave, his steps slowing.

Emma looked at Austin. She thought he was a friend of Harley's, but Harley liked Greer. "You should go to the canoe races," she told him.

"Where's Harley going?" he asked, starting to head after her.

Emma needed to stop him. She raised her voice. "Where's Eee-saw? I need to find him but he's not around."

"He's not in my bunkhouse. He's in Hawk's Beard," he said, but he kept on going.

"Harley likes Greer!"

That stopped him. At the same time, another boy popped up from behind one of the cabins. "Austin! C'mon. Let's beat these guys! We can outrow them!"

Lanny's son. Not as goofy as his father.

"Ah, fuck it. Sure."

"No swearing," said Emma as Austin went to join Lanny's son. After a minute, she followed after them, turning down between the cabins and toward the lake. She stopped on the top of the rise. People were grabbing canoes and forming groups. Everyone was there except Harley . . . and Jamie.

She looked over to where the trail started to Haven Commune. There were several big fir trees there. She blinked. There was a ghost hand on the tree!

She gasped and looked around quickly. Where was *Jamie*? Where was *Harley*?

She turned to go back the way she'd come. Harley could still be at that maintenance building.

But then the ghost hand disappeared. There was a flash of light. Off binoculars, she thought. Like Ryan's.

Emma's heart was pounding. She placed a hand to her chest, afraid her heart might hurt itself, banging against her ribs. Slowly, a man appeared from behind the tree. He was looking down at the group by the water.

Emma's mind went blank. *HIS EYES! HIS EYES!*

She could see *his eyes*!

But . . . no, those scary eyes weren't his. They were someone else's. Not the man who'd hurt her. Who'd cut the scar into her back.

Her eyelids fluttered and she tried to pull herself under control. Not let it take her over this time. She always saw *his eyes* when she was scared.

She managed to squint her eyes open and look at him, but now he was disappearing behind the trees. Had he seen her? She didn't know. But . . . she felt a rush of relief. He was *not* the man who'd hurt her. That man was gone. *Long gone.* This man looked like . . . an older . . .

She gasped.

*Cain!*


"Greer . . ."

Harley caught up with him as he was heading into his apartment. He glanced back at her and waited, but his expression wasn't encouraging.

"I'm going to find cell service. I was wondering—"

"I'll show you the way. Give me a minute." He disappeared inside the building while Harley waited outside, half thrilled, half worried.

"What are you doing here?" a woman's voice suddenly demanded.

Harley jerked as if stung and turned around. Allie was now standing in the doorway to the maintenance building, where Greer had just passed through. She couldn't see her features distinctly as the gray outside light of day was behind her, shadowing her features, but it didn't matter. Her cold tone gave her feelings away.

"Um . . . Greer's showing me where I can find cell service."

"He's taking you to the hut?"

"I guess so. If that's where it is . . ."

"Guess I'll see you both there, then. I'm on my way there now."

She suddenly stalked toward the edge of the forest. Harley thought it might be an act of defiance, but she just kept on going.

Greer reappeared, carrying a backpack and holding a flashlight. He switched it on and said, "Batteries are still good," then switched it off. "Was that Allie? I heard voices."

"Uh, yeah. She said she'd meet us at the hut."

Greer took that in, then said, "She doesn't give a shit that Marlon died. He's replaceable. Just a maintenance guy. A servant."

"I know. I heard her with Cru-Ella."

He almost smiled. "I'll probably get fired for taking you into the woods, but I want to make a call, too."

"Who are you calling?"

"My dad. We didn't leave on the best of terms. It's stupid to stay mad, though, right?"

"Right."

"Marlon died today . . . it makes you think . . ."

Harley nodded, not trusting her voice.

"Okay, let's go." Greer pulled himself together and led them to the same area that Kendra, and now Allie, had disappeared into, which was a barely discernible trail. Harley glanced back toward the lake, where she could hear shouts and laughter, but the bunkhouses obscured her view. She looked up at the sky and thought it seemed darker than it had earlier.

*        *        *

They were almost to Haven when Jamie felt the dizziness. *I'm going to pass out*, she thought in wonder, and sank to her knees.

"Are you all right?" Sunny Dae was beside her in a moment. Her worried voice was watery and came from afar. The gray sky bore down on her, and she crumpled into Sunny Dae's arms.

# Chapter 25

Rona watched her husband paddling maniacally, trying his best to beat out Lanny, who had kept his lean, lanky form into middle age and looked damn good, while Donovan had grown puffy and red-faced, dissatisfied grooves etching beside his mouth. She'd aged better than he had, but this morning she'd seen the same dissatisfied lines bordering her lips and was suffused by despair. Alcohol abuse wasn't helping, she knew that, but how would she cope without her liquid helper?

But this wasn't about her. It was about Marlon's death. In her mind's eye she saw that Greer kid pressing rapidly and rhythmically on his chest, but the old guy's ticker just couldn't take it.

She had to shake off this melancholy, yet she didn't know how. Hope had told them there were sandwiches and bags of potato chips waiting for them whenever they wanted lunch, and some people had meandered back toward the lodge, but most of the idiots were still racing. Neither Brooke nor Wendy was participating. She thought Brooke was back at the cabin and Wendy was probably wrangling with Caleb. Or maybe, while everyone was engaged in the canoe racing, they'd gone back to his bunkhouse or somewhere and had sex. The possessive way he raked his hands along her arms and around her waist expressed a sexual vibe that even Donovan had remarked on.

Well, she didn't want to be clambering into a canoe, either, but she didn't want to give Donovan the right idea. He was full of questions, that husband of hers. Always was, but being at Camp Love Shack had his little pig eyes constantly checking her out, capturing her reactions, his calculator mind making connections, coming to conclusions.

*He cleaned out the canoe . . .*

She pressed her lips together. If he wasn't watching her, his eyes were all over the young counselors and CITs, especially the ones with tits and asses squeezed into itty-bitty bikinis. Not that the other dads didn't notice, but at least they had some discretion. Donovan's eyes were like those cartoon characters whose peepers shot out of their head at the sight of luscious female curves.

She sighed. Brooke had the right idea. Dump the husband.

*And get your life together, girl.*

She glanced behind her and saw Emma standing up on the rise. She'd been there for quite a while, and was she wringing her hands? Her gaze ran back and forth across the camp, like slow-moving windshield wipers. What was she looking for?

Rona, too, swept her eyes over the assembled group. She knew most of the parents and alumni, at least by name, though a few escaped her. That one guy . . . he seemed sort of familiar, but she couldn't place him. She could see the back of his head and his light brown hair, but she couldn't see his face.

Was it getting darker?

Rona shifted her gaze to the sky, then the hills to the west. The trees were slowly being swallowed by an oozing gray fog.

"Oh, shit . . ."

Jamie awakened slowly, her ears ringing, her skin feeling buzzy. She'd only fainted a few times in her life, but she recognized the same physical signals. Her limbs felt leaden. She didn't think she could raise her arms or move her legs yet. Above her was a timbered ceiling and she could smell the scent of pine.

She was lying on a cot and covered by a fluffy pink duvet.

*Where am I?*

The answer came when she saw Joy's worried face swimming above her. She was in Joy's apartment, her bedroom.

"You're awake," she said with relief. "How are you feeling? You gave Sunny Dae quite a scare."

"I'm . . ." Jamie licked her dry lips.

"Here. I've got some herbal tea."

She helped Jamie sit up. Jamie's head still felt cottony, but she was coming back. Joy placed the warm cup in her hands and encouraged Jamie to take a drink. She did so, carefully.

"Chamomile," said Joy.

Jamie tried to quiet the clamoring in her head that warned her everything about Haven was suspect. Sunny Dae was here and she brought and cooked the food that fed Camp Fog Lake. There was no reason to be so jumpy. The tea was definitely chamomile and felt restorative. She drank some more and said, "I need to use my cell phone."

"Oh, I'm sorry. We don't have cell service here."

"Sunny Dae said it was good by the northernmost yurts."

"Oh, well, yes. No one can use it, though. It's only for the men."

"The men? You're serious?"

"We're just the women," she said reasonably.

Jamie's feeling of unrest intensified. "Where's Sunny Dae?"

"She's . . ." Joy's voice petered out as she looked over her shoulder. Jamie looked past her, through the open door to Joy's small living area, but there was no one there.

Jamie set the tea aside and tried to get to her feet. She realized she had no shoes.

"Oh, don't get up yet. I gave you a little something to keep you quiet. You didn't tell us you were pregnant," she gently chided.

"What did you give me?" Jamie demanded, her heart jumping in fear. "I'm not pregnant."

"Yes, you are. And you're too tense. You'll lose the baby, if you don't relax. Lie back down."

Jamie sank back onto the cot, more because Joy's words were pinging around in her brain and she needed a moment to think than because she was heeding her advice. She'd fainted once when she'd become overheated as a child playing in hundred-degree weather. She'd fainted a second time when she was first pregnant with Harley.

"I can't be pregnant," she said. "I mean, I can, but I'm not. I wouldn't be able to carry a child, even if I were."

"Who says?"

"Everyone. Every doctor. My uterus is incapable of carrying to term."

"Hmmm."

Once again Joy looked off into space.

"What did you give me?" Jamie asked again.

"Natural herbs. Just a mild relaxer. I was worried about you."

Jamie would have liked to argue that she had no right to drug her with anything, natural herbs, or no, but she didn't have the strength. Pregnant . . . *pregnant*? No. And even if she was, it would only end in heartbreak.

"I really need to make a call."

"Maybe if you talked to Josh, he would allow it," she said doubtfully. "Pastor Rolff never will."

"Your father . . ."

"He's everyone's father. We all love him." Her tone was sardonic. "Did you know he took my daughter away from me? Just gave her away. Told my mother we were all sick and he didn't want to take care of another one of us, so he gave Arianna away. But she came back to Haven. I didn't know it was her, when she came back! She was seventeen. How could I know? They never told me till after she was gone. I let him guide her. I didn't know who she was. She was very spiritual. Her parents had raised her right.

"And then he killed her. Up on the ledge. He thought she was sick, but she wasn't. He killed her when she was seventeen."

"Your father killed your daughter?" asked Jamie.

Joy swept a hand toward the fireplace that Jamie could see through the open doorway. "I had matching urns once. Now there's just one. He kept the hemlock ashes in it. Poured them over Arianna. She was already dead. The sheriff said she was strangled, but he poisoned her first."

"How do you know all this?" Jamie's mouth was dry and her pulse was pounding, yet there was a lassitude creeping through her at the same time, the herbal drug filtering through her veins. Frightened, she squeaked out, "Did you poison me?"

Joy looked horrified. "Oh, goodness. I'm trying to save you! I don't know what Sunny Dae has planned, but she brought you here for a reason!"

Jamie looked into Joy's delusional blue eyes.

She was in deep, deep trouble.

"The fog always makes things worse for her," said Joy.

Was she talking about Sunny Dae? Arianna? Someone else? "Sunny Dae has a wedding," Jamie struggled to say.

She slowly shook her head. "Lark ran away last night. I

could have told them she was in love with someone else. She came to us as a runaway, too. Pastor Rolff would never let her go."

"Who is she in love with?" Jamie wasn't sure she'd actually asked that out loud, her mind was dull and smothered, but she must've because Joy answered, "Esau Hemphill. They fell in love last month when the Hemphills stayed here. You could see it a mile away. Mr. Hemphill was not happy, but his wife helped them get together. After they left, Lark kept making my father happy, taking care of him, but it was a facade. She pretended to be so dutiful. But she's gone now."

*Gone now?* "Where . . . is . . . she?"

"Dead," she answered tearfully. "She ran away to meet Esau, but they're both dead . . ."


Harley had tramped after Greer for half an hour when they encountered the fog. One moment it wasn't there, the next it was. Slowly swirling its way around both her legs and Greer's.

"Greer," she said, trying to keep the alarm out of her voice. She knew the tales of the fog in this area were just myth, but fear was making her heart pound erratically nonetheless.

He stopped, looked around, then dropped his backpack to the ground, digging inside it. As he did, the fog seemed to reach around him and into the pack as well.

*Get a grip.*

"Marlon borrowed the compass," he muttered. He seemed unaware of the fog, which felt like it was swallowing them up.

"Greer. The fog," Harley said pointedly.

"Yeah, we better get a move on. Can't find the compass, so we'll have to dead reckon."

*In this fog?*

Harley followed after him again, but closer. She had to be careful not to give him a flat tire.

Emma paced outside Foxglove. Jamie was gone. Harley was gone.

But she'd seen *Cain*. It was *Cain*.

He had the ghost hand. He was the one she'd made out with.

*HIS EYES . . . HIS EYES!!*

No! No, no, no. Not him, she reminded herself sternly. Not Cain.

She hadn't had sex with Cain, but he'd had sex with someone else!

Brooke? One of the Three Amigos . . . *amigas* . . . Not Rona . . .

*Wendy.*

Brooke and Rona were sitting on their bunks, neither saying much. Wendy was with Caleb. The rest of their cabinmates were who knew where. Out in the fog, still. Like the guys. Donovan had pooh-poohed them earlier when they'd worried about fog.

"You still believe that shit?" he'd laughed. "The *sentient* fog?"

"You're the one who said the fog 'thinks,'" Rona had snapped back, then she and Brooke had headed back to their cabin. They'd shuttered the windows and lit two candles because it was damn dark outside, even though it was the middle of the afternoon.

Emma came in, her brows tucked together, her body rigid. She began pacing and then started tidying up, lining up everyone's belongings, lingering over a small carved deer by Harley's cot. She said, "It's dark."

"The fog comes in June," Brooke murmured.

"It's July," remarked Emma.

"Close enough," Rona said, eyeing Emma. "What's wrong?"

Emma stood stock-still for a moment. "Cain had sex with Wendy."

Rona felt electrified. "What?"

"I didn't have sex with Cain, but he was able."

"Cain had sex with Wendy?" Rona pushed.

"Rona, stop," Brooke murmured.

"You know Cain, Emma?"

Brooke chattered, "I just want the fog to leave. How long do you think that's going to take?"

"Emma?" Rona wasn't going to be diverted.

"You rowed in the fog last time," said Emma.

"I knew you saw us! Jesus! Brooke . . ." Rona glared at Brooke, who shook her head helplessly. She didn't know what to do.

"I saw Cain," Emma said. "He was older. Like us."

Brooke's heart jolted. "You mean, you saw Cain . . . *now*?"

"Bad things happen at Camp Love Shack. I told Harley not to come. Harley's not here." Emma's chest started to rapidly rise and fall.

"Where did you see Cain?" demanded Rona.

Emma turned to look at the shuttered window, the one on the lakeside of the cabin. Then she started shrieking in a way that put Brooke's hair on end.

"Shit, Emma!" Rona sputtered.

"Oh, my God," gasped Brooke.

"It was Wendy!" Emma clasped her shirt with both hands as if she were going to rend it. "She was screaming!"

Marissa and Kiley suddenly burst into the cabin. "Who's screaming?" Kiley demanded in fright.

Marissa was shaking, her gaze flying all over the cabin as she clutched at Kiley's arm.

"That was Emma." Rona recovered faster than Brooke.

"It was nothing . . . nothing . . . Emma was just showing us a scream."

"What?" Marissa asked.

Emma said, "I saw Cain."

"You were pretending?" Kiley demanded of her. As fear receded, anger took its place. "You scared the crap out of us!"

"It's okay." Marissa let go of Kiley and moved to stand near Emma. "Who's Cain?" she asked.

"He had sex with Wendy."

"What?" asked Kiley.

"A long, long time ago," Rona told her daughter quickly.

"She was screaming," Emma said, not to be deterred.

Kiley stared at her in consternation. "Was it that good, or that bad?"

"Oh, my God." Rona ran her hands through her hair. "What are you two doing together?" she asked a bit desperately. "I thought you were both after the same guy? Niles . . . something."

"Harwick," Kiley supplied, lowering her voice as if she expected someone to be listening in. "Not that it's any of your business, but we've been kind of faking. Niles's dad saw me and Niles together and he started following us around. Marissa's friends with Niles, so he and I asked her to help get him off our case. Now he doesn't know if Niles is with me or Marissa."

"Niles is definitely with Kiley," said Marissa. "He's just good to talk to."

"You're not having sex," Emma said to her.

"Definitely not."

"Marissa's boyfriend broke up with her," Kiley put in.

"Cam?" Emma's head swiveled toward Marissa.

"Yes . . . Cam. We were . . ." Marissa's lower lip began to tremble and she looked away. "Goddammit, I'm tired of crying. No swearing, I know, Emma. But I'm just . . . I'm just so pissed off at him!"

"Better to be pissed off than sad," Kiley advised. "I think I spend most of my relationships pissed off."

"Are the guys still out in the fog?" asked Brooke. Like Rona, she wanted to change the subject from Cain, though her nerves were buzzing.

"I don't know. We were in the lodge. Hope was lighting the candles they're going to use for the vigil tonight."

"Good luck with that in this fog," muttered Rona.

"We're already using up the candles. I don't care, but Ella had a fit," said Kiley.

"Cru-Ella," Emma stated flatly, and both Kiley and Marissa choked out a laugh.

"There's not going to be a candlelight vigil unless the fog clears," Rona predicted.

Brooke looked toward the shuttered windows, though there was nothing to see. "It feels like it's settled in."

There was a knock on the door. "Everything okay in there?"

Hope's voice.

"Yep. All's well," said Brooke.

"We heard screaming," she said.

"I saw Cain," Emma told her.

A pause, and then, "Try not to scream and unnerve everyone."

Her footsteps retreated.

"Where's Jamie?" Emma asked Marissa.

"I think she's still with Sunny Dae. And Harley's with Greer."

"I want them back."

"Me, too."

"I want to tell them that I saw Cain, but they're out in the fog. And I never gave Eee-saw his message." She pulled a folded-up note from her pocket and added gravely, "He's not at the camp. He's out in the fog, too."

\* \* \*

Wendy stood outside the lodge with Caleb, who held her forearm in a death grip, the same way he had practically from the moment they arrived at Camp Fog Lake. It was on the tip of her tongue to ask if he really thought she'd run off with this thick pea soup covering everything, making objects indistinct past a yard or two, but that would give him carte blanche to bend her over his knee for being insubordinate . . . if he could find anywhere in this camp to do it.

It was almost funny, how impotent he was at finding a place to discipline his wife. Yet, she couldn't show any amusement or he would double down on his efforts. Not that she didn't deserve it. She did. She'd killed a man . . . and much more. She was just wondering if he was the right person to mete out her punishment. Earlier today, when he'd tried to coax her to join in the canoe races, she'd had a physical reaction—heart galloping, palms sweating, insides liquefying . . . or at least it felt that way. She couldn't make herself get into that boat and she'd flat-out refused to join him. She knew he was now just itching to paddle her.

But there was no way she could have followed through. She felt faint remembering that night: the musty, earthy smells of the lake, the hardness of the oar in her hands, the fear that tasted metallic in her mouth. How many times had she struck Cain with the rock before they'd rolled him into the canoe? She'd collapsed afterward, could scarcely remember rowing to the middle of the lake.

But she could still see Rona poking him with her oar and declaring him dead. And she could still hear the splash that followed rolling him overboard.

And she remembered how difficult it had been clambering into that oversized canoe to discard Cain's body while Emma had stood on the shore, staring into the fog at them, or so it had seemed.

She shivered now, and Caleb's grip tightened ever more.

"We're leaving this place," he growled.

"Not without Esau," she said tightly. No matter what befell her at Caleb's hands, she was, and would always be, uncompromising when it came to her son.

"Where has he gotten to?"

"Back to Haven Commune." She'd come to this conclusion after worrying herself sick about him. It was the only answer that made sense. She'd been a compassionate ear when he'd admitted his feelings for Lark, though she'd known there was no hope for a real relationship between them. Lark was betrothed to Josh and Caleb had plans for their son that didn't include an unimportant waif from Haven Commune. Caleb, for all his glowing talk about the commune, sneered at Haven in hidden moments, calling it a "kumbaya cult" after their month there. The renowned Pastor Rolff had been much diminished by his deteriorating health and his chosen successor, his son, Josh, couldn't measure up, earning Caleb's scorn. But Caleb, who would rather cut off his right hand than admit he'd made a mistake, had pretended Haven Commune was a gift from God, only privately venting his deep disappointment and anger.

Now, Caleb ground his teeth. "He went back for that little witch? Is that what you're saying?"

"I hope he's with her. Because if he's not, where is he?"

"You *hope* he's at Haven?" He shook her arm hard.

"Well, then, where is he, Caleb? Where is he?" She let a trace of hysteria enter her voice. Yes, she hoped he was at Haven because that at least was an answer.

He finally lessened his grip a bit. "That little whore's getting married tonight. Hope is on her way to the commune now. Hope told me herself."

"Who's in charge of Camp Fog Lake if she's not here?" Now she didn't have to force the hysteria.

"We don't need a director. We're all adults."

"But you want to leave! I'm not going without Esau."

"You want to go to that commune again? You want to look for him there?" he challenged.

"Well, the fog . . ."

"Yes, the fog. We can go out to the road, though. Find our way out to our car. Get some cell service. This weekend was a mistake from the start."

They'd only come because Esau was a counselor. She hadn't wanted to come, but she'd been worried about her son. She'd do anything for him.

Once upon a time she'd have done anything for Caleb, and of course, that's why she was in this predicament. To win him back, she'd lied, cheated, and killed.

She was a whore and a murderess, yes. But she would do it all over again to have her son. Her heart clutched.

*Please, God. Let him be at Haven.*


September walked up the steps of the small home in Portland's West Hills. The lots were large, houses palatial, many with spectacular views of the city below and up the Willamette River, north past the dual white arcs of the Fremont Bridge. However, the Luft-Shawks' home was a modest bungalow tucked onto a small, pie-shaped lot. She knew it was a rental with only Jedidiah Shawk's name on the lease.

She'd debated off and on all day about just stopping by today. It was Sunday and tomorrow was the Fourth of July. Jake had tried to convince her to stay home and spend the afternoon in bed, and she'd almost laughingly succumbed, but when she said she'd be right back, he smiled, shook his head, and said, "Bullshit, Nine."

"It's just a background interview. I want to know about R.J. Everly's class at the Glory to God school."

"What do you think you're going to learn?"

"I'll tell you all about it later . . . in bed."

She smiled to herself, remembering as she pressed the bell. She heard a rather annoying *bzzzzz* inside. No melodic chimes.

The man who cracked open the door had a wisp of white hair, huge bags under wary brown eyes—and the barrel of a .38 pointed at September's chest.

She froze in place.

"Mr. Shawk?" she questioned carefully after several silent moments.

"Who are you?"

"Detective September Rafferty. Put your gun away," she ordered coldly.

He withdrew the .38. "It isn't loaded." He then opened the door. "You the one who called me?"

"Yes, sir." September stayed put and kept her eyes on the gun as Shawk laid it atop a small console and lifted his hands.

"I can't help you," he said, his voice quavering.

"Is your wife home?"

"Eh?"

"Your wife. Is she home?" September said distinctly.

His mouth worked for several moments, before he said, "She can't help you, either."

"May I talk to her?"

"Eh?"

September wasn't completely sure he was as deaf as he was making out, but she asked loudly again, "May I talk to her?"

He seemed to have a debate with himself and finally waved her inside. "Georgia's in the bedroom," he said and led the way through the house.

September inhaled what smelled like chicken soup. The house was closed up, the drapes drawn against the dark afternoon. He led her down a short hallway with a bathroom on one side and the door to the bedroom on the other.

"Georgie?" he called in his wavering voice. "You have a visitor."

Georgia Luft-Shawk was sitting up in bed, propped by

several pillows. Her gray hair was askew and the skin of her face fell in soft folds. She smiled at September and regarded her curiously. "Hello."

"She says she's a policewoman." Jedidiah sounded like he thought that was highly unlikely. "She wants to ask about the camp."

September's first instinct was to correct him. She wanted to ask about the Glory to God school. She half-expected Georgia to be as wary as her husband, but she seemed to take September's presence in stride.

"I'm sorry I'm in bed. The cancer's taking its toll."

"Oh, I'm sorry."

"Has something happened at the camp? Hope Newell is very capable. I thought it would be better this time."

"I don't really know about the camp," admitted September.

"We couldn't keep it after Arianna died, you know. They tried to say it was murder, but she didn't pour those ashes over herself. She wanted to be part of them, their group, their clan, and that's where she came from. It was like she knew, even though we couldn't tell her the truth. We couldn't keep her away." She smiled sadly.

"Arianna was . . . ?"

"Our daughter. Rolff gave her to us. He said she was damaged, but she was perfect."

"They killed her," said Jedidiah.

"You don't know that," Georgia argued gently. "She fell in love with Rolff's preachings. She was a true believer. They had no reason to kill her." A frown darkened her face. "I don't know about the others who died on Suicide Ledge. Joy was in charge of the camp, then, but she—"

"She was the one who wasn't right in the head," Jedidiah quavered, adding to the narrative.

For someone hard of hearing, he certainly was following their conversation.

"She wasn't as strong as Hope," Georgia tempered.

"She's a very nice person, but things get away from her. Don't speak ill of her, Jed."

"It's the plain truth, that's all. Joy's not right. And if you want to find Arianna's killer, look no further than Haven Commune. Rolff could hold 'em in line when he was younger, but Josh can't. He's a poor substitute, and a killer. Josh killed his brother, Adam. Drowned him in the lake cuz he knew what Josh was up to."

"Jed!"

He threw up his hands in surrender. "Always sneakin' around our camp, gettin' in the girls' cabins. He wasn't even part of it, but he was always there. Sniffin' at the girls."

"Jed!" she cried louder.

"He's not the only one. They're all killers. You might as well know. Been scared to tell on 'em. Thought they'd murder us in our beds, but it's time the truth was told. Our Lord wants it to come out. Josh Ulland is the reason Joy had to close the camp, and he's the reason we closed our school. Tried to do Rolff a favor by taking the boy and it nearly ruined us."

"Don't blame Rolff!" She turned to September. "We bought all the property together, Jedidiah and me and Rolff and Cornelia. We split it up and he started Haven Commune, and we had Camp Fog Lake. Such a lovely spot. All those summer campers." Tears filled her eyes. "We couldn't have children, but then Rolff gave us Arianna."

"Seventeen years later, Josh took her away," said Jed.

"We don't know that!" Georgia stated fiercely, her cheeks turning a hot pink.

"Yes, we do," he said in his shaky voice, regarding her tenderly. "Yes, we do."

September was silently absorbing their history, but in the pause that followed, she asked, "You said you closed a school. Glory to God?"

Georgia got herself under control, but she'd stopped looking at her husband. "That's right. After Arianna's death, we didn't want to run the camp. Rolff asked if Joy could be in charge and we stepped away. We knew the people who'd started Glory to God—lovely and caring people—but they needed to sell and so we took over. We had some troubled souls attending, but they found their way through our Lord."

When she hesitated, September looked to Jedidiah, but he didn't seem to want to go another round with his wife.

"What happened?" September asked. R.J.'s name was on the tip of her tongue, but she was hoping to hear it from them.

"Like Jed said, Rolff sent Josh to us," Georgia finally admitted. "They were having some problems." Jedidiah was staring at her. Almost daring her to continue. She closed her eyes and said miserably, "And he had relations with one of the girls. She was a tainted woman, God rest her soul. There were several boys involved. But when she died of alcohol poisoning, the school got blamed."

"Do you know the names of these other boys?"

Georgia's eyelids flickered open. "What does that have to do with the camp?"

"Maybe nothing," September answered honestly. "I'm trying to find someone who knew Richard—R. J. Everly— who attended the Glory to God school."

Georgia's gasp mirrored the one Jedidiah had given when September had first called him. "R.J. was a friend of Josh's! Josh was always the leader, but R.J. was right there!"

Finally, someone who knew R.J.! "Where is Josh now?"

"The commune. Haven Commune. Rolff and he eventually made up and he's back there," she answered. "Why do you want him?"

"R.J. was the victim of a homicide I'm trying to solve. You may have seen it on the news. I'm trying to interview his friends, family, acquaintances . . . I heard about the class at Glory to God that effectively shut down the school."

"R.J. was . . . at a crossroads. He wasn't a bad kid," said Georgia.

Jedidiah got back in the conversation. "Josh, Brody, and R.J. . . . Josh influenced everyone. You be careful, if you go see him at Haven."

"Was *Brody Daniels* one of his friends?"

"Yes, ma'am," said Jedidiah.

"Oh, yes, dear. Brody Daniels. He only spent a short time with us, but it was enough. He's the only one who turned for the good. God's love shined on him and he went on to great things. Do you know who he is?" asked Georgia. "He's on the path to glory."

*I wouldn't bet on it,* thought September, but she kept her thoughts to herself.

# Chapter 26

Marissa and Kiley decided to leave Foxglove and head back to Bird's Foot cabin together. No one wanted to be in the fog alone.

Rona stood up from her bunk. "Emma, I don't want to belabor the point, but what was Cain doing when you saw him *now*?"

She tilted her head, thinking hard, and finally said, "Mixing in."

"Could you have been mistaken?" Brooke suggested. "I think . . . I heard that Cain is dead."

"You killed him and rowed him out to the lake."

Rona and Brooke looked at each other, their worst fears confirmed.

"So, you did see," stated Rona. "Let's stop playing this game."

"You said his name and dragged the canoe. The fog was there. You didn't talk to each other anymore."

"Emma, he was raping Wendy," Rona whispered tensely. "That's why she was screaming."

"We had to fight him off her," said Brooke.

"We needed to save Wendy," Rona agreed.

"Are you sure you saw him?" Brooke asked, hoping against hope she was mistaken, even if he was alive.

"Yes."

Emma headed for the door.

"You're going out in the fog?" Brooke questioned.

"I have to find Jamie and Harley . . . and Eee-saw."

When she was gone, Brooke latched the door behind her. Rona said, "I don't like the feeling of this. Better check the back door, too."


It was dark when Jamie woke up. She had no idea what time it was. A series of candles quivered in the faint breath of air. She could smell incense, maybe sandalwood?

She realized there were dozens of candles. All around her bed.

*Oh, my God, what is this?*

She got to her feet, feeling woozy, and Joy appeared from the gloom of the other room. "Are you ready?" she queried.

"Ready?" Jamie asked cautiously. Her throat was dry and her head ached.

"To join with Pastor Rolff. He's waiting."

"Where's Sunny Dae?"

"She's here. Don't worry. You're safe."

She clasped Jamie's hand and led her forward, barefoot across the wooden floor. With her free hand, Jamie surreptitiously checked her pocket. With relief, she felt her cell phone, still in place.

"You're to take a bath first. We have one ready. And then we have the ceremonial robe."

"What . . . ? No, I need to get back. I was only supposed to be here a little while. Everyone will be looking for me."

Joy put her finger to Jamie's lips and whispered so softly Jamie could scarcely hear her. "It's best if you just go along. And don't tell anyone you're pregnant already."

"I'm not—"

"Shhhh."

Already? *Already?* "Where are you taking me?"

"To the wedding."

"You said there was no wedding!"

"This is your wedding, not Lark and Josh's."

"For God's sake, I'm married, Joy! This is nuts! What are you doing? I'm not going anywhere!"

She wrenched her arm free and ran blindly to the door and outside into a velvety, gray fog. Sticks cut into her bare soles but she barely noticed. She didn't know which way was which. She had to hide. Hide until the fog lifted. Every worry she'd felt about the commune was validated and then some!

She ran forward with her arms outstretched and smacked into another person, tumbling them both to the ground. It turned out to be Lark, who grabbed Jamie's arms and said urgently, "*Run!*"

Jamie ran.


"There it is," said Greer.

Harley looked past him. A small building with natural shingles and roof, moss covering everything, barely discernible in the gray gloom. Immediately, Greer grabbed his phone from his back pocket and Harley did the same.

"Got anything?" Greer asked several moments later.

"No. You?"

"No. Let's move around to the other side."

There wasn't much of a clearing around the hut. It had an abandoned feel and Harley guessed that's exactly what had happened to it. Whatever its purpose had once been, it had been left to the elements.

Except there was a woven basket by the front door. Very much like the ones Sunny Dae used to transport items from Haven Commune to Camp Fog Lake.

"I'm getting nothing," said Harley as she followed Greer.

He swore softly. "Maybe the fog. Maybe we just can't connect right now. It worked when I was here before."

"Why were you here?"

He shook his head. "Just looking for cell service, like now. C'mon. Let's go inside."

The door hung raggedly on a rusted hinge that groaned as Greer pushed on it. Inside, the hut was damp and smelled of musty plants and weeds. A blackberry vine had worked its way around the dirty broken pane.

A green, rolled-up sleeping bag sat on the rough wooden floor.

"Someone's been here," she noted.

"Camping . . ." Greer agreed. Beyond the sleeping bag there was an unzipped backpack leaning against the wall. Whoever was squatting at the hut had taken most of his or her belongings from the pack.

"What do you think we should do now?" Harley asked.

"We can keep going farther toward the main road, checking for cell service."

"Deeper into the woods?"

"It'll be slow going. There's no path. But the closer we get toward the road, the better chance we have."

Harley hesitated, mentally chewing on her lip. She didn't want to leave her mom and Emma and Marissa. They barely knew where she was as it was. Hopefully, Marissa had told them . . . although Mom hadn't been seen since she'd gone in search of Sunny Dae. Worrisome.

"Don't they have Wi-Fi at Haven?" she asked.

"That's what I heard." He didn't sound sure.

"Maybe the fog'll be a problem there, too. I really need to talk to my mom."

"We can go toward the main road, or if we head due west, we'll run into the trail between Camp Fog Lake and the commune. The hut's about due east from Suicide Ledge, but there's no trail. We can follow the trail back to camp, then catch the one toward Haven, if you want."

"I don't know."

Greer had been looking at everything but her, it seemed, but now he focused on her, his gaze dropping to her lips. "Maybe we should go back."

"Yeah," she said, but there was no conviction in her tone.

"Or we could stay here for a bit . . . although we don't know when whoever belongs to that"—he pointed to the sleeping bag—"will return."

"I guess we should go . . ."

They left the hut together and he pulled the groaning door shut behind them. Then they aimed in the direction from which they'd come, following the barely legible trail they'd taken in, Harley letting Greer lead the way again.

After a while, Harley said, "You and Allie had a fight."

He turned his head slightly to answer her. "You know we did."

"Yeah."

They traveled a bit farther, then he turned his head again. "It's not working. I gotta end things with her." He sounded so dispirited that Harley kept her thoughts to herself, but she couldn't ignore how her heart lifted at the news. She was glad he was in front of her, so she didn't have to pretend she was sorry.

They'd gone about a quarter of the distance back, when he stopped and turned around to really look at her. "I think—" he started when a long, low moan sounded through the fog.

Harley instinctively moved nearer to Greer and he pulled her close. They stood in an embrace, hearts thumping against each other's chest, listening hard.

"Was that . . . human?" Harley whispered.

"It's over there." He leaned toward the southeast, closer to camp, but east of the trail they were following, toward the densest part of the woods.

". . . help me . . ." a female voice warbled.

"That's Allie." Greer's arms dropped Harley. "Where is she?"

"I don't know. She went off the same direction Kendra did."

Greer took off at a faster clip and Harley hurried behind him. It wasn't a straight shot. They ducked tree limbs and rounded thorny bushes.

"Where are you?" Greer called, veering off the trail toward where it had sounded as if the plea had come from.

His answer was painful weeping.

He crashed forward and Harley came after him. "Allie?" he called. "*Allie?*"

Harley followed on his heels.

"Allie?" he called again.

"Greer? Greer!" Allie was full-on crying. "I'm here. I'm here! Oh, thank God!"

He charged forward in the direction of her voice. One moment he was in front of Harley, the next he'd fallen out of sight. She was in headlong pursuit and the only thing that saved her from tumbling after him was his disappearance. She put the brakes on her own momentum but her feet slid over the muddy edge of a deep pit.

*Holy shit!*

"*Greer!*" she screamed, scrabbling around in the dirt, her flailing hand catching an exposed root, just stopping her fall.

"Harley, stop!" he yelled back.

"I'm stopped. I'm stopped." She drew a quaking breath. "Are you all right?"

"*No!*" Allie shrieked. "No, No. *Oh, God.* Do you see? Do you see?"

Harley dragged herself back from the lip of the pit. The legs of her jeans were covered in mud and her clothes were streaked with dirt, twigs, and leaves. She crawled back carefully to the pit's rim.

It was deep. Six feet under . . . the size of several large

coffins. Harley could just make out Allie huddled in one corner, hugging herself, a dark scratch down the side of her face. Greer was nearer, but on one knee. His leg looked funny . . . his ankle turned at an unnatural angle. An electric shiver shot down Harley's spine.

But it was the body at the bottom of the pit that they were both looking at that got her the most.

Cam was lying in the muck, staring up at her with black eyes. If he wasn't dead, he sure as hell was giving a great impression.

Harley sat down hard on the ground and put her head between her knees, gulping air.

September parked across the street from Brody Daniels's house, checked each way for traffic, and then hurried across the road and up the front walk and steps. She noted again what a beautiful and manicured home it was, just as she had the several times she'd dropped by, hoping to catch him in, failing each time.

She was working on her own time today, as she had been all weekend. Jake was right—it was her need to solve a puzzle that drove her. When she'd been let go from the department a year or so back because of budget cuts, she'd become embroiled in what amounted to private investigations, but she'd found herself constrained by the inability to search information from official databases, a real pain in the ass. She also couldn't say she was with the department to potential sources and witnesses, and without that authority she'd been hamstrung in ways she sometimes took for granted now that she was back with the Laurelton Police Department.

However, being completely free, she also hadn't had to worry about protocol as much, and, after knocking on Brody Daniels's door and ringing the bell and receiving no response yet again, she resorted to trying to peer through the front windows of the house. If she were a private citizen she could try to find a way in, breaking the law if she had to, claiming she'd thought she heard something and begging for forgiveness, if it came to that. But as a member of the police force she needed to see or hear something, anything that made her believe she needed to enter the house to save someone or catch a criminal in the act; something that would give her cover for her actions and could be verified as her reason for forcible entry.

It was a paradox, in its way. She thought about miming—in case anyone was watching—that she'd seen something galvanizing through the window. Some reason for her to break in. But then what? If the house was as empty and vacant as it appeared, she would have a hard time explaining just what she'd seen.

Giving up that idea, she walked off the porch and around the side of the house to the backyard. If Brody Daniels saw her, she would think of something. There were no neighbors in her direct line of sight, so she wasn't worried the department would get a call, but she couldn't afford to break the law and lose her job.

There was a side door, sturdy and locked with a window that showed a small hallway that likely led through a laundry room and maybe into the kitchen. Apart from breaking and entering, she was stuck firmly on the outside. She walked farther around the back. There was a covered, rear deck that looked out on a recently mowed and clipped backyard. A mimosa tree's delicate pink flower petals quivered in a slight breeze.

And on that breeze she caught the odor of decay. One she was familiar with in the course of her work. Human remains.

She hurried down the walkway to the front of the house again, but the scent disappeared. Retracing her footsteps to the backyard, she got a pungent whiff.

Here, then, was reason to enter.

Carefully, she pulled her Glock from its hip holster and

walked back to the side door with the window. She banged on the door with her hand once more, and when that got no response, she hit the butt of her gun against the double-paned glass window, shattering it in two tries. Knocking out the vicious hanging shards of glass with her elbow, she reached a hand in and turned the lock.

Once inside, the stench greeted her like a fist in the face. Covering her nose and mouth with her hand, she stepped carefully through the laundry room and into the kitchen.

Brody Daniels lay sprawled across the top of the island, his face turned toward her, his tongue out and his features slackened, his body already beginning to dissolve. A thin rope was tightly wound around his neck.

She backed out of the house, gulped air as soon as she was outdoors, and called in the suspicious death.

# Chapter 27

"I'll get help," Harley said as soon as she'd pulled herself together. "Is he . . . Is he . . ." She couldn't say it.

"He's gone," Greer confirmed.

Allie started wailing and Harley felt another wave of dizziness. "Who killed him? Who did this?" she asked.

"He was in the pit when I fell in!" Allie cried. "I've been calling and calling for help! What took you so long?"

"We got here as soon as we heard you," Greer said tightly.

"But you fell in! You fell in!"

Greer said to Harley, "I can throw you the flashlight, but can you find your way back?"

"Yeah . . . yeah, I can." Could she? The fog was a gray blanket. Tree limbs and trunks would suddenly appear as if by magic right in front of you, flashlight or no flashlight.

Greer tossed the flashlight up over the lip of the pit and Harley scrambled to corral it before it rolled back in.

"Can you find the trail we walked in on?" Greer was tense. It didn't help that when Allie wasn't wailing, she was moaning and crying.

"Yes," Harley said, even though she harbored serious doubts.

"Come back soon!" Allie begged.

"I will. You'll be okay?" She meant the question for Greer, but Allie said, "No! I'm never going to be okay!"

"We'll be fine," was Greer's grim answer. "Take care."

"You, too."

Harley switched on the flashlight, which sent out a fuzzy cone of illumination that barely cut into the gray curtain. She got her bearings as best she could, and tried to find where she and Greer had veered off the path in the direction of Allie's moans.

Emma stood outside Hawk's Beard bunkhouse, where Esau would be if he wasn't out in the fog. She didn't like being in the fog. She knew it couldn't think, like Donovan had told them around the campfire, but she didn't like it. Bad things happened in the fog. She was worried about Jamie and Harley. Her chest felt tight.

Maybe she could leave the note on Esau's bed, but which one was it? She didn't know.

A body came out of the fog and Emma cried out in fear and stumbled away from it. But it was just Donovan.

"What are you doing here?" he asked.

"I want to know where Eee-saw's bed is."

"Planning to cradle-rob? What? Am I too old? We could pick up where we left off."

Emma was pretty sure he was teasing her. "I don't think so," she said. "I need to leave Lark's message for Eee-saw."

"Who's Lark?"

"I can't talk about it."

"What's the message? If I see Esau I'll tell him."

"It's a note. For Eee-saw's eyes only. I was supposed to

give it to him yesterday and now he's in the fog some-where."

He put out his hand. "I'll put it on his bed. Under his pil-low. How's that?"

"You can't read it."

"I won't," Donovan promised.

"I don't believe you."

"Well, then, you're on the horns of a dilemma. Either leave the note with me, or wait for Esau. You can't go in the bunkhouse."

"Why can't I?"

"It's not a good idea. A bunch of guys being guys. They're not . . . kind."

"They would make fun of me?"

"It's just better if you give the note to me. Now, I'm going in. You want to hand it over?"

"You won't read it?"

"I won't read it."

Very reluctantly, Emma handed Donovan the note. She felt bad. She thought she should give it to Esau herself. Donovan was trying to be nice. She thought it might be hard for him to be nice. He hadn't been nice when he was younger.

She just hoped Esau got the message.


As soon as the door to Hawk's Beard closed behind her, Donovan unfolded the note. It was only a few words.

*Don't come tonight. He knows. I'll find a way to get away.*

*Huh*, he thought, then refolded the note and put it beneath Esau's pillow. The bunkhouse was empty. None of the other guys had come back inside. He didn't feel like staying in-side, either.

* * *

Wendy went with Caleb to Esau's bunkhouse and nearly ran into Donovan, who was just leaving. "Is Esau here?" she asked anxiously.

Donovan shot a glance at Caleb. Wendy could tell the two men didn't like each other, but that was neither here nor there.

"Wendy's worried about our son. We plan to leave. This place . . ." He looked around as if he could see through the fog. "I have real work to do and we don't want to waste the rest of our holiday weekend."

"Is he there?" Wendy persisted.

"No. But maybe he connected with his girlfriend," said Donovan. "I don't give a shit about this fog. I'm not just hanging out in the bunkhouse like a scared little girl. Lanny and me are heading back to archery. Just shoot through the fog. See if you can hit the target."

"There is no girlfriend!" declared Caleb.

"Lark?"

"How do you know about Lark?" Wendy inhaled on a gasp.

"Emma mentioned her. She had a note for Esau that I put on his bed."

"What note? Is it still there?" Caleb demanded.

"What did the note say?" Wendy asked on a dry throat.

"I didn't look. I'll see you later . . ." He drifted into the fog, swallowed up in moments.

Caleb shot into the bunkhouse and Wendy followed. If one of the guys was naked or doing God knew what, she could ask forgiveness later. As it was, the bunkhouse was empty. Caleb found the note, read it, and crumpled it into his palm.

"Did you know?" he demanded.

"No. About what?"

"They were planning to meet. She's meeting him." He opened his hand and Wendy snatched the note from him, smoothing it out enough to read it. "She told him *not* to meet her," she corrected him.

"Oh, he met her. That's what he did. We need to warn Josh that she's a cheating whore."

He headed out the door, but when she didn't immediately follow, he stopped just outside the bunkhouse. "Are you coming?"

"In this fog, Caleb?"

"We'll get the car and drive to Haven."

She wanted to beg him to wait until the fog lifted, but knew that would never work.

*But if you just stepped into the fog, disappeared, turned to smoke, he wouldn't be able to find you. You could look for Esau on your own. Go to Haven. Make sure he's all right.*

She said, "Let me go back to Foxglove and gather my things."

That made sense to him. "I'll get mine. Meet me at Snakeroot. We'll leave from there."

"Okay."

Wendy melted into the fog.


"Lanny?"

Donovan had secreted the bottles of Grey Goose and Captain Morgan behind the huge archery target. Lanny and his son, Lendel, had both imbibed. So had that Austin kid. They'd been tippling off and on since the start of this whole weekend debacle, first Lanny's pint of Patrón tequila—like that was going to work in this crowd—then onto Donovan's stash.

Lanny had a thing for Brooke. He'd as much as admitted she'd been in his thoughts off and on for years and had hoped she'd be here.

His boy, Lendel, seemed like a pretty straight shooter, but that Austin kid was a fox in a henhouse. Donovan understood. He was made the same way.

He expected them to be at archery but couldn't sense them in the fog. He felt his way toward the barrel of rubber-tipped arrows, set against the side of one of the cabins, Trillium, he thought it was named.

"Hey, man. Lanny? Lendel, are you here? I'm getting an arrow." He reached around inside the barrel and was shocked to cut himself on something sharp. He jerked back and saw he'd sliced his finger. "What the fuck?"

Gingerly, he felt around inside again and eventually withdrew a long, feathered shaft with a wicked-looking arrowhead attached.

He brought it close to his face. Shit. Was it made of . . . obsidian?

"Hey, I found a—"

*THWACK.*

Donovan fell back at the impact. Something had hit him. He glanced down and was stunned to see the feathered end of an arrow sticking out of his abdomen.

"Wha . . . ?"

*THWACK. THWACK.*

Two more arrows sprouted in his right thigh. He cried out in fear and shock and crumpled to the ground. Out of the gloom came a man, a hunter, bow at his shoulder, an arrow nocked and ready and aimed down at him.

"Oh, my God!" Donovan immediately held up his hands. "Stop! Stop! You shot me! You shot me! Stop!"

The man immediately lowered the bow as he came forward, his eyes examining the arrows already bristling from Donovan's stomach and thigh. Fear turned to fury. "You shot me, you fucker! You see? You see? You shot me! Oh, my God!"

The man set the bow and arrow on the ground beside Donovan. His hands were encased in surgical gloves.

"You see?" Donovan repeated, hysteria building. "You've got to get help. Jesus, this hurts. You idiot. You fucker! Who the hell are you? Where'd you get these arrows? Wait . . . I know you! I saw you!!!"

The man sat back on his haunches. "I know you know me. That's the problem. You saw me this afternoon."

"You're Cain!"

"Your wife—she's your wife, now—and her friends tried to kill me. And you knew, all this time."

"No, no . . . well, no, yes. I thought something like that. I saw the canoe . . . But you were with Wendy, not Rona. It's not Rona's fault! It's Wendy's!"

"You know too much."

"It's not my fault!" Donovan could hardly believe it. "You—you meant to hit me? It's a mistake. They're the ones who know. They're the ones that did it to you! It's not my fault! I didn't try to drown you! How . . . how did you . . . ?"

"Survive?"

"You've got to get me help. This was just a mistake. I know it was a mistake."

"The cold water woke me up. I got to shore because God needed me alive. He sent Marlon to find me."

"Marlon?"

"All these years he was silent, but then this weekend— here you all are. It was just a matter of time before he broke."

"I won't tell anyone. I promise." He killed Marlon. Is that what he was saying? Where was Lanny? And Lendel? Anyone?

"You *will* tell," Cain said regretfully. "And the three of them will, too, now." He lifted the arrow.

"What? Stop! No. I promise! I promise!" Tears were running down Donovan's face and he started blubbering.

"The good Lord believes in retribution."

Cain jammed the point of the arrow through Donovan's throat.

Donovan stared in shock. He lifted a hand to his neck and felt the warm blood pumping. Cain had deliberately hit one of his carotid arteries. He clutched his throat in a vain attempt to stop the bleeding.

But Cain wasn't done. He pulled a vial from his pocket and opened it. He then grabbed Donovan's face, forced his mouth open, and poured something onto his tongue. Donovan gagged, but was helpless to stop whatever it was from going down his throat.

Then without preamble, the man jerked his arrow out of Donovan's throat. Donovan tried to scream but Cain punched him in the face. He lay dying. He felt the blinding wrench of pain as Cain wrenched the arrow from his stomach. All he could do was moan, but in his mind, Donovan was screaming and screaming. Cain then tried to rip out the two arrows from his thigh. Pain exploded. It was everywhere! Inside him, too. He could feel it.

*Poison hemlock!* he shrieked in his mind, minutes before he died.


The pole lamp on the maintenance shed that normally spread illumination all across Camp Fog Lake's courtyard was now little more than a blurry, distant star. The ground was dark, but a flashlight beam was raking across it as Wendy headed back to Foxglove cabin. She froze in place and waited as it went past her, the illumination nearly reaching her in the swinging arc back and forth. She caught a glimpse of who was holding the flashlight. Hope. She was sweeping the ground in front of her with the light in order to see, on some mission of her own. Wendy almost called out to her but thought better of it.

\* \* \*

"Did you hear that?" Brooke asked tensely. "That cry?" She found herself ripping at her nails again and curled her fingers into two fists.

"That does it. I'm grabbing Kiley and Donovan and we're all getting the hell out," muttered Rona, beginning to wrap up her sleeping bag. The candles flickered in the sudden movement.

"Through this fog?"

"The car's at the main road. It's not that far. Come on. Get your stuff."

"Are you serious?" Brooke demanded. She nearly reminded Rona that it was her idea to come to the camp, but what did it matter now? "That cry sounded like it was by the lake."

"You want to go to the lake in the fog and find someone who cried out?" Rona demanded.

The cabin door rattled and Brooke let out a cry herself.

"It's me, Wendy. Unlock the door!"

"Shit," muttered Rona, and let her in.

"Caleb wants to leave, but I've got to find Esau."

"Emma saw Cain today," said Brooke.

"What?" Wendy asked faintly, propping herself with one hand against the wall.

"Cain. He's alive. He's here!"

"*What?*" Wendy said again.

"That cry down by the water . . . what if it's Cain? Hurting someone else?"

"Brooke, come on." Rona tried to laugh but it fell short.

Wendy said, "Cain is dead. We killed him."

"*You* killed him," Rona reminded her swiftly. "We were just trying to save you. But I've been thinking about it. I've thought about it a long, long time, but I've just ignored it."

Wendy shook her head. "I can't talk about this. I need to

find my son and leave. I'm meeting Caleb. He's getting the car."

"He wasn't raping you." Rona had stopped wrapping up her bag and was gazing hard at Wendy. "He never was. That was a lie you brought us all into, but you were *seeing* him. He was the guy. I remember him around. You were seeing him on the sly. He wasn't one of the counselors."

"I was raped!" she insisted.

But Brooke was remembering more, too. "You were wrapped around him like a burr and only started screaming when you saw us."

"You were enjoying it!" Rona confirmed.

"He was seeing Emma!" Wendy practically shrieked.

"Emma wasn't really with anyone. They all wanted her, but she didn't feel the same," said Brooke.

"She was a tease," agreed Rona.

"Ask her!" Wendy cried. "Ask her!"

"That's your defense?" demanded Rona. "Emma Whelan's memory?"

"I was raped!" Wendy insisted, turning back blindly toward the door. She yanked it open and ran outside. One of the candles blew out in the rush of her departure. "We have to leave. Hope's already gone. I saw her go by. She's left us!"

"Where was she going?" demanded Rona, rushing to the door with Brooke right behind her.

There was no answer. They could only hear Wendy's hurried footsteps fading out in the fog.

"Hope left us?" Brooke repeated.

"Thanks a lot, bitch," Rona muttered, infuriated.

Brooke stared into the blank fog. "We can't just let Wendy go out there alone."

"She's going to Caleb."

"What if she doesn't make it? What do we do then?"

"We don't care!"

"I care!" Brooke shot back.

Rona stared Brooke down. She really, really did not want this to be her problem.

"Well . . . fuck . . . shit . . . okay, yes." Rona shouldered her way past Brooke into the gray wall outside.

# Chapter 28

Jamie lay on the ground north of the camp, breathing hard. Her bare feet were bleeding, but she barely felt them. She was far from the trail south to the camp, but at least she was safe, for the moment. She didn't know if her panicked race away from the commune was completely necessary, but when Lark had whispered, "Run!" she'd taken off on primal instinct.

And something was wrong at Haven. It wasn't just Joy's delusions. Something was seriously wrong. Maybe it hadn't been when Mary Jo was here, or maybe it had been and that's why she and Stephen left when they were so young.

She listened hard. She was cold, lying on the ground behind a thick grouping of shrubs, a canopy of fir trees overhead, the fog wisping around her. It wasn't as thick here. Maybe it was moving out. She didn't know how to feel about that because the fog was a shroud. When it was gone she would be exposed.

Had Joy really planned to marry her to Rolff? Good grief! That's sure as hell what it had sounded like. Some kind of cult wedding? What the hell? Now, away from her, Jamie just shook her head in disbelief.

She pulled her cell phone from her pocket and looked at the lit-up screen.

*Oh, my God. Two bars!*

She swiped the phone to her favorites list and punched in Cooper's number, aware silent tears had filled her eyes. But the moment she touched the screen to connect, she heard footsteps coming her way. She switched the phone off, glad she'd put it on silent when she'd arrived at the camp. But a moment later, the screen lit up as Cooper tried to respond to her aborted call. She stopped the call, then pressed the phone facedown onto the ground.

She held her breath. The footsteps had stopped, but she sensed the person was still there. Were they just being cagey? Listening? Was the threat even real?

She closed her eyes and tried to slow her breathing, willing herself into invisibility. She couldn't allow them to find her in any case.


With relief, Harley found the trail she and Greer had taken from the camp and began heading in that direction, following the diffused, bobbing white dot from her flashlight through the wall of gray surrounding her on all sides.

She was moving slowly, her focus on her feet, making sure she didn't stray off the path. She'd followed Greer so closely she hadn't paid a ton of attention to what was around her, not that she'd been able to see much.

Greer . . . and *Cam* . . .

She bit her lower lip hard to keep from sobbing. She tasted blood.

*Hurry*, she told herself. *Hurry.*

Then she heard something ahead of her. A crashing

through the underbrush. A person? Moving fast? Help? Or . . . something else . . .

Immediately she switched off the flashlight and gently backed away from the trail, her progress almost noiseless until she stepped on a twig that made a light cracking sound at the same moment she pressed up against the bole of a large Douglas fir. Quickly, she slipped behind it, pulling in her shoulders and laying her cheek against the rough bark, trying to make herself as small as possible.

*Mom . . . Emma . . . Greer . . .* she thought, eyes closed, praying a little.

The crashing changed to fast footsteps. Someone taking a real risk of running into something in this thick blanket.

She held her breath and risked opening her eyes. A flashlight circle was jerking around in front of someone's progress. She couldn't see them from her vantage point.

As if sensing her, the person swept the light her way. She stayed as still as death. After a moment or two, the light retreated and the person went on in the direction of the dilapidated hut.

*A man*, Harley thought. *No one up to anything good.*

She was about to step out of her hiding spot and scurry as fast as she could toward the camp, when she heard more approaching footsteps. This person was moving more carefully, their steps hesitant but methodical. Maybe someone from the camp? Someone she could trust?

*But what if it's not? What if they're the person who dug the pit?*

She stayed still. Again, she risked one tiny look when they were just about opposite her. This person didn't stop and "sniff the air" like the last one. This one plodded forward. A woman, this time, Harley thought. Was she meeting the man at the hut?

Should she follow them? Maybe there was cell service at the hut now. Maybe she could contact Cooper. Who, at the camp, could she completely trust? Hope? She was related to Allie somehow. Surely she would want to save her niece, or whatever their relationship was. Mom hadn't been there. She was in the fog, too! But maybe she was with Sunny Dae. Harley hoped so. Unless maybe she'd made it back to camp? Marissa was trustworthy, but she'd put Cam before her family and now Cam was dead.

*Oh, God . . .*

Emma. Emma would help her. How, she didn't know, but at least Emma was straightforward about everything.

Was the fog lifting a little? She thought she could see a little bit farther than before.

Though she wanted to follow the two figures through the fog to the hut, she chose the route back to the camp and Emma.


Emma stood in the doorway of the lodge. The mean girls had lit a few candles and were talking about the vigil. Emma didn't think it was going to happen. It was still too foggy. She had told them it was too foggy, but they ignored her. One of them leaned in and whispered to the one named Ella something about Marlon and Emma being the same.

*Cru-Ella*, Emma thought, looking around the room. She wanted Harley to be here in the lodge with her, but Harley wasn't here.

She didn't like the fog. It was mean, like the mean girls. But Harley was out in it and so was Jamie.

And so was Cain. She didn't like him, either. Not anymore.

She left the lodge and carefully headed back in the direction of Foxglove cabin, holding her arms in front of her.

Where was Marissa?

The thought of being with Cooper's daughter—stepdaughter—lifted her spirits a little and she increased her pace.

Where was the cabin?

Emma blinked and blinked but the fog was still there and the cabin wasn't.

She stood stock-still, listening. She couldn't hear anything. Her chest felt tight. She had trouble breathing.

She was lost.


"Where's Wendy?" Rona demanded as she and Brooke reached Snakeroot bunkhouse just as Lanny and Lendel were entering it.

"Hi, Brooke," Lanny said with his somewhat goofy smile.

Rona made a garbled sound of disgust. "Jesus, Lanny, you want to flirt? This isn't the time. Where's Wendy?"

"If I knew I'd tell you, but I don't know."

"She was supposed to meet Caleb here," said Brooke.

Lendel had stepped inside and now he stuck his head back out. "No one's here."

"Well, shit," muttered Rona.

"What's going on?" asked Lanny. "You wanna come in?" He swung the door wider. "We were supposed to meet Donovan at archery. See how we would do in the fog, but he wasn't there. Now I guess we're just waiting for the fog to clear, so . . . ?"

"Thanks, but no thanks," Rona said drily.

He spread his hands. "Come back if you change your mind."

Rona and Brooke moved off, toward the trail that led to Haven Commune. Rona looked in the direction of the lane that would take them back to the main road. "If they went to their car, more power to 'em. I'm not going to worry about Wendy anymore. We saved her once and she didn't even need saving. I've got my own family to think of."

"If Cain is here . . . alive . . ."

"Then we didn't kill him. Fine. Good," she hissed. "I

don't have to think about that anymore! And let's be honest, Wendy was the one who smacked him with the rock. And it wasn't rape. She wants us to think it was, but she was with Cain by choice. I know she was. You know it, too."

"She was fighting him off," Brooke murmured. But there was truth in Rona's words. She did know that. But she didn't believe it was all the truth. "She was terrified."

"Yeah. Terrified that we'd see through her act."

"You're so hard on everyone, Rona!'"

"You want to keep looking for her, fine. I want Kiley and Donovan and fucking *cell service*!"

"She wants to find Esau and he's probably at the commune. She won't leave without him."

"What are you saying? You're thinking about going there?"

"I don't know, Rona. Maybe." Brooke was annoyed and tired of fighting. She, too, wanted to leave.

"Well, don't let me stop you. But if you're not with me when I've got Kiley and Donovan, we're leaving you. I'm heading back to find Kiley, now. I don't know where the hell Donovan is."

She turned around and headed in the direction of the lodge, as Bird's Foot was the closest cabin to it.


Harley gasped aloud and stumbled a little, hit by a sudden thought.

*That second person, that woman, was Hope!*
*And Hope has walkie-talkies!*

She took a moment, resting her hands on her knees. It wasn't that she was racing fast, but her heart was thundering and her insides felt shredded.

Cam was dead. *Dead.*

She shook her head and stood up. Her mind was jumping all over the place. Walkie-talkies would work, wouldn't they? Even in the fog? Or maybe the fog wasn't the reason the cell phones wouldn't work. Maybe they just needed to try harder to find bars.

Was she making a mistake? Should she have followed Hope . . . and whomever *she* was following?

Too late now. She was committed.

Who'd dug that pit? Was it meant for animals . . . or *humans*?

Greer . . . she had to save Greer, and Allie. Remembering the sight of Greer's torqued ankle, she clamped down on a full-body shiver.

Oh, shit. Was her flashlight beam growing dimmer?

Drawing several calming breaths, Harley pulled herself together and forged onward.


The tech team took pictures of Brody Daniels's slumped body, examining it closely before hauling it away on a gurney. As the doors to the coroner's van slammed shut, September asked one of the techs to confirm the cause of death.

"Strangulation, I'd say, but there are blisters on his body. He came in contact with something fairly recently that caused that."

"I saw those," she agreed. "Could they be related to his death?"

The tech shrugged.

September watched them leave, then called George again. He'd grumbled a bit about somebody trying to ruin his holiday weekend, but when she told him about finding Brody Daniels's body, he'd dropped the grievances and gotten to work.

"As far as I can tell, Josh Ulland is living at a place called Haven Commune, which was run by his father, Pastor Rolff Ulland, until a few years ago when Josh took over."

"I'm going there," she'd told him determinedly.

"Weather's no good. Go tomorrow."

September hadn't answered. She didn't need to argue with George. She'd spoken to their boss, Captain Calvetti, who'd told her to contact the Winslow County Sheriff's Department, which she had, but no one was doing anything tonight.

There was wisping fog and damp cold at Daniels's house, and she had to admit the idea of being home and snuggling up with Jake had real appeal. Maybe she would drive by Brooke Daniels's apartment and see if she was back yet, then she would make her decision.


Hope reached the dilapidated hut in the woods and stopped at the door, which was slightly ajar. She pushed it with her finger and it made a groaning sound.

"Josh?" she whispered.

It was dark inside. However, she could make out his belongings. And she could sense him. He'd played tricks on her and Adam all the while they'd been growing up.

"I know you're in here," she stated calmly.

"The name isn't Josh," he said.

Apprehension feathered along her arms. Josh had made himself an alter ego long ago. A personality who assumed all the blame for any wrongdoing. When Josh was in "Cain" mode, he was dangerous. But as his big sister, Hope was one of the few people who could get through to him. She had to protect him from himself.

"Shouldn't you be getting ready for your wedding?"

"You know Lark betrayed me."

"I talked to Mom. She's at Haven, waiting for you."

"She's waiting for *Esau*," he corrected her, "but he's not coming."

Hope's breath caught. "Did something happen to Esau? Did you do something to him?"

"You are too quick to judge me, Hope."

"Why don't we go back to Haven. I know Lark is there. I have a walkie with me. We can call her."

"Lark is not my mission tonight."

"What is?"

"Retribution."

He came out of the hut like a striking snake. To Hope's shock, he wrapped his hands around her throat. He'd never done that before! He'd always listened to her. She'd had some sway!

As if reading her mind, he ground out, "You think you're smarter than me, but you're not. I know a lot of things."

She tried to speak but his fingers closed tighter.

"I know you've always plotted against me. You and Adam. You both told Father about my trips to the camp."

Hope dug and scrabbled and slapped against his deadly grip. Spots formed in front of her eyes.

"It was your fault I had to kill Fern and Christopher— called himself Ryan at the camp. Such a do-gooder. Tried to 'save' Fern from me. And no one has to save *me*, Hope. Not you . . . not Mother . . . God is with me."

A black curtain slowly descended over her, blanking out the hut, the fog, and the twisted snarl of her brother's face.

Brooke was indecisive. She didn't want to charge through the fog alone. She knew Rona was right, really. Wendy could make her own choices, and some of those choices had seriously affected Brooke's own life. And anyway, she didn't have a flashlight in hand. Hers was at the cabin.

She retraced her footsteps to Foxglove. Opening the door, she realized the candles had all blown out. It was darker inside than out. When someone suddenly stepped from the cabin's depths, she screamed.

Emma said in a thin voice, "I got lost. I can't find the matches."

Brooke patted her chest, then realized how scared Emma was. Well, that made two of them. "Let me see if I can find them."

Harley heard the short scream at the same moment the trail ended. She could have cried with relief. She'd made it! She was at Camp Fog Lake.

But where had the scream come from?

One of the farther cabins. One closer to the lodge . . .

Fear grabbed her once more. Emma? Was it Emma?

She ran through the fog, hands in front of her in case she miscalculated and ran into something.

A moment later, she did just that. Slamming into another body. They both tumbled to the ground.

"Fuck!" spat Austin.

Harley scrambled away from him and kept going.

"Hey! Harley! *Hey!* We're all at the lodge, getting ready for the vigil. Where've you been? Join us . . ."

She reached Foxglove cabin and saw Brooke and Emma lighting candles. "Emma," she said, her nose suddenly burning with unshed tears.

She barreled straight for her aunt and embraced her hard, even though she knew Emma loathed being touched.

Emma stiffened, but Harley clung to her, silently crying on her shoulder. Then slowly Harley felt a hand awkwardly pat her head.

# Chapter 29

Jamie lay flat on the ground, her cheek pressed into a muddy swatch of ground, stiff grasses, twigs, dirt, and small rocks her bed. She was freezing cold. June? Hah. It felt like winter.

She'd moved farther north as soon as the footsteps had receded, away from the commune. Cooper had tried to phone her back several times after her aborted call. Though she'd had the cell facedown on the ground and on silent, she'd seen the glow surrounding the edges. The fear she would be seen had forced her to lie down atop the phone, and then as soon as she could she'd moved deeper into the woods . . .

And lost cell signal.

Should she go back? Was she being ridiculous? Maybe Huntington's wasn't the culprit, but Joy was definitely delusional.

Maybe Lark, too?

And yet . . . there weren't really any men at Haven other than Rolff and the mysterious Josh she had yet to meet. It was a community of women, almost living life from another century. Was there something deeper going on?

*Maybe you're the idiot. Maybe your lunacy over Mary Jo made you as delusional as Joy is.*

"Ms. Whelan?"

She heard Sunny Dae's voice and she almost wanted to cry with relief. Instead she waited, thinking, worrying and weighing what was true.

But Sunny Dae was sanity.

Making a decision, she picked herself off the ground and brushed dirt off her stained shirt and pants. Her torn feet, which she had barely noticed earlier, were making themselves known now, throbbing and jabbing her with every move.

"Over here," Jamie said, trying to move toward Sunny Dae's voice through the fog.

Sunny Dae materialized like a saving angel. She took one look at her and said on a sigh, "Oh, no. I should have never left you with Joy. Sometimes, seldom, but sometimes she lives in her own world. I was getting ready for the wedding, although with this fog . . ."

"It's getting lighter, though, isn't it?" Jamie felt like she could see farther.

"I hope so. Come on. You can stay at my place and . . . oh, your feet." She clucked her tongue in dismay. "I'll take care of them at my apartment and then we'll get you back to the camp."

"Thank you," Jamie said, heartfelt. "And it's not Whelan, it's Haynes," she reminded her. "I got married in April."

"Of course. And now you're having a baby."

"I'm not actually having it," Jamie reminded her. "Mary Jo is our surrogate."

"Here we are."

They passed by several yurts to enter the main courtyard. In the drifting fog, Jamie saw about twenty women wearing crowns of flowers, all dressed in white.

The wedding, she realized.

Although it was odd the way they were all standing in a

semicircle, seemingly waiting for her and Sunny Dae to appear. There was no sign of Lark.

"Get the rope!" Lanny ordered, outside the maintenance shed. Austin, Niles, Lendel, and several other guys were scrambling to find whatever they could to rescue Greer and Allie.

Marissa stood next to Harley, practically *on* Harley, as she was in deep shock after Harley had told her about Cam's death. She seemed to want to practically dive inside Harley's skin to hide. Emma stood by, wearing her worried frown.

Ropes, shovels, a pick-ax, blankets, black plastic tarps, a thermos filled with hot tea . . . the band of would-be rescuers were arming themselves. Niles and his father were part of the group, working together for once, it appeared.

Ella's band of counselors was standing by as well. Harley had grudgingly thanked them for the thermos as it was Ella's idea, though Tina and Warren had taken over the kitchen.

As soon as they were ready, Harley and the men headed out, flashlight beams dancing ahead of them. Emma insisted on going as well, though Harley managed to talk Marissa into staying with Kiley without too much trouble. She was a complete wreck.

When the group reached the woods and the barely discernible trail that led to the hut, Harley was put in the lead. As soon as she felt she was close to where the pit was, she started hollering Greer's name and soon he yelled back. That energized the group, which crashed through the woods like a herd of buffalo. Everyone was gung-ho and focused, so there was very little questioning of Hope's whereabouts. That might come later.

It was easy enough getting Allie out. She was wild-eyed and scared, but she was eager and athletic and she grabbed the rope and scampered up the slippery, muddy sides of the pit as the men pulled her up. Allie then threw herself on the ground and started bawling with relief. Greer stayed down in the pit while Lanny rappelled down to help wrap a rope around Cam's body and bring him up. The odor of death was growing and Harley had to stagger away when she witnessed the bloated body. Cam had clearly been dead for a few days.

Greer was pulled up and Lanny followed.

Harley wanted to throw herself in Greer's arms, but it wasn't the time or place. His face was white and though he tried to hobble, he was helped along by Lendel and Niles as they worked their way back to the trail. Lanny and Niles's father rolled Cam's body in the tarp and lashed it around him with baling twine. Allie refused the hot tea but Greer drank it and managed to coerce her into having some. Like Harley, she wanted to throw herself at Greer, but she was forced to walk out on her own. Lanny tried to ask her how she fell in the pit, but apart from saying she was mad and just took off and it was covered with fir boughs, she didn't have much more to add.

Definitely a trap of some kind, Harley determined.

As they drew closer toward the camp, Emma stopped short, letting the rest of the group go around her, an island in the stream.

"What's going on?" Harley asked. The fog appeared to be lessening, at least on lower elevations. Emma, spying a curling wisp of fog wrapping around her right leg, picked up her leg and shook it off. "I want to find Jamie."

"We have to head back toward the camp and take the other trail to the commune, then."

"You said the phone bars were this way." She pointed toward the hut, up the trail, and into the fog.

Harley closed her eyes. She felt weary beyond belief. Yes, she'd told the rescuers that she and Greer had gone to the hut in search of cell service. "We didn't find cell service, though," she reminded.

"Did you look hard?"

"Yes! Both Greer and I tried." When Emma didn't move, she admitted, "But it was foggier. Maybe that was the problem."

"I'm going to go."

"Emma, no. We need to go back to the camp with everyone. And anyway, you don't have a cell phone."

"You do," she said reasonably.

"Okay . . . yes, but I want to check on Greer. And there was . . . someone was staying at the cabin. Their belongings were strewn around."

"Eee-saw?" She perked up.

"I don't know who. I didn't see them. But I don't think it's safe to go there."

"I don't want to go back to the camp."

"I'm not all that crazy about it anymore, either, but we have to."

"You go ahead," said Emma. "I'll go find Jamie."

"Wait! Wait a minute." Harley calculated how long it would take to do as Emma wanted. She wasn't eager to hand over her cell phone, and she didn't want Emma wandering around by herself in the first place. "I'll take you to the hut if you promise we'll go right back to the camp."

"I promise," she said solemnly.

Harley turned back to Greer, who was being propped up by Niles and Lendel. "I'm okay," he told her.

"I have to go."

"Be careful," he warned, his serious tone causing the hair on her arms to stand on end.

She nodded, then turned back to Emma, who was already plodding ahead.


Rona had been tramping down the lane toward the main road, entertaining thoughts of getting the car and driving back for Kiley and Donovan. There was a key taped inside the wheel . . . well, hopefully, unless Donovan had removed it.

The fog had lessened on this side of the camp and she was able to see farther in front of her. What a goddamn relief. She heard voices in the fog and slowed her steps.

". . . not leaving without him!" Wendy declared. "I'm going back!"

Caleb muttered something Rona couldn't quite catch. Not wanting to step into their continuing argument about Esau, which this undoubtedly was, she started walking carefully backward. But a few words reached her ears and she stopped and strained to listen.

". . . tricked me . . . you weren't ever . . . God's eyes are on you . . . 'and the inhabitants of the earth have been made drunk with the wine of her fornication' . . ."

"You are so full of shit!" Wendy's voice came clear and strong.

Rona sensed Wendy was coming her way so as noiselessly as possible she hurried back the way she'd come. Forget the car. She would find Kiley, and wherever the hell Donovan was, he could find her.

To her shock, she suddenly came face-to-face with a man standing in the middle of the road.

"Cain?" she said in disbelief.

He pulled back his fist and knocked her flat. She lay on the ground, trying to think. She lost consciousness shortly after he picked her up and threw her over his shoulder.


Wendy's lips were clamped together in a thin line as she headed back toward the camp and the still-menacing fog. She'd lied and cheated to be married to him, and he'd turned out to be a mean-spirited, overbearing bastard. Twenty years . . . *twenty years*!

Was it over now? Was it finally over? Was she ready to break away completely from him?

Her mother had never liked Caleb. Had thought his piety was all an act, but Wendy hadn't listened. He'd been so good-looking in high school. So good at sports. So attentive. So popular! She'd made the mistake of flirting with that bad boy, Dean, and well . . . doing some stuff. When Caleb found out, he broke up with her and she thought she'd die. And then she'd found out she was pregnant! Glory hallelujah!

When she told him he went white, but he did the right thing. He told his parents and, though they'd initially scorned Wendy for trapping their son, they'd also done the right thing. The wedding was planned.

Wendy, newly graduated, had been pressured into being a CIT at Camp Fog Lake by Rona and Brooke. As soon as she was engaged, however, she pulled the plug on that plan. Well, she'd *intended* to, but then she miscarried. She saw the blood in the toilet and knew it for what it was. She told no one of her misfortune and cried herself to sleep that night.

She could hardly face Caleb. She lost weight and grew pale . . . and never canceled the trip to Camp Fog Lake. Caleb was perplexed when she decided to go anyway. He thought it unseemly for his pregnant fiancée to go to a co-ed camp, but he was on his way to a sabbatical anyway, so, why not? She never intended to cheat. She really didn't. But there he was. Cain. He didn't say where he came from, but she figured he was from that cult on the other side of the lake. He was attractive and smooth and she saw him as the snake in the Garden of Eden, a tempter by nature. Even so, she never would have gone with him if it weren't for Emma Whelan. Emma got all the guys without even trying. She just had a sort of blithe disregard for anyone but herself that guys seemed to go nuts over. An "it" factor. She sensed that Cain, like everyone else, wanted Emma. He stayed in the shadows, more myth than reality to the rest of her friends, but Wendy was always looking for him, keenly aware of him when he was watching from behind the shrubbery.

Then one day he grabbed her. Just jumped out of the bushes and dragged her back with him. He made love to her as if he were starving for her. She felt the exact same way . . . and way, way back, in a dark, hidden corner of her mind, she thought: *Maybe he'll get me pregnant.*

And he did.

And she thought about that when she killed him. Whore, murderess, evil temptress, liar . . . she was all that and more. But God gave her Esau anyway! God knew she wasn't all bad.

Except Esau was missing and Cain was alive, according to Emma.

What if Cain knew Esau was his son? What if he'd done something to him? Wendy had encouraged Esau and Lark's blossoming relationship when they were at the commune. Over the years she'd fallen out of love and lust with her husband, and she'd also learned to agree with her mother: his piety was a sham.

*Be careful, daughter,* Mama had said. *The dog that bites at the tires and catches the car never knows what to do with it once he's caught it.*

She hadn't initially understood. She'd wanted Caleb. She'd wanted to be married to him. And to do that she'd needed to be pregnant.

But now she knew what it meant to "catch the car" and find out you don't really want it. Twenty years of marriage . . . twenty difficult years . . .

She was ready to let that car drive away on its own.

And she was going to Haven Commune to find her son.

Harley tried to hurry Emma up, but she always moved at a deliberate pace. She was holding the flashlight and Harley wanted to take it from her, but sometimes Emma could be stubborn and Harley didn't want a fight. This was a bad idea. Except that Harley was starting to worry about Mom, too. As soon as they got back to the camp, Harley was going to head up the trail to Suicide Ledge and Haven Commune and find her. She didn't even want to think that maybe she wasn't there. How long had she been gone? Hours and hours. That wasn't like her. But she had no way to contact them besides walkie-talkies.

Which reminded her that Hope had come this way.

Harley slowed her steps abruptly and Emma almost ran into her.

"I think we should be really quiet on our approach," she told her aunt.

"If it's Eee-saw, then—"

"What if it's not?" Harley cut her off. "What if it's . . ."

"Cain?" put in Emma when Harley trailed off.

"Yeah, him. Or, some other bad dude—and I mean *bad*. We have to be careful. I saw a guy come this way. Couldn't see who he was exactly. But I think Hope was following him."

"Was she quiet on her approach?"

"I don't know. But just follow my lead, okay?"

"Okay."


Rona woke up slowly. She was on her back, on the floor, staring at a rough board ceiling. Her head thundered, and it took her a moment to remember that Cain had knocked her unconscious.

She jerked at the memory and suddenly his face was above hers and he was staring down at her. She felt his hands close around her neck, slowly squeezing. They stared at each other and Rona realized he was enjoying himself.

"You tried to kill me," he whispered. "But I'm still here."

*Cain . . .* she mouthed.

"God has seen fit to bring all of you back to me."

She thought of Wendy, fighting on the road with Caleb. And Brooke . . . had she really gone to Haven Commune?

*You should have gone with her. You'd be safe.*

"Are you planning to kill me?" Her voice was barely audible. Fear was sliding icily through her veins, but she struggled not to show it.

"It's your fault. I didn't know it was possible to kill till you showed me. You and Wendy and Brooke," he sneered.

"That's a lie. You killed Fern and Ryan—"

"That was betrayal," Cain defended himself. "She betrayed me. You and those other two bitches threw me into the lake! And your friend, Wendy—she lied about me! I've never raped any woman. They've all wanted me."

Dully, Rona realized the rules were whatever he made them. Fern's and Ryan's deaths didn't count. It was what she and Wendy and Brooke had done to him that mattered.

"Betrayal deserves death," he said, as if he'd read her thoughts. "Hope betrayed me."

*Hope?*

"Where's Hope?" she dared to ask. She needed her senses back. She needed to find a way to get free. Fight. Warn Brooke and Wendy.

"Suicide Ledge," he said with satisfaction.


There were voices. Two voices, Harley thought as she and Emma drew near to the hut.

". . . Suicide Ledge," a man's voice said.

Harley immediately grabbed Emma's hand and took the flashlight, turning it off. Through the cracks in the hut's walls she could see the uncertain light from another flashlight, a bright one. Emma sucked in a breath, but Harley placed her finger over her aunt's lips and shook her head. Harley edged carefully forward with Emma right behind her.

"What did you do to her?" a woman's voice asked. Rona. But she sounded dull, the words slow and slurred.

"The same thing I did to Adam. He betrayed me, too. Told Father on me and he beat me with a strap. Blistered my behind. But all I was doing was following in his footsteps. I didn't kill Arianna. I know my mother thinks I did, but that wasn't me. Father knew I knew. He sent me away for a while, but I came back. And then *you . . . you* and *your friends . . .* Marlon had to put me together again. An accident, we told everyone, but I stayed out of sight until after the camp closed. Joy suspected. I had to make a deal with her to keep her quiet. She thinks I'm Josh and that I'm getting married today to lovely, pure Lark."

"Who's Josh?"

*SLAP!*

Harley jerked at the sound and so did Emma.

"*I am!*" he yelled. "*And that lovely, pure bitch is fucking my son!*"

*SLAP!*

Emma stepped forward in fury, but Harley was swifter. She ran past Emma and burst through the hut's door as Josh, leaning over Rona, reared up in surprise. Without thought, Harley cracked the flashlight against his head. It knocked him sideways, but he was still on his feet. He roared at her and lunged, but Harley slammed the flashlight beneath his chin, then darted back outside into the fog. He staggered after her, roaring and swearing.

Emma stuck out her foot.

He tripped and sprawled on the ground. Harley smacked him on the head one more time, but he wouldn't give up. He threw himself upward and lunged for her, his hands clawing, snagging her shirt.

But Rona had found the bright flashlight and now shone it up at him from where she lay. Blood, black in the harsh light, ran down his temple.

"Come at me and I'll break your teeth in," Harley snarled, dancing away.

He shot a look at Emma.

She said, "Cain."

He spat on the ground and lurched away into the under-brush.

Harley immediately ran to Rona, who was trying to sit up. "My throat," she whispered.

"Don't say anything. Don't do anything," warned Harley.

"We've got to warn Wendy and Brooke."

"I'll do it."

Rona sank back down, closed her eyes, and muttered, "You're a real badass."

"Emma, stay with her, please." And then she was gone.


Jamie wiggled her bandaged feet. She was sitting on a chair in Sunny Dae's apartment, which was much like Joy's but with a real kitchen, not just a microwave. Herbs hung from the ceiling along with pots and pans. Something was simmering on the stove and Sunny Dae had changed into a white dress, but had an apron over it.

"What are you making?" asked Jamie.

"It's for the groom. A drink of virility. He will be at-tended by all the women of Haven."

"I'm not getting married," she said on a strained laugh.

Sunny Dae frowned and said, "Lark is marrying Josh."

"Okay, good. Joy thought Lark was . . ." She broke off, feeling slightly embarrassed about her fear-driven flight. She changed the subject. "So, Josh is the only man here? Besides Rolff?"

She nodded. "Men are really only good for one thing, aren't they? Giving us children," she said unexpectedly.

Jamie thought she must be joking. "Let me think, men must be good for at least one other thing."

Sunny Dae turned back to her simmering pot. "I'm Rolff's second wife. I didn't want him to marry a third and he hasn't. Joy seems to have that all mixed up."

"Well, good," Jamie responded, not sure quite what to say.

"But Rolff didn't want any competition, either, so there are no other eligible men except for Josh. Unfortunately, neither of them knows the meaning of fidelity, so they fornicate with whomever they please. Cornelia has passed from this world." She sighed. "Sometimes I think she's the lucky one."

Jamie kept silent.

"Pastor Rolff has a wonderful reputation. His sermons were so inspiring, they could make you weep. I still can get tears in my eyes, remembering. But he was a man, pure and simple, and his usefulness is over."

"Well, that . . . seems kind of harsh." Jamie wondered what the herbs were hanging above her. She didn't recognize them. She got up and walked carefully to look at a long stem of a dried plant, thinking she really needed to find her shoes. She reached a hand forward.

"Don't touch that," Sunny Dae snapped.

Jamie yanked her hand back. "What is it?" she asked, but she knew, she already knew.

"Poison hemlock. It does have medicinal purposes, but you have to be very careful."

Jamie stared at the older woman, whose aproned, round figure and gentle expression were in contrast to her iron capability. "Was it really alcohol poisoning that sickened Kendra?" she asked carefully.

"I don't think so," Sunny Dae admitted.

Jamie felt a sudden surge of adrenaline through her system that made her feel light-headed. Her instincts about the commune had been on the money. "Someone poisoned her?"

She looked incredibly sad. "I'm a good person. I've always only wanted what's best for my children and Haven Commune."

"You . . . you poisoned Kendra?" Jamie asked, her throat hot.

"No. No. Of course not. But, God forgive me, I planted the idea that Cornelia had Huntington's in Rolff's brain. I didn't know the idea would take root so deeply. I just wanted him for myself. Rolff thought Cornelia had passed the disease onto Joy and onto Arianna. I was the one who told him about poison hemlock. He watched Joy like a hawk, waiting for symptoms that would never come. Then she was pregnant with Arianna and his obsession about both of them grew. I was afraid that as soon as the baby was born, he would kill them both. But then God sent an answer. The Luft-Shawks had always wanted a child. They could have Arianna and Joy could run the camp for them. Joy was told the baby died at birth. She never knew. She got the camp and that got her away from her father. It saved her, too."

"You're saying Rolff poisoned Kendra?" Jamie had seen the older man and didn't see how that was possible.

She sighed. "I believe that was Josh. Or, more accurately, Cain."

"Cain?" Jamie's heart flipped over painfully.

"He renamed himself in his teens. Anything bad he did, it was Cain's fault. He was with my younger son, Adam, when he drowned. Josh said it was an accident, but Rolff blamed him anyway. Josh then switched and said it was Cain's fault. Everything thereafter was Cain's fault."

*I didn't have sex with Cain but he was able.*

"Cain slew his younger brother, Abel," said Jamie.

Sunny Dae held her gaze and nodded.


Allie was shaking and shaking and the layers of blankets over her shoulders and around her torso couldn't seem to warm her up. She sat on a chair in the lodge surrounded by

Ella and her posse, and all looked at Greer and Lanny and everyone involved in the rescue through wide, scared eyes.

Marissa felt like she was having an out-of-body experience. Her mind had only grasped a few salient points, but from what she'd learned, Cam had fallen into the pit and died sometime after breaking up with her. She couldn't think beyond that, though the conversation whirled around her.

". . . Hope has the walkie . . ."

". . . Harwick's taking the truck to his car . . ."

". . . tried the hut where there was service before, but no bars . . ."

". . . candlelight vigil at the lakeshore . . ."

That last comment was from Ella. She and her followers rose as one and grabbed their candles. Kiley was with them, but she looked over at Marissa and silently asked if she wanted to join them. Marissa had the strange desire to laugh. With everything else, they wanted to keep with the vigil? Like any of them gave a shit about Marlon or anyone else.

Her nose suddenly burned with unshed tears. It was all so unreal. She should have gone with Harley and Emma. She should have insisted. She wanted her family around her.

"Hey."

She looked up as Greer—whose ankle was strapped to two pieces of wood, a makeshift splint designed by Warren—slid a few chairs closer. His pale face revealed the pain he was feeling but he didn't complain.

"How're you doing?" he asked kindly.

That did it. The tears ran down her cheeks. She didn't know Greer all that well. He'd been Harley's boyfriend, but Marissa had never really gotten to know him. She'd been jealous of their relationship, she knew now, and she'd wished they would just break up. She almost wanted to apologize now.

The chorus of blood-curdling shrieks that sounded from the lake caused Marissa to jerk in alarm. Greer got to his feet and hurriedly and awkwardly limped toward the door.

Brooke, from Foxglove, and Lendel's dad, Mr. Zenke, had been talking to each other, but they anxiously followed Greer.

Cru-Ella stumbled into the lodge, fog racing in around her. "There's a dead man in the canoe!"

Brooke waited half a beat as that sunk in, then pushed past Ella and the other traumatized counselors and headed through the drifting fog to the water's edge. She'd done her damnedest to stay away from that shore, away from the site of their crime, but she was past that now.

The largest canoe had been righted and a man's body was lying inside, an arrow shaft sticking out of his thigh. Blood had poured from a wound in his throat. His eyes were open and staring upward into a clearing but dark sky.

Donovan. Oh, God! *Donovan! Why?*

She staggered backward, felt faint.

Cain was behind this. He'd killed Donovan. And she had no doubt he'd dug the pit Allie had fallen into. Some kind of trap meant for . . . ? She didn't know. But she knew she and Rona and Wendy weren't safe.

The fog was lifting. She could go on the trail. Maybe Wendy and Caleb had left and were safe, but Kiley was still here, and Donovan, so Rona must still be around.

She bent over, felt physically sick. Her brain swirled and she clamped down on her emotions with an iron fist. She had to warn Rona.

Lanny had joined her and his harsh gasp was like a dash of cold water. Brooke straightened. She wasn't going to wait around and wring her hands. She ran back up the hill from the lake.

"Where're you going?" yelled Lanny, but she didn't answer because she didn't really know.

\* \* \*

"So, is Josh still getting married today, then?" asked Jamie. She was feeling anxious and uncomfortable. A lot of time had passed and though she'd foisted herself on Sunny Dae, she now wanted to leave, and yet felt somehow that that wouldn't be acceptable.

"Lark is in love with someone else." Her voice had turned flat.

"You don't approve."

She sighed. "We hoped . . . we all hoped . . . that she would be the reason Josh settled down. He was Cain a lot, in the old days. Rolff sent him to Georgia and Jedidiah's boarding school—the Luft-Shawks," she clarified, "but he didn't last there, either. He and his friends got into trouble, the school closed, and he came home. He had his eye on Fern. She was a beauty, no doubt, but she didn't feel the same. She was running away with Christopher, whose family had left us a few years earlier, when . . . she met her demise."

*He killed her.* Sunny Dae didn't say it, but Jamie could tell she believed Josh/Cain had killed Fern Galbraith and possibly Christopher Ryan Stofsky as well. When she was back home, she would tell Cooper about it, see if a case could be made now that implicated Josh Ulland.

Which made her wonder why Sunny Dae was being so forthright with her. A whisper of intuition swept over her. What did Sunny Dae want from her?

Carefully, she asked, "Are you worried for Lark?"

"Not anymore." She took a pot that was just starting to bubble off the stove. There was no scent to speak of, apart from something earthy and weed-like. Jamie's eyes followed her as she poured the hot liquid into a rust-colored earthernware pot.

"What is that?" she asked, hearing how tight her voice was.

"Just a tincture."

Bull. Shit.

"I really need to get my shoes and get back." Jamie looked toward the apartment's front door.

"You can't go till after the wedding."

"Oh, I can't stay. I know my daughter and sister are waiting for me. And I called my husband. You have cell service here. So glad! I got through to him while I was hiding from Joy," she lied. "He's coming here soon to pick me up. He's a detective with the River Glen Police Department. What time is the wedding? I don't think you said." She was rattling on and sweat was beading at her temples.

"I don't think you're being truthful, Mrs. Haynes. I want you to help me trap him, when he gets here. He doesn't trust any of us, but if you play your part right, he'll believe he's helping you escape. Then we'll feed him the poison."

She sounded so reasonable. Like she expected Jamie to just go along. "Well, that can't happen."

"He's trying to kill your sister's friends. He blames them for nearly drowning him. I blamed them a long time, too, but I didn't know the extent of Cain's perfidy. We've all tried to pretend it isn't happening again. He did stop for a long time," she added earnestly. "But now he's hunting again. When Kendra stumbled out of the woods, I really hoped it wasn't what I thought it was. I wanted to believe she really was seeing someone else, that it was alcohol poisoning. But now I believe she was just the prologue. He wants the three women who tossed him in the lake and anyone associated with them."

"I can help . . . my husband will help stop him."

"I don't really want the police. You can help me on your own."

"Why me?" Jamie asked, her mind racing.

"Because you're here. Because you're interested in Haven. I suppose it goes without saying that Josh . . . Cain . . . is the reason Mary Jo and her family and Stephen's family left.

She miscarried soon after she was with Josh, which was probably a blessing, though I believe she assuages her guilt now by carrying babies full term."

"I'll go call Cooper again . . ."

Jamie hurried to the door on feet that sent new pains shooting from her soles. Outside, the white-dressed women were waiting. She tried to skirt around them. Joy was not among them. Neither was Lark.

They closed in a little nearer. "It's time Cain found his way to the hell from which he sprang," one of them said.

"You were sent to help us."

Once again Jamie took Lark's words to heart.

She *ran*.


Wendy's legs ached as she climbed toward Suicide Ledge, the crest of the trail between the camp and the commune. The fog was shifting below but the higher she reached, the thicker it became. The sun had made the fog a light gray but it was sinking into the horizon and the haze was growing darker. She could see only a few feet in front of her. But her thoughts were simply a prayer that her son was safe. Nothing else mattered.

She reached the top and stopped short. A body lay on the slab. A woman.

Heart fluttering, inwardly shrieking, she tiptoed around it.

Hope was lying on her back, eyes closed, arms crossed over her chest. There were white flowers on thick stalks scattered around her. An urn lay tipped on its side, ashes spilled onto the ground.

She opened her mouth to shriek but it took a long moment before any sound came out. Then she screamed to the skies for all she was worth.

Down the trail, Harley heard her and figured the sound came from Suicide Ledge or thereabouts. She doubled her pace, swearing at the lingering fog.

Brooke heard the scream, too, though more faintly as she was farther from the source, a ghostly sound that seemed to bury itself in her soul.

Cain, head aching, blood trickling down his head and into his mouth, smiled grimly at the fear in that terrified female voice. He assumed it was the little bitch who'd attacked him at the hut and slowed him down. Good. God's retribution was at hand.

# Chapter 30

One look at Hope and Harley fell to her knees, listening hard to hear if she was breathing. "CPR? Have you given her CPR?" she demanded of Wendy.

"No . . . I . . . no."

Harley clasped one of her hands over the other and started pushing rhythmically on Hope's chest. In her head was the tune of "Stayin' Alive"—how she'd learned to count for CPR.

"He . . . he did this," Wendy said. "Cain! He did this! He did this! You don't know him . . . but he did this."

"We've met," Harley muttered tersely.

"He wants to kill me! He wants to kill us all!"

"Because Esau's his son?"

She gasped and staggered as if hit by a blow. "No! No. He blames us . . . What a thing to say. How did you . . . why did you say that?"

Harley didn't have time or the energy to fill her in. She leaned down to listen, but Hope wasn't breathing. Her lips were blue. Harley closed her eyes and continued.

And then out of the gloom came Cain. Harley saw him

first. Her pulse leapt, but she couldn't abandon her post. Wendy saw him at the same moment as he lurched toward her. "There you are!" he crowed.

"Stay away from me," she warned him. "Stay away!"

*Stayin' alive. Stayin' alive . . .*

"Thought our son could steal my girl, did you?"

"You stay right there. Don't move." Wendy backed away slowly.

*Ah, ha, ha, ha, stayin' alive . . .*

Cain paid no attention to Harley. Just lumbered by her as if she wasn't there. He grabbed Wendy's arm and she started screaming and hitting at him.

"Stop!" Harley yelled.

And then Wendy's husband shot into view—Caleb. He yelled something at the top of his lungs and Cain swung around on him, knocking Wendy off her feet.

"*No!*" Harley screamed as Wendy pin-wheeled her arms, falling backward, stumbling out of control toward the cliff edge. Caleb jumped forward to grab her just as Cain gave him a hard push. In utter disbelief and terror, Harley watched Wendy and Caleb fly over the cliff together.

Then Cain turned hot eyes on her.

Quivering all over, Harley stood up. She knew Hope was gone. She knew Cain had sacrificed her like he'd sacrificed Fern and that girl before her.

Then Brooke was there, appearing as if by magic.

And before Harley could hardly react, her mom appeared from the other direction, her face white and set, a rock nestled in her palm. Cain's back was to her. He didn't see her. He only saw Brooke.

Harley wanted to warn them, scream at them to run and hide, but she saw the look from Mom's eyes and merely whimpered, "Hope's dead."

Brooke said, "Everyone knows it's you, Cain. You can't get away. The people you caught in the pit are free."

"The pit was for you and your friends, bitch. It wasn't meant for the blundering fools it caught."

"The police are on their way."

He grinned at her. "Such a lying, pretty mouth."

"They've taken the truck. Donovan Hemphill was still alive and named you as his attempted killer."

"*Liar!*" He leapt at her.

But Mom was quicker and so was Harley. They jumped at the same moment. Mom crashed the rock down on his head with all her force she could muster. Harley dived for his legs. Brooke elbowed him in the face. Blood gushed and he staggered back, roaring with fury.

He kicked at Harley and she bit hard into his calf muscle. With a shriek of rage he jerked away, reeling into the fog, heading in the direction of the commune.

Mom suddenly sat down hard and put her head between her knees, shaking so hard Harley thought she might fall apart.

"Mom, Mom . . ." she whispered, putting her arms around her as Brooke also slowly sank to the ground beside them.

Harley caught Brooke's gaze, silently asked if one or both of them should go after him.

"Don't," said Mom. "They're waiting for him."

# Epilogue

September looked over the top of her computer monitor across the squad room. She could hear the familiar squeak of George's desk chair even before she saw him bent forward, peering closely at his own screen. Above the general low hum of conversation among other officers, Captain Calvetti's indistinct voice rose and fell as she spoke to someone on the phone inside her glass-enclosed office. Fourth of July was over and everyone was back at work and had been all of this truncated week, while the news coming out of Winslow County and the deaths surrounding Camp Fog Lake and Haven Commune dominated the news cycle.

September was putting the finishing touches on the report she had on the now deceased Joshua Ulland, who was allegedly responsible for a number of homicides over the course of the holiday weekend. Even before the sheriff's department had learned of the deaths, they'd been alerted to trouble when one young woman was hospitalized for supposed alcohol poisoning and Camp Fog Lake's handyman, Marlon Kern, had died of what had initially appeared to have been cardiac arrest. In light of the suspicious deaths at and around the camp, those two incidents were under further review.

As soon as September had learned about Ulland's alleged involvement, she'd contacted Detective Barbara Gillette of the Winslow County Sheriff's Department and told her what she'd learned about Richard Everly's connections to both Joshua Ulland and Brody Daniels. Now she was laying it down on paper, so to speak, keeping it in terms of what she knew to be true, which was that the three men had been acquaintances and friends at the Glory to God school, that their misdeeds had contributed to the school's closure, and that both Everly and Daniels had been recent victims of homicide. She'd also added that Everly was a gifted hacker who'd been hired by Daniels to find who was amplifying an internet smear campaign against his wife, Brooke Daniels, and that person appeared to be the opportunist Everly, who was working on his own agenda as well. The through-line between Everly and Daniels appeared to be the reason both had been killed.

Those were the facts of September's report, but since the news broke on Ulland's alleged rampage, she'd spoken directly with Detective Gillette and freely voiced her opinions.

"Josh Ulland killed both R.J. and Brody Daniels to keep them quiet. They knew him from Glory to God, had gotten into trouble with him there, or at least had covered up for him. Before Camp Fog Lake opened up their alumni weekend, Ulland was targeting Brody Daniels's wife as a means to control or use Daniels. There's no record of Daniels's time at Glory to God, though I believe a deeper dive into his past will uncover that the accusations of sexual misconduct at that school involved Daniels in some way. With his ascendance in the financial world, Daniels was desperate to keep his time at Glory to God deep in the rearview, but Ulland had other ideas. Maybe he was blackmailing Daniels, or maybe it was something personal."

"It was something personal," Detective Gillette had interjected. In their own preliminary investigation, the sheriff's department learned that it appeared Ulland's main aim for his alleged killings was to get revenge on three women from his past, one of them being Brooke Daniels, who'd attacked him when she and Rona Keegan had discovered him raping their friend, Wendy Hemphill. Hemphill, along with her husband, Caleb, were two of the deceased from the current mass killing at and around Camp Fog Lake.

Gillette had gone so far as to postulate that Brody Daniels's initial interest in his wife, Brooke, was because he knew of Josh Ulland's obsession with her, though he didn't know why.

September had continued her own narration, saying, "Everly likely hit up Ulland for money as well as Daniels. When Ulland caught wind of it, he killed Everly, who was too untrustworthy, and broke into his home on Carmine Ridge, stealing his laptop and/or whatever else Everly used in his hacking enterprise. Everly's death freaked out Daniels, who must have known he was likely next on Ulland's hit list."

"Somewhere in there Ulland learned about Camp Fog Lake's parent/alumni weekend," Gillette had put in, nodding. "He likely knew one or all of his three quarries, Brooke Daniels, Rona Keegan, and Wendy Hemphill, were attending."

"He had to take care of Daniels before that weekend to get him out of the way, if he was going after his wife," September had realized. She'd added that Ulland likely planned to kill his targets using poison hemlock as it had been determined that, though the official cause of Brody Daniels's death was strangulation, he'd been given poison hemlock, probably in liquid form, which had splashed on him and blistered his skin.

Detective Gillette had then filled her in on some pieces of information that hadn't quite hit the airwaves. Almost twenty years earlier, Ulland was now believed to be behind the death of a girl named Fern Galbraith, whose body had been found at a place called Suicide Ledge, about halfway between what had then been Camp Fog Lake—Camp Love Shack, as it was "affectionately" known—and Haven Commune, Josh Ulland's home. Galbraith's body was found left in the same ritualistic way—arms folded over the chest, sprinkled with ash—as Ulland's sister, Hope Newell, had been discovered over the past weekend. Galbraith's death had long been believed to be half of a murder/suicide plot perpetrated by Fern's lover, Christopher Ryan Stofsky. At least that's the narrative Pastor Rolff Ulland of Haven Commune had heartily endorsed and which the sheriff's department had accepted. Now Galbraith's case was going to be reopened.

Gillette had spoken personally with members of Haven Commune about Josh Ulland and, on condition of anonymity, they'd painted a stark and ugly picture of Joshua Ulland's character. Before "Camp Love Shack" closed, Ulland had used the camp for his sexual exploits as his father, Pastor Rolff, had expressly forbidden his son from becoming involved with anyone from the commune. Ulland had been scheduled to marry Fern Galbraith, but she'd had no interest in him. She hadn't, apparently, had any interest in Christopher Stofsky, either; he was merely a friend trying to help her escape a marriage she didn't want. Josh Ulland had killed them both. According to his mother, Sunny Dae Ulland—who'd been remarkably stoic when her son staggered into the commune, collapsed, and died of an apparent "brain bleed" the previous Sunday—her son could never abide betrayal.

The sheriff's department was still trying to piece together all the ins and outs of what had happened at the environs around Camp Fog Lake over the past weekend. Interviews were ongoing. One surprising note was that one of the people who'd physically fought with Joshua Ulland was Jamie Haynes, the wife of River Glen Police Department detective

Cooper Haynes. His stepdaughter, Jamie Haynes's daughter, Harley Woodward, had also had a hand in keeping Joshua Ulland from harming more people.

September finished up her report and handed it in to Captain Calvetti. There was a lot more to the story, that was clear, but her own official involvement was over.

Three weeks after Camp Fog Lake closed, Harley sat in a pew at the memorial service for both Caleb and Wendy Hemphill alongside her mother, her aunt, and her stepfather. Marissa hadn't joined them. Since returning from camp she'd stayed at her mom's place, which was close to the Dornbrenners—Cam's family—and Cam's parents and Marissa were comforting one another in their grief. Harley and everyone had tried to help, but it was just going to take time.

Harley glanced down the pew to the people seated across from them on the other side of the aisle. Greer was there, his leg cast to the knee, and though he was seated by Allie, who was a second cousin to Hope, he had made it clear to her that there was no relationship between them any longer. Allie had apparently accepted this news, though Harley suspected she was just trying to show how amenable she was as a means to keep hanging around him, and hope he'd realize he'd made a mistake. Harley could have told her that wasn't going to work. Greer had told Harley that, if she was willing, he'd like another chance.

She smiled to herself. Hell yes, she was willing.

Remembering where she was, she settled back and tried to concentrate on the funeral . . . but her mind wandered a bit. She and Marissa had gone together to see Kendra, who'd been released from the hospital and was making a full recovery. They'd exchanged information on the camp and Kendra had admitted that Cain was the older man she was seeing. "Yeah, I was drunk, but I wasn't that drunk," she admitted, negating the alcohol poisoning. "Cain put that stuff in my mouth. I spit it out. But I guess it was poison. Nobody was listening to me!"

Harley had finally got it: *Cain . . . in my mouth . . .* She wished she'd been able to decipher that message correctly at the time. Who knew . . . it might've saved a lot of death and destruction. She tried to apologize to Kendra, who told her to forget it.

"It wasn't your fault I made such shitty choices. I'm just glad to still be here!"

The hymn the organist had been playing ended and the minister said solemnly, "And now Caleb and Wendy's son, Esau, would like to speak about his parents . . ."

Harley looked toward the front of the small church with its curved overhead pine beams and the large, circular stained glass window of Mary and the baby Jesus, which took most of the far wall. She watched Esau walk up the stairs to the lectern, his expression sober.

"Eee-saw," said Emma.

"Eee-saw," Harley repeated softly.

Mom looked over at them and gave them the evil eye.

When it all hit the fan after Hope's death and Josh's staggering departure into the fog, it was decided that Harley should be the one to go back to the camp and alert them to what happened. Brooke was sent to the main road in search of cell service, and Mom, who was weak and couldn't walk well, as her bandaged feet were cut and bloodied, stayed with Hope.

The fog had been lifting as Harley reached the camp, but even so she'd barely gotten back and was standing near the sheet-metal mirror when she heard the thumping. She'd stared at the door and then gotten both Greer and Lanny Zenke to come over and pull the screws to open the door. Esau had tumbled out, gagged and tied. He'd been rushed to the hospital but, though drugged, had recovered. He'd said that Joshua Ulland had grabbed him and thrown something over his mouth that had knocked him out. Before he lost consciousness, Ulland had said he was his father and he couldn't have Lark. Esau didn't know who had screwed the door shut, but the general consensus was that it had been Hope. Had she known Esau was in there? Was she trying to harm him, or just save him from Josh, should Josh decide maybe it wasn't worth it to save his son after all . . . ? Impossible to know what her motivations were, but Esau survived and connected with Lark, who'd previously been unable to meet with him. Hope and Josh's half sister, Joy, had told Mom that Esau and Lark were both dead, but Joy, who apparently wasn't a reliable source, had luckily been mistaken.

A DNA test had proven Esau was an Ulland, which Esau was still getting used to.

They listened to Esau's words and Harley looked toward the pew where he'd been seated. She could just see Lark through the heads of other mourners. Emma hadn't managed to get Lark's note to Esau because Josh had intervened by kidnapping him. But things had worked out between them. She hoped for the same for her and Greer.

The service ended forty minutes later, and everyone stood and made their way outside into a warm late July day.


Brooke stood beside Rona on the church lawn, turning her face to a small but welcome breeze. Rona had spent some time recovering in the hospital, which had freaked out Kiley, but Rona had assured both her daughter, whom she was delighted was showing that she cared about her mother, and Brooke that she was fine, totally fine.

Now, watching the mourners leave the white clapboard church, Rona said, "So, you're dating Lanny?"

"No. Where'd you get that? We've had a few lunches. That's all."

"Lunches lead to dinners, which lead to after-dinner

drinks, which lead to make-out sessions on the couch, taking chocolates out of each other's mouths, and sex on the living room floor."

Brooke actually laughed—the first time she'd done that since the events at the camp and the mind-boggling horror and grief of learning about Brody's death. She was still grappling with being a widow, but as Brody's suspected financial dealings kept coming to light, snowballing, she'd been forced to come to terms with her new life *tout de suite*.

She was relieved that only her name was on the deed to the house. She hoped she would be able to keep it.

"Where'd you come up with all that?" she asked Rona.

"I mighta lived it."

"What do you mean? You had sex with someone? Recently?"

Donovan's death had hit Rona harder than she'd expected. She'd thought she had no feelings left for him whatsoever, but that hadn't been the case. She was still getting over it, and was half-embarrassed, half-belligerent to admit she'd used sex as a coping means.

Rona cleared her throat and threw Brooke a sheepish look. "Last night, actually."

"Oh, my God. Who?"

"Steve Burckman."

"Steve . . . *Burckman*? *The asshole?*"

"Who said he was an asshole?"

"You did! At Camp Love Shack! When Donovan asked you if you had sex with him!"

"Oh. Well, I didn't have sex with him *then*."

Brooke eyes filled with tears of mirth. She wondered if she was having some kind of attack. It wasn't that funny, but she wanted to roll on the ground and howl.

"Have you seen him lately?" demanded Rona. "My God, he's in shape. And you know what? He doesn't drink. Gave it up."

"Is that what you're going to do?" Brooke asked, struggling to get her wild emotions under control.

"Who knows?" She threw up her hands. "Life's crazy. I'm just glad you and I are friends again."

"As long as we stay out of jail."

They'd admitted leaving Josh for dead following their fight with him, when they'd believed they were saving Wendy from him, but they hadn't admitted to rowing him out to the lake and no one had asked. Maybe something more would come to light, or maybe it wouldn't. In either case, it felt like a huge weight had been lifted off Brooke's shoulders.

"If we go to jail, we'll be jailbird friends," said Rona. She linked her arm through Brooke's. "Wanna move in together?"

"Hell, no."

"I don't know, I see you changing your mind . . ." she said with a slow smile.

Brooke shook her head. Rona did have powers of persuasion that she'd fallen for, time and again, but . . .

*Hell, no!*

*Three weeks*, Jamie thought, cleaning up the kitchen after dinner. She'd gone to Wendy and Caleb's funeral to support Harley, and Cooper had gone to support her. He'd been worried, alarmed, at her call that hadn't gone through when she was at Haven, and that worry had led to action. He'd called the sheriff's department and gotten them to check on the camp, which was where he'd believed Jamie to be. Then the dads and alumni had shown up at the hospital with Cam Dornbrenner's body and everything had ramped up.

Jamie could barely remember hitting Josh Ulland with the rock. She'd picked up the stone when she'd heard screaming and shouting, wild voices, one of them being

Harley's. She'd been hurrying away from Haven on tender, hurting feet, but her urge to escape kept her going. She did remember not wanting Harley to follow after Josh, and she'd meant what she'd said that Haven would take care of him. She didn't know what all the herbs were in Sunny Dae's kitchen, but the women ran the place, whether the men knew it or not, and she'd made it clear she would use whatever means she saw fit to achieve her ends. Had Josh really died of a brain bleed . . . ? Maybe. It was just as likely, in Jamie's biased opinion, that Sunny Dae and the women of Haven had helped Josh along to the afterworld with a con-coction of their own.

But some good had come out of the crazy events at Camp Fog Lake. Jamie had actually connected with Mary Jo!

Mary Jo had been shocked to learn that Jamie had gotten embroiled with Josh Ulland at Camp Fog Lake. When Jamie told her Sunny Dae had inferred that Mary Jo had gotten pregnant by Josh . . . possibly against her will, Mary Jo had quickly denied the rumor, saying Rolff wouldn't allow Josh to have sex with any of them. Even so, Jamie got the impres-sion she might be on the right track. In any case, after their conversation, Mary Jo seemed to ease up a bit in her "good-ness," actually becoming more human. A strange kind of bonding had occurred between them, and the result was Jamie was happier and more settled.

As Jamie stacked the dishwasher, the back door opened and she heard Emma and Duchess enter from a brief eve-ning constitutional. The dog's toenails tippy-tapped down the hallway and then they came into view, Duchess whining for a treat. Emma had tried to capture Twink again, upon her return from camp, but the wily feline seemed to sense her motives and stayed just out of reach. Emma had finally given up. Bob Atchison was still recovering from a heart at-tack and it looked like Faye would become the permanent director of Ridge Pointe, so therefore Twink was safe. Whether she still attacked Jewell's stinky feet was another matter, and whether Emma herself would stay at Ridge Pointe was yet to be decided as well.

A door slammed upstairs and Harley bounded down the stairs. She looked . . . amazingly pretty in a short, black sundress and sandals, her dark hair clipped into a loose ponytail, her eyes dramatic with eyeliner and mascara.

"Wow," Jamie said.

"I know, right?" Harley batted her eyes at her and Jamie laughed.

Harley had applied to Portland State University, determined to study criminal justice. It didn't hurt that Greer Douglas was transferring to the same school. When Jamie had asked about her graduation trip to Great Britain, Harley had shrugged and said she could travel "across the pond" next summer . . . when Greer might join her.

Emma's intense stare took in Harley's "look."

"So?" Harley asked her as she attempted to stop Duchess's whining by grabbing the dog's rope toy and playing tug-of-war.

"You're a real badass," said Emma.

Cooper, who'd been on a phone call in their bedroom, came down the stairs and within earshot at that moment. "Meeting Greer?" he asked.

"That's the plan. Emma, want a ride back to Ridge Pointe?"

"Yes."

She followed Harley outside with Duchess on their heels.

Alone, Cooper looked at Jamie and Jamie looked at him.

"Well?" he asked.

Jamie opened the junk drawer and looked down at the pregnancy test she'd taken. Her period was three weeks late.

Please turn the page for an exciting sneak peek of
Nancy Bush's next thriller
**THE SORORITY**
coming soon wherever print and e-books are sold!

# PROLOGUE

"HI, Ethan!"

"Hey, Ethan!

"Yoohoo, *Ethan!*"

"*ETHAN!*"

Ethan Stanhope looked over at the girls waving frantically at him from the front steps of River Glen High School. *Freshmen*, he smirked to himself. He nodded toward them with his usual half-smile and chuckled as they fell all over themselves in hysterical giggles. He was a senior. And captain of the water polo team. And king of the prom this year, although he'd taken off his crown as soon as the foil and glitter piece of junk was laid on his head and then placed it atop Celine Ergon-Smith's instead. From her wheelchair she gazed up at him in adoration, her cheeks turning pink. He didn't know why she was in the chair; some kind of birth defect he never knew the name of. He then bumped fists with Celine, smiled at her, ignored his "queen," and the crowd had gone wild.

The queen was Mia Jordan, his girlfriend. Ex-girlfriend now as she'd iced him out ever since he'd fooled around

with Roxy at Gavin's parents' pool house during the senior
barbecue. He'd told Mia that nothing had happened between
him and Roxy, and really not much had. Roxy was a tease,
which he could admit he kind of liked. It was just . . . well,
there'd been less than a month of school left at that time and
he'd wanted to do something else. Be with someone else before there was no more school, no more seeing everybody
everyday.

*Sorry, Freshmen*, he thought as he chirped his tires and
drove his silver BMW from the school parking lot. *I am
fuckin' outta here.*

Friday was graduation and his classmates were once again
gathering at Gavin's afterward. His parents had purposely
left again, tacitly allowing Gavin to have the party for his
class. But Ethan didn't really want to go if Roxy wasn't there,
and he'd asked her if she would be there and she'd simply
shrugged. He didn't know what that meant, but she'd been
hard to pin down since the pool party. He just felt . . . unsatis-
fied. He remembered kissing Roxy in the pool house. She
hadn't really kissed him back, though. She'd just stood there.
And then she'd told him to back off. He was too aggressive,
which had pissed him off. Who the hell was she to tell him?

But then she'd pushed him back onto the pool house cot
and slowly pulled down his pants to stare at his engorged
cock. And when she'd leaned over him, he'd groaned aloud
in anticipation, but all she'd done was kiss his dick and then
give it a friendly pat. "Not tonight," she'd said.

"When?" he demanded.

"Probably not ever."

She'd then sauntered out of the pool house and he'd had
to wait a while to cool his blood before nonchalantly following after her. But then, of course, one of Mia's friends had
seen Roxy leave the pool house and then she saw him coming out a few minutes behind her. From that point on there
was no talking Mia out of it. Everyone assumed he and
Roxy had had sex and though Ethan had half-heartedly

stated that they hadn't, Gavin had thrown back his head and roared and said, "Sure. Wink, wink," exaggeratedly closing one eye a couple of times and grinning like an idiot. Ethan let him think what he would. Why not?

Of course Roxy said nothing had happened between them as well, but Mia hadn't believed her. She'd called Roxy a slut, which had pissed Roxy off, even though she was one. A real bitch, teaser, slut. Yet, Ethan would never say so, because he still thought there was a chance they might get together tonight, again at Gavin's, now that he and Mia were unofficially through. After that last barbecue he'd gone home to learn Roxy had left red lipstick on his skin, and the realization had made him groan some more and engage in a little self-love.

He wanted more.


Friday afternoon, following graduation ceremony and family duties, Ethan called Gavin to ascertain when to arrive. He didn't want to be the first one to show up, but if Roxy was there . . .

"Nobody's here," Gavin informed him on a disgusted sigh. "Nobody good, anyway." A pause. "Mia's here."

"Hey, Mia's good," Ethan protested. "She's always good. We don't hate each other."

"You sure about that?"

"Why? She say something?"

"It's all her 'sisters'. They're standing around like in judgment, man."

"Is Roxy there?" He tossed the question in lightly, but Gavin was all over it.

"Stop thinking about her. It's messing with your head and we're done here. School's over. Graduation's over! Foxy Roxy's probably out screwing someone else. You know that's who she is."

"It wasn't like that with us."

"So you say, so you say . . . Get over here and cheer these bitches up or get 'em outta here. I'm gonna get hammered and maybe get laid, but not with any of them."

"I'll be there." Ethan felt his hopes sink. If Roxy wasn't there, he really didn't want to go.

And he really didn't want to see Mia, and the rest of her posse. Leigh and Kristl and that Natalie. God, she was the worst. And the other one . . . Allie. Gavin had tried to make it with her but she was needy and whiny and he'd given up after one make-out session. Ethan could have told him. None of them were worth anything but Mia, and even she had gotten on his nerves. It annoyed him that she'd stopped talking to him, but it was a relief, too. He could go about whatever he wanted now.

And what he wanted was Roxy.

An hour and a half later he showed up at Gavin's. Maybe nothing had been happening earlier, but the party was in full swing now. Some of the guys were really wasted and loud, and so were some of the girls. Not Mia's group. They were all standing together and looking dead sober. Okay, maybe Allie was staggering a bit, but the others were grim as parents surveying the lot of them. He saw Mia's black hair, clipped back at her nape like always. She was talking to Jeremy Orsini, a total piece of shit.

Natalie lifted her chin. She'd zeroed in on him as soon as he'd entered through the back gate and was coming his way. She, too, had black hair, but unlike Mia, whose skin glowed with good health, Natalie's pallor was pale as death. Natalie was totally Goth. And she was grim like that, too. Mia said she was the leader of their group. Well, good for her. She was another piece of shit.

He watched Natalie lean toward Kristl, who was the tallest and heaviest of their group. Kristl was looking over at him, too. She wore a one-piece swimsuit instead of a bikini to probably contain the flab. He waved frantically at them all, pretending to be crazily overjoyed to see them. No one waved back, although Leigh, who'd always been nice, surreptitiously lifted a few fingers. Leigh had light brown hair and was sort of cute, but she was flat-chested and Mia said she was emotional. Not as bad as Allie, maybe, but who needed the aggravation.

Roxy was nowhere in sight. How she was even part of their group was a mystery.

He got himself a beer, but then another girl, younger, he decided, since he didn't know her, talked him into a glass of punch. He drank half of it, and then set it down as some more people arrived. It was just getting dark and the air was starting to chill, so Ethan headed around the side of the house and to his BMW to retrieve his jacket. He nearly ran into Mackenzie Laughlin on the way, staggering a bit to avoid her as she was just standing in the driveway by one of the SUVs, eyeing the house, clearly thinking over whether to join the party. He'd recently seen her in the school play, *Oklahoma*, which Mia had talked him into going to. Mackenzie hadn't been half bad. He couldn't remember the name of her character, but he could remember part of the song she'd sung.

"*I'm just a girl who can't say no,*" he warbled badly, half laughing. He was no singer.

Mackenzie eyed him carefully, but didn't say anything. He started to feel a little foolish for making fun of her. As he shouldered past her toward the street where his BMW was parked, she said, "You don't want to drive in your condition."

His condition? "I've barely had anything to drink," he protested. Had his voice slurred? That was . . . weird.

"You need a ride? I'm leaving." The words sounded dragged from her. She clearly didn't mean what she'd said.

"You just got here."

"Yeah, well . . . I'm not staying."

"Yeah, well . . . I'm just getting my coat." He heard his voice and thought he'd said those words pretty clearly.

Mackenzie gave him a look he couldn't decipher, then headed back to an older model Ford Explorer that was parked on the opposite side of the street from Ethan. Ethan leaned into his SUV and half fell on the seat as he snagged his coat. In a way he was kinda sorry to see Mac go. She was friends with Mia and her group, but a bit of an outsider. And there was something about her parents . . . oh, yeah . . . her dad had died a few years back. That was too bad.

Back at the party Ethan grabbed another glass of punch and sank into one of the lounge chairs around the pool, which really irked Miles, who'd been sitting there apparently. The world was spinning and he lay back and fell asleep. When he came to, he realized most everyone had moved indoors. He thought about Roxy. She wasn't here, so why was he? He saw his drink and someone had put ice in it. He picked it up and swallowed about half of it. He looked toward the pool house, but it was dark. However, the plate glass windows of the main house were brightly lit from within and he could see through the dining room to the kitchen. Mia was standing with the rest of her group. He felt a pang in his heart. She'd ditched him and he wasn't the kind of guy who should be ditched.

Staggering up, he walked back around the pool house through the gate and down the drive. When he got behind the wheel of his rig he saw that someone had left him some food, sealed up on a paper plate beneath plastic wrap. Mia, maybe?

He started the car but sat there for a while. Maybe Mackenzie was right. He shouldn't drive. He certainly felt odd.

He didn't know how long he'd sat there before he shook his head. Fuck it. He didn't live that far away.

He pulled into the street and glanced in the rearview mirror. Someone was standing in the road behind him. Mia? Was she waving?

No. It wasn't Mia . . . he didn't think.

And they weren't waving. They were giving him the finger.

Well, shit. He threw the BMW into gear and roared away. He wanted to drive to the ends of the earth, but then remembered vaguely that there was some obligation he needed to do for his parents, so he headed home.

He didn't know that he'd be dead within the hour.

Visit our website at
**KensingtonBooks.com**
to sign up for our newsletters, read
more from your favorite authors, see
books by series, view reading group
guides, and more!

**BOOK** **CLUB**
# BETWEEN THE CHAPTERS

Become a Part of Our
**Between the Chapters Book Club**
Community and Join the Conversation

**Betweenthechapters.net**